BY WATER

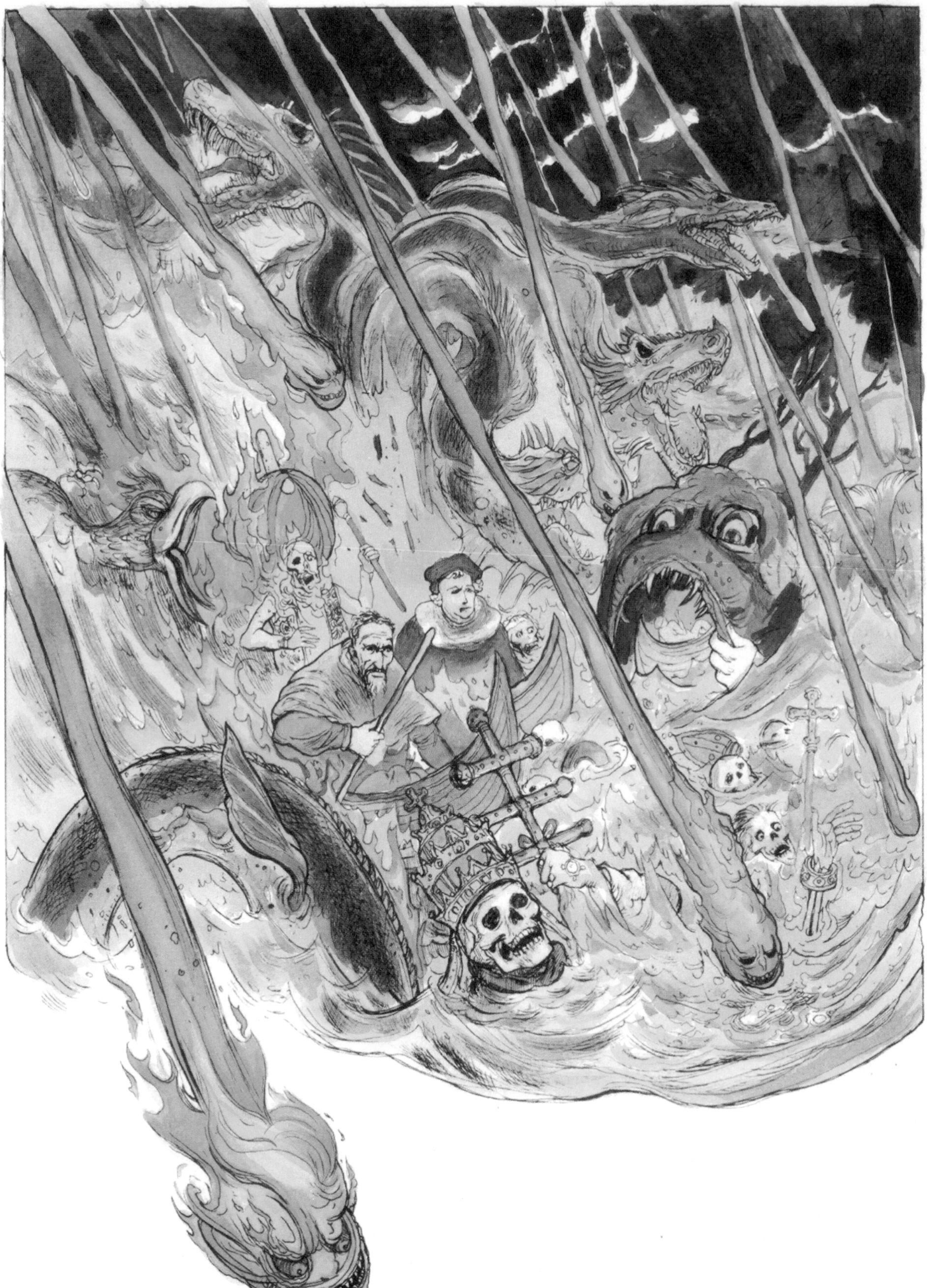

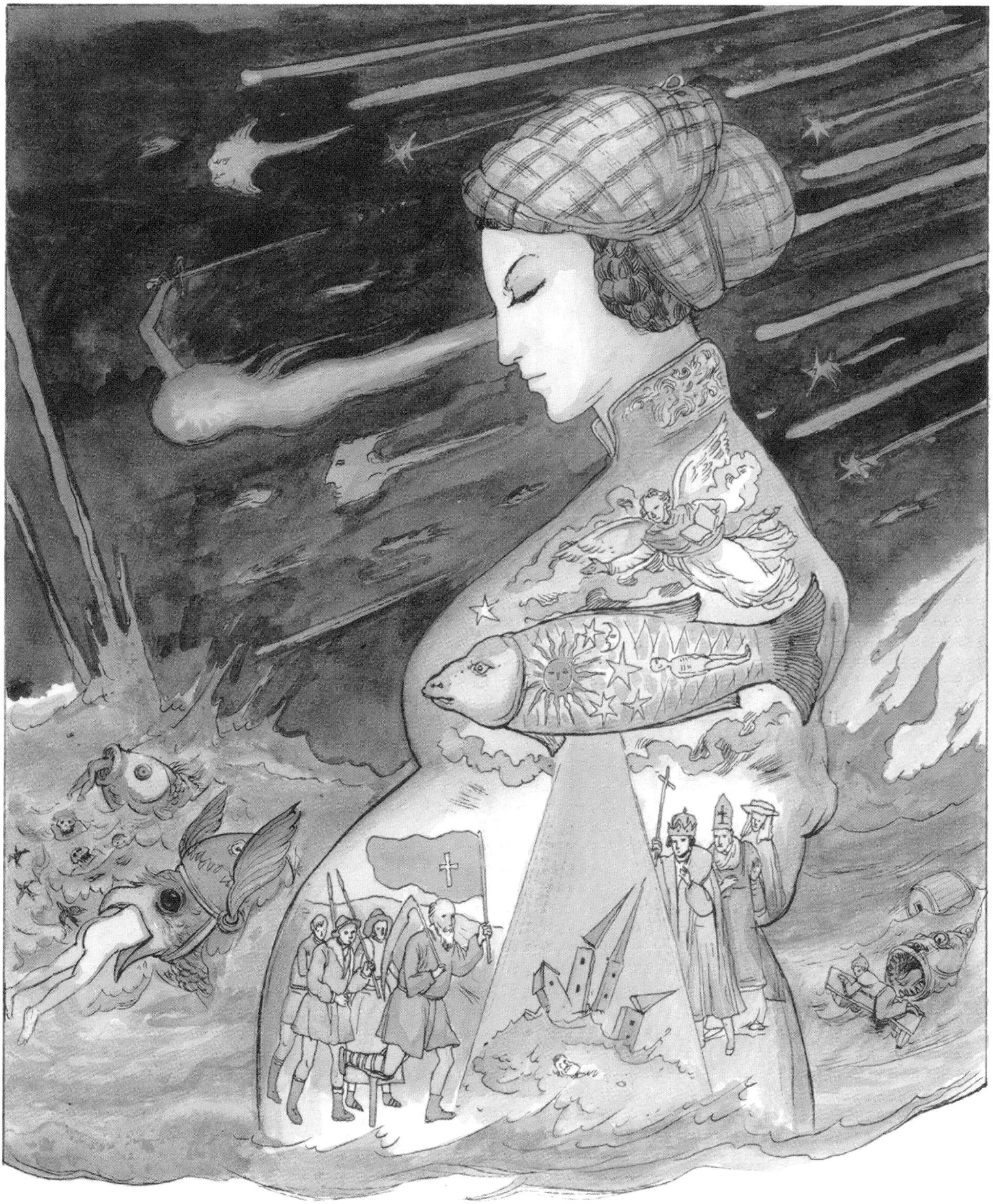

HEROES OF THE RADICAL REFORMATION

BOOK ONE

By Water

THE FELIX MANZ STORY

JASON LANDSEL

SANKHA BANERJEE, ART
RICHARD MOMMSEN, SCRIPT

Plough

Plough

Published by Plough Publishing House
Walden, New York
Robertsbridge, England
Elsmore, Australia
www.plough.com

Plough produces books, a quarterly magazine, and Plough.com to encourage people and help them put their faith into action. We believe Jesus can transform the world and that his teachings and example apply to all aspects of life. At the same time, we seek common ground with all people regardless of their creed.

Plough is the publishing house of the Bruderhof, an international Christian community. The Bruderhof is a fellowship of families and singles practicing radical discipleship in the spirit of the first church in Jerusalem (Acts 2 and 4). Members devote their entire lives to serving God, one another, and their neighbors, renouncing private property and sharing everything. To learn more about the Bruderhof's faith, history, and daily life, see Bruderhof.com. (Views expressed by Plough authors are their own and do not necessarily reflect the position of the Bruderhof.)

Library of Congress Cataloging-in-Publication Data

Names: Landsel, Jason, author. | Banerjee, Sankha, illustrator.
Title: By water : the Felix Manz story / Jason Landsel with Casey Kurtti
   and Richard Mommsen ; artist Sankha Banerjee.
Description: Walden, New York : Plough Publishing House, [2023] | Includes
   bibliographical references. | Audience: Grades 10-12.
Identifiers: LCCN 2022030966 (print) | LCCN 2022030967 (ebook) | ISBN
   9781636080536 (paperback) | ISBN 9781636080543 (ebook)
Subjects: LCSH: Manz, Felix, 1500-1527--Comic books, strips, etc. |
   Anabaptists--Switzerland--Comic books, strips, etc. | Christian
   martyrs--Comic books, strips, etc. | Graphic novels.
Classification: LCC BX4946.M24 L35 2023 (print) | LCC BX4946.M24 (ebook)
   | DDC 843/.914--dc23/eng/20220722
LC record available at https://lccn.loc.gov/2022030966
LC ebook record available at https://lccn.loc.gov/2022030967

Printed in the United States of America

TO THE READER

STUDENTS WILL KNOW that the Reformation began when Martin Luther nailed his "Ninety-Five Theses" to a church door in 1517. While reading *Renegade,* a graphic novel about Luther, I realized that this format would be a great way to tell a lesser-known and far more dramatic part of Reformation history, the story of the Anabaptists of the Radical Reformation. These Reformers were more daring than Luther and faced intense persecution for their beliefs at the hands of both Catholic and Protestant authorities. Their courage and vision helped establish goals that we still aspire to today: economic justice, peaceful social reform, and freedom of conscience.

So I began seriously researching the Anabaptist movement, which started in the Swiss city of Zurich in 1525. (Their enemies called them Anabaptists, or "rebaptizers," because they didn't recognize infant baptism – one had to choose to become a Christian.) I read dozens of books and traveled to locations in Europe including the street where Felix Manz lived, a cave where he may have hidden, and the place where he was drowned.

The title comes from an early Anabaptist text describing the punishments threatening anyone who was rebaptized: along with torture and loss of property both men and women faced execution "by water, by fire, or by sword." All named characters in this book are historical figures, and the plot follows documentary sources, though some scenes have been imaginatively recreated.

THE ANABAPTIST STORY IS PERSONAL FOR ME. I belong to the Bruderhof, a Christian community that practices the biblical tenets of early Anabaptism such as believers' baptism, community of goods, and conscientious objection to military service. And I married Doris Waldner, who has Hutterite roots; her ancestors have been living a life of sharing and nonviolence in Christian community for centuries. They were driven from one land to another and eventually fled Russia during the 1870s when the tsar threatened to force them into the military. My wife's family settled in what is now South Dakota, where Hutterites still live and work together today. Preserving her heritage and presenting it to our children has been an inspiration throughout this project.

I would like to thank my coauthors Sankha Banerjee and Richard Mommsen for their teamwork throughout the process, and Casey Kurtti and Oriol Malet for their editorial contributions.

Dauntless conviction was one of the marks of the first Anabaptists. I hope this book inspires you to stand up boldly and firmly for what you know is right and true.

Jason Landsel
June 2022

Episode One
THE DREAM

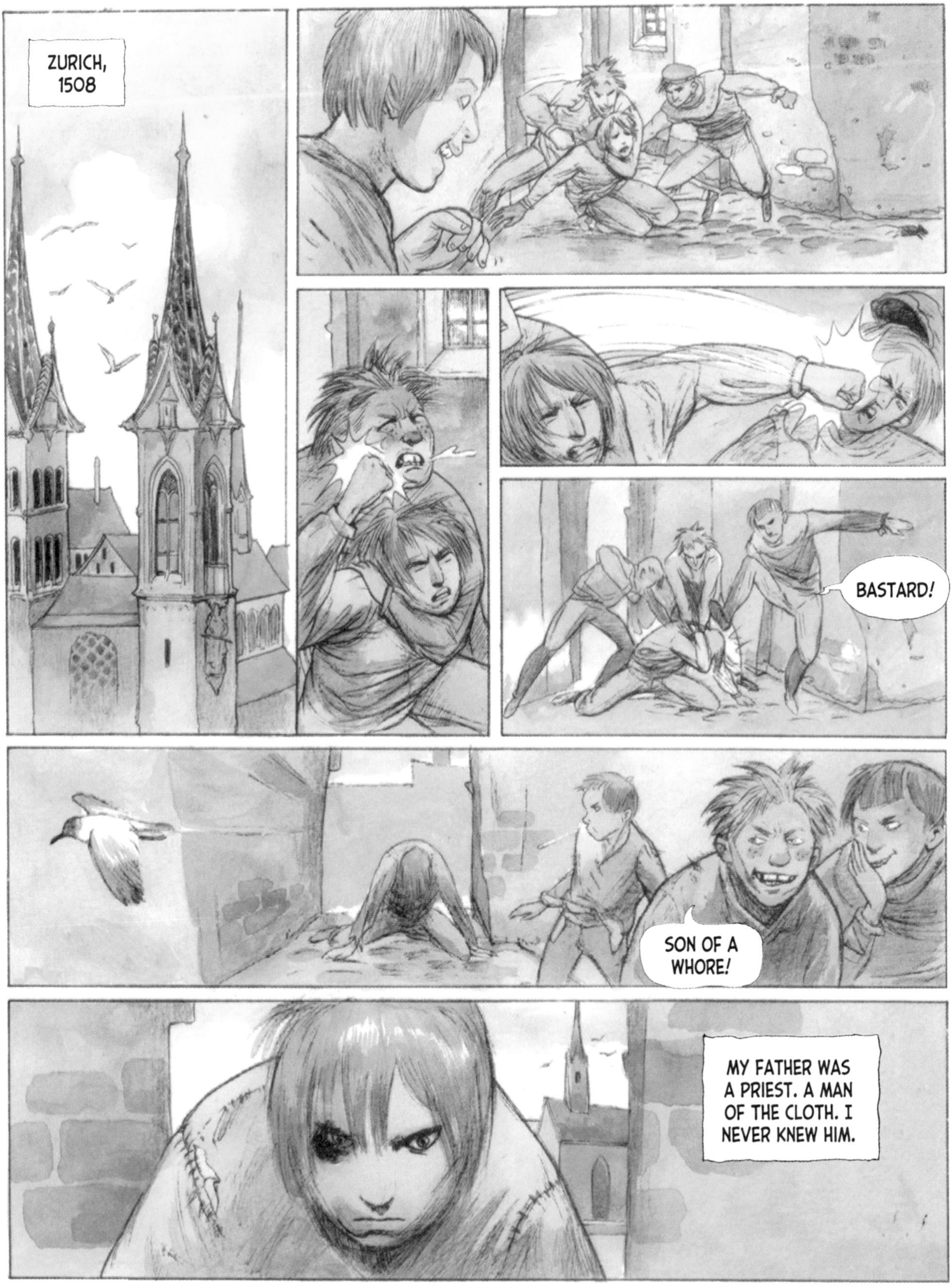
ZURICH, 1508
BASTARD!
SON OF A WHORE!
MY FATHER WAS A PRIEST. A MAN OF THE CLOTH. I NEVER KNEW HIM.

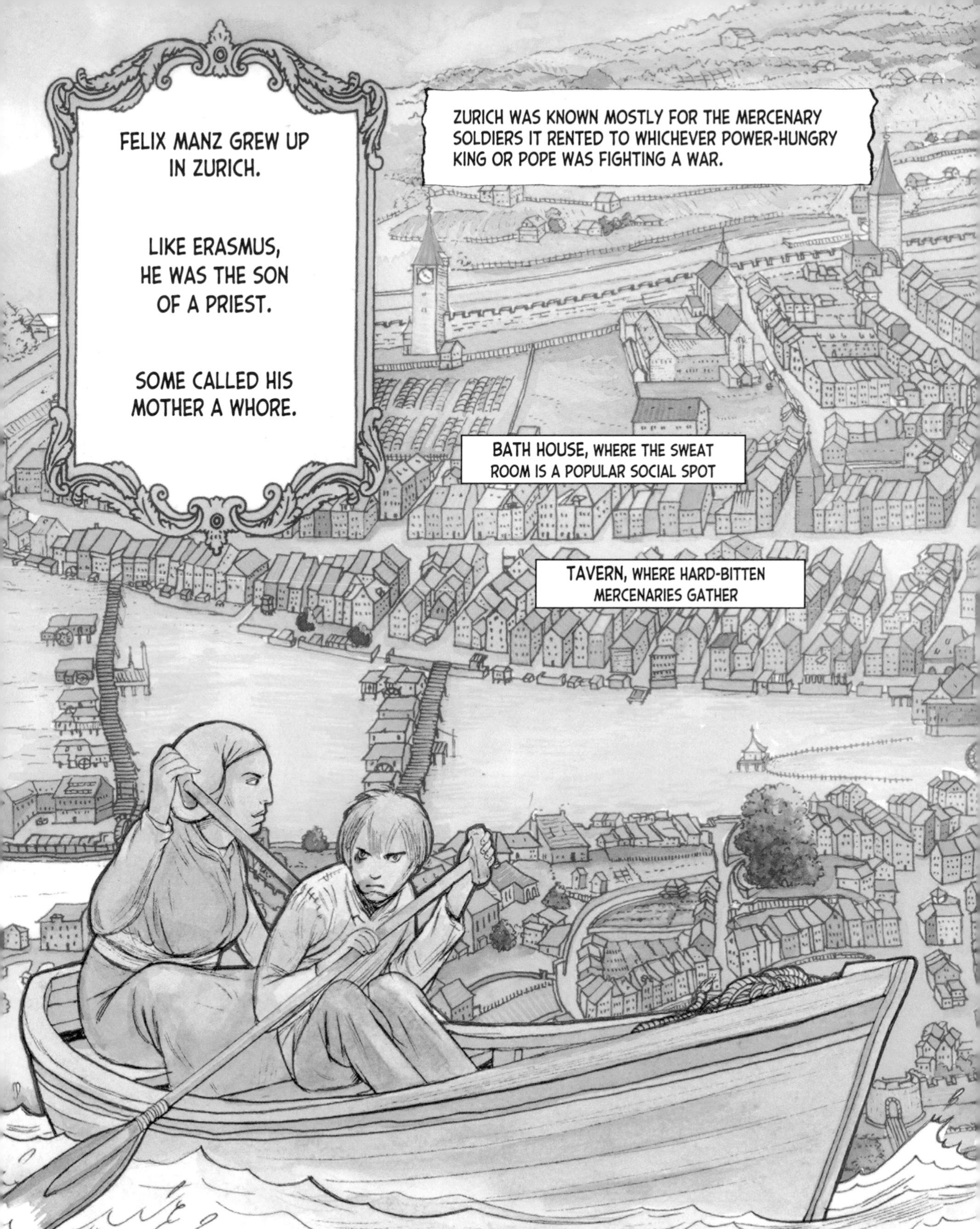
FELIX MANZ GREW UP IN ZURICH.
LIKE ERASMUS, HE WAS THE SON OF A PRIEST.
SOME CALLED HIS MOTHER A WHORE.
ZURICH WAS KNOWN MOSTLY FOR THE MERCENARY SOLDIERS IT RENTED TO WHICHEVER POWER-HUNGRY KING OR POPE WAS FIGHTING A WAR.
BATH HOUSE, WHERE THE SWEAT ROOM IS A POPULAR SOCIAL SPOT
TAVERN, WHERE HARD-BITTEN MERCENARIES GATHER

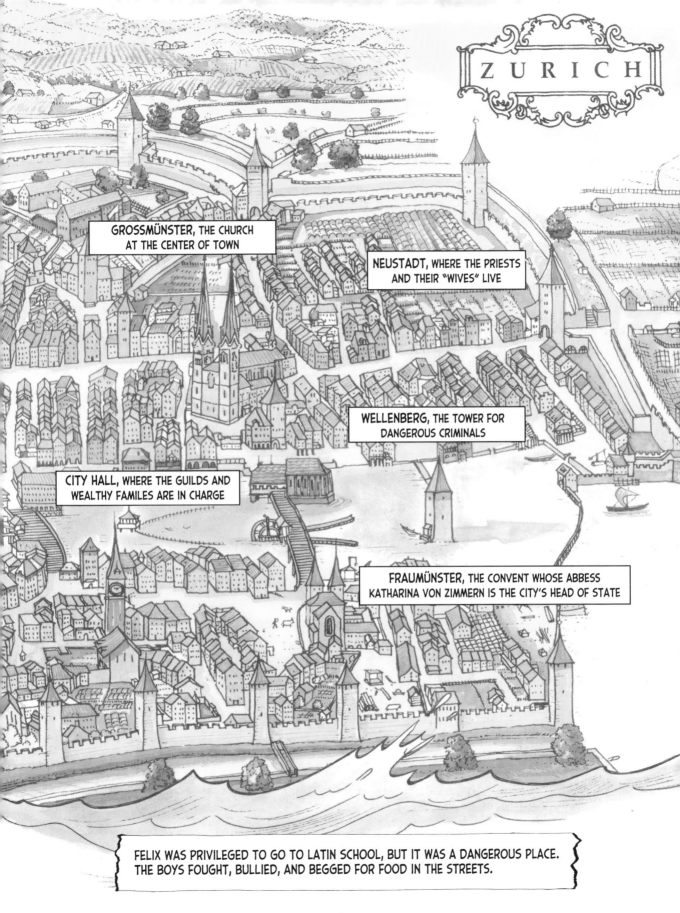

ZURICH

GROSSMÜNSTER, THE CHURCH AT THE CENTER OF TOWN

NEUSTADT, WHERE THE PRIESTS AND THEIR "WIVES" LIVE

WELLENBERG, THE TOWER FOR DANGEROUS CRIMINALS

CITY HALL, WHERE THE GUILDS AND WEALTHY FAMILES ARE IN CHARGE

FRAUMÜNSTER, THE CONVENT WHOSE ABBESS KATHARINA VON ZIMMERN IS THE CITY'S HEAD OF STATE

FELIX WAS PRIVILEGED TO GO TO LATIN SCHOOL, BUT IT WAS A DANGEROUS PLACE. THE BOYS FOUGHT, BULLIED, AND BEGGED FOR FOOD IN THE STREETS.

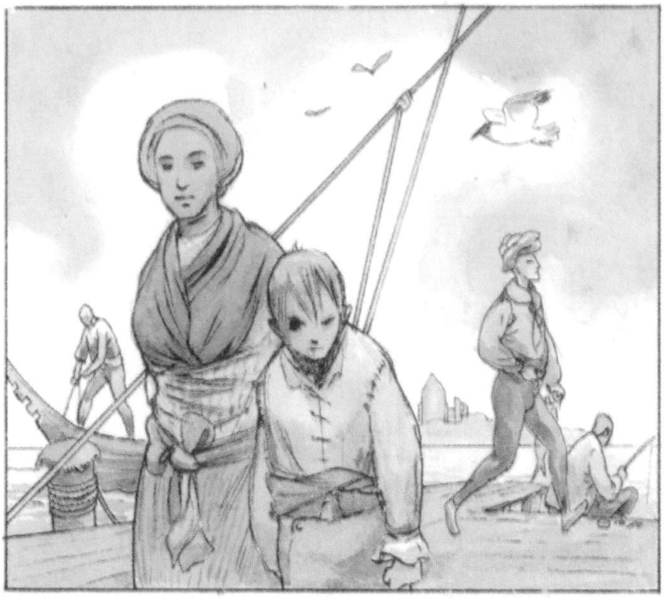

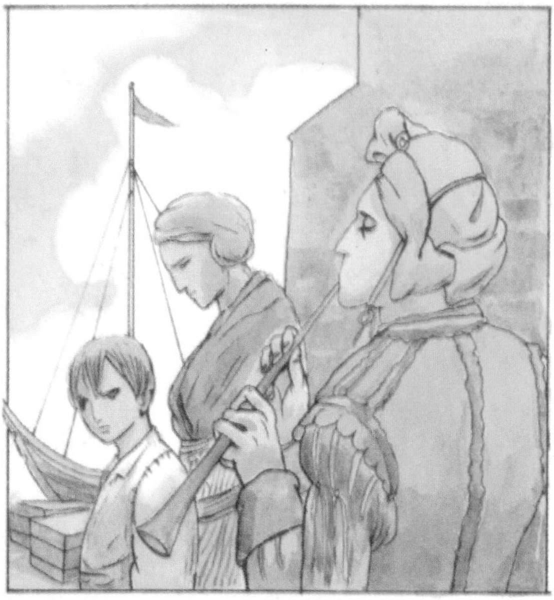

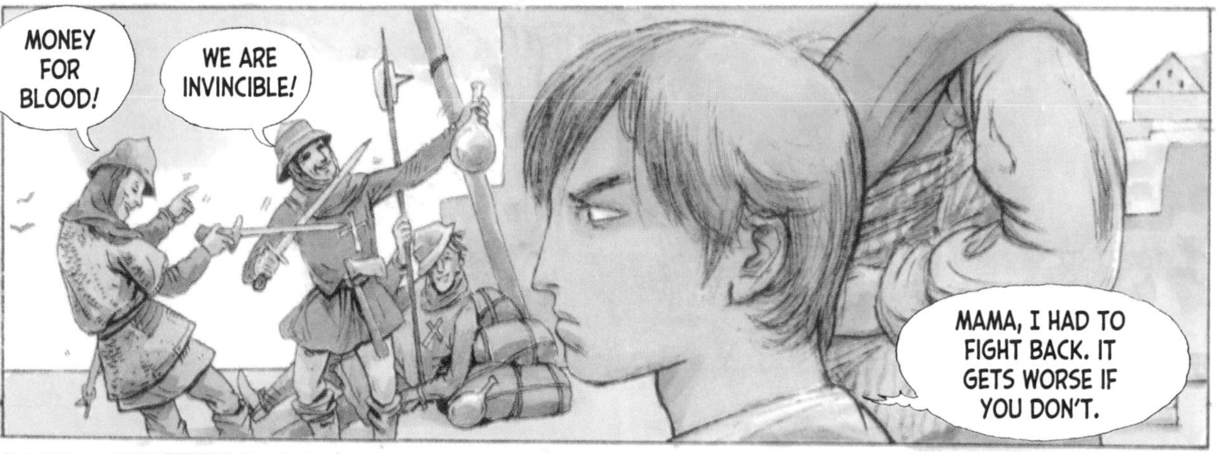
MONEY FOR BLOOD!
WE ARE INVINCIBLE!
MAMA, I HAD TO FIGHT BACK. IT GETS WORSE IF YOU DON'T.

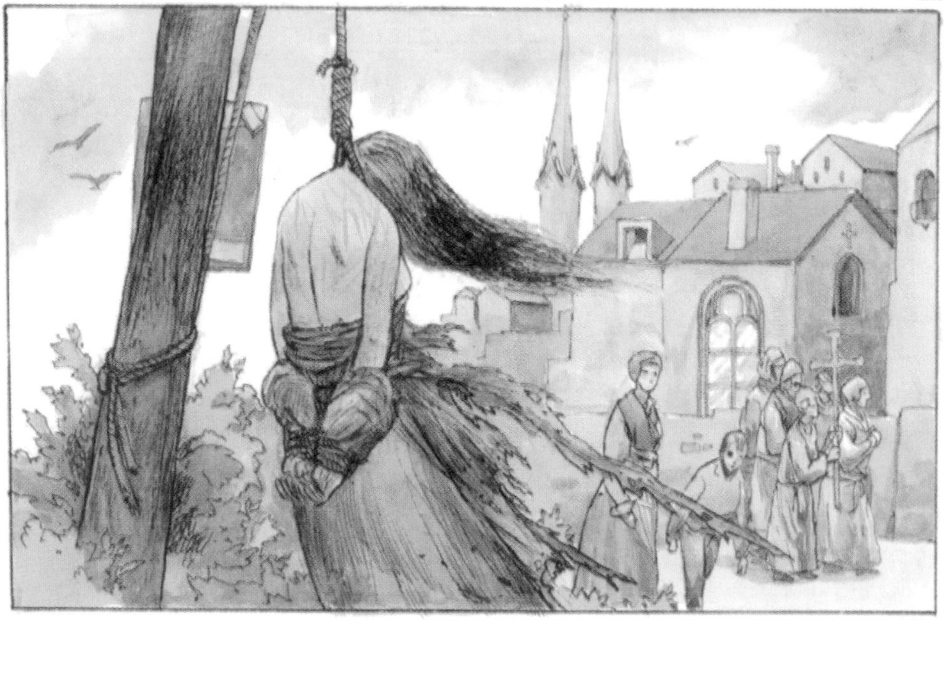

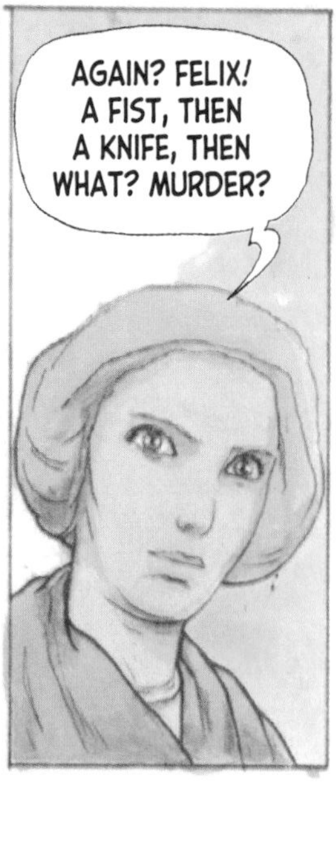
AGAIN? FELIX! A FIST, THEN A KNIFE, THEN WHAT? MURDER?

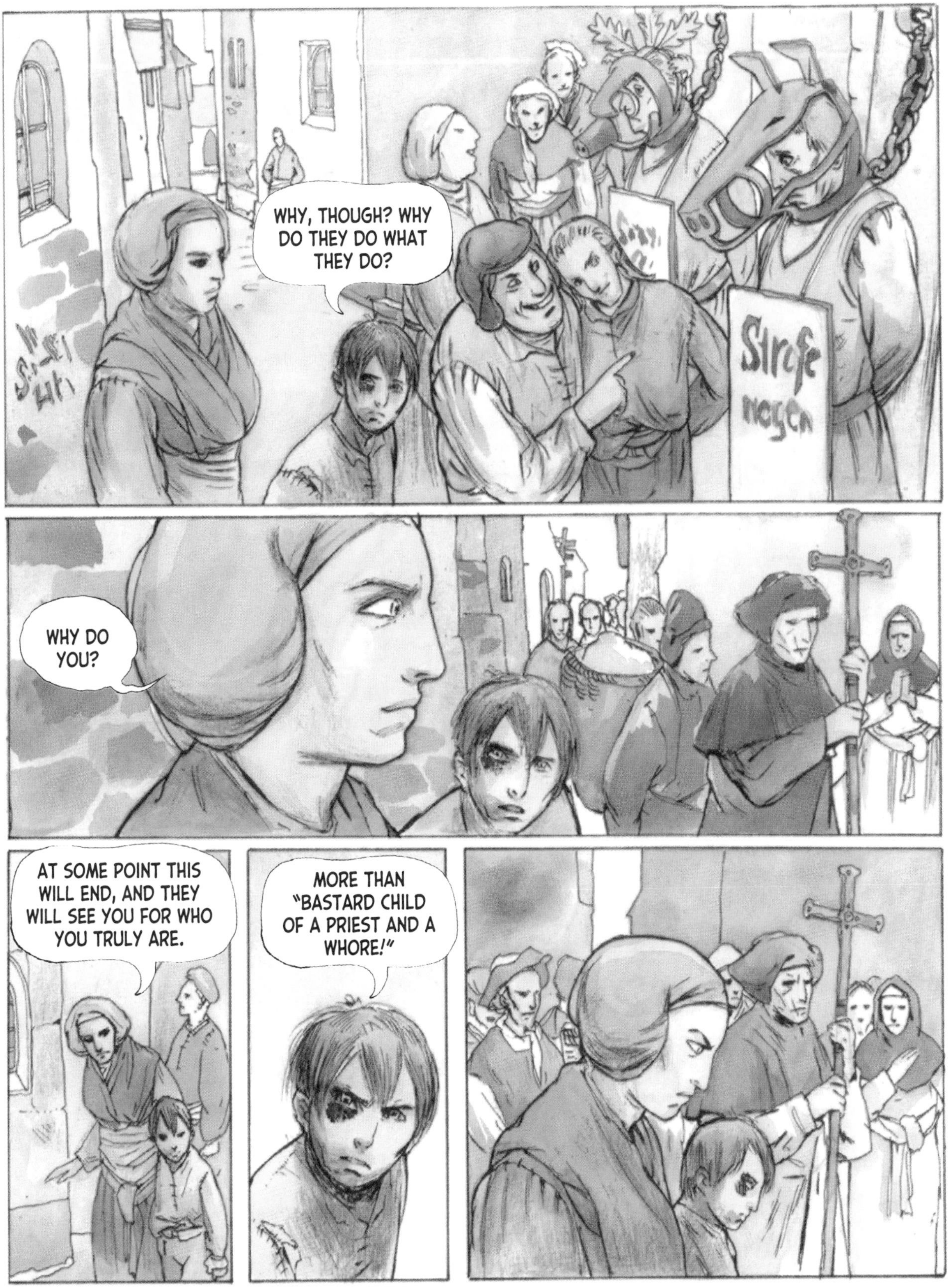
WHY, THOUGH? WHY DO THEY DO WHAT THEY DO?
Strafe
WHY DO YOU?
AT SOME POINT THIS WILL END, AND THEY WILL SEE YOU FOR WHO YOU TRULY ARE.
MORE THAN "BASTARD CHILD OF A PRIEST AND A WHORE!"

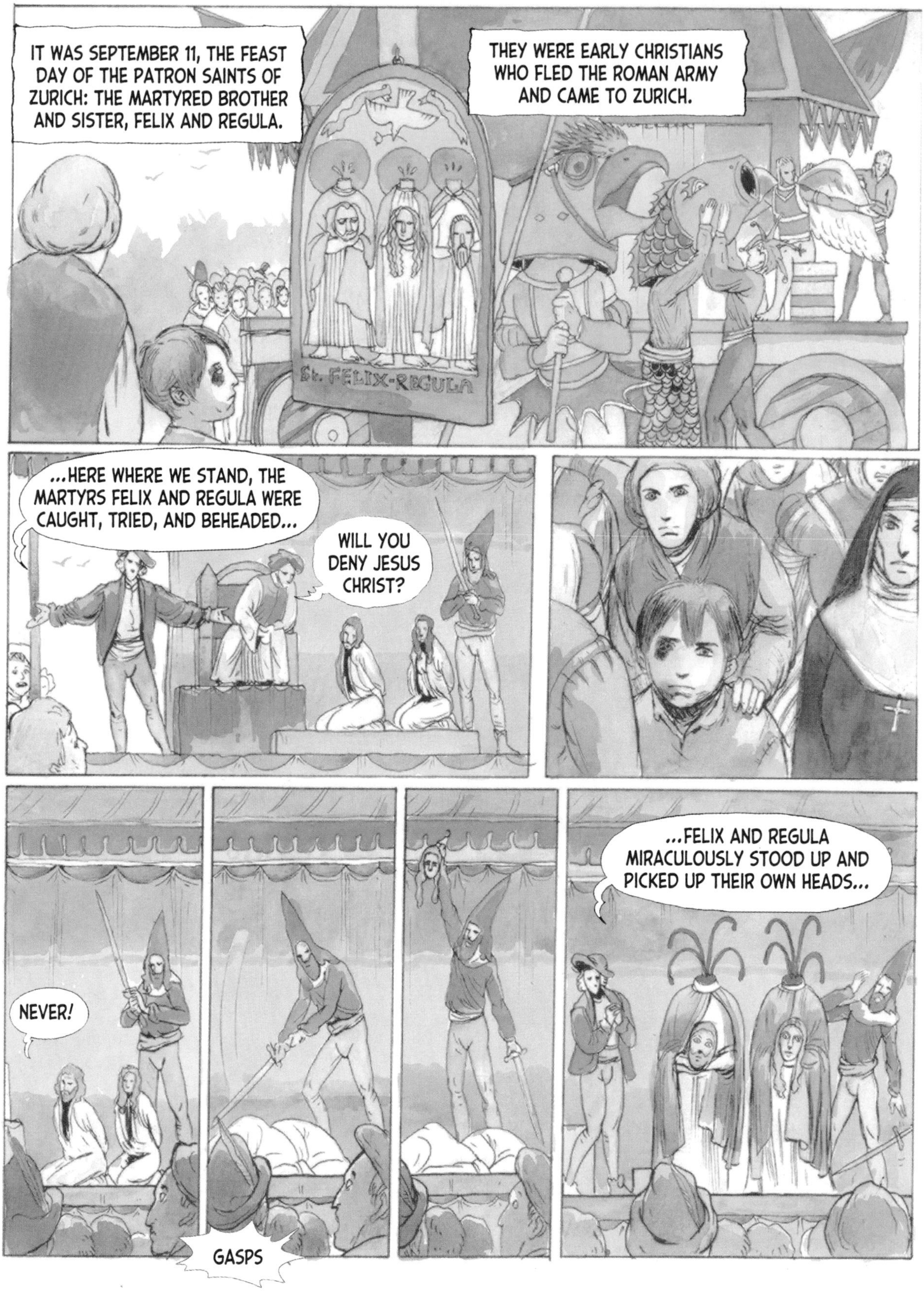
IT WAS SEPTEMBER 11, THE FEAST DAY OF THE PATRON SAINTS OF ZURICH: THE MARTYRED BROTHER AND SISTER, FELIX AND REGULA.
THEY WERE EARLY CHRISTIANS WHO FLED THE ROMAN ARMY AND CAME TO ZURICH.
St. FELIX-REGULA
...HERE WHERE WE STAND, THE MARTYRS FELIX AND REGULA WERE CAUGHT, TRIED, AND BEHEADED...
WILL YOU DENY JESUS CHRIST?
NEVER!
GASPS
...FELIX AND REGULA MIRACULOUSLY STOOD UP AND PICKED UP THEIR OWN HEADS...

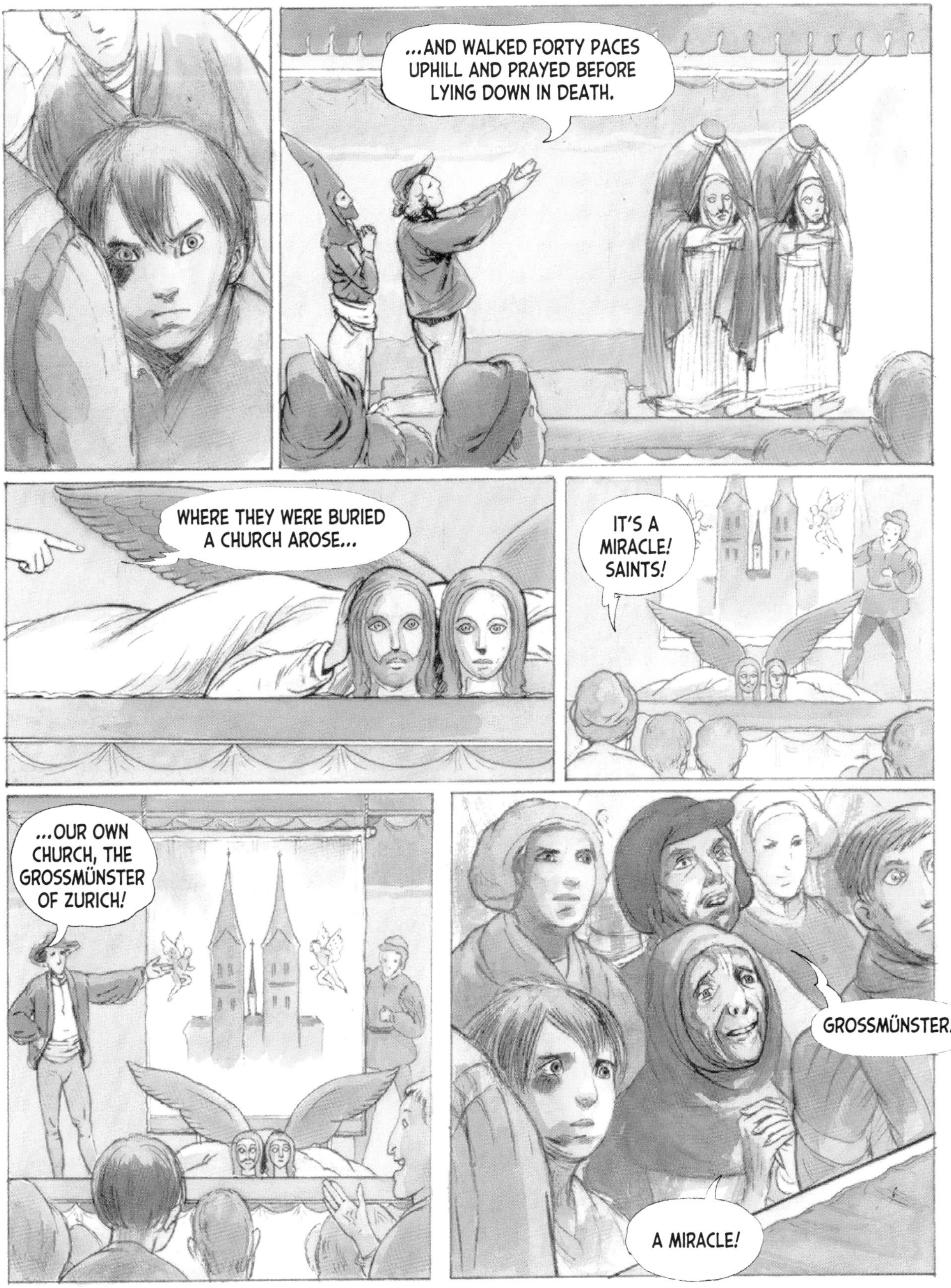
...AND WALKED FORTY PACES UPHILL AND PRAYED BEFORE LYING DOWN IN DEATH.
WHERE THEY WERE BURIED A CHURCH AROSE...
IT'S A MIRACLE! SAINTS!
...OUR OWN CHURCH, THE GROSSMÜNSTER OF ZURICH!
GROSSMÜNSTER!
A MIRACLE!

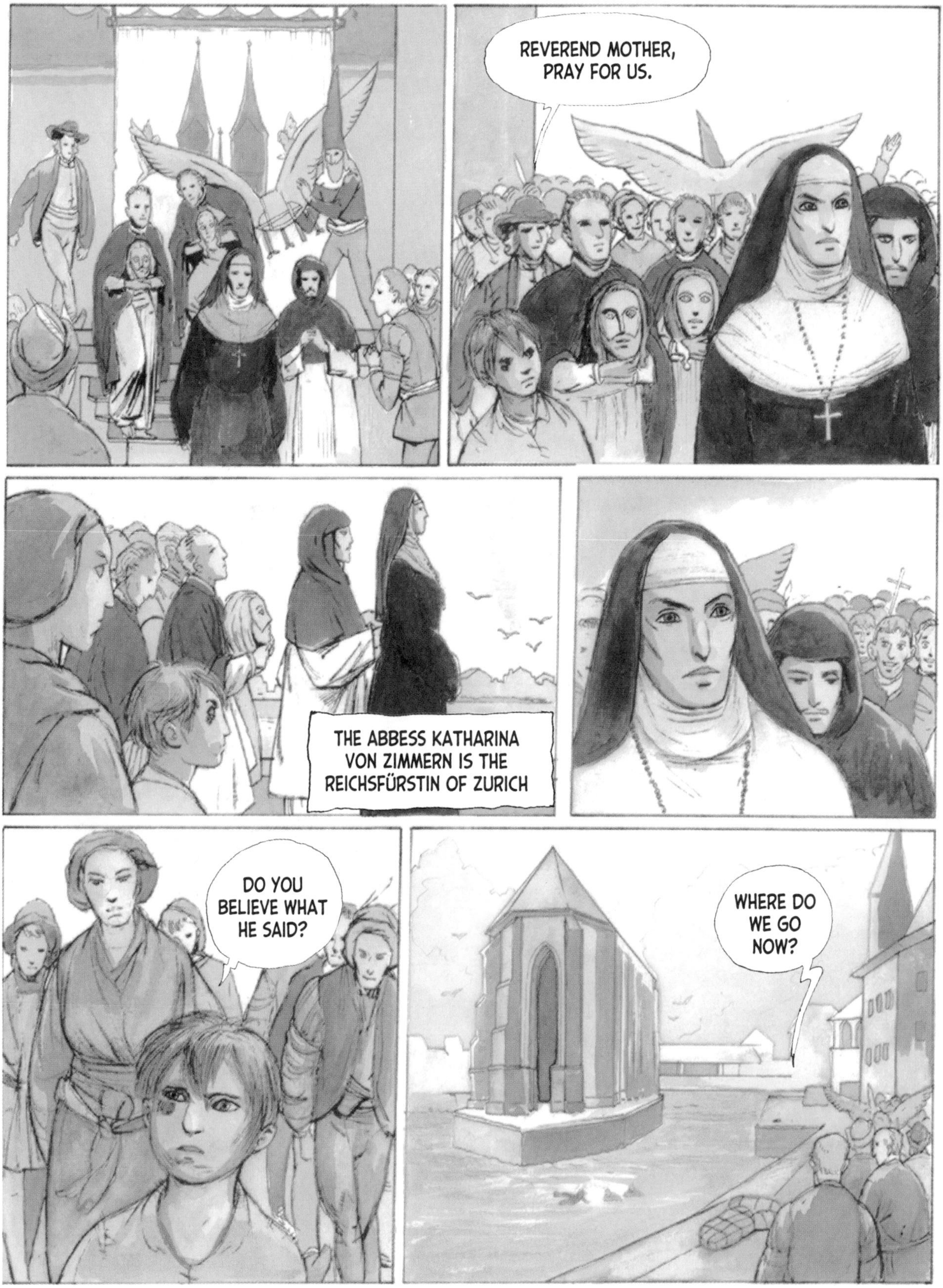
REVEREND MOTHER, PRAY FOR US.
THE ABBESS KATHARINA VON ZIMMERN IS THE REICHSFÜRSTIN OF ZURICH
DO YOU BELIEVE WHAT HE SAID?
WHERE DO WE GO NOW?

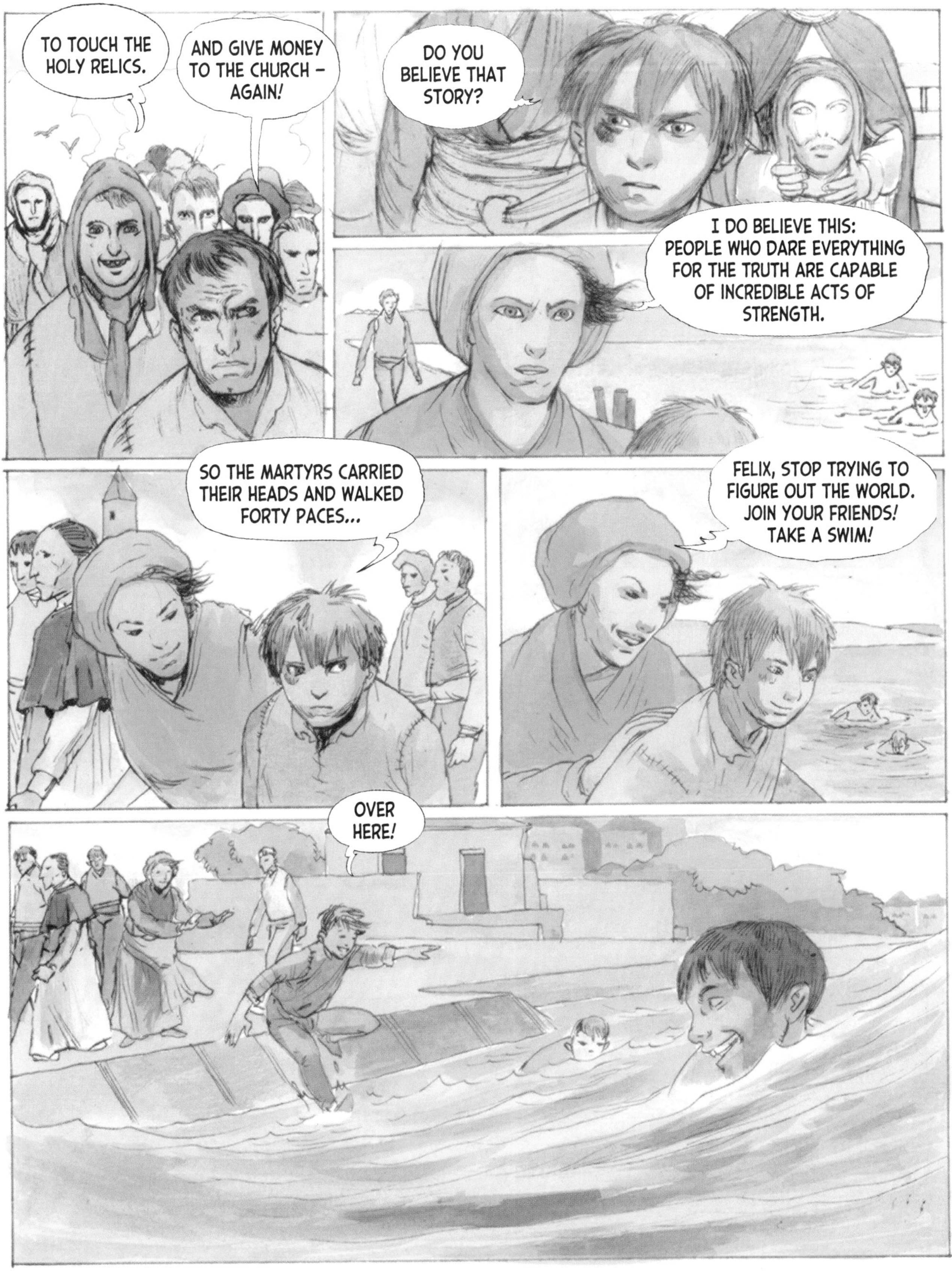
TO TOUCH THE HOLY RELICS.
AND GIVE MONEY TO THE CHURCH – AGAIN!
DO YOU BELIEVE THAT STORY?
I DO BELIEVE THIS: PEOPLE WHO DARE EVERYTHING FOR THE TRUTH ARE CAPABLE OF INCREDIBLE ACTS OF STRENGTH.
SO THE MARTYRS CARRIED THEIR HEADS AND WALKED FORTY PACES...
FELIX, STOP TRYING TO FIGURE OUT THE WORLD. JOIN YOUR FRIENDS! TAKE A SWIM!
OVER HERE!

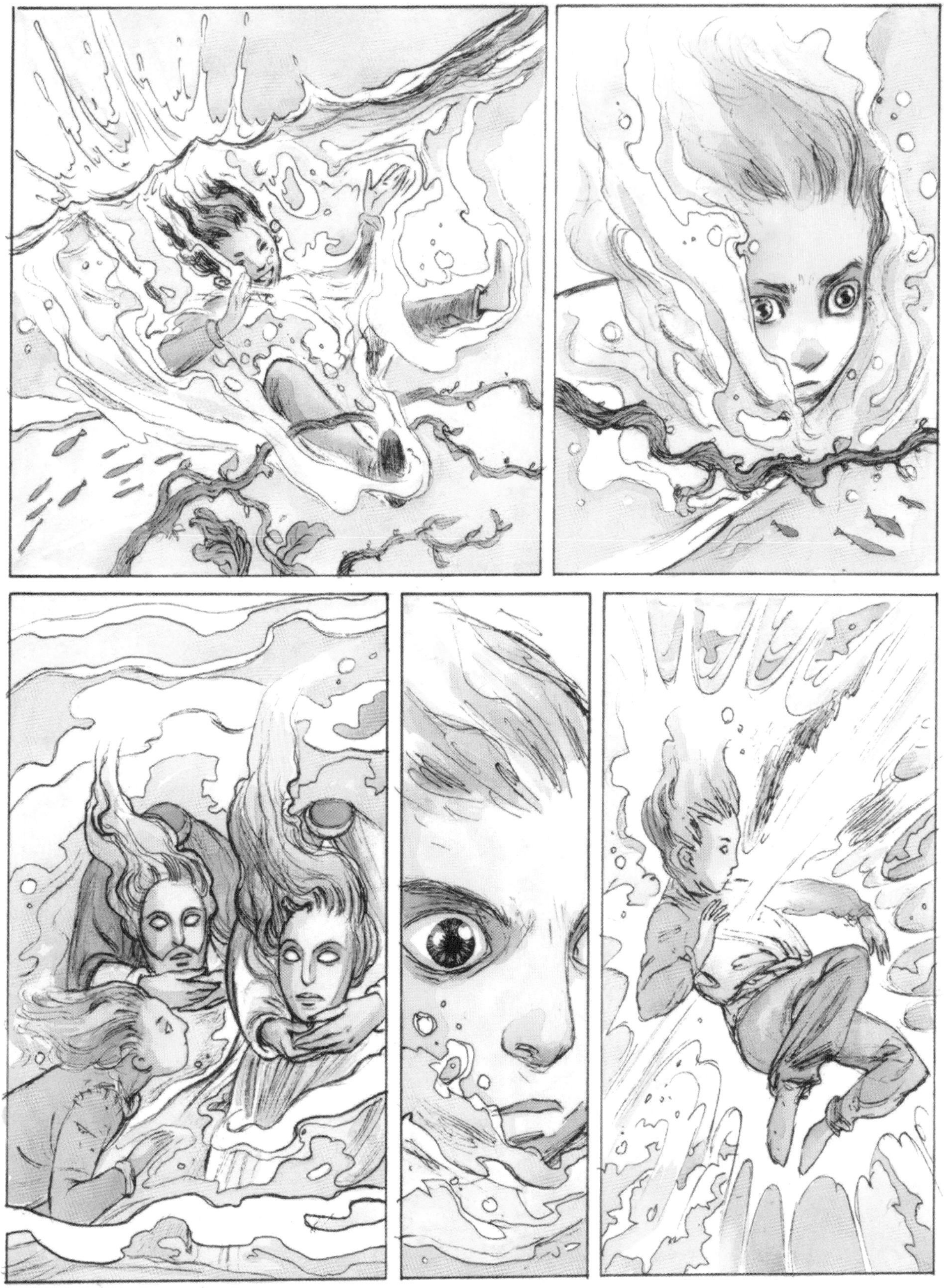

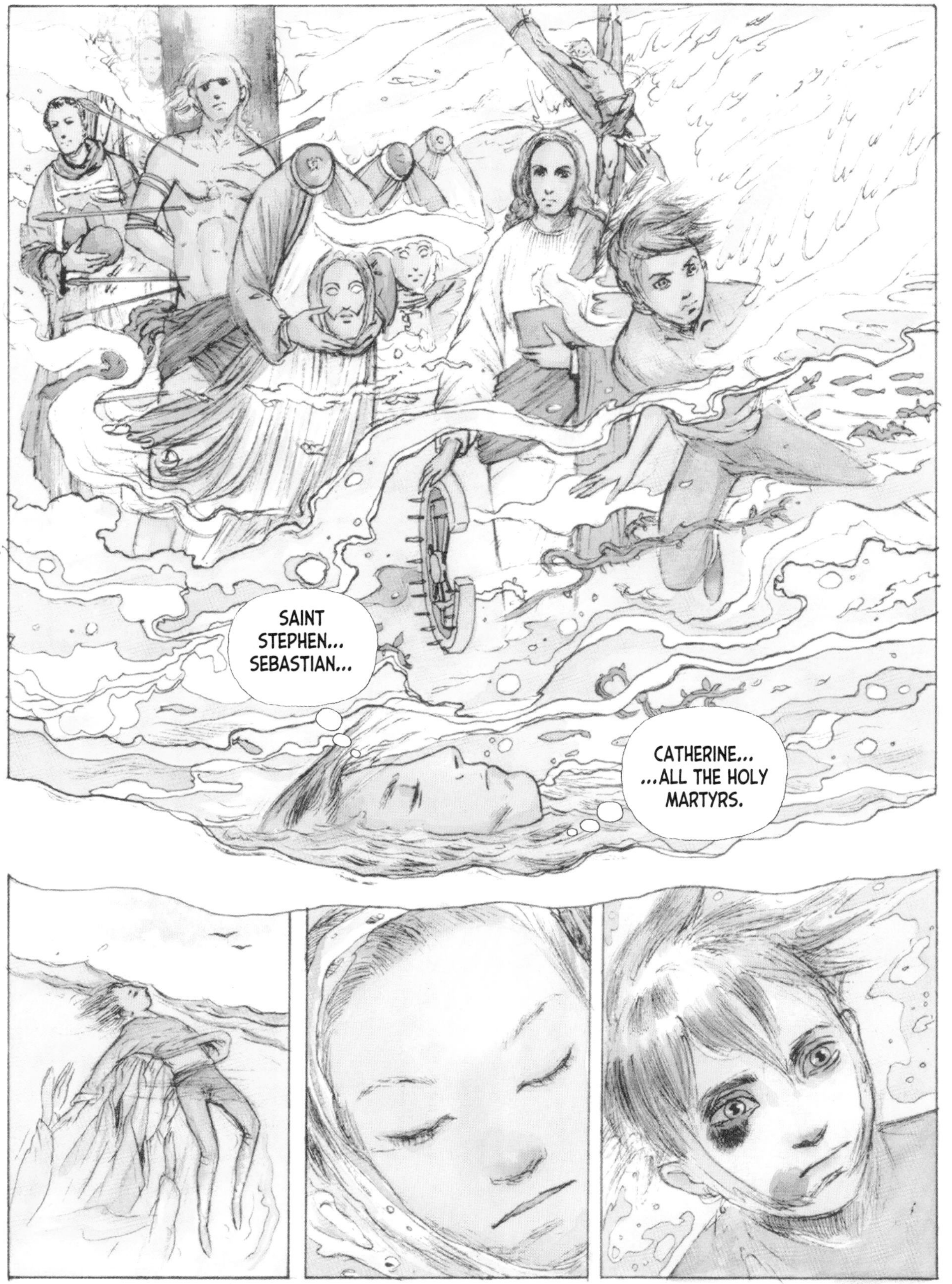
SAINT STEPHEN... SEBASTIAN...
CATHERINE... ...ALL THE HOLY MARTYRS.

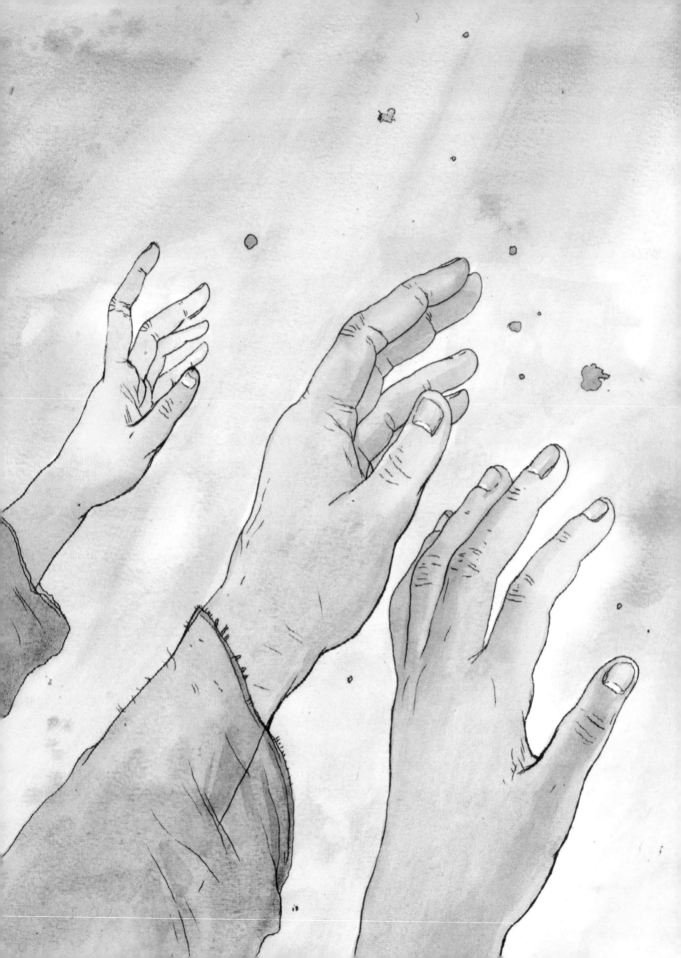

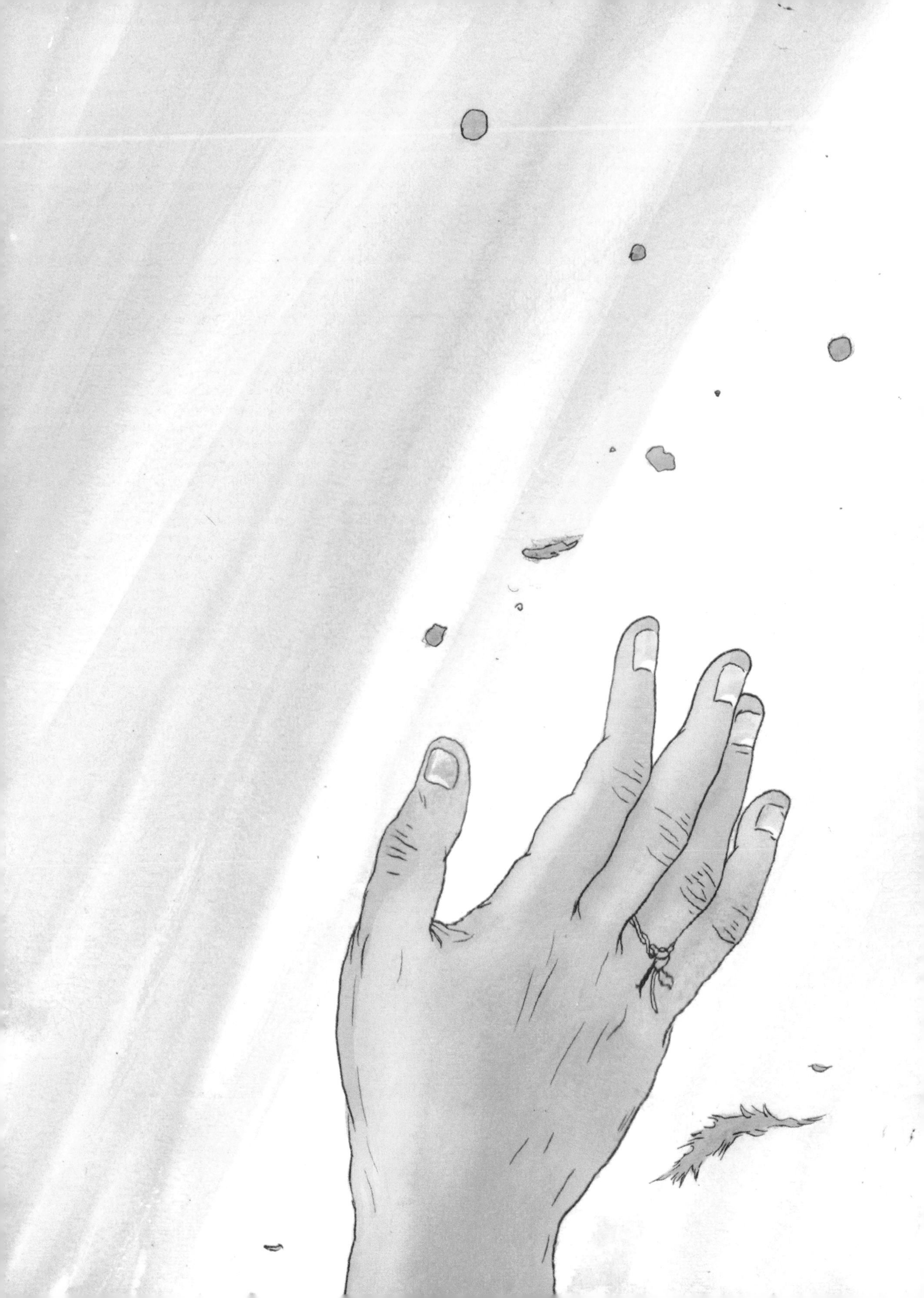

Episode Two
UTOPIA

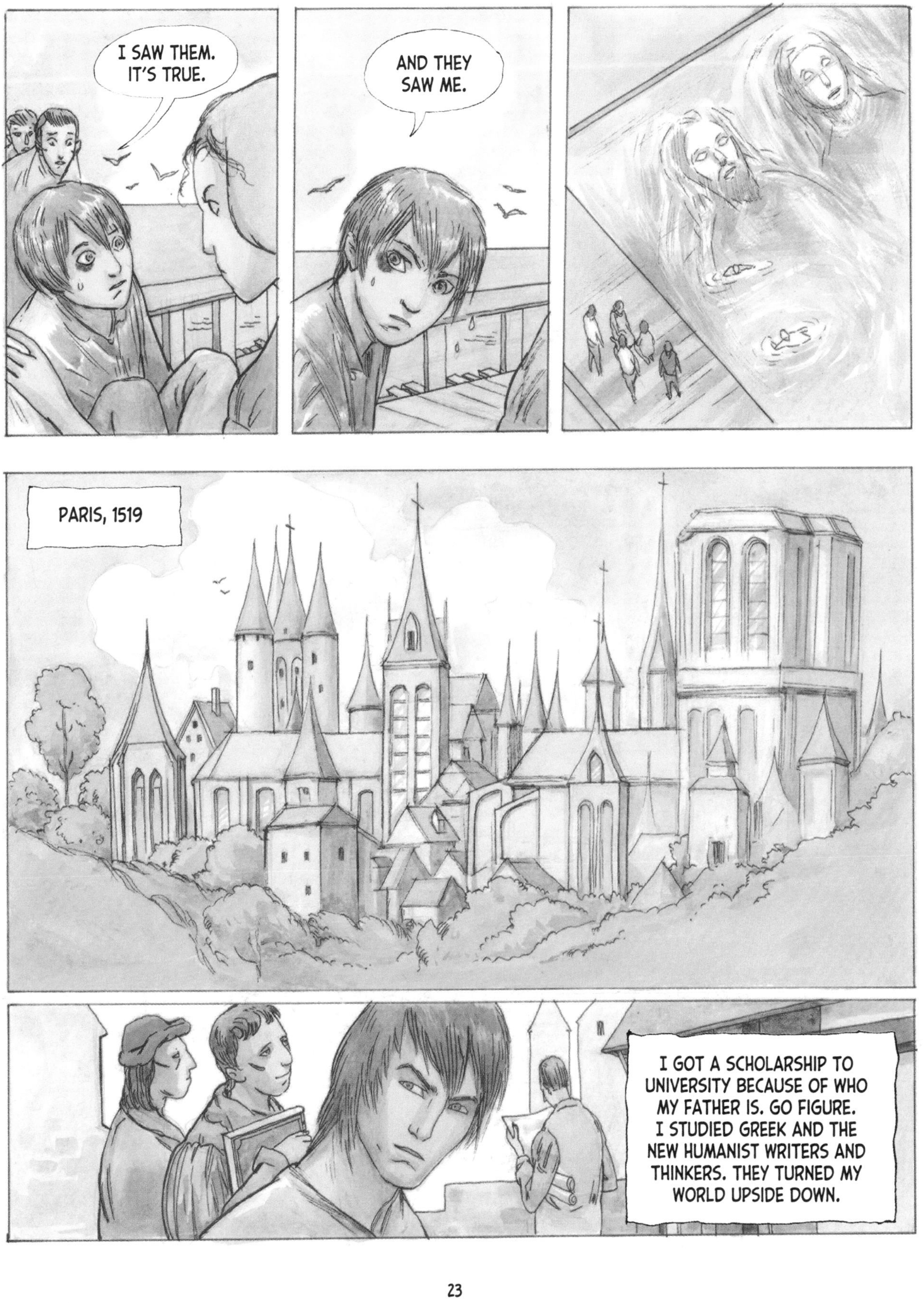
I SAW THEM. IT'S TRUE.
AND THEY SAW ME.
PARIS, 1519
I GOT A SCHOLARSHIP TO UNIVERSITY BECAUSE OF WHO MY FATHER IS. GO FIGURE. I STUDIED GREEK AND THE NEW HUMANIST WRITERS AND THINKERS. THEY TURNED MY WORLD UPSIDE DOWN.

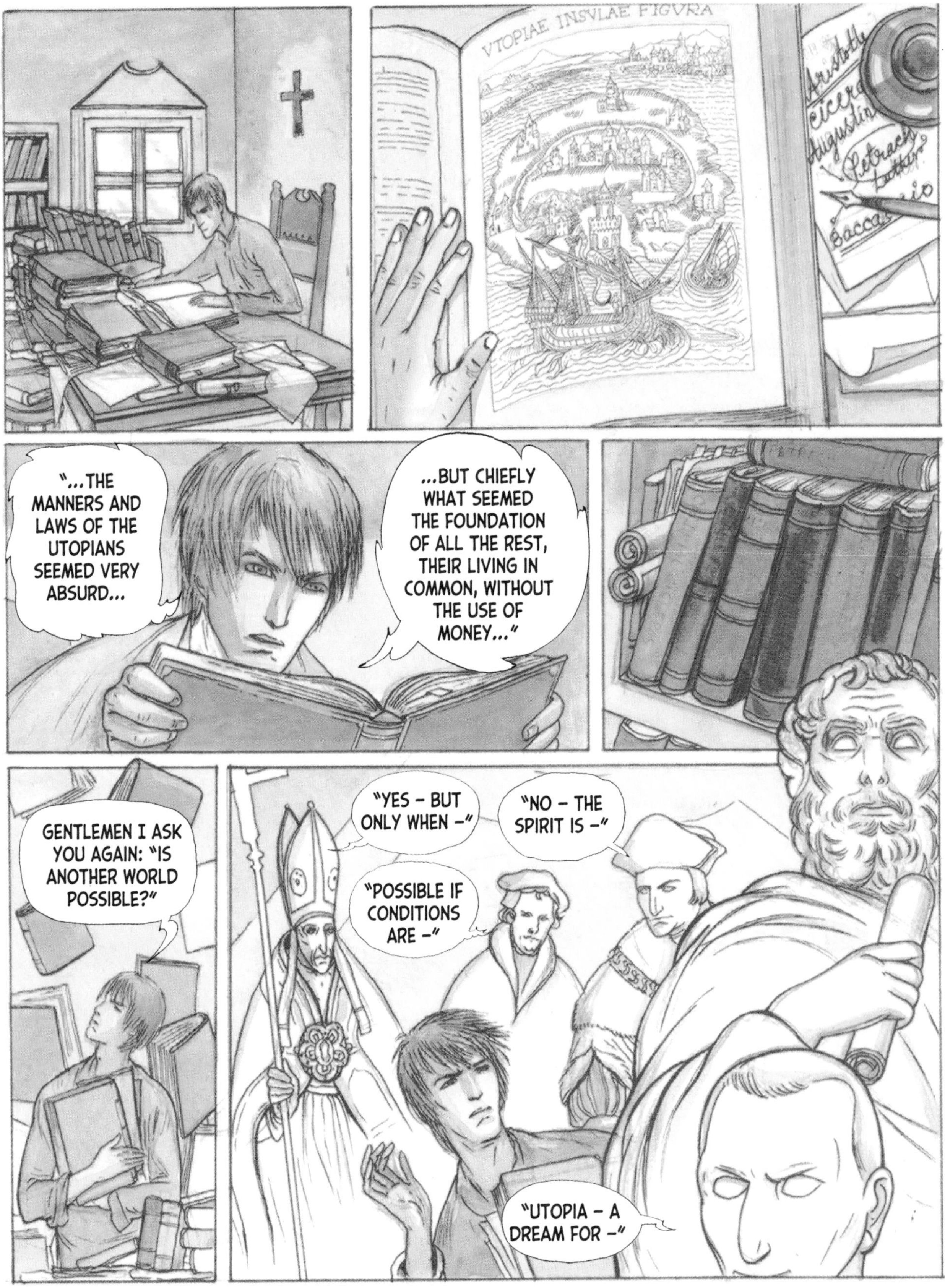
VTOPIAE INSVLAE FIGVRA
"...THE MANNERS AND LAWS OF THE UTOPIANS SEEMED VERY ABSURD...
...BUT CHIEFLY WHAT SEEMED THE FOUNDATION OF ALL THE REST, THEIR LIVING IN COMMON, WITHOUT THE USE OF MONEY..."
GENTLEMEN I ASK YOU AGAIN: "IS ANOTHER WORLD POSSIBLE?"
"YES – BUT ONLY WHEN –"
"NO – THE SPIRIT IS –"
"POSSIBLE IF CONDITIONS ARE –"
"UTOPIA – A DREAM FOR –"

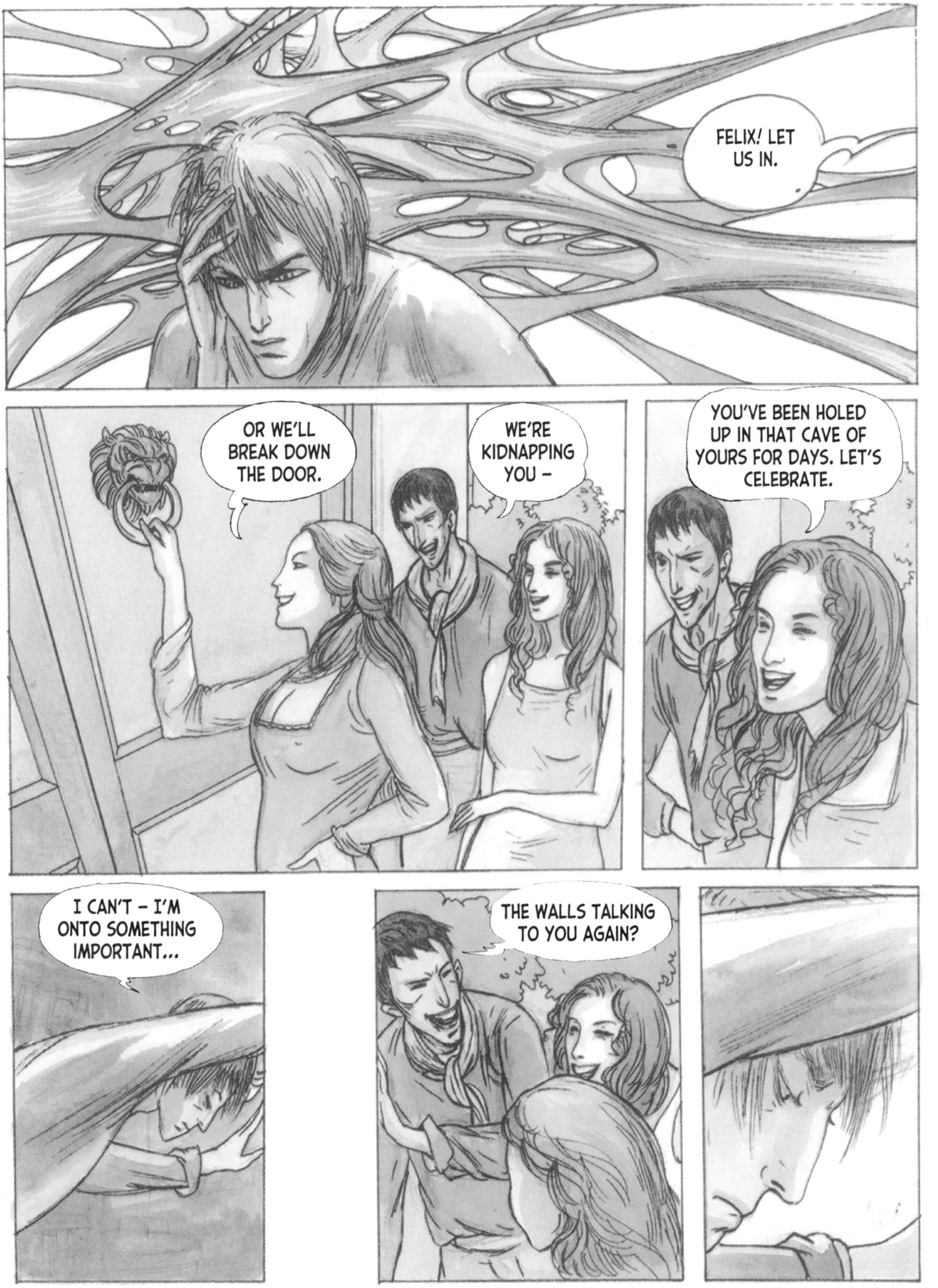
FELIX! LET US IN.
OR WE'LL BREAK DOWN THE DOOR.
WE'RE KIDNAPPING YOU –
YOU'VE BEEN HOLED UP IN THAT CAVE OF YOURS FOR DAYS. LET'S CELEBRATE.
I CAN'T – I'M ONTO SOMETHING IMPORTANT...
THE WALLS TALKING TO YOU AGAIN?

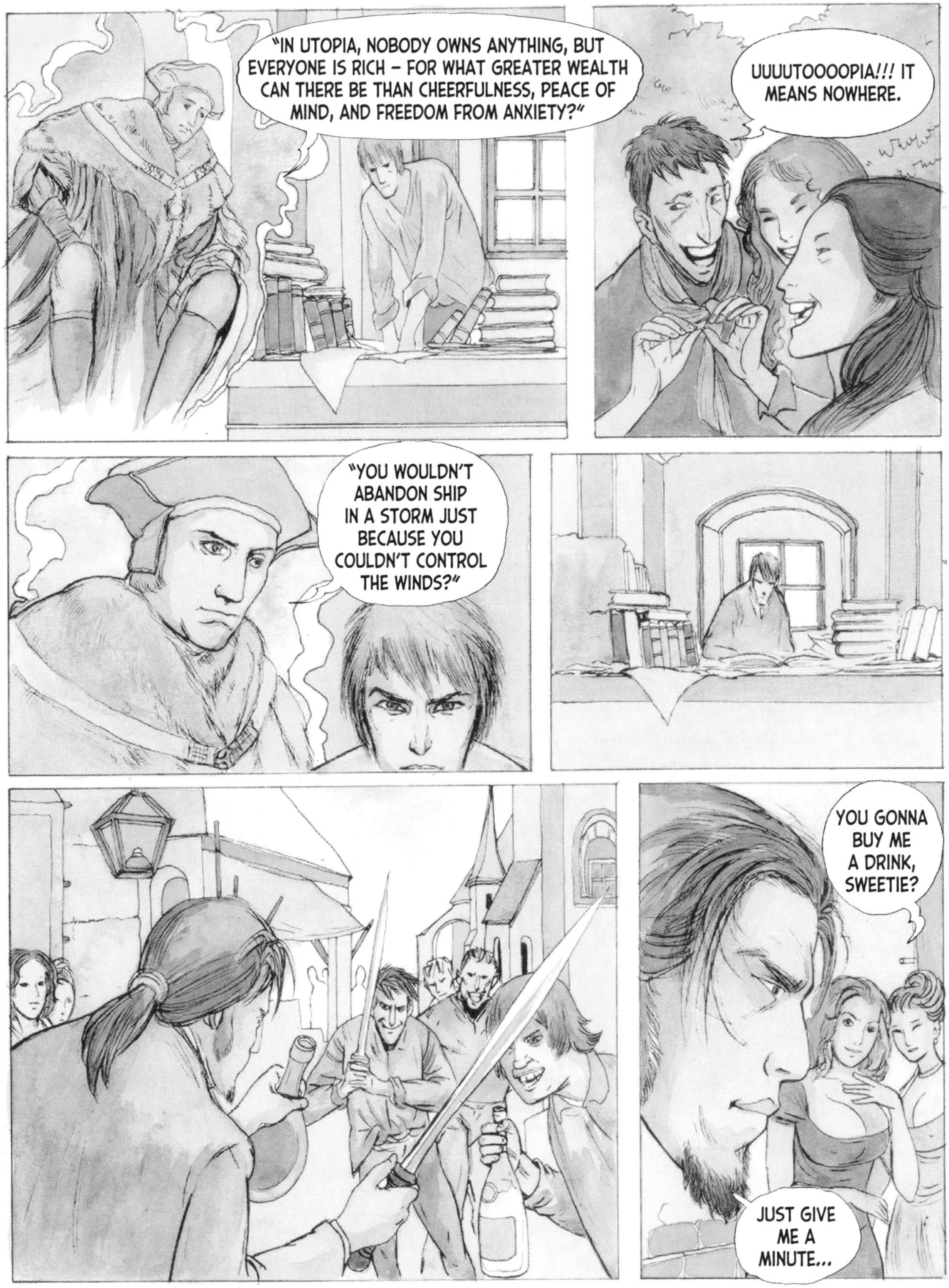
"IN UTOPIA, NOBODY OWNS ANYTHING, BUT EVERYONE IS RICH – FOR WHAT GREATER WEALTH CAN THERE BE THAN CHEERFULNESS, PEACE OF MIND, AND FREEDOM FROM ANXIETY?"
UUUUTOOOOPIA!!! IT MEANS NOWHERE.
"YOU WOULDN'T ABANDON SHIP IN A STORM JUST BECAUSE YOU COULDN'T CONTROL THE WINDS?"
YOU GONNA BUY ME A DRINK, SWEETIE?
JUST GIVE ME A MINUTE...

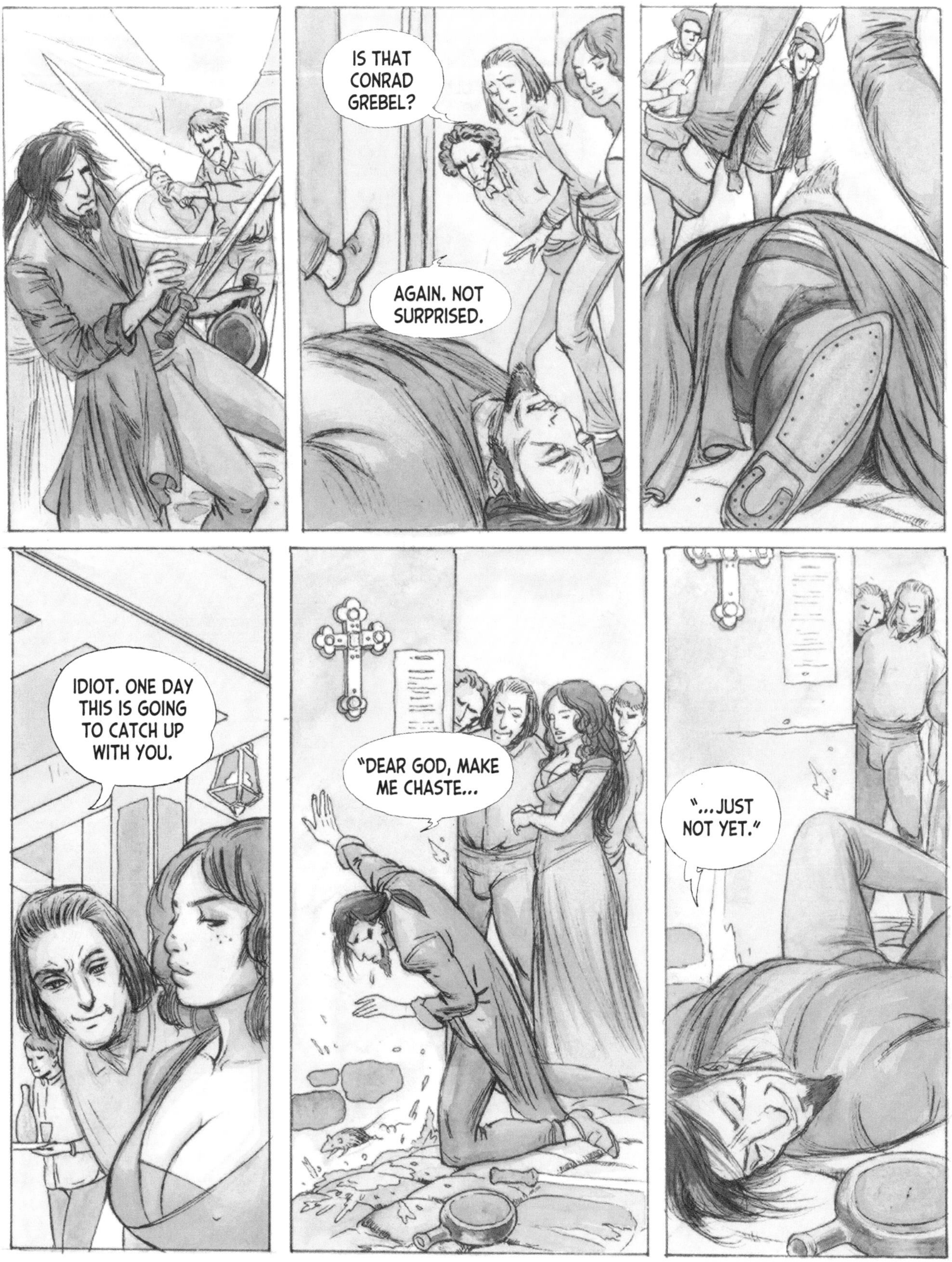
IS THAT CONRAD GREBEL?
AGAIN. NOT SURPRISED.
IDIOT. ONE DAY THIS IS GOING TO CATCH UP WITH YOU.
"DEAR GOD, MAKE ME CHASTE...
"...JUST NOT YET."

Episode Three
THE BLACK DEATH

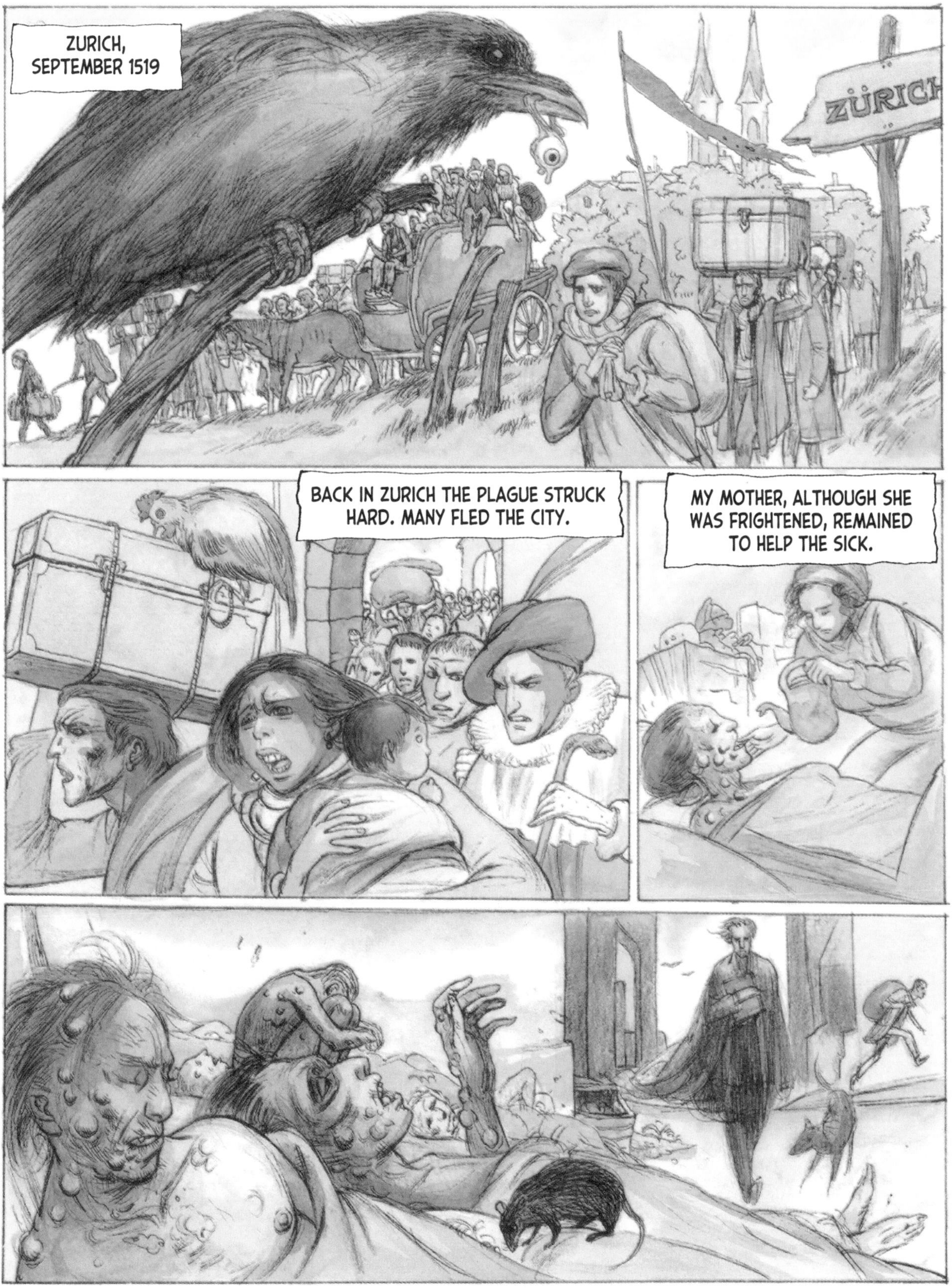
ZURICH, SEPTEMBER 1519
BACK IN ZURICH THE PLAGUE STRUCK HARD. MANY FLED THE CITY.
MY MOTHER, ALTHOUGH SHE WAS FRIGHTENED, REMAINED TO HELP THE SICK.

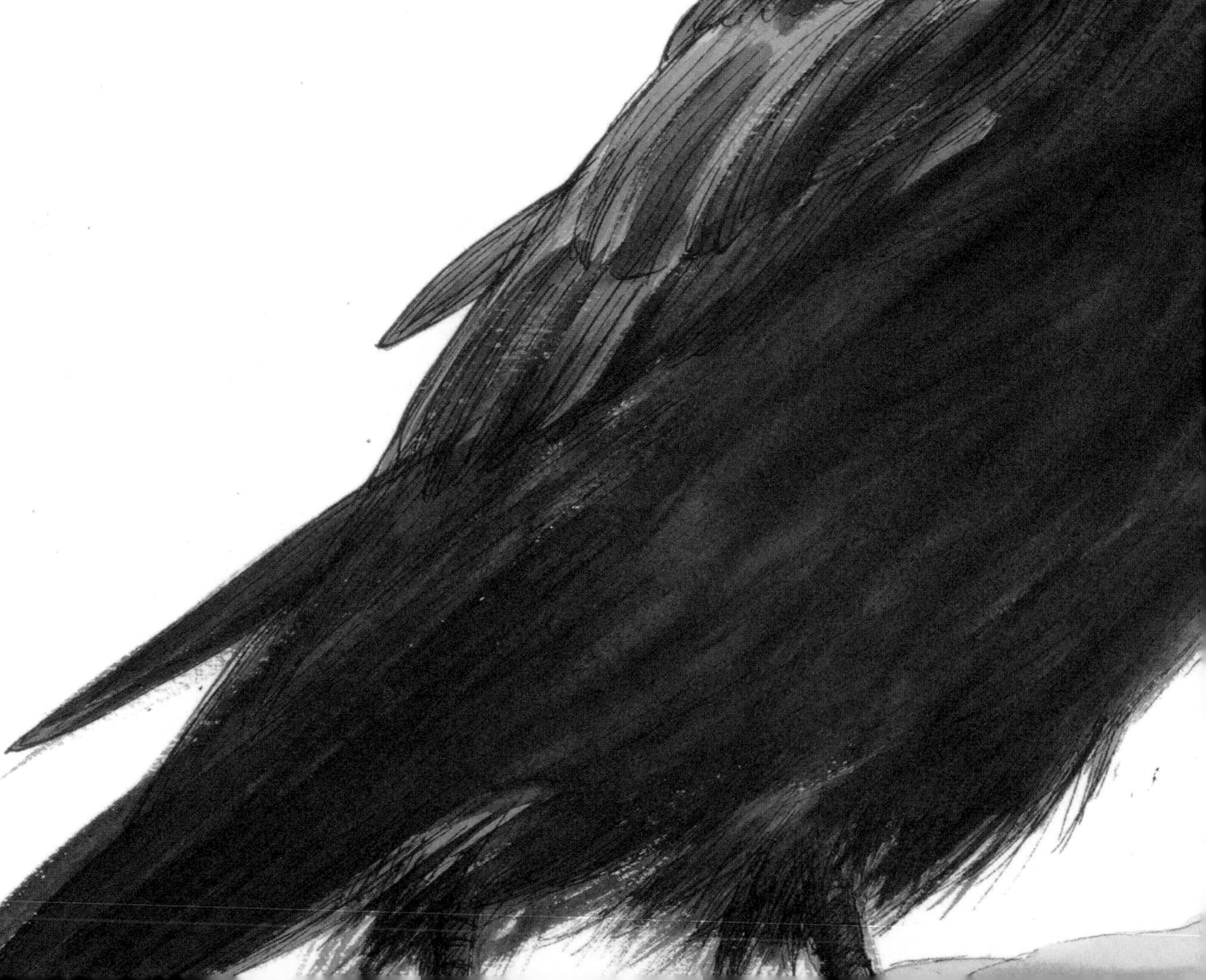

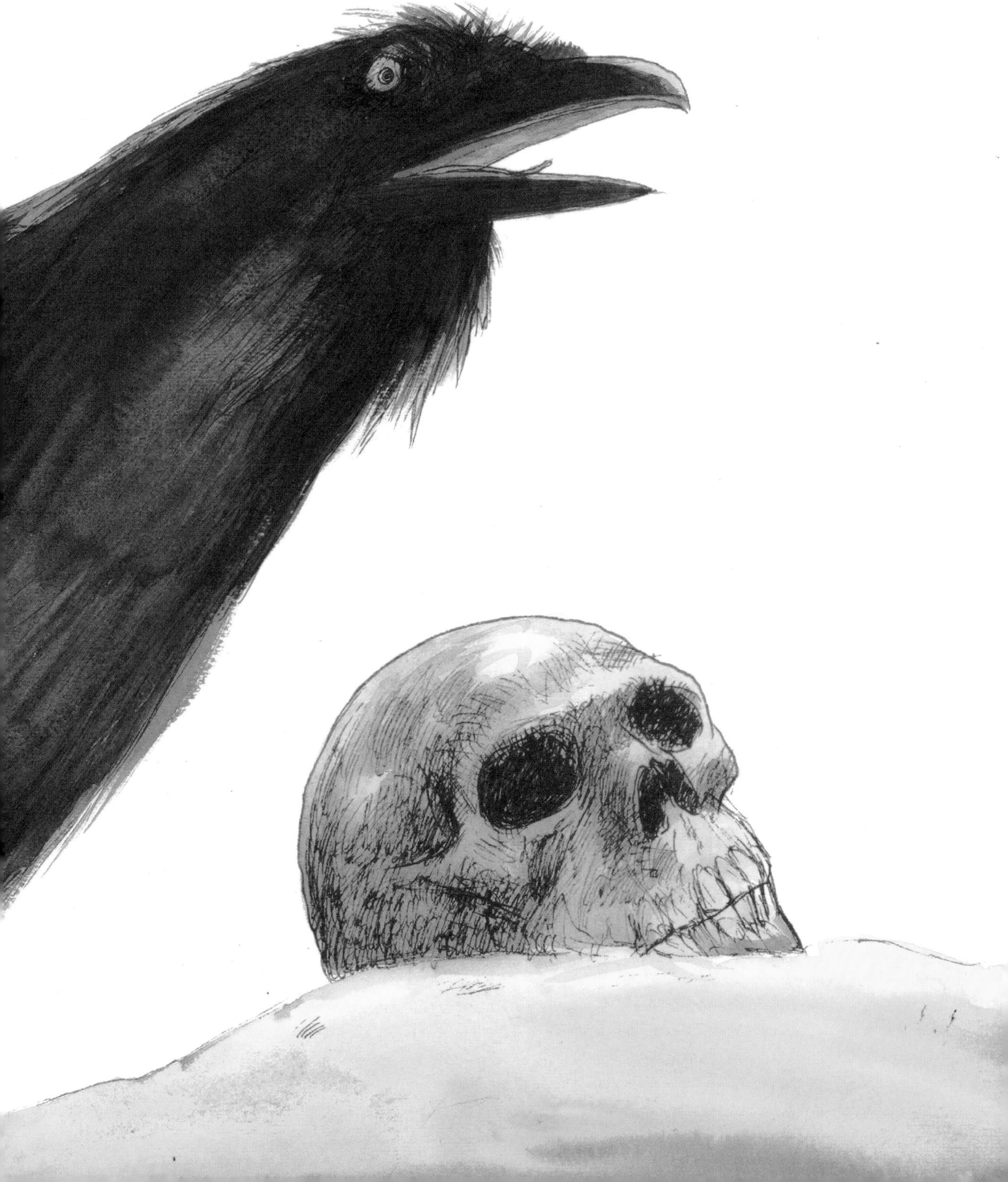

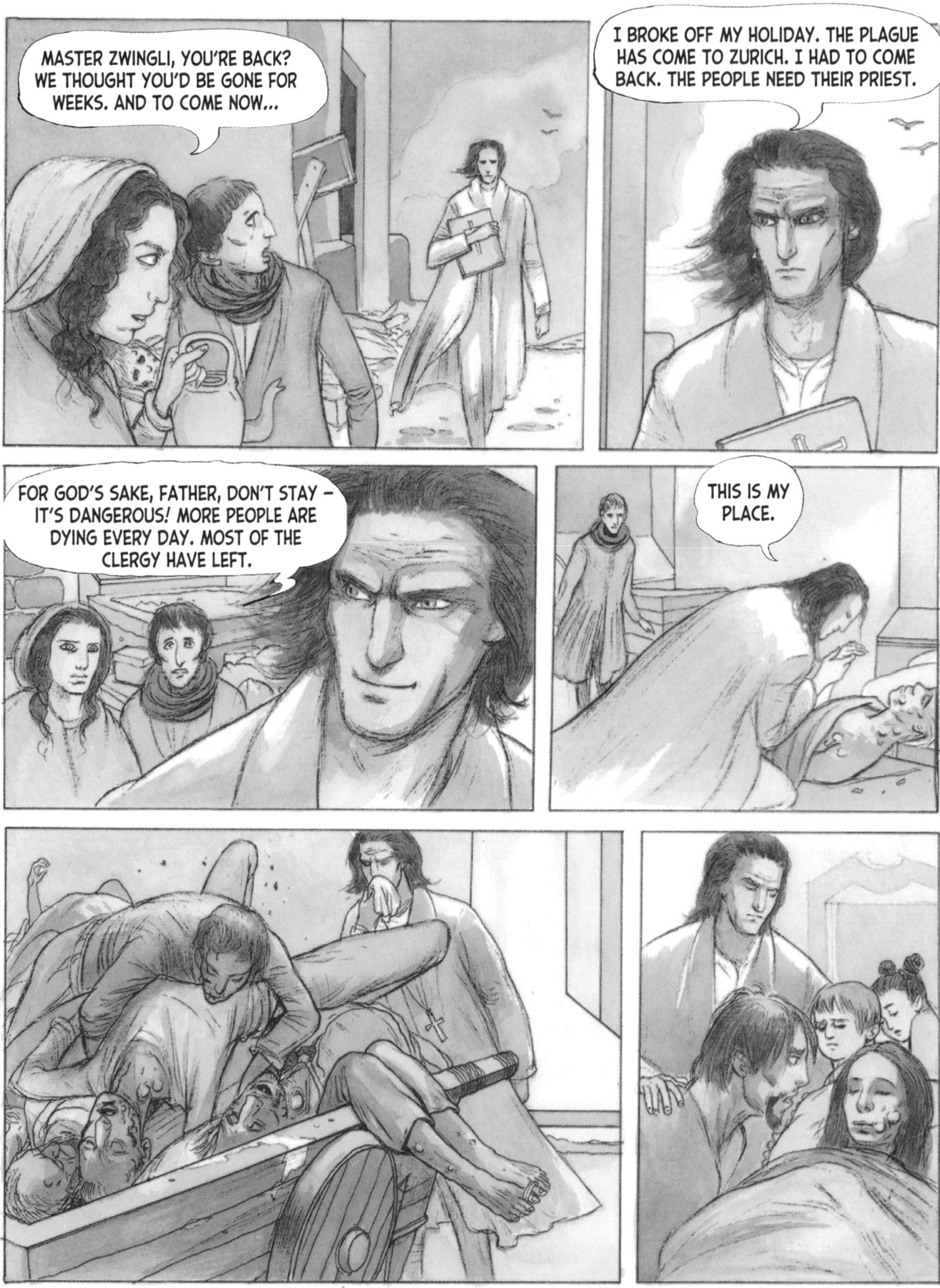
MASTER ZWINGLI, YOU'RE BACK? WE THOUGHT YOU'D BE GONE FOR WEEKS. AND TO COME NOW...
I BROKE OFF MY HOLIDAY. THE PLAGUE HAS COME TO ZURICH. I HAD TO COME BACK. THE PEOPLE NEED THEIR PRIEST.
FOR GOD'S SAKE, FATHER, DON'T STAY – IT'S DANGEROUS! MORE PEOPLE ARE DYING EVERY DAY. MOST OF THE CLERGY HAVE LEFT.
THIS IS MY PLACE.

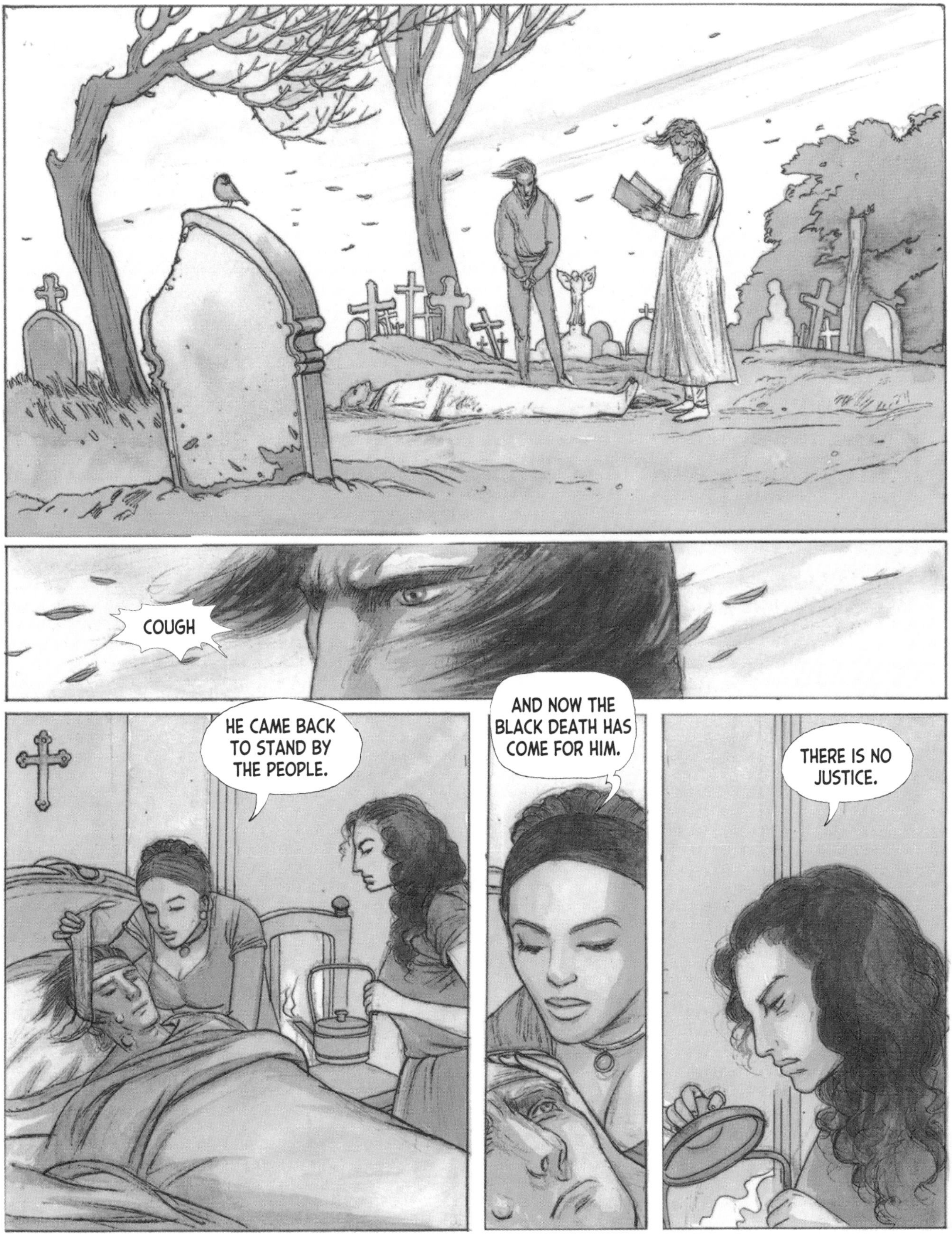
COUGH
HE CAME BACK TO STAND BY THE PEOPLE.
AND NOW THE BLACK DEATH HAS COME FOR HIM.
THERE IS NO JUSTICE.

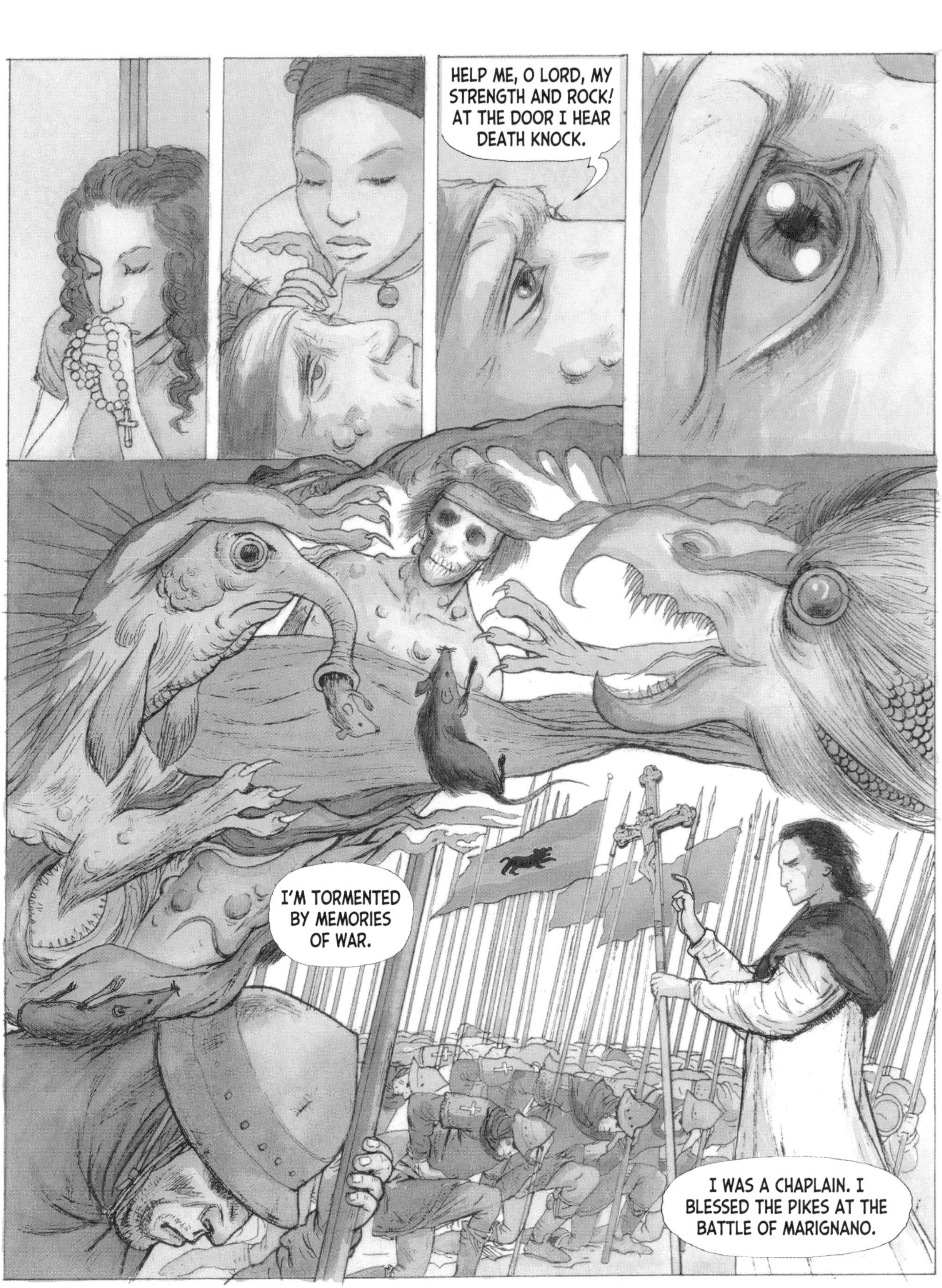
HELP ME, O LORD, MY STRENGTH AND ROCK! AT THE DOOR I HEAR DEATH KNOCK.
I'M TORMENTED BY MEMORIES OF WAR.
I WAS A CHAPLAIN. I BLESSED THE PIKES AT THE BATTLE OF MARIGNANO.

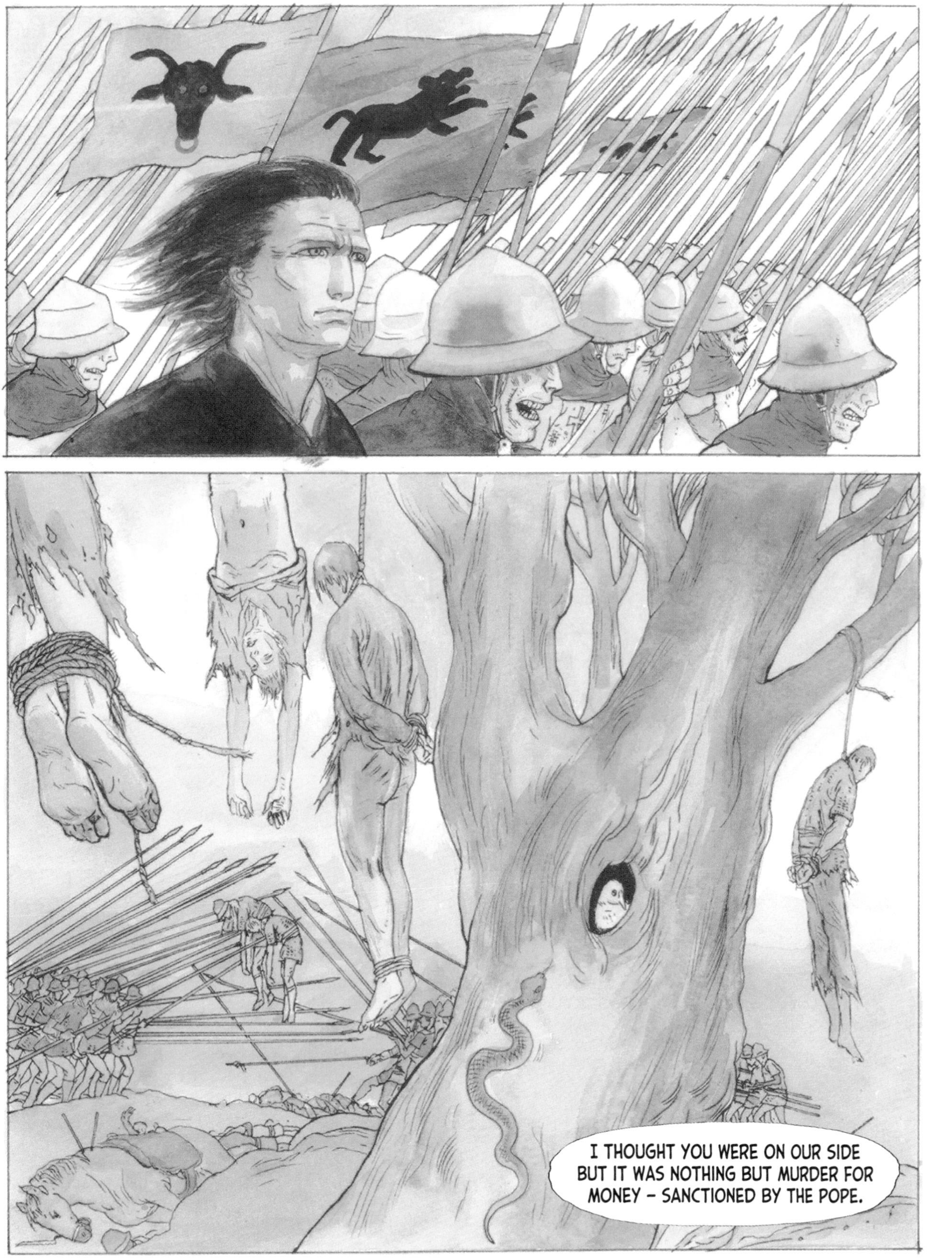
I THOUGHT YOU WERE ON OUR SIDE
BUT IT WAS NOTHING BUT MURDER FOR
MONEY – SANCTIONED BY THE POPE.

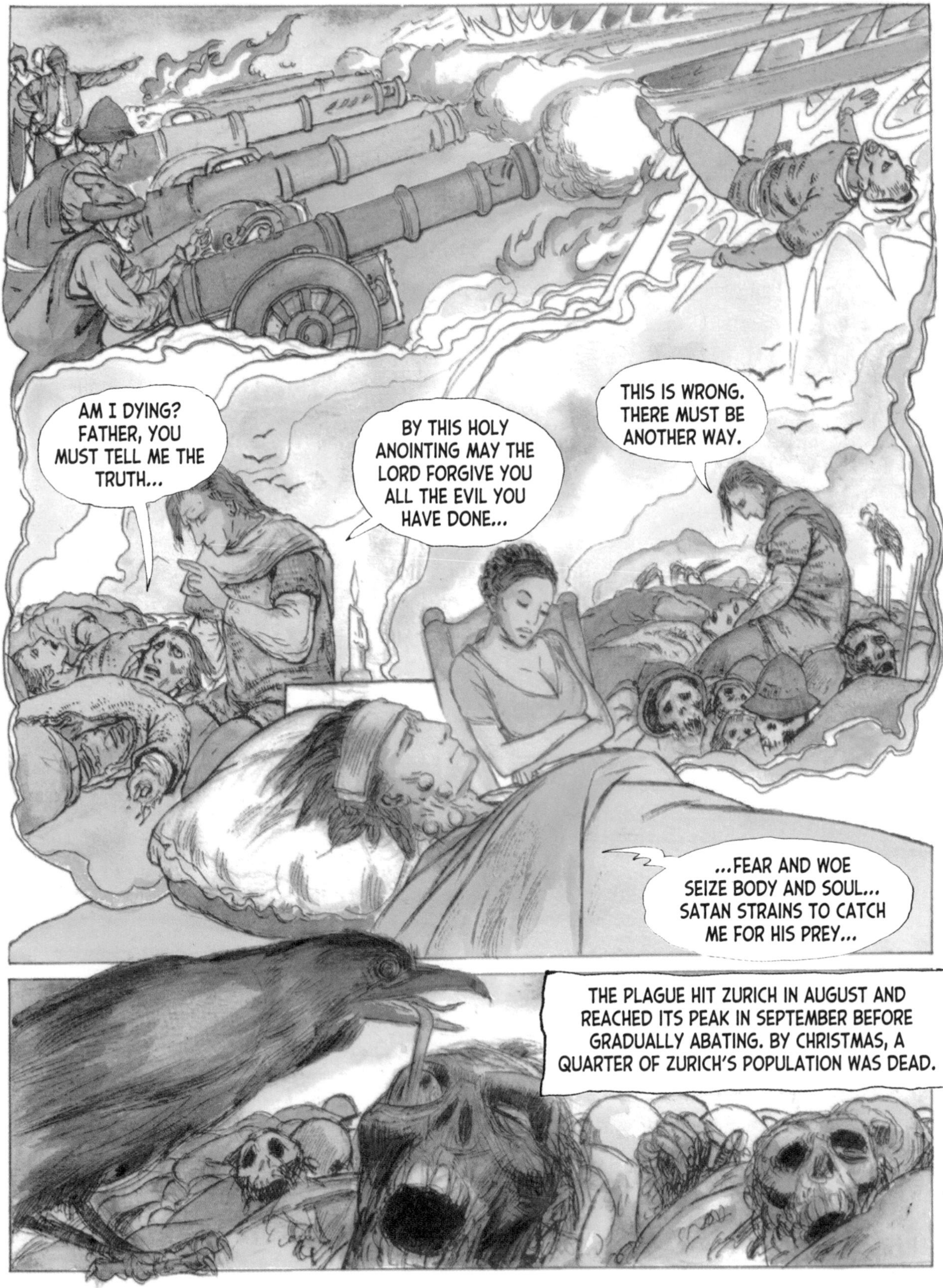

AM I DYING? FATHER, YOU MUST TELL ME THE TRUTH...
BY THIS HOLY ANOINTING MAY THE LORD FORGIVE YOU ALL THE EVIL YOU HAVE DONE...
THIS IS WRONG. THERE MUST BE ANOTHER WAY.
...FEAR AND WOE SEIZE BODY AND SOUL... SATAN STRAINS TO CATCH ME FOR HIS PREY...
THE PLAGUE HIT ZURICH IN AUGUST AND REACHED ITS PEAK IN SEPTEMBER BEFORE GRADUALLY ABATING. BY CHRISTMAS, A QUARTER OF ZURICH'S POPULATION WAS DEAD.

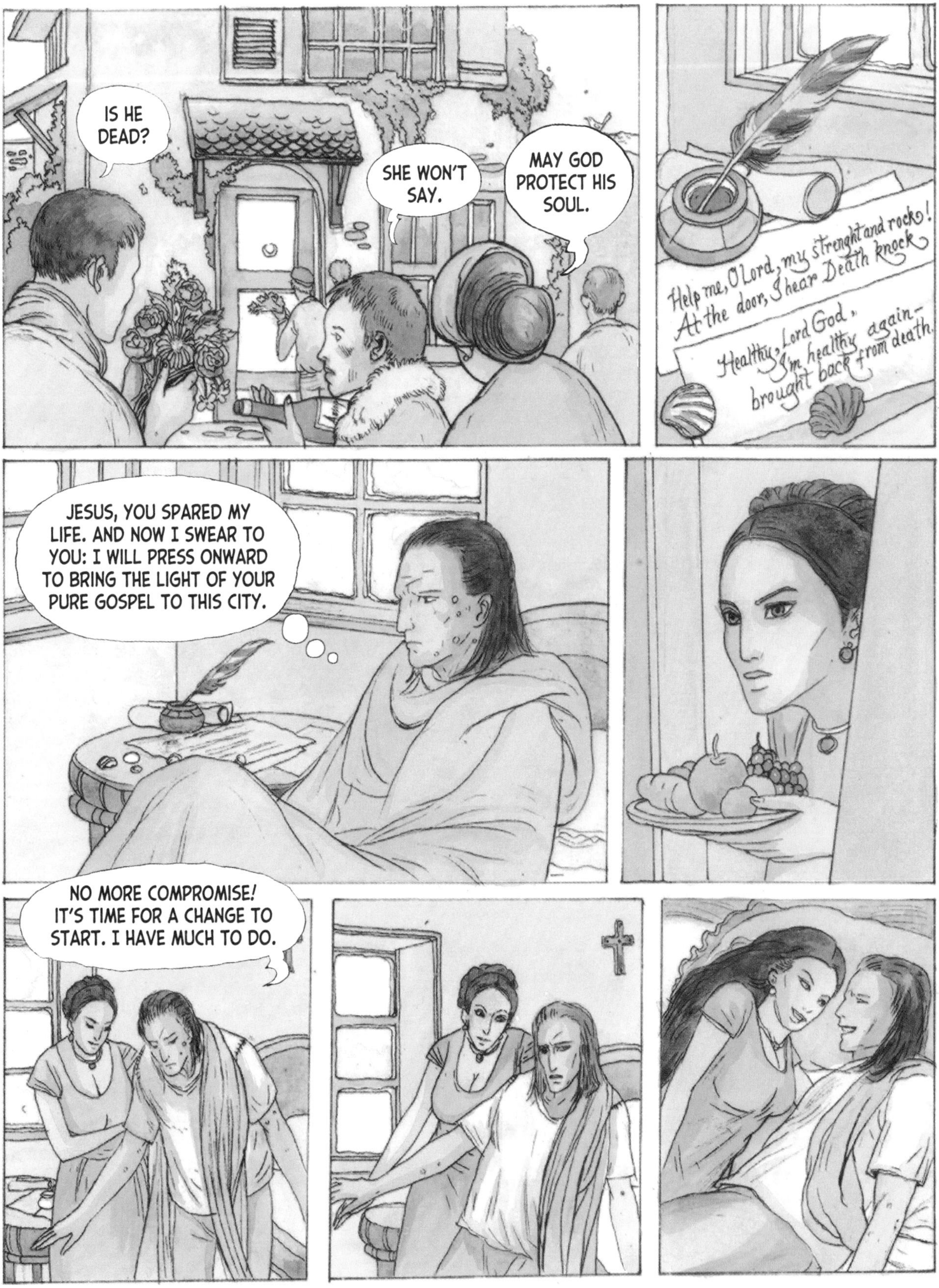
IS HE DEAD?
SHE WON'T SAY.
MAY GOD PROTECT HIS SOUL.
Help me, O Lord, my strenght and rock! At the door, I hear Death knock
Healthy, Lord God, I'm healthy again— brought back from death.
JESUS, YOU SPARED MY LIFE. AND NOW I SWEAR TO YOU: I WILL PRESS ONWARD TO BRING THE LIGHT OF YOUR PURE GOSPEL TO THIS CITY.
NO MORE COMPROMISE! IT'S TIME FOR A CHANGE TO START. I HAVE MUCH TO DO.

Episode Four
THE TEACHER

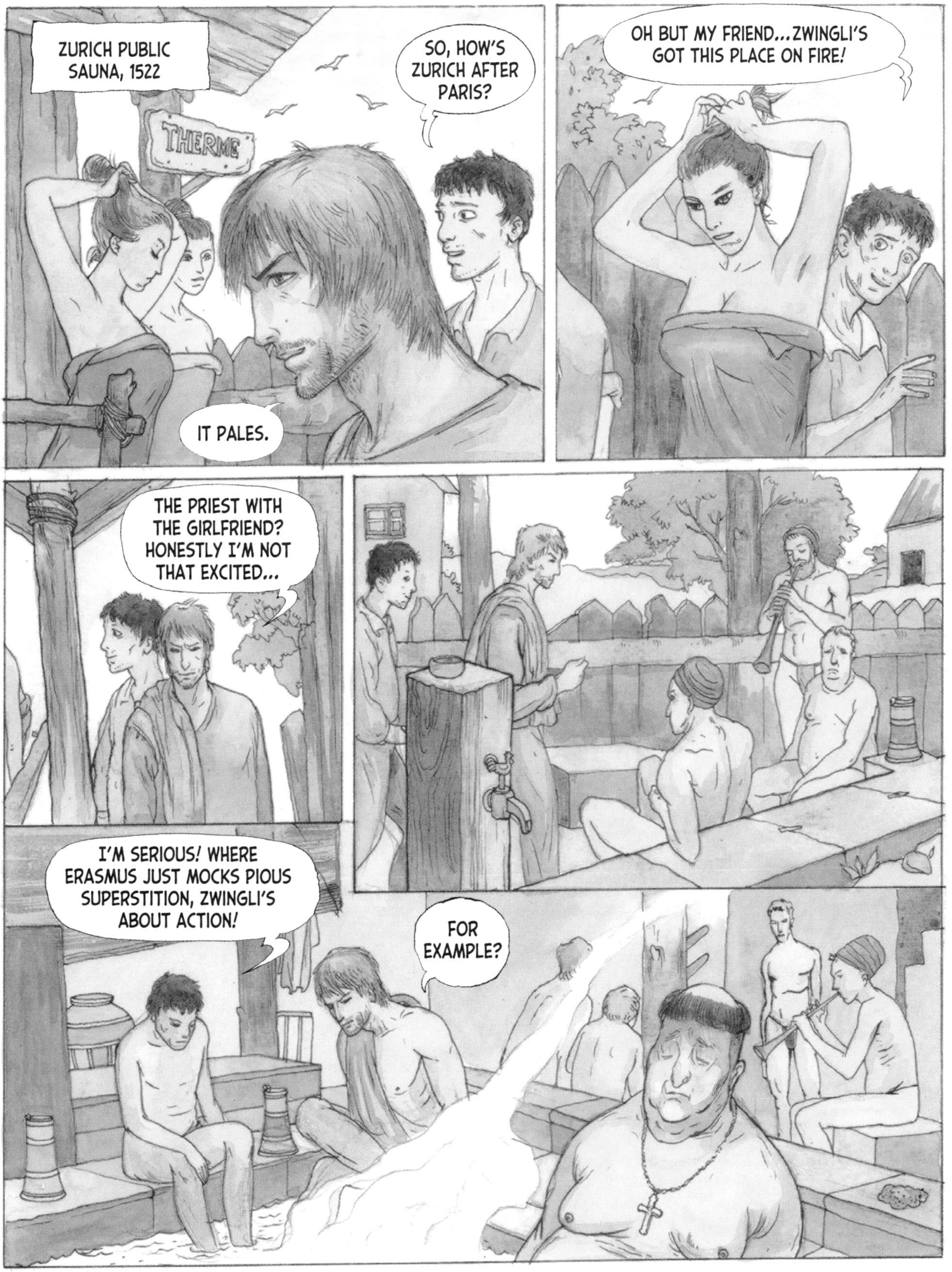
ZURICH PUBLIC SAUNA, 1522
SO, HOW'S ZURICH AFTER PARIS?
THERME
IT PALES.
OH BUT MY FRIEND...ZWINGLI'S GOT THIS PLACE ON FIRE!
THE PRIEST WITH THE GIRLFRIEND? HONESTLY I'M NOT THAT EXCITED...
I'M SERIOUS! WHERE ERASMUS JUST MOCKS PIOUS SUPERSTITION, ZWINGLI'S ABOUT ACTION!
FOR EXAMPLE?

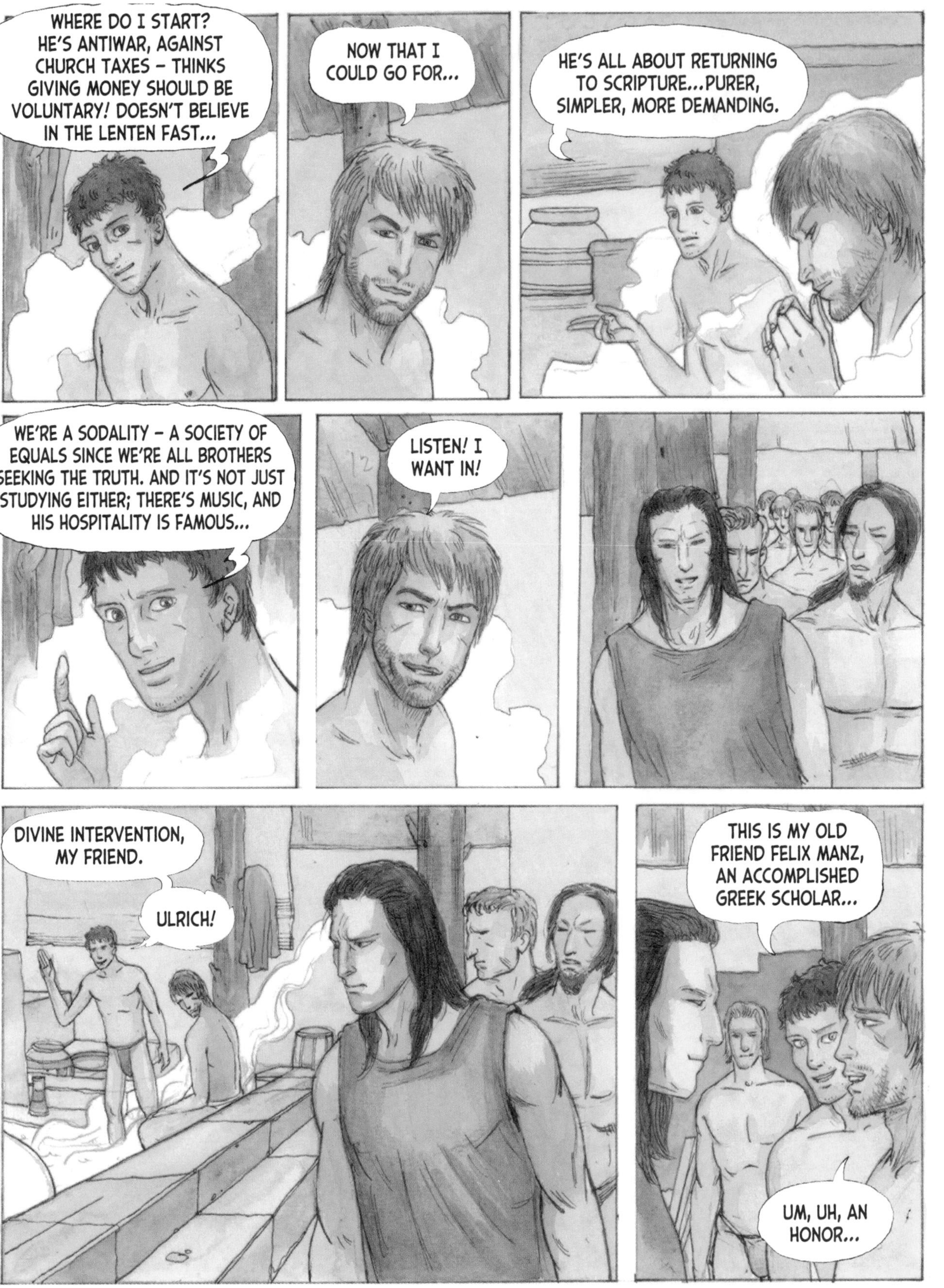
WHERE DO I START? HE'S ANTIWAR, AGAINST CHURCH TAXES – THINKS GIVING MONEY SHOULD BE VOLUNTARY! DOESN'T BELIEVE IN THE LENTEN FAST...
NOW THAT I COULD GO FOR...
HE'S ALL ABOUT RETURNING TO SCRIPTURE...PURER, SIMPLER, MORE DEMANDING.
WE'RE A SODALITY – A SOCIETY OF EQUALS SINCE WE'RE ALL BROTHERS SEEKING THE TRUTH. AND IT'S NOT JUST STUDYING EITHER; THERE'S MUSIC, AND HIS HOSPITALITY IS FAMOUS...
LISTEN! I WANT IN!
DIVINE INTERVENTION, MY FRIEND.
ULRICH!
THIS IS MY OLD FRIEND FELIX MANZ, AN ACCOMPLISHED GREEK SCHOLAR...
UM, UH, AN HONOR...

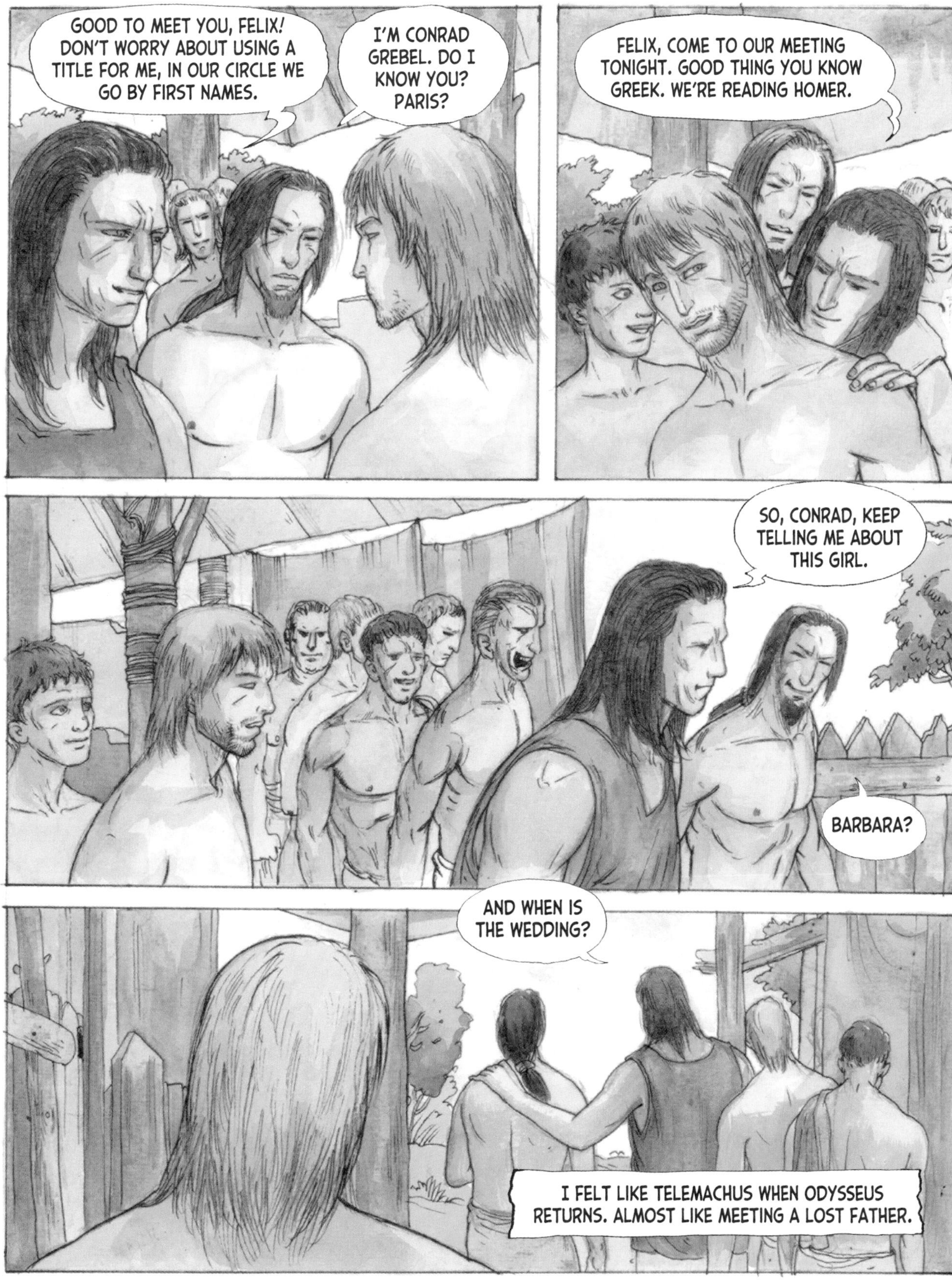
GOOD TO MEET YOU, FELIX! DON'T WORRY ABOUT USING A TITLE FOR ME, IN OUR CIRCLE WE GO BY FIRST NAMES.
I'M CONRAD GREBEL. DO I KNOW YOU? PARIS?
FELIX, COME TO OUR MEETING TONIGHT. GOOD THING YOU KNOW GREEK. WE'RE READING HOMER.
SO, CONRAD, KEEP TELLING ME ABOUT THIS GIRL.
BARBARA?
AND WHEN IS THE WEDDING?
I FELT LIKE TELEMACHUS WHEN ODYSSEUS RETURNS. ALMOST LIKE MEETING A LOST FATHER.

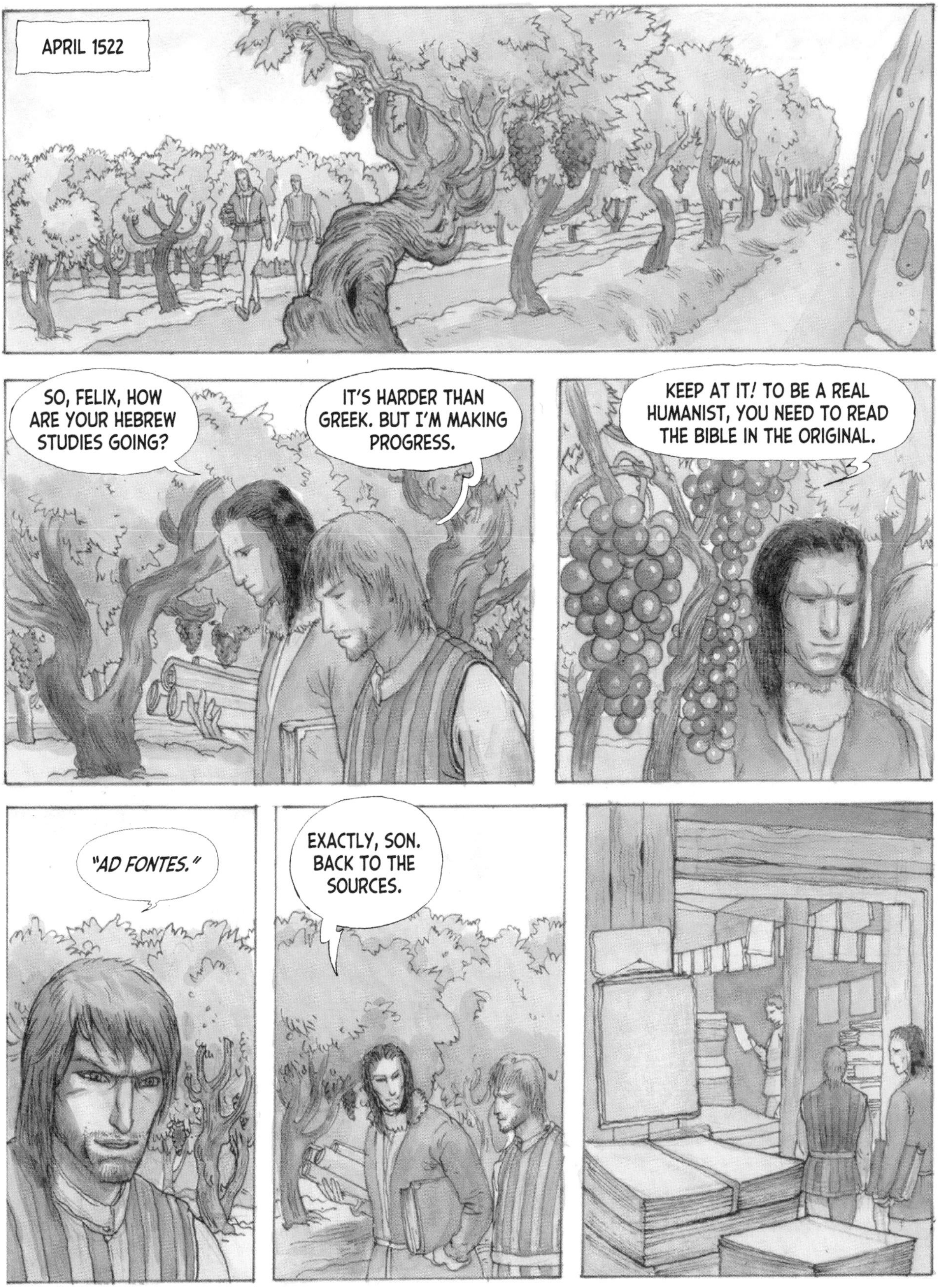
APRIL 1522
SO, FELIX, HOW ARE YOUR HEBREW STUDIES GOING?
IT'S HARDER THAN GREEK. BUT I'M MAKING PROGRESS.
KEEP AT IT! TO BE A REAL HUMANIST, YOU NEED TO READ THE BIBLE IN THE ORIGINAL.
"AD FONTES."
EXACTLY, SON. BACK TO THE SOURCES.

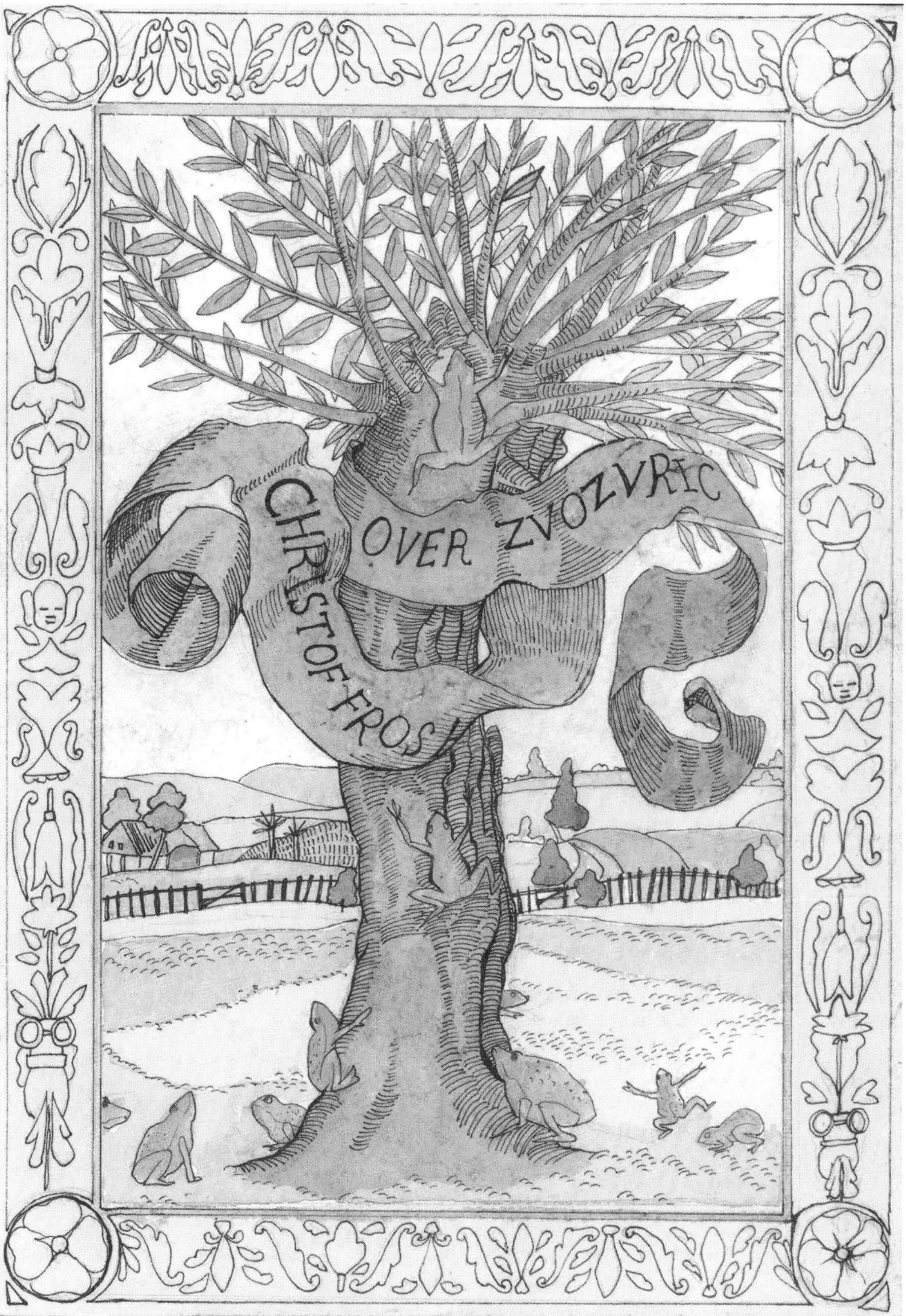
CHRISTOF FROS
OVER ZVOZVRIC

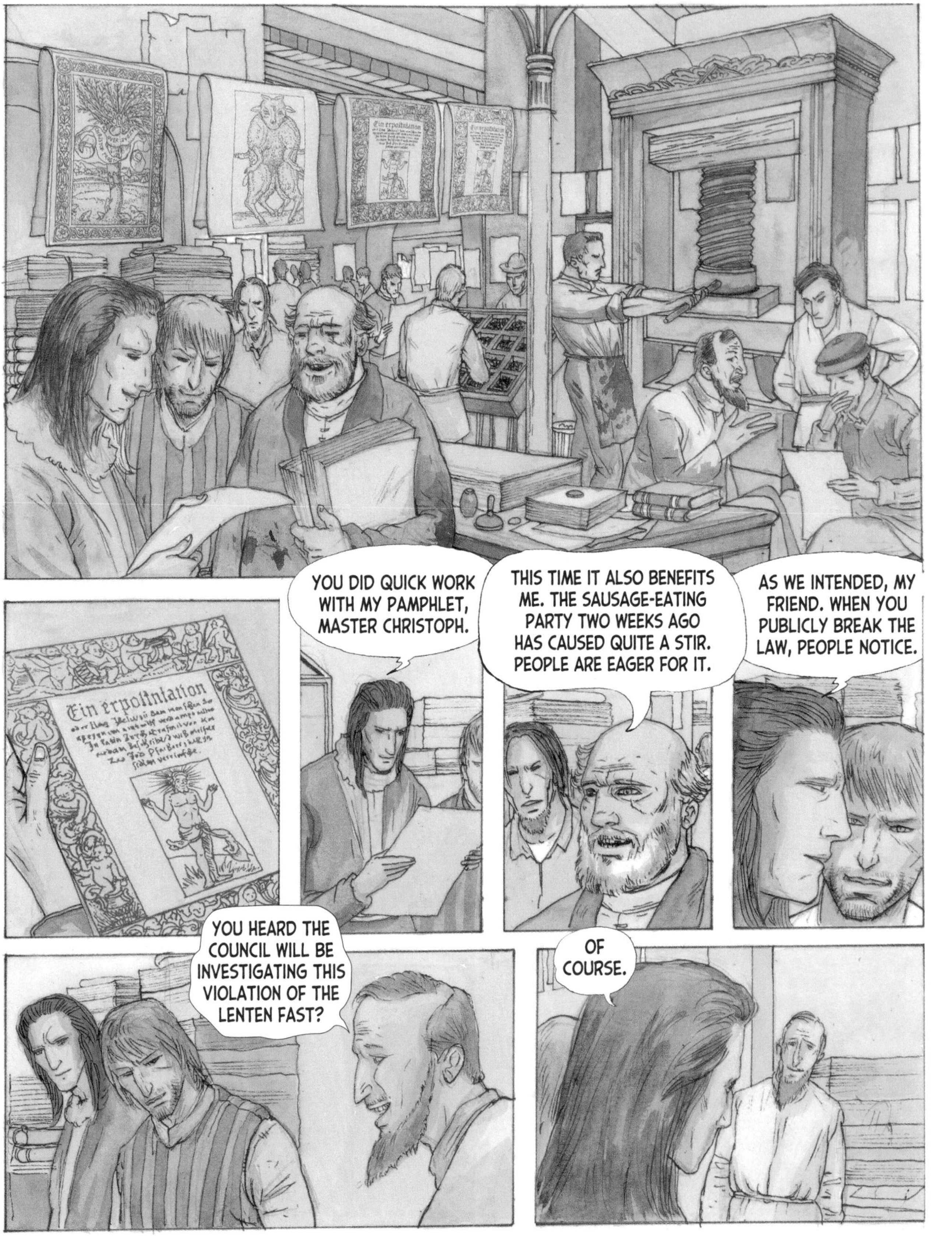
YOU DID QUICK WORK WITH MY PAMPHLET, MASTER CHRISTOPH.
THIS TIME IT ALSO BENEFITS ME. THE SAUSAGE-EATING PARTY TWO WEEKS AGO HAS CAUSED QUITE A STIR. PEOPLE ARE EAGER FOR IT.
AS WE INTENDED, MY FRIEND. WHEN YOU PUBLICLY BREAK THE LAW, PEOPLE NOTICE.
YOU HEARD THE COUNCIL WILL BE INVESTIGATING THIS VIOLATION OF THE LENTEN FAST?
OF COURSE.

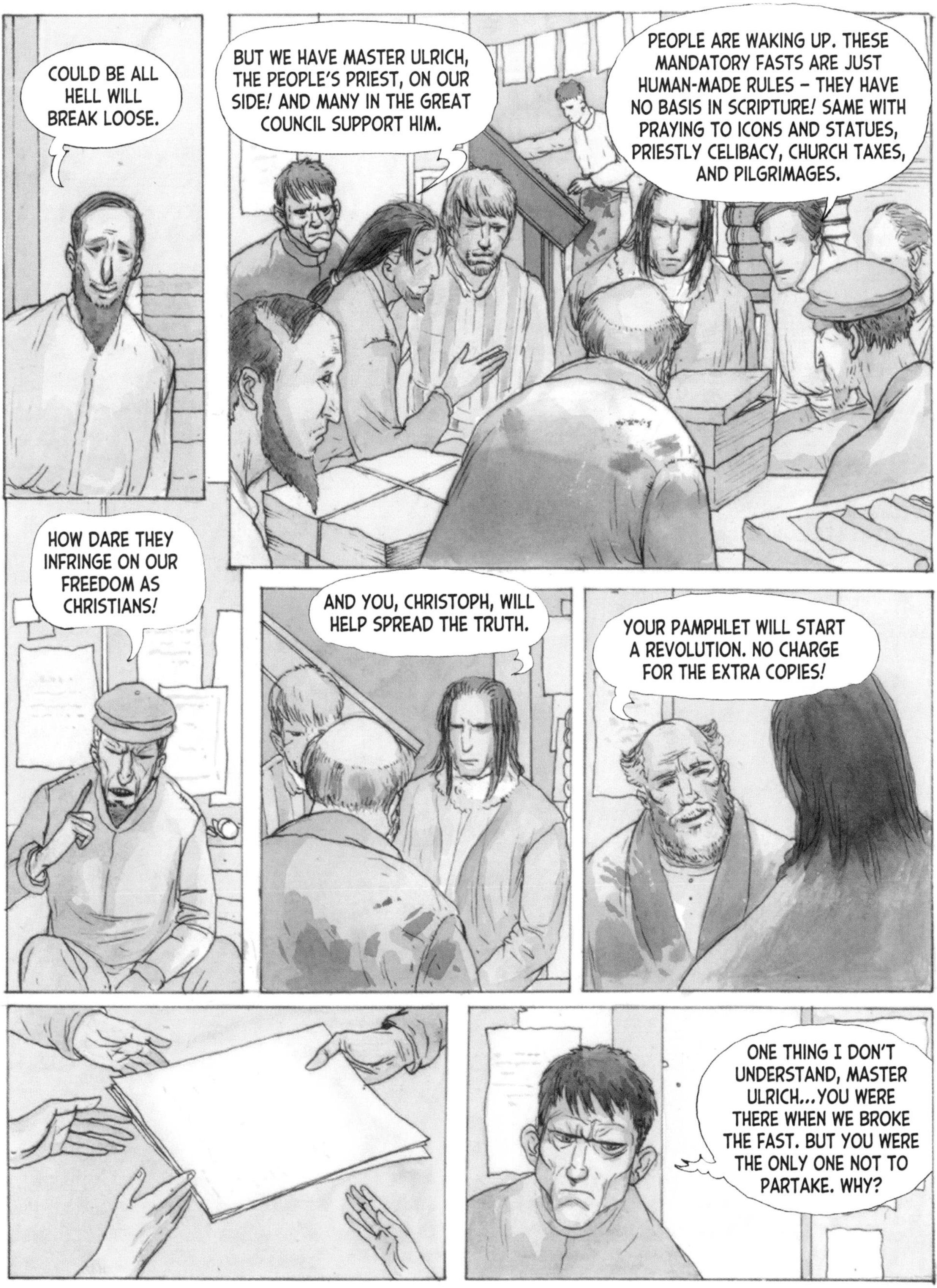
COULD BE ALL HELL WILL BREAK LOOSE.
BUT WE HAVE MASTER ULRICH, THE PEOPLE'S PRIEST, ON OUR SIDE! AND MANY IN THE GREAT COUNCIL SUPPORT HIM.
PEOPLE ARE WAKING UP. THESE MANDATORY FASTS ARE JUST HUMAN-MADE RULES – THEY HAVE NO BASIS IN SCRIPTURE! SAME WITH PRAYING TO ICONS AND STATUES, PRIESTLY CELIBACY, CHURCH TAXES, AND PILGRIMAGES.
HOW DARE THEY INFRINGE ON OUR FREEDOM AS CHRISTIANS!
AND YOU, CHRISTOPH, WILL HELP SPREAD THE TRUTH.
YOUR PAMPHLET WILL START A REVOLUTION. NO CHARGE FOR THE EXTRA COPIES!
ONE THING I DON'T UNDERSTAND, MASTER ULRICH...YOU WERE THERE WHEN WE BROKE THE FAST. BUT YOU WERE THE ONLY ONE NOT TO PARTAKE. WHY?

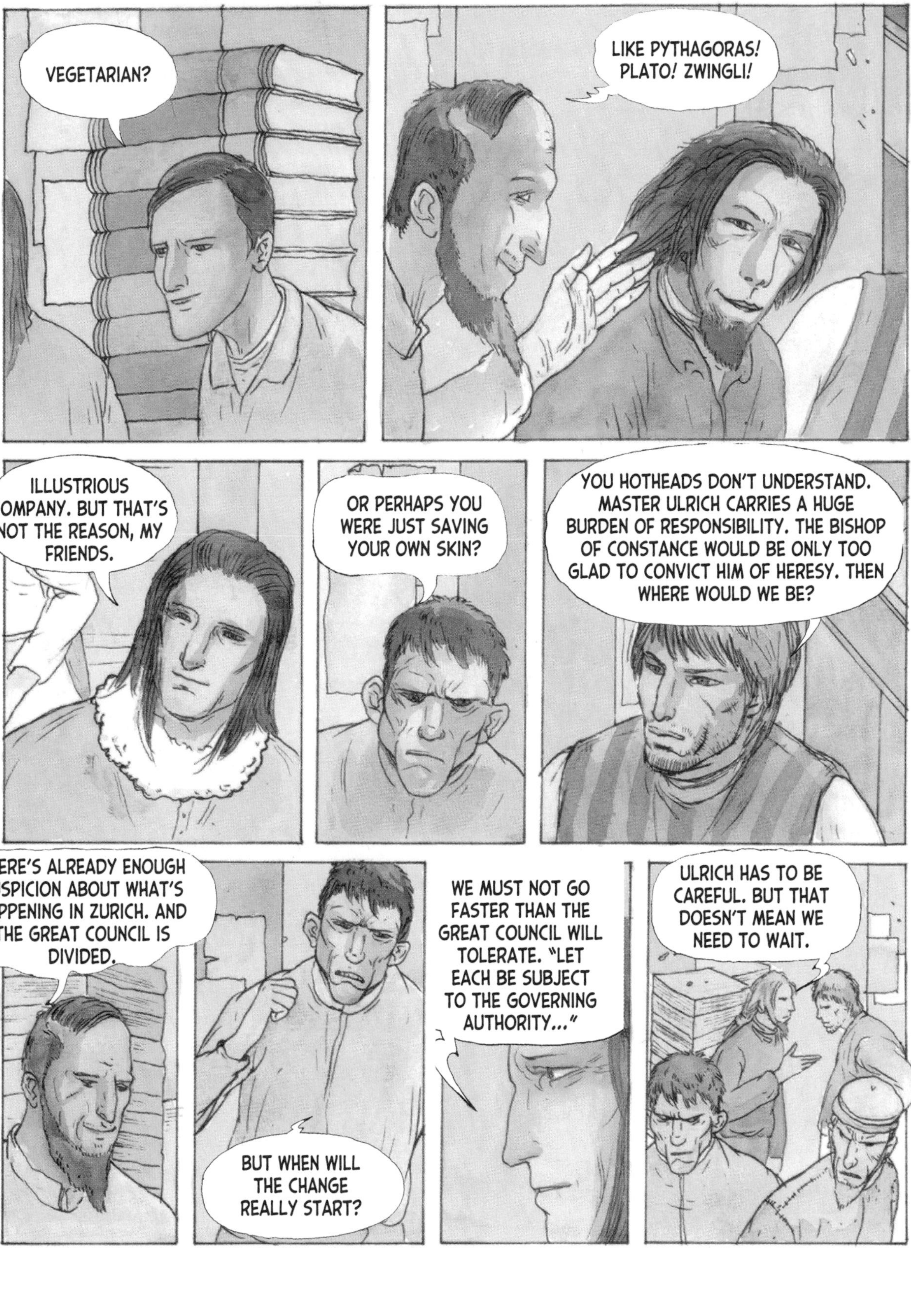
VEGETARIAN?
LIKE PYTHAGORAS! PLATO! ZWINGLI!
ILLUSTRIOUS COMPANY. BUT THAT'S NOT THE REASON, MY FRIENDS.
OR PERHAPS YOU WERE JUST SAVING YOUR OWN SKIN?
YOU HOTHEADS DON'T UNDERSTAND. MASTER ULRICH CARRIES A HUGE BURDEN OF RESPONSIBILITY. THE BISHOP OF CONSTANCE WOULD BE ONLY TOO GLAD TO CONVICT HIM OF HERESY. THEN WHERE WOULD WE BE?
THERE'S ALREADY ENOUGH SUSPICION ABOUT WHAT'S HAPPENING IN ZURICH. AND THE GREAT COUNCIL IS DIVIDED.
BUT WHEN WILL THE CHANGE REALLY START?
WE MUST NOT GO FASTER THAN THE GREAT COUNCIL WILL TOLERATE. "LET EACH BE SUBJECT TO THE GOVERNING AUTHORITY..."
ULRICH HAS TO BE CAREFUL. BUT THAT DOESN'T MEAN WE NEED TO WAIT.

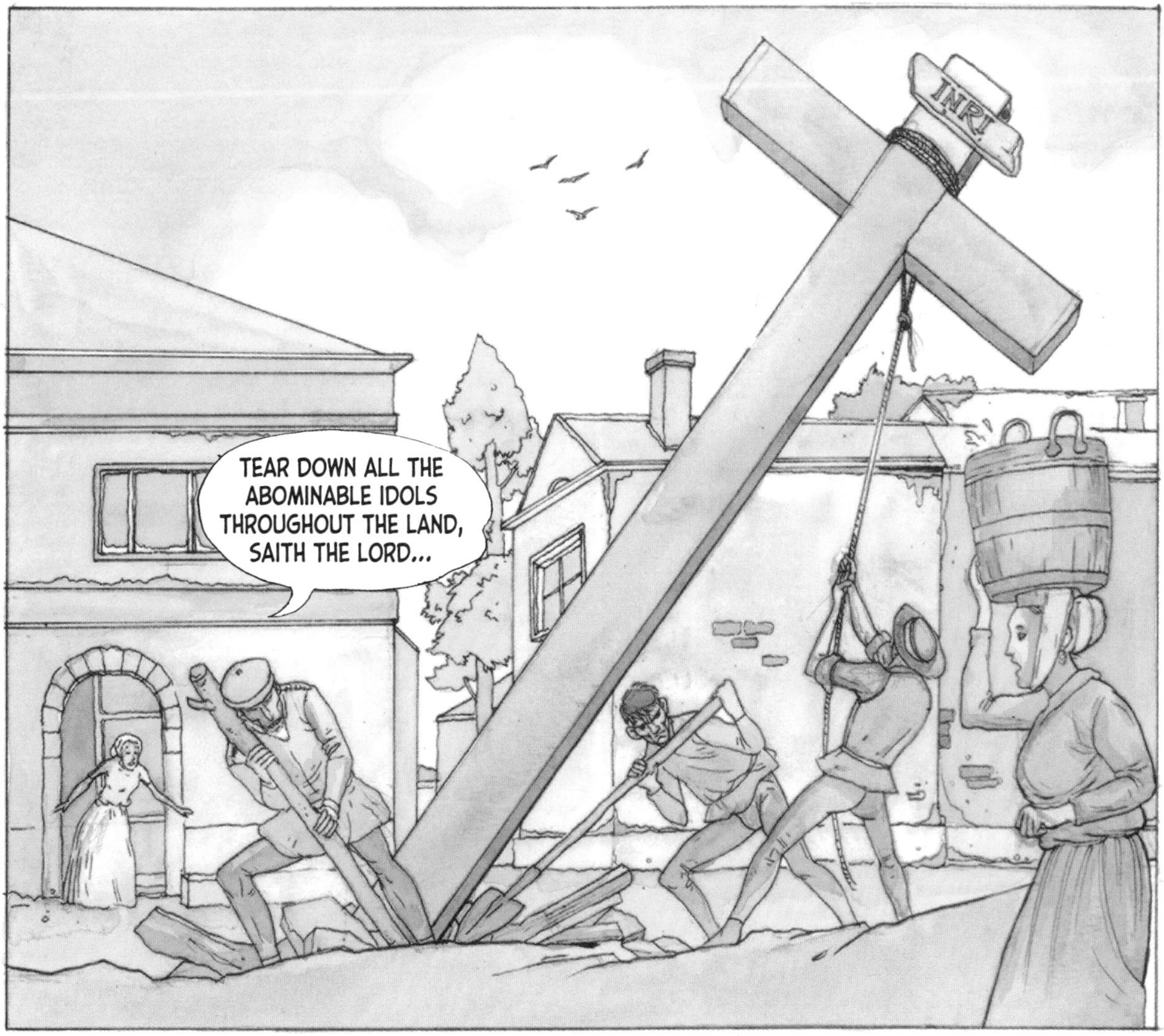
INRI
TEAR DOWN ALL THE ABOMINABLE IDOLS THROUGHOUT THE LAND, SAITH THE LORD...

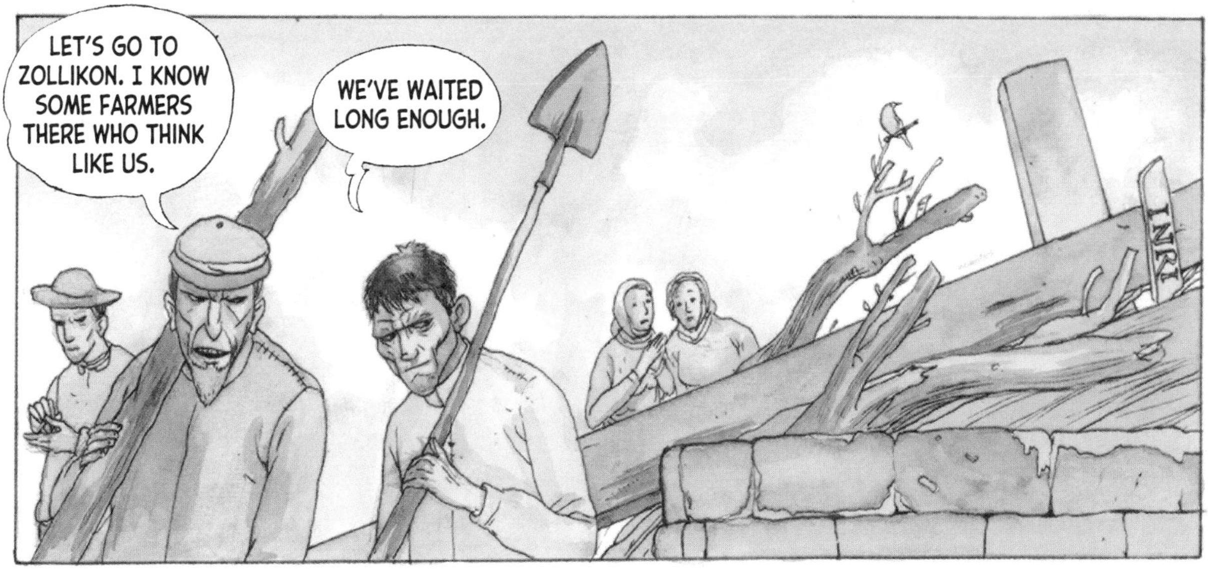
LET'S GO TO ZOLLIKON. I KNOW SOME FARMERS THERE WHO THINK LIKE US.
WE'VE WAITED LONG ENOUGH.
INRI

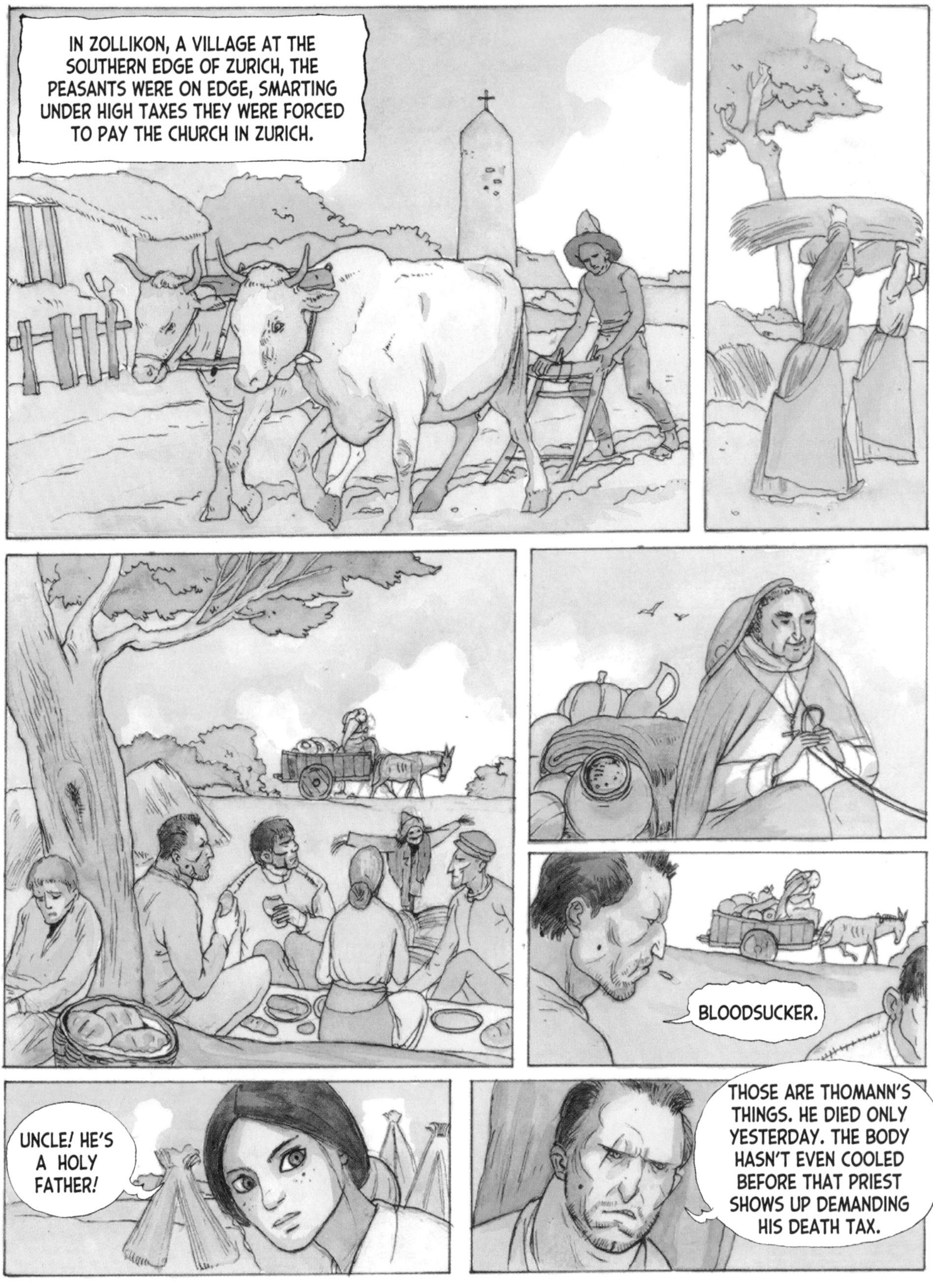
IN ZOLLIKON, A VILLAGE AT THE SOUTHERN EDGE OF ZURICH, THE PEASANTS WERE ON EDGE, SMARTING UNDER HIGH TAXES THEY WERE FORCED TO PAY THE CHURCH IN ZURICH.
BLOODSUCKER.
UNCLE! HE'S A HOLY FATHER!
THOSE ARE THOMANN'S THINGS. HE DIED ONLY YESTERDAY. THE BODY HASN'T EVEN COOLED BEFORE THAT PRIEST SHOWS UP DEMANDING HIS DEATH TAX.

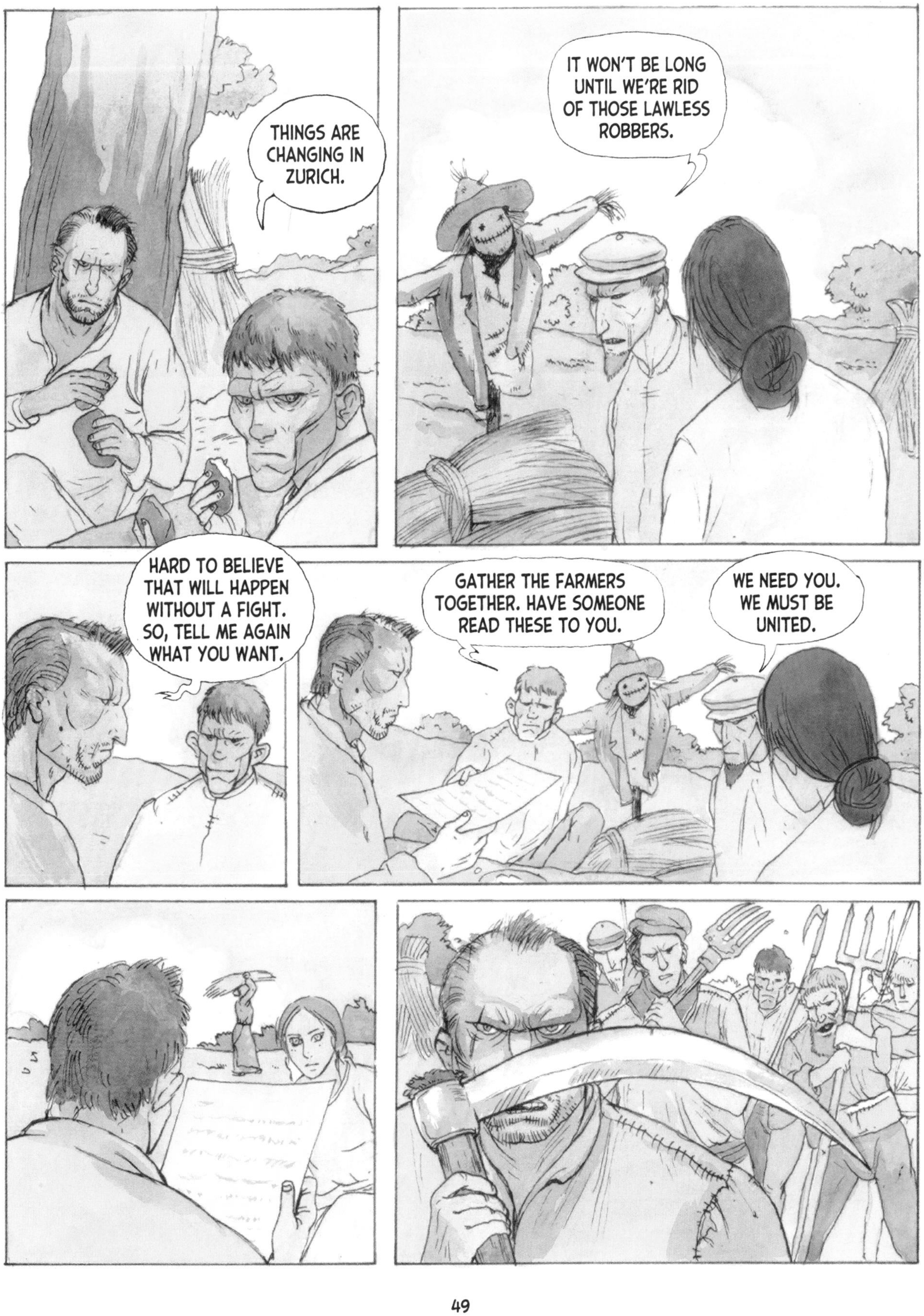
THINGS ARE CHANGING IN ZURICH.
IT WON'T BE LONG UNTIL WE'RE RID OF THOSE LAWLESS ROBBERS.
HARD TO BELIEVE THAT WILL HAPPEN WITHOUT A FIGHT. SO, TELL ME AGAIN WHAT YOU WANT.
GATHER THE FARMERS TOGETHER. HAVE SOMEONE READ THESE TO YOU.
WE NEED YOU. WE MUST BE UNITED.

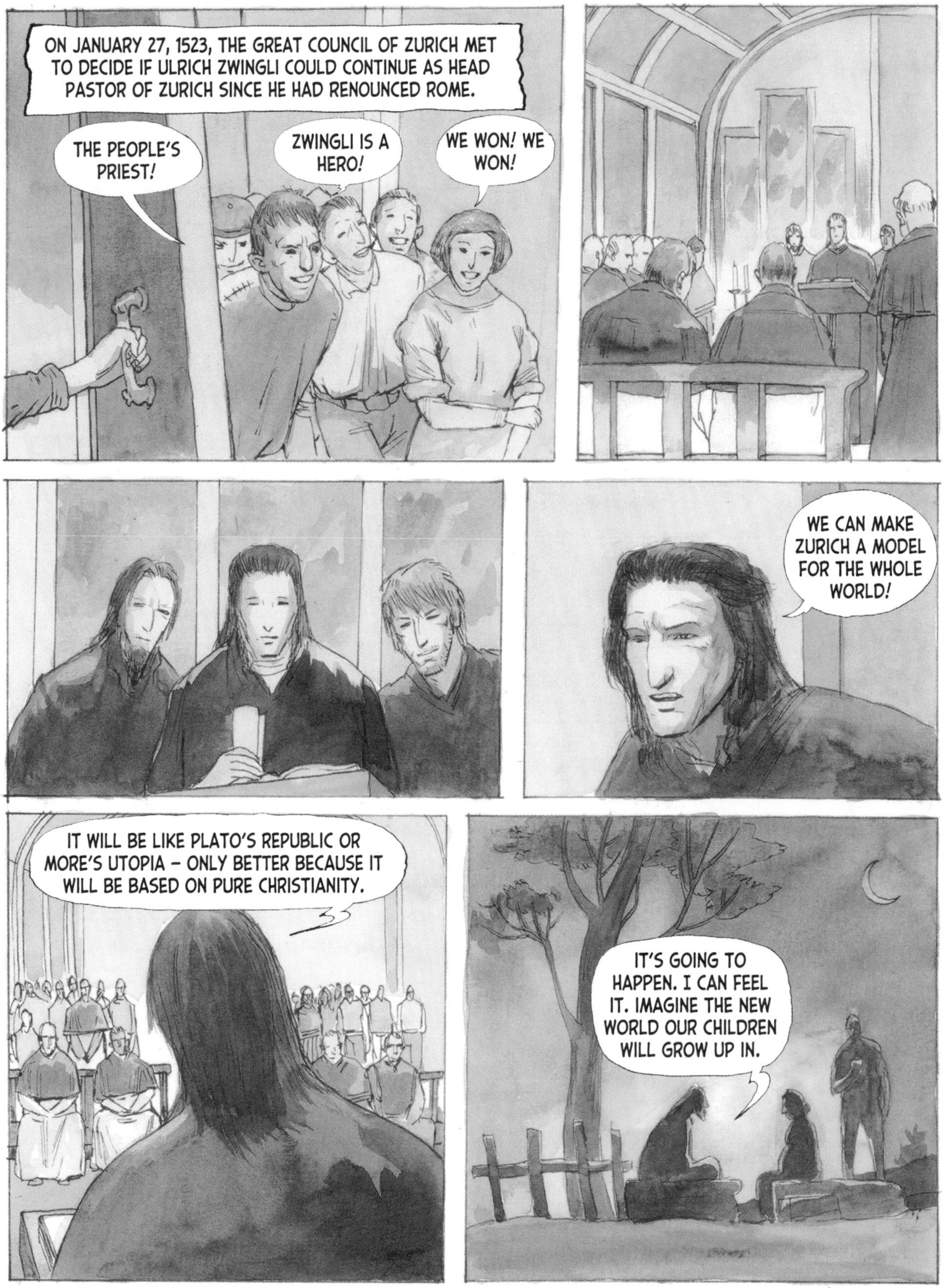
ON JANUARY 27, 1523, THE GREAT COUNCIL OF ZURICH MET TO DECIDE IF ULRICH ZWINGLI COULD CONTINUE AS HEAD PASTOR OF ZURICH SINCE HE HAD RENOUNCED ROME.
THE PEOPLE'S PRIEST!
ZWINGLI IS A HERO!
WE WON! WE WON!
WE CAN MAKE ZURICH A MODEL FOR THE WHOLE WORLD!
IT WILL BE LIKE PLATO'S REPUBLIC OR MORE'S UTOPIA – ONLY BETTER BECAUSE IT WILL BE BASED ON PURE CHRISTIANITY.
IT'S GOING TO HAPPEN. I CAN FEEL IT. IMAGINE THE NEW WORLD OUR CHILDREN WILL GROW UP IN.

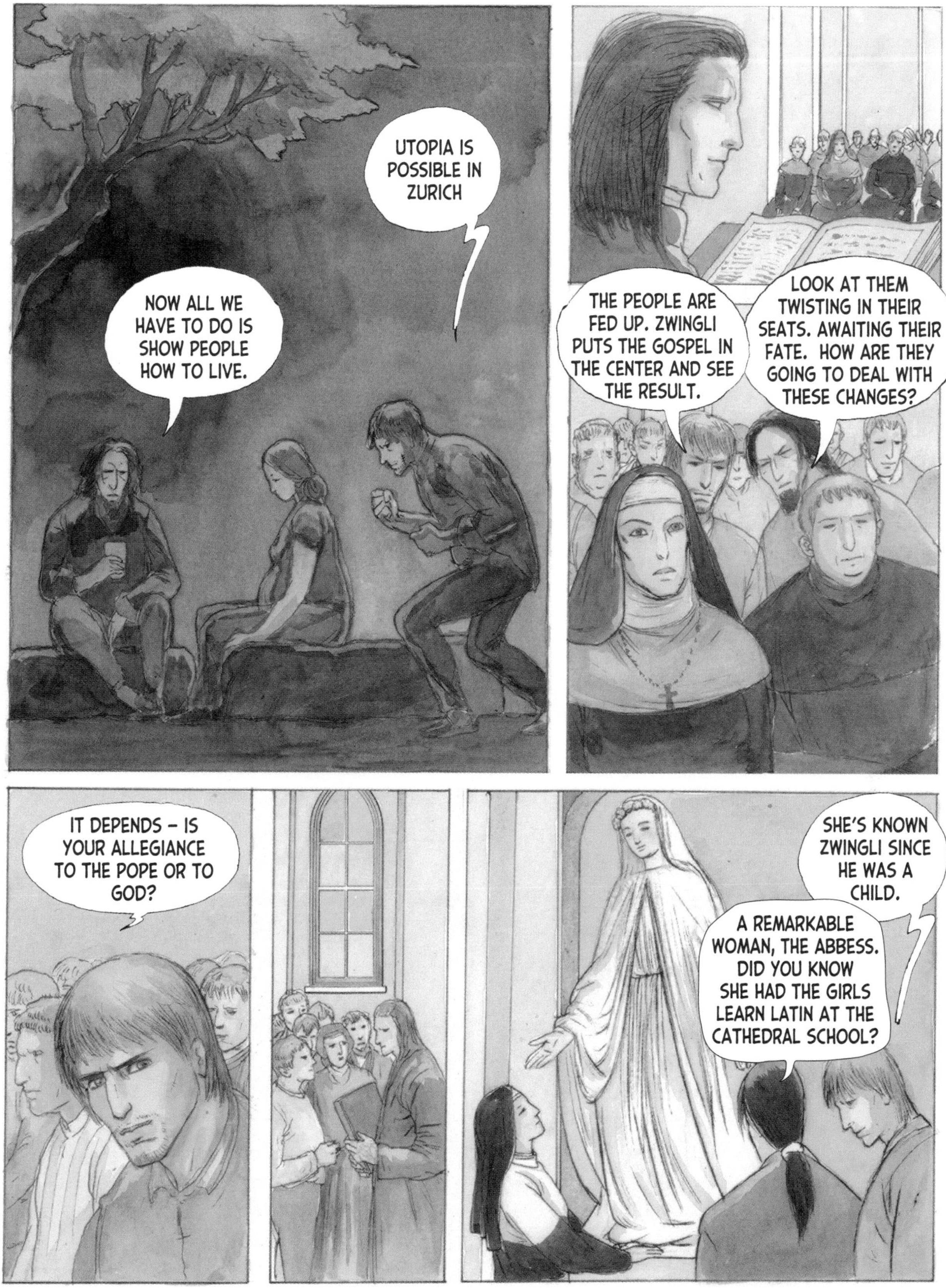
UTOPIA IS POSSIBLE IN ZURICH
NOW ALL WE HAVE TO DO IS SHOW PEOPLE HOW TO LIVE.
THE PEOPLE ARE FED UP. ZWINGLI PUTS THE GOSPEL IN THE CENTER AND SEE THE RESULT.
LOOK AT THEM TWISTING IN THEIR SEATS. AWAITING THEIR FATE. HOW ARE THEY GOING TO DEAL WITH THESE CHANGES?
IT DEPENDS – IS YOUR ALLEGIANCE TO THE POPE OR TO GOD?
SHE'S KNOWN ZWINGLI SINCE HE WAS A CHILD.
A REMARKABLE WOMAN, THE ABBESS. DID YOU KNOW SHE HAD THE GIRLS LEARN LATIN AT THE CATHEDRAL SCHOOL?

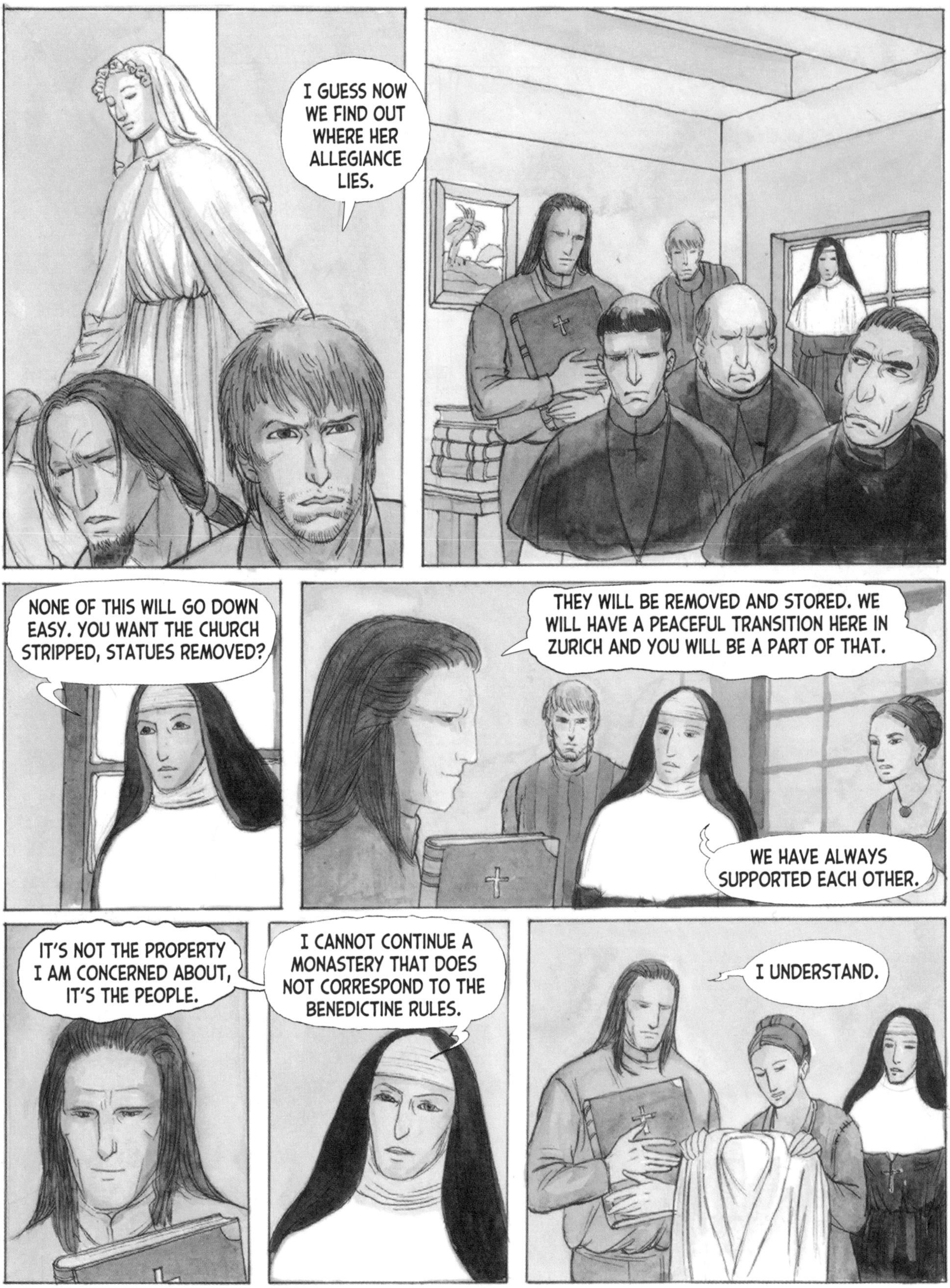
I GUESS NOW WE FIND OUT WHERE HER ALLEGIANCE LIES.
NONE OF THIS WILL GO DOWN EASY. YOU WANT THE CHURCH STRIPPED, STATUES REMOVED?
THEY WILL BE REMOVED AND STORED. WE WILL HAVE A PEACEFUL TRANSITION HERE IN ZURICH AND YOU WILL BE A PART OF THAT.
WE HAVE ALWAYS SUPPORTED EACH OTHER.
IT'S NOT THE PROPERTY I AM CONCERNED ABOUT, IT'S THE PEOPLE.
I CANNOT CONTINUE A MONASTERY THAT DOES NOT CORRESPOND TO THE BENEDICTINE RULES.
I UNDERSTAND.

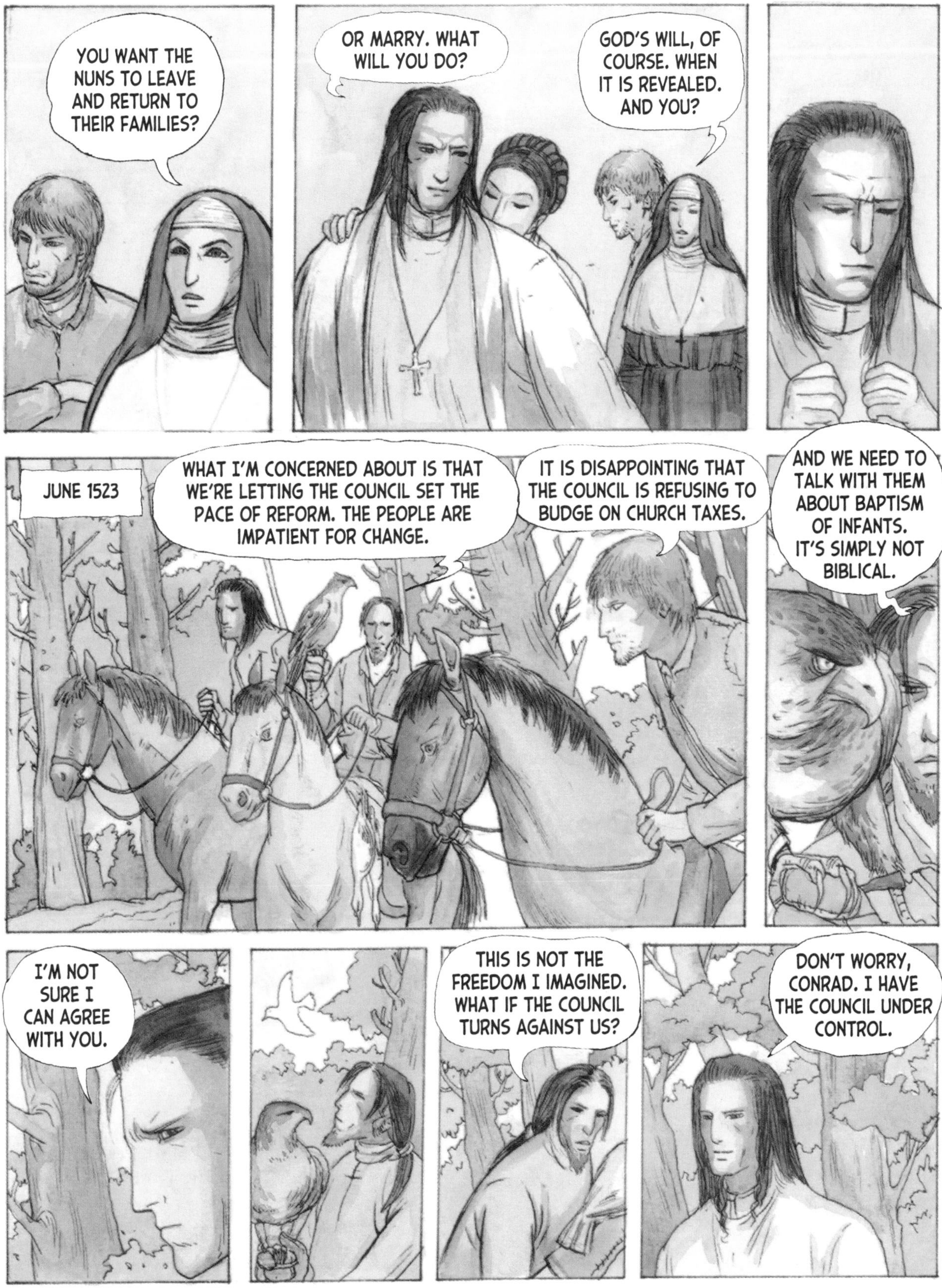
YOU WANT THE NUNS TO LEAVE AND RETURN TO THEIR FAMILIES?
OR MARRY. WHAT WILL YOU DO?
GOD'S WILL, OF COURSE. WHEN IT IS REVEALED. AND YOU?
JUNE 1523
WHAT I'M CONCERNED ABOUT IS THAT WE'RE LETTING THE COUNCIL SET THE PACE OF REFORM. THE PEOPLE ARE IMPATIENT FOR CHANGE.
IT IS DISAPPOINTING THAT THE COUNCIL IS REFUSING TO BUDGE ON CHURCH TAXES.
AND WE NEED TO TALK WITH THEM ABOUT BAPTISM OF INFANTS. IT'S SIMPLY NOT BIBLICAL.
I'M NOT SURE I CAN AGREE WITH YOU.
THIS IS NOT THE FREEDOM I IMAGINED. WHAT IF THE COUNCIL TURNS AGAINST US?
DON'T WORRY, CONRAD. I HAVE THE COUNCIL UNDER CONTROL.

I'M CONFIDENT THAT BEFORE TOO LONG OUR OPPONENTS WILL BE EXILED FROM ZURICH.

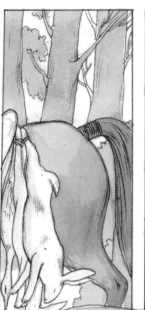

GET HIM, PRINCESS!

IT SEEMS STRANGE TO DEPEND ON THE STATE, WHICH ENFORCES ITS WILL THROUGH VIOLENCE. I DON'T SEE WHERE SCRIPTURE SUPPORTS IT.

WHAT DO YOU SAY, ULRICH?

WE MUST USE THE POWER OF THE STATE TO DO GOD'S WORK. TOGETHER WE'LL ABOLISH SUPERSTITION. WE'LL FEED AND CLOTHE THE POOR. WE'LL PUT AN END TO FOREIGN WARS. ALL TO THE GLORY OF GOD!

BUT ONLY IF YOU STICK WITH ME. WE NEED TO KEEP PEACE AND GOOD ORDER. OTHERWISE WE'LL HAVE REBELLION AND ANARCHY.

Episode Five
THE CONFLICT

APRIL 2, 1524

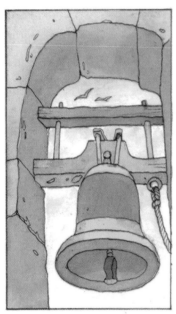

IT'S BEEN TWO YEARS SINCE I MET HIM. HE'S GIVEN ME SO MUCH, OPENED MY MIND.

BUT SOMETHING'S CHANGED. HE'S MORE INTERESTED IN POLITICAL INFLUENCE THAN THE TRUTH.

HERETIC!

YOU'RE GOING TO HELL!

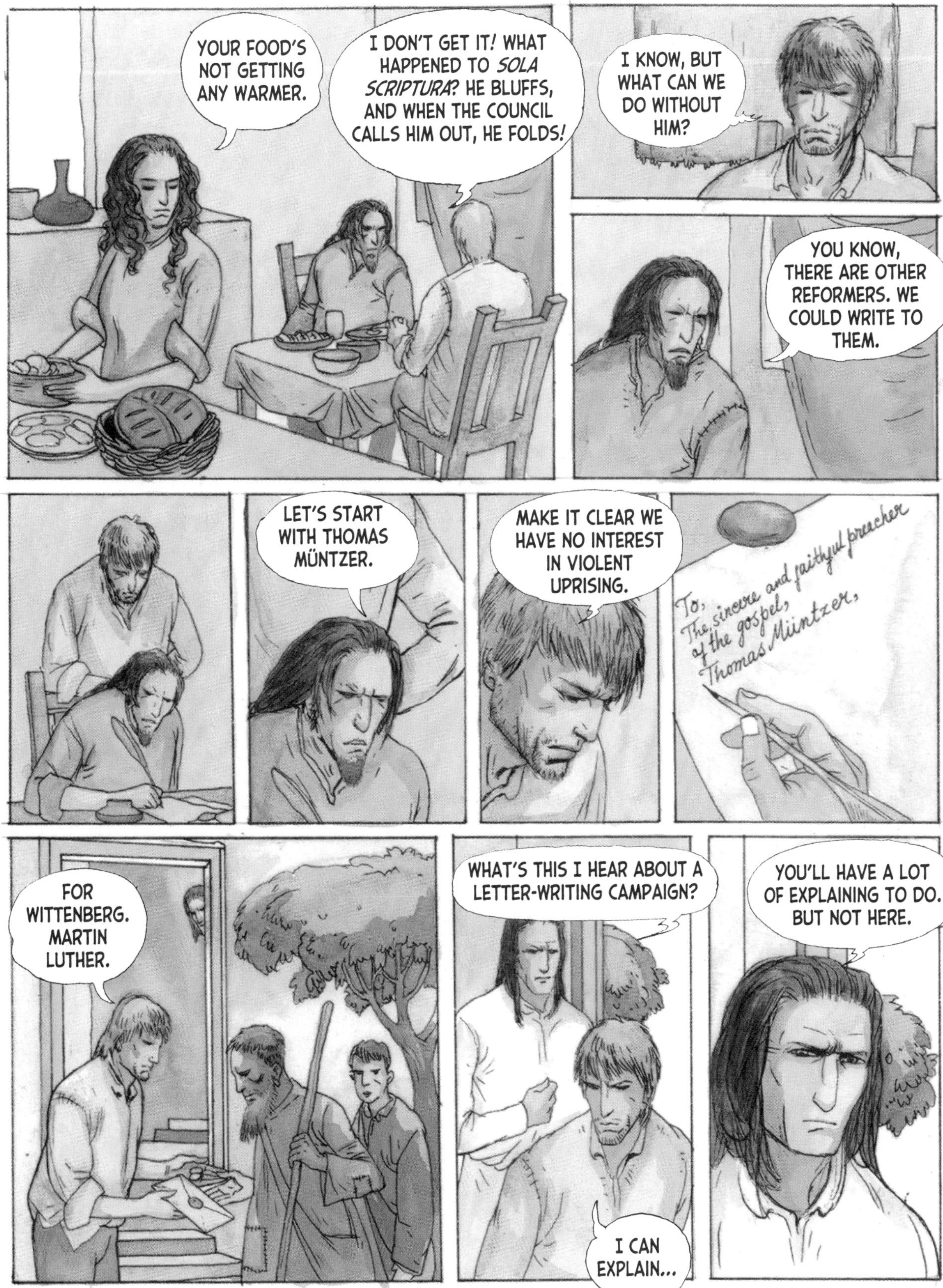
YOUR FOOD'S NOT GETTING ANY WARMER.
I DON'T GET IT! WHAT HAPPENED TO *SOLA SCRIPTURA*? HE BLUFFS, AND WHEN THE COUNCIL CALLS HIM OUT, HE FOLDS!
I KNOW, BUT WHAT CAN WE DO WITHOUT HIM?
YOU KNOW, THERE ARE OTHER REFORMERS. WE COULD WRITE TO THEM.
LET'S START WITH THOMAS MÜNTZER.
MAKE IT CLEAR WE HAVE NO INTEREST IN VIOLENT UPRISING.
To, The sincere and faithful preacher of the gospel, Thomas Müntzer,
FOR WITTENBERG. MARTIN LUTHER.
WHAT'S THIS I HEAR ABOUT A LETTER-WRITING CAMPAIGN?
I CAN EXPLAIN...
YOU'LL HAVE A LOT OF EXPLAINING TO DO. BUT NOT HERE.

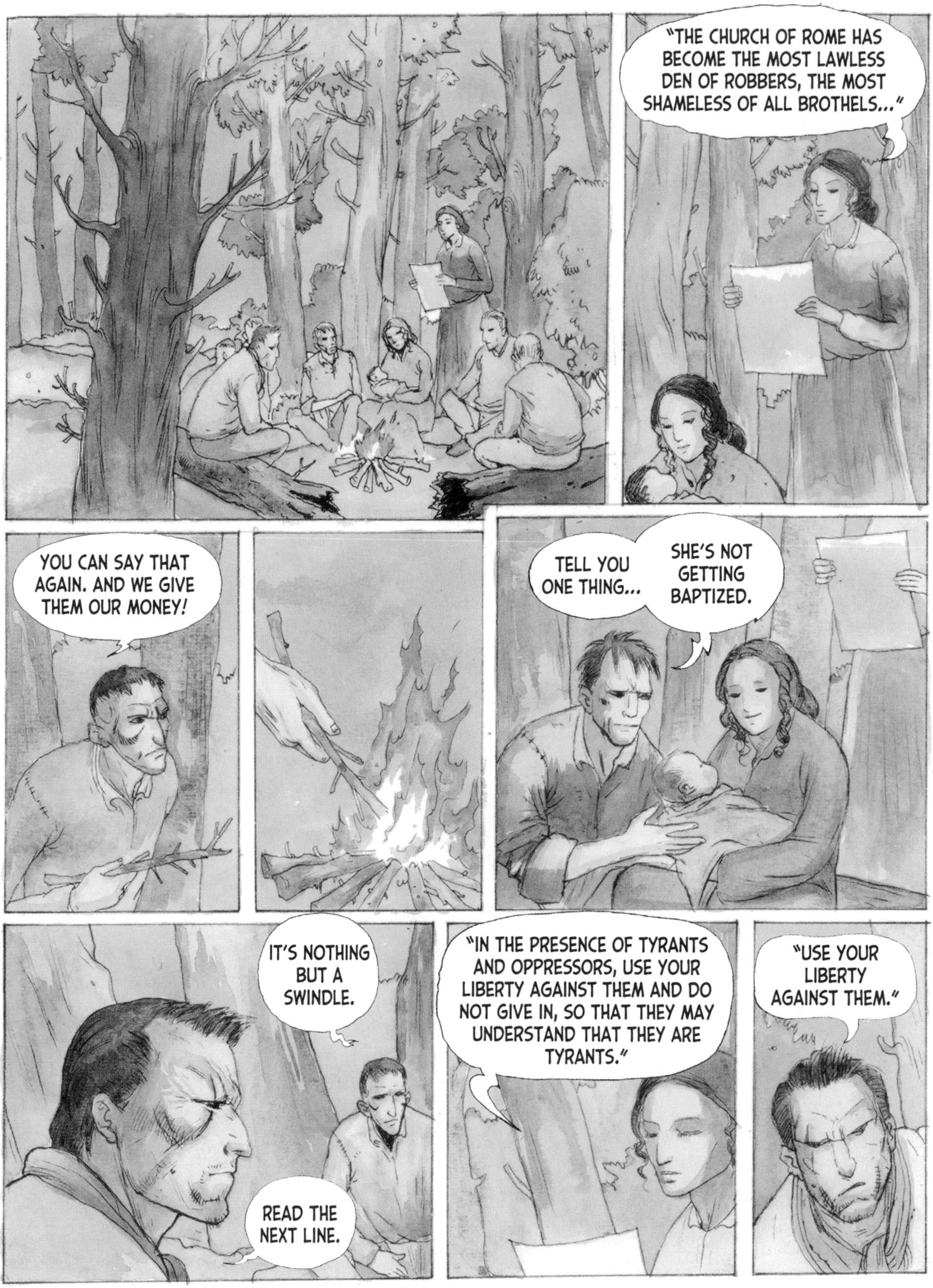
"THE CHURCH OF ROME HAS BECOME THE MOST LAWLESS DEN OF ROBBERS, THE MOST SHAMELESS OF ALL BROTHELS..."
YOU CAN SAY THAT AGAIN. AND WE GIVE THEM OUR MONEY!
TELL YOU ONE THING...
SHE'S NOT GETTING BAPTIZED.
IT'S NOTHING BUT A SWINDLE.
READ THE NEXT LINE.
"IN THE PRESENCE OF TYRANTS AND OPPRESSORS, USE YOUR LIBERTY AGAINST THEM AND DO NOT GIVE IN, SO THAT THEY MAY UNDERSTAND THAT THEY ARE TYRANTS."
"USE YOUR LIBERTY AGAINST THEM."

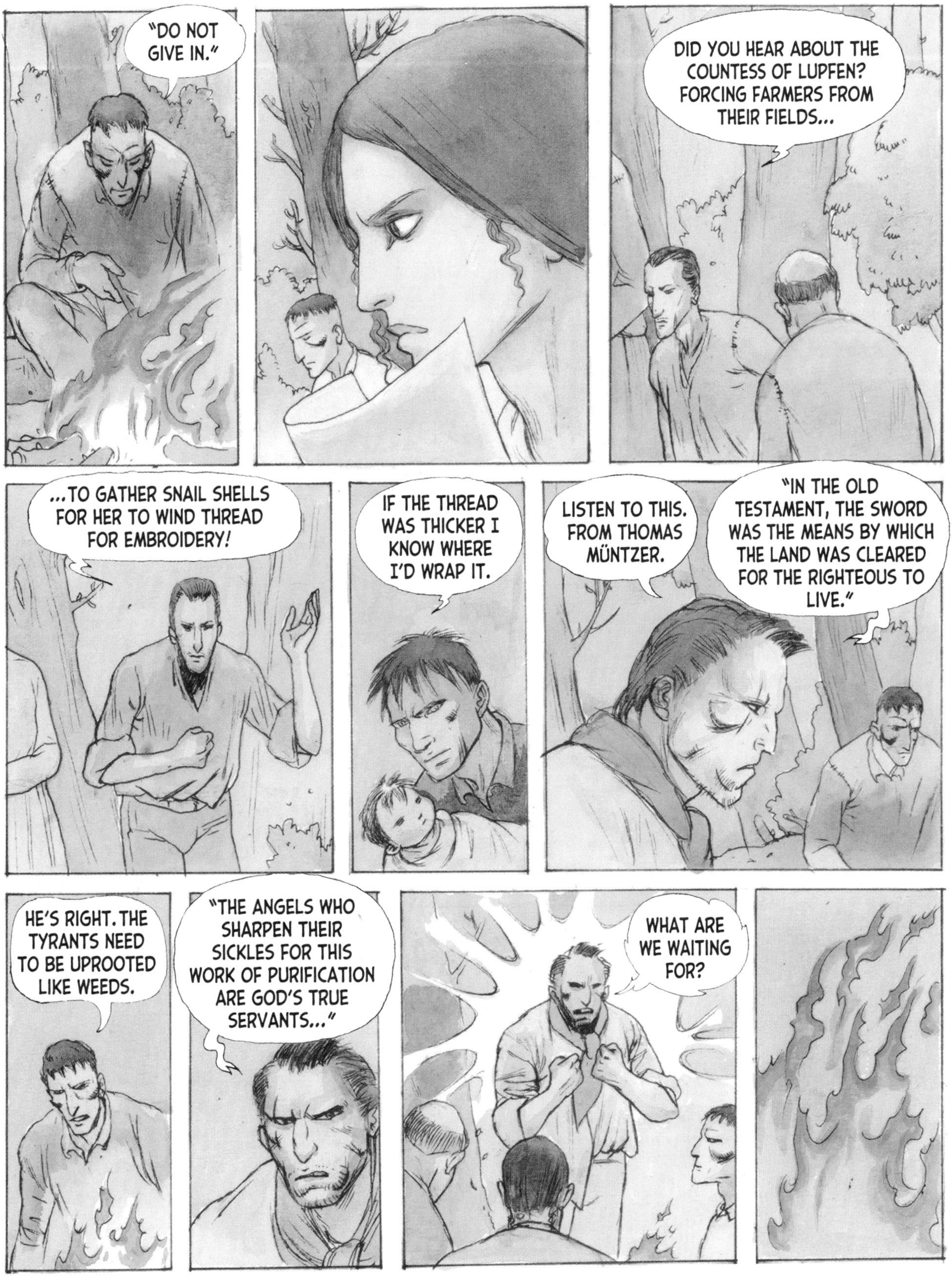
"DO NOT GIVE IN."
DID YOU HEAR ABOUT THE COUNTESS OF LUPFEN? FORCING FARMERS FROM THEIR FIELDS...
...TO GATHER SNAIL SHELLS FOR HER TO WIND THREAD FOR EMBROIDERY!
IF THE THREAD WAS THICKER I KNOW WHERE I'D WRAP IT.
LISTEN TO THIS. FROM THOMAS MÜNTZER.
"IN THE OLD TESTAMENT, THE SWORD WAS THE MEANS BY WHICH THE LAND WAS CLEARED FOR THE RIGHTEOUS TO LIVE."
HE'S RIGHT. THE TYRANTS NEED TO BE UPROOTED LIKE WEEDS.
"THE ANGELS WHO SHARPEN THEIR SICKLES FOR THIS WORK OF PURIFICATION ARE GOD'S TRUE SERVANTS..."
WHAT ARE WE WAITING FOR?

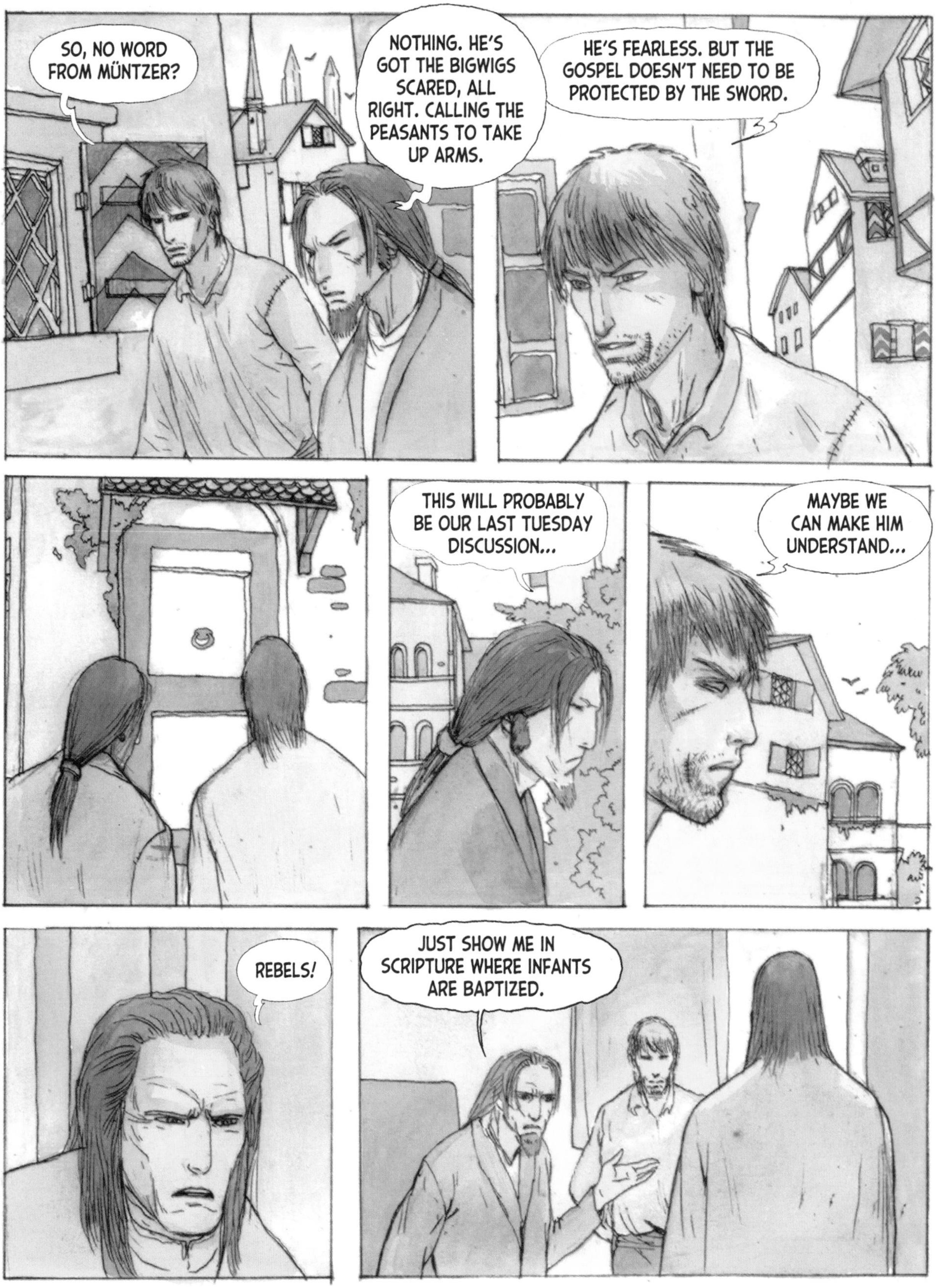
SO, NO WORD FROM MÜNTZER?
NOTHING. HE'S GOT THE BIGWIGS SCARED, ALL RIGHT. CALLING THE PEASANTS TO TAKE UP ARMS.
HE'S FEARLESS. BUT THE GOSPEL DOESN'T NEED TO BE PROTECTED BY THE SWORD.
THIS WILL PROBABLY BE OUR LAST TUESDAY DISCUSSION...
MAYBE WE CAN MAKE HIM UNDERSTAND...
REBELS!
JUST SHOW ME IN SCRIPTURE WHERE INFANTS ARE BAPTIZED.

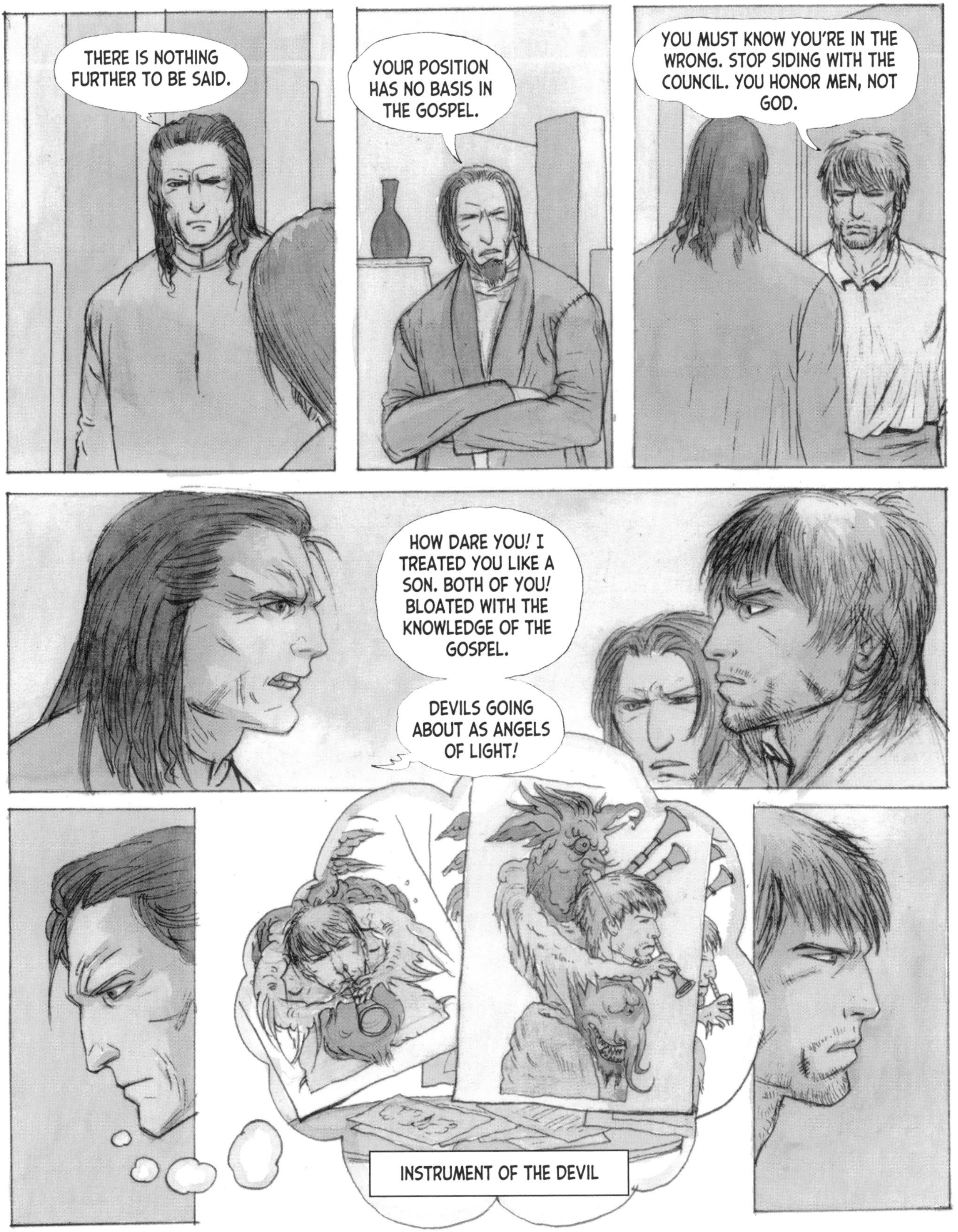
THERE IS NOTHING FURTHER TO BE SAID.
YOUR POSITION HAS NO BASIS IN THE GOSPEL.
YOU MUST KNOW YOU'RE IN THE WRONG. STOP SIDING WITH THE COUNCIL. YOU HONOR MEN, NOT GOD.
HOW DARE YOU! I TREATED YOU LIKE A SON. BOTH OF YOU! BLOATED WITH THE KNOWLEDGE OF THE GOSPEL.
DEVILS GOING ABOUT AS ANGELS OF LIGHT!
INSTRUMENT OF THE DEVIL

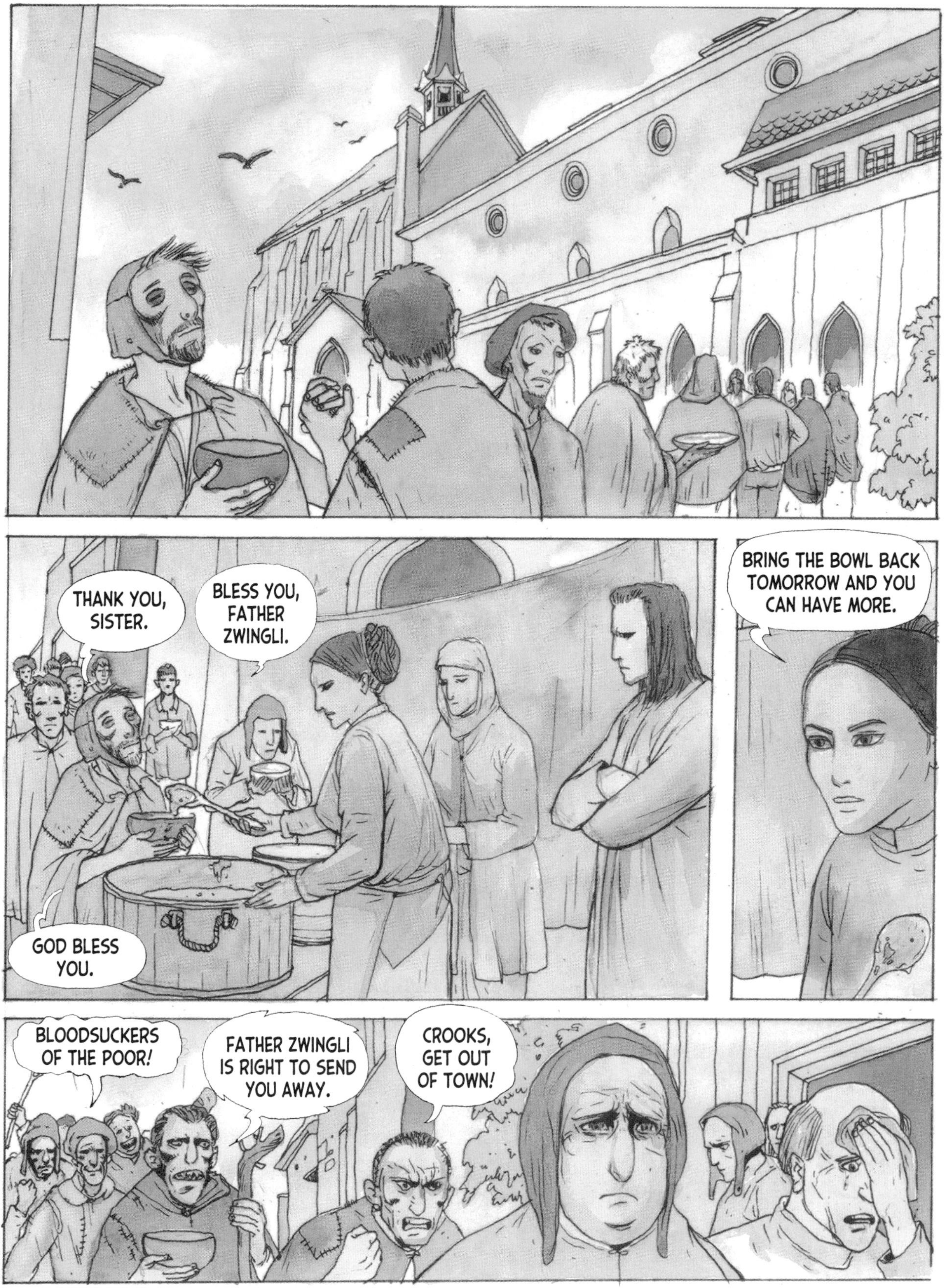
THANK YOU, SISTER.
BLESS YOU, FATHER ZWINGLI.
GOD BLESS YOU.
BRING THE BOWL BACK TOMORROW AND YOU CAN HAVE MORE.
BLOODSUCKERS OF THE POOR!
FATHER ZWINGLI IS RIGHT TO SEND YOU AWAY.
CROOKS, GET OUT OF TOWN!

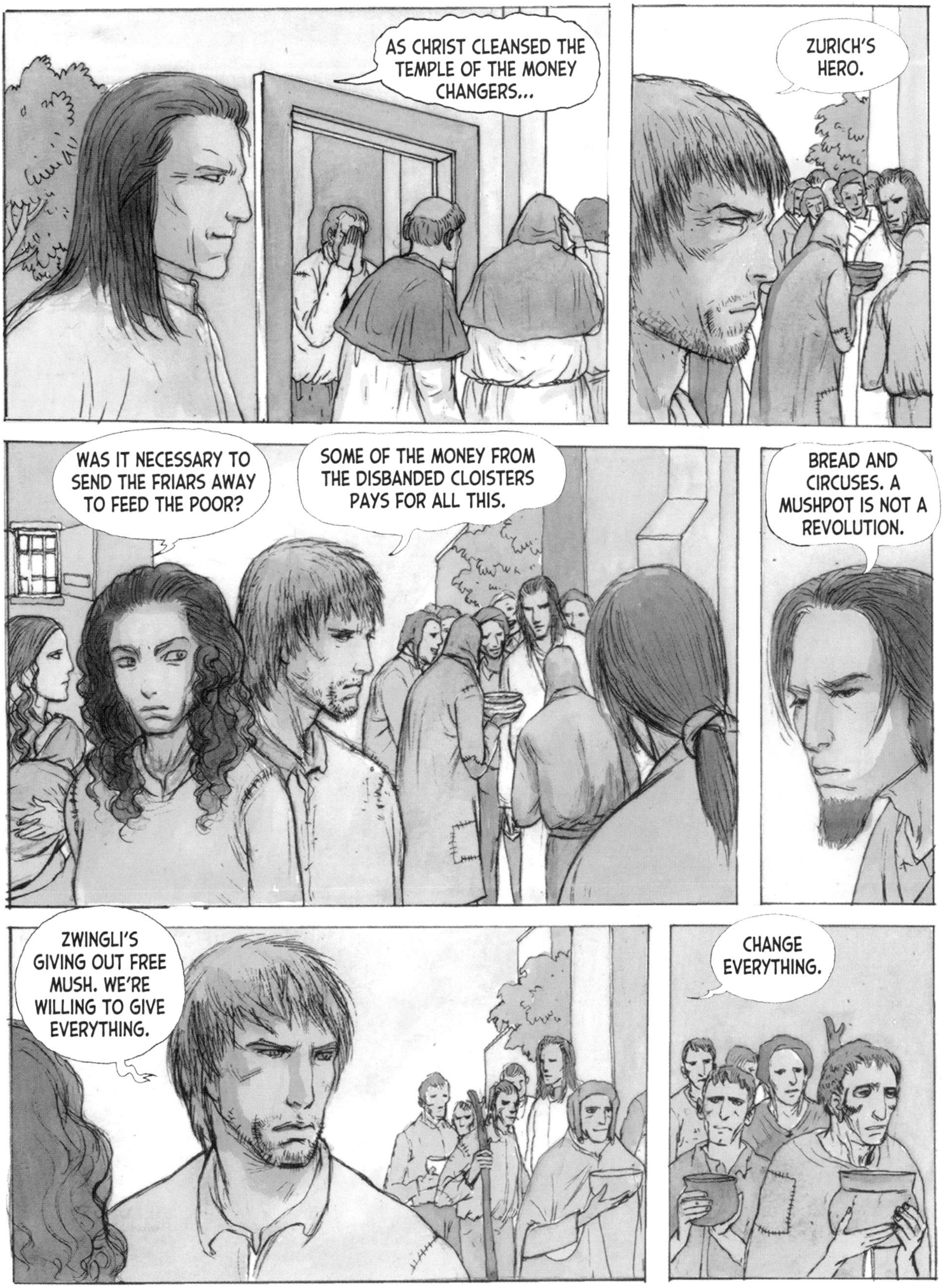
AS CHRIST CLEANSED THE TEMPLE OF THE MONEY CHANGERS...
ZURICH'S HERO.
WAS IT NECESSARY TO SEND THE FRIARS AWAY TO FEED THE POOR?
SOME OF THE MONEY FROM THE DISBANDED CLOISTERS PAYS FOR ALL THIS.
BREAD AND CIRCUSES. A MUSHPOT IS NOT A REVOLUTION.
ZWINGLI'S GIVING OUT FREE MUSH. WE'RE WILLING TO GIVE EVERYTHING.
CHANGE EVERYTHING.

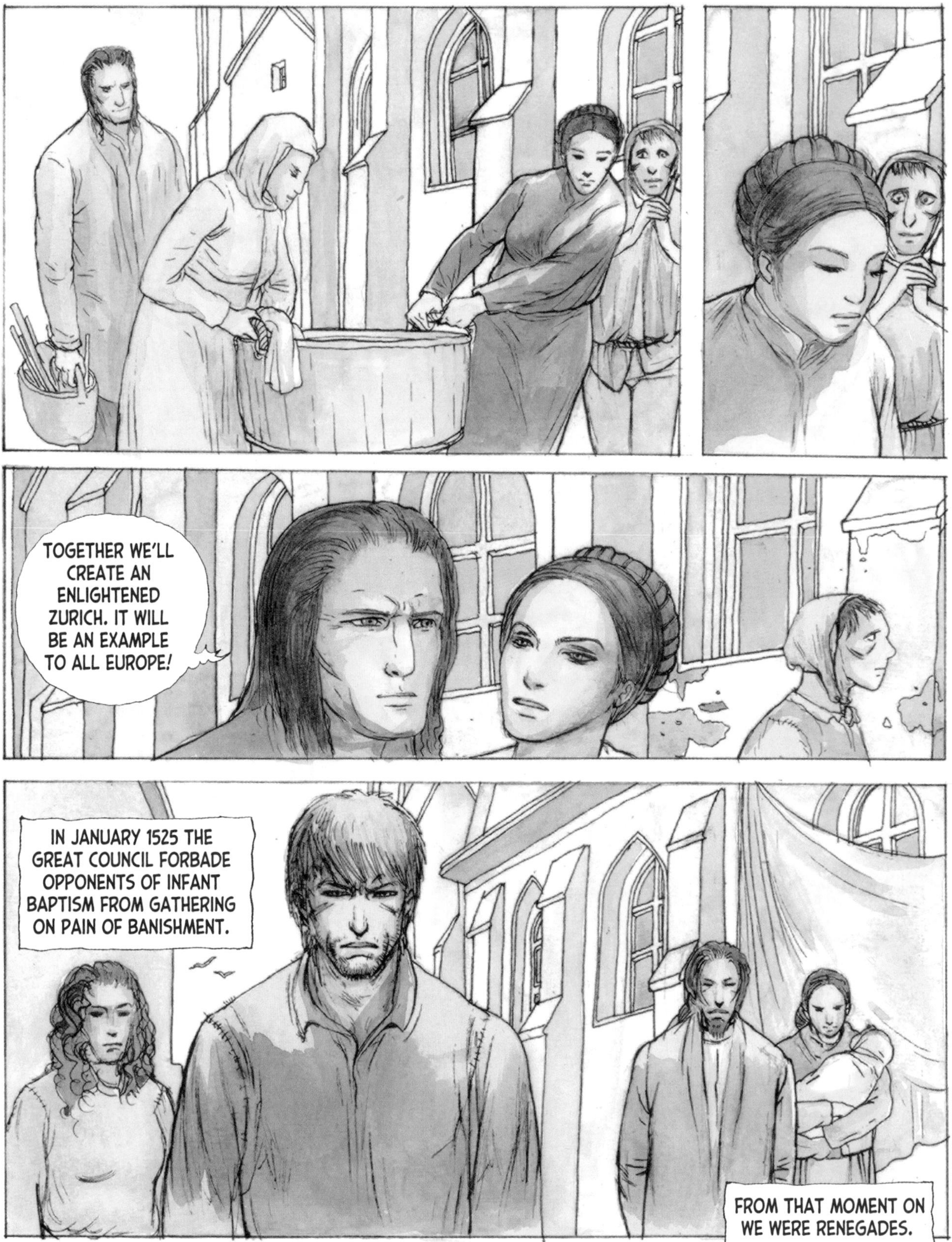
TOGETHER WE'LL CREATE AN ENLIGHTENED ZURICH. IT WILL BE AN EXAMPLE TO ALL EUROPE!
IN JANUARY 1525 THE GREAT COUNCIL FORBADE OPPONENTS OF INFANT BAPTISM FROM GATHERING ON PAIN OF BANISHMENT.
FROM THAT MOMENT ON WE WERE RENEGADES.

Episode Six
THE BAPTISM

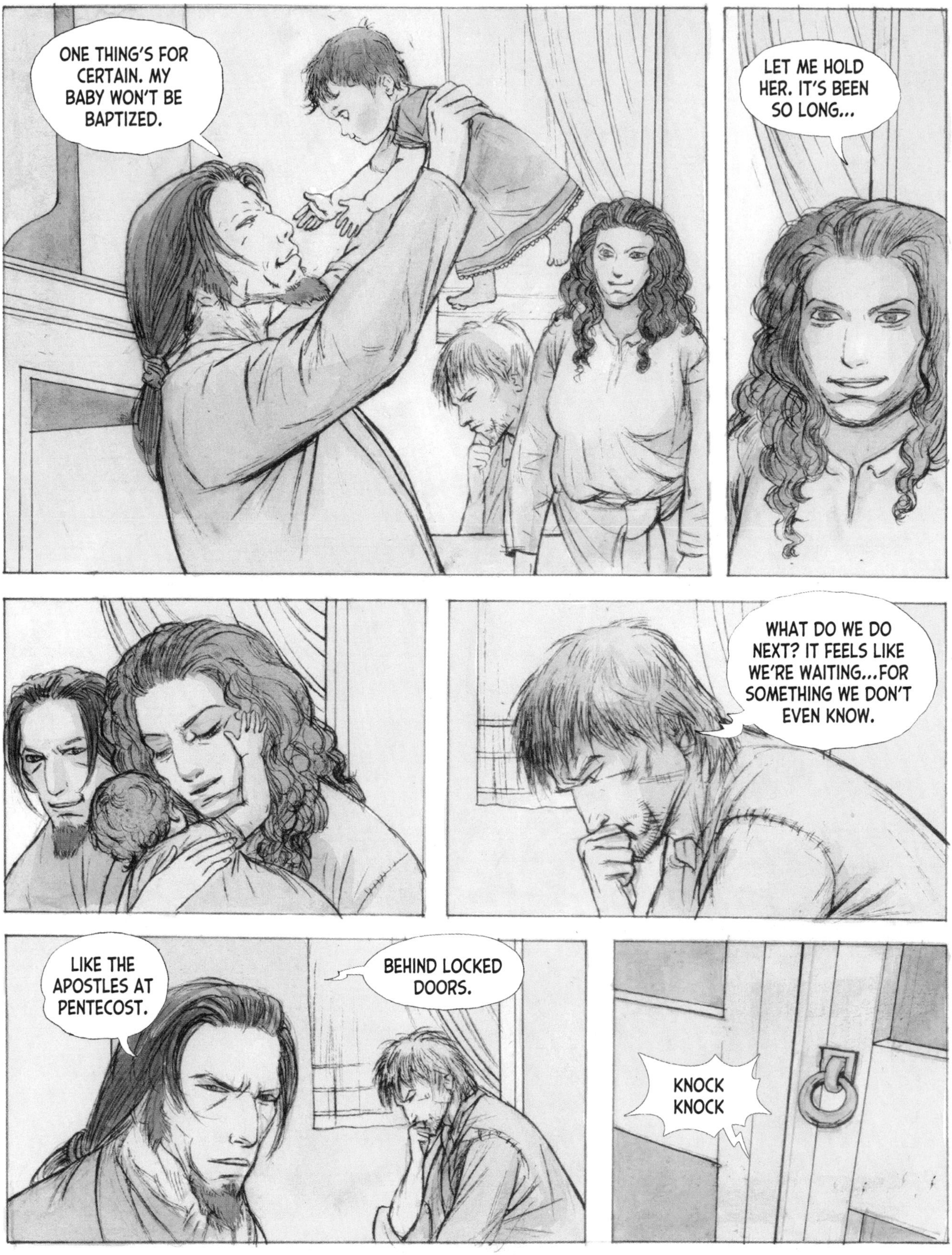
ONE THING'S FOR CERTAIN. MY BABY WON'T BE BAPTIZED.
LET ME HOLD HER. IT'S BEEN SO LONG...
WHAT DO WE DO NEXT? IT FEELS LIKE WE'RE WAITING...FOR SOMETHING WE DON'T EVEN KNOW.
LIKE THE APOSTLES AT PENTECOST.
BEHIND LOCKED DOORS.
KNOCK KNOCK

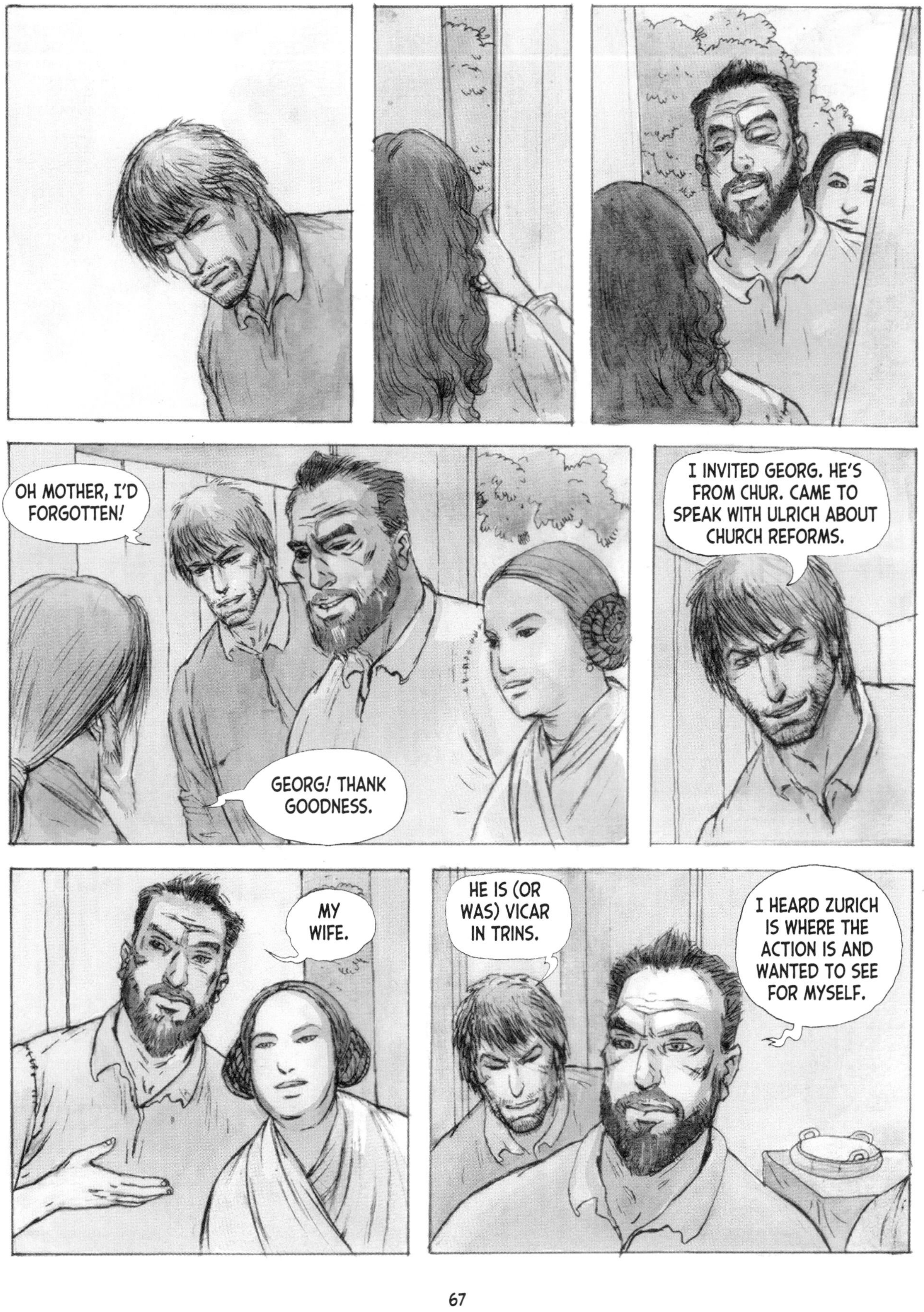
OH MOTHER, I'D FORGOTTEN!
GEORG! THANK GOODNESS.
I INVITED GEORG. HE'S FROM CHUR. CAME TO SPEAK WITH ULRICH ABOUT CHURCH REFORMS.
MY WIFE.
HE IS (OR WAS) VICAR IN TRINS.
I HEARD ZURICH IS WHERE THE ACTION IS AND WANTED TO SEE FOR MYSELF.

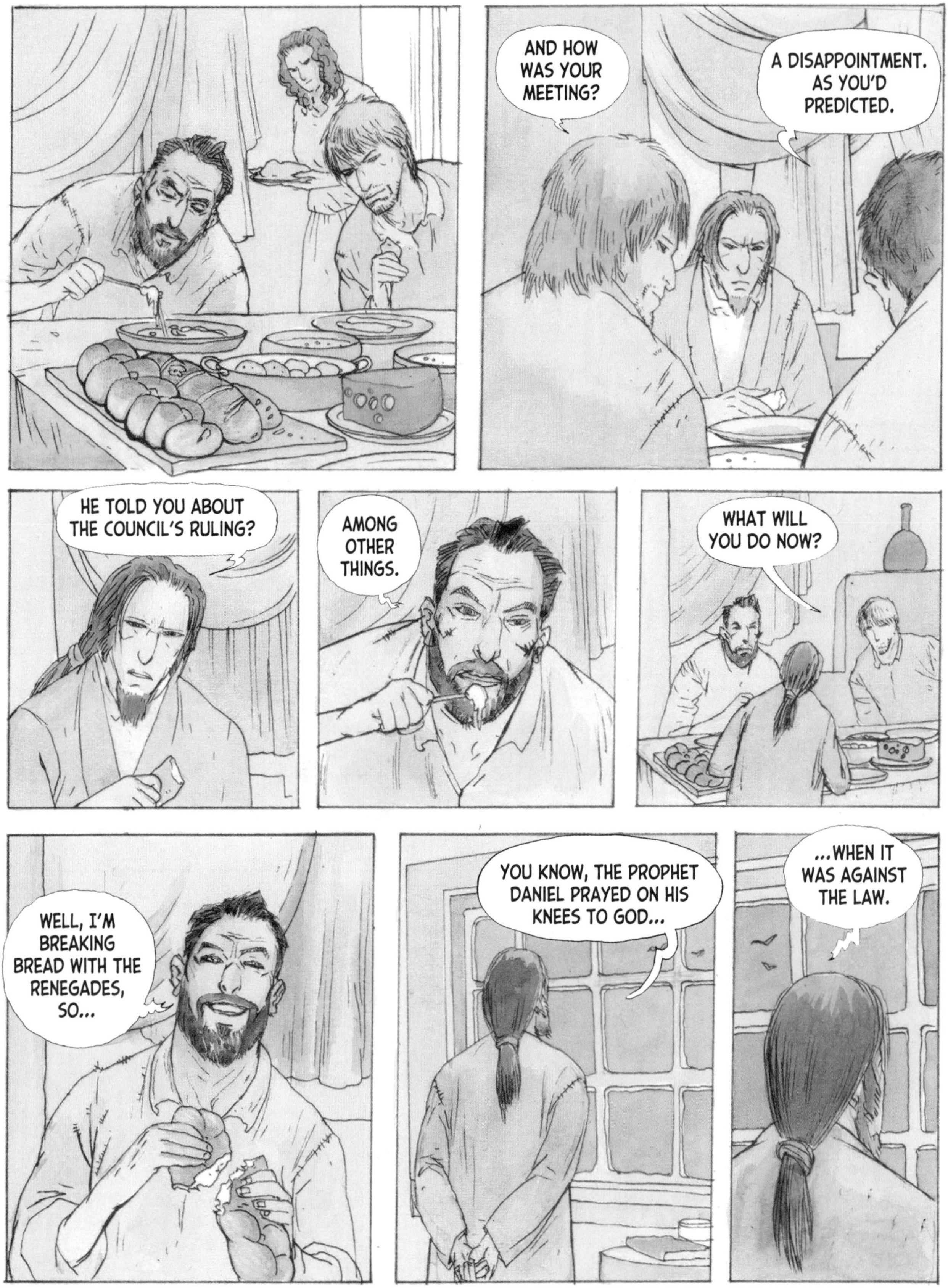
AND HOW WAS YOUR MEETING?
A DISAPPOINTMENT. AS YOU'D PREDICTED.
HE TOLD YOU ABOUT THE COUNCIL'S RULING?
AMONG OTHER THINGS.
WHAT WILL YOU DO NOW?
WELL, I'M BREAKING BREAD WITH THE RENEGADES, SO...
YOU KNOW, THE PROPHET DANIEL PRAYED ON HIS KNEES TO GOD...
...WHEN IT WAS AGAINST THE LAW.

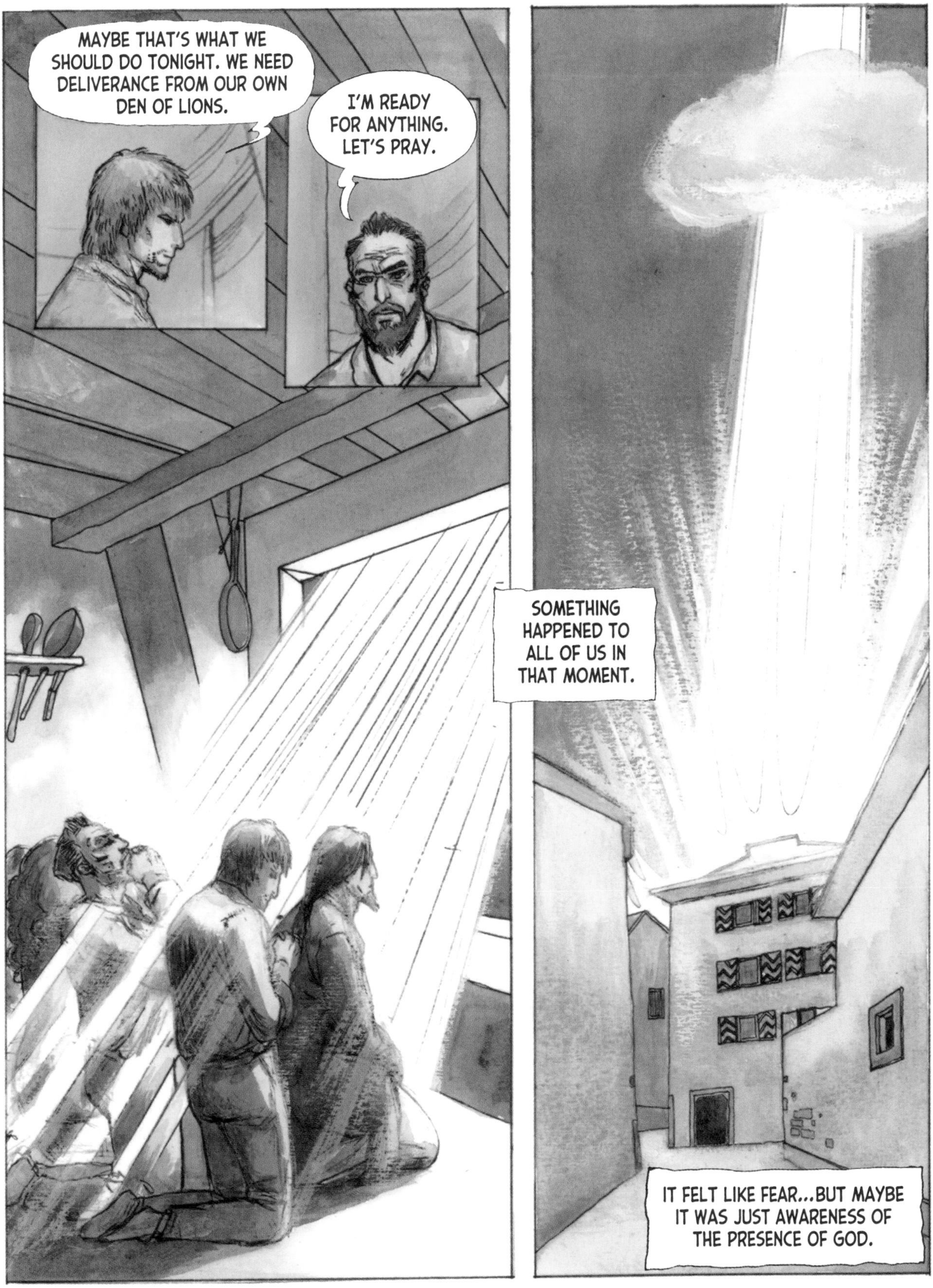
MAYBE THAT'S WHAT WE SHOULD DO TONIGHT. WE NEED DELIVERANCE FROM OUR OWN DEN OF LIONS.
I'M READY FOR ANYTHING. LET'S PRAY.
SOMETHING HAPPENED TO ALL OF US IN THAT MOMENT.
IT FELT LIKE FEAR...BUT MAYBE IT WAS JUST AWARENESS OF THE PRESENCE OF GOD.

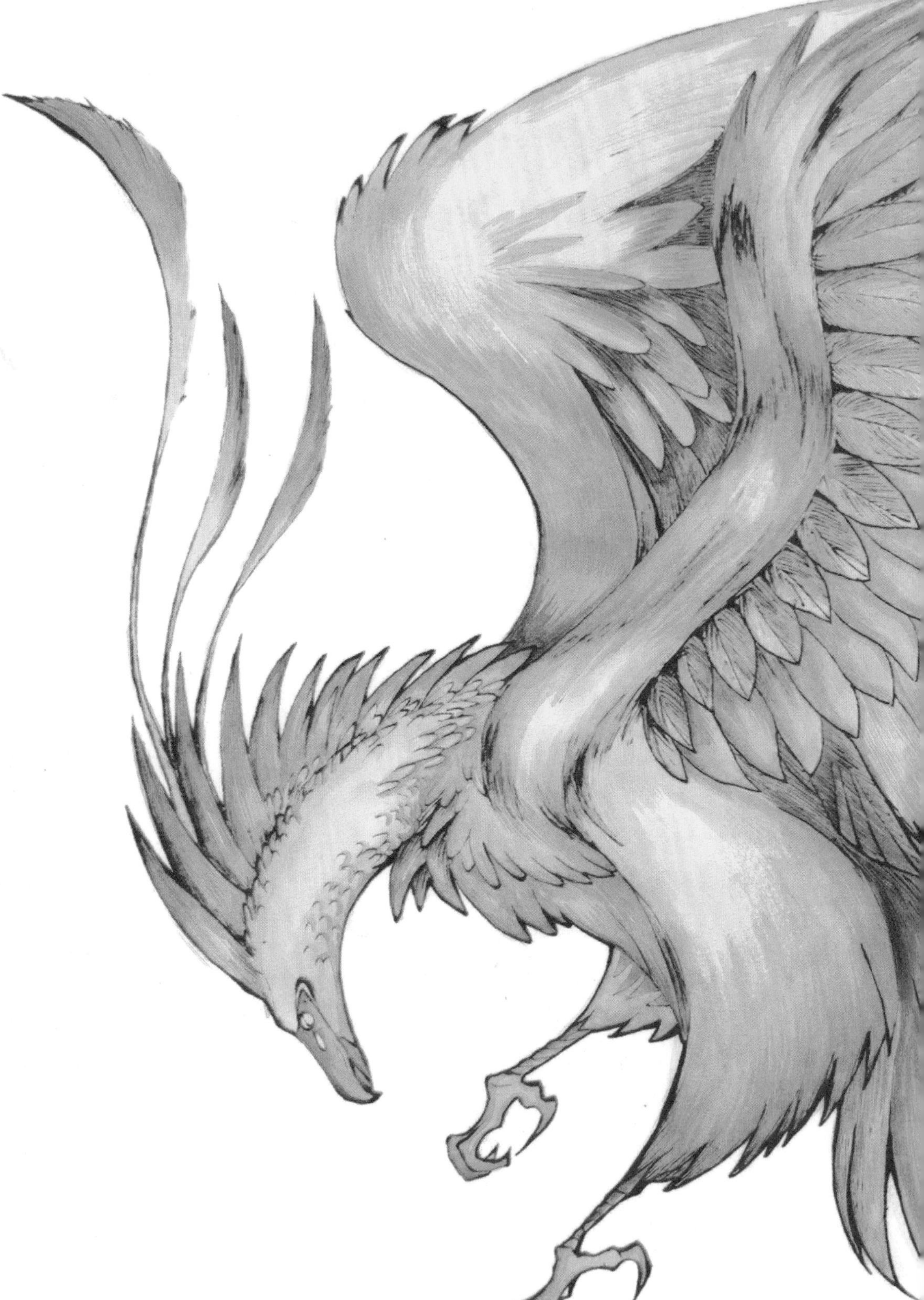

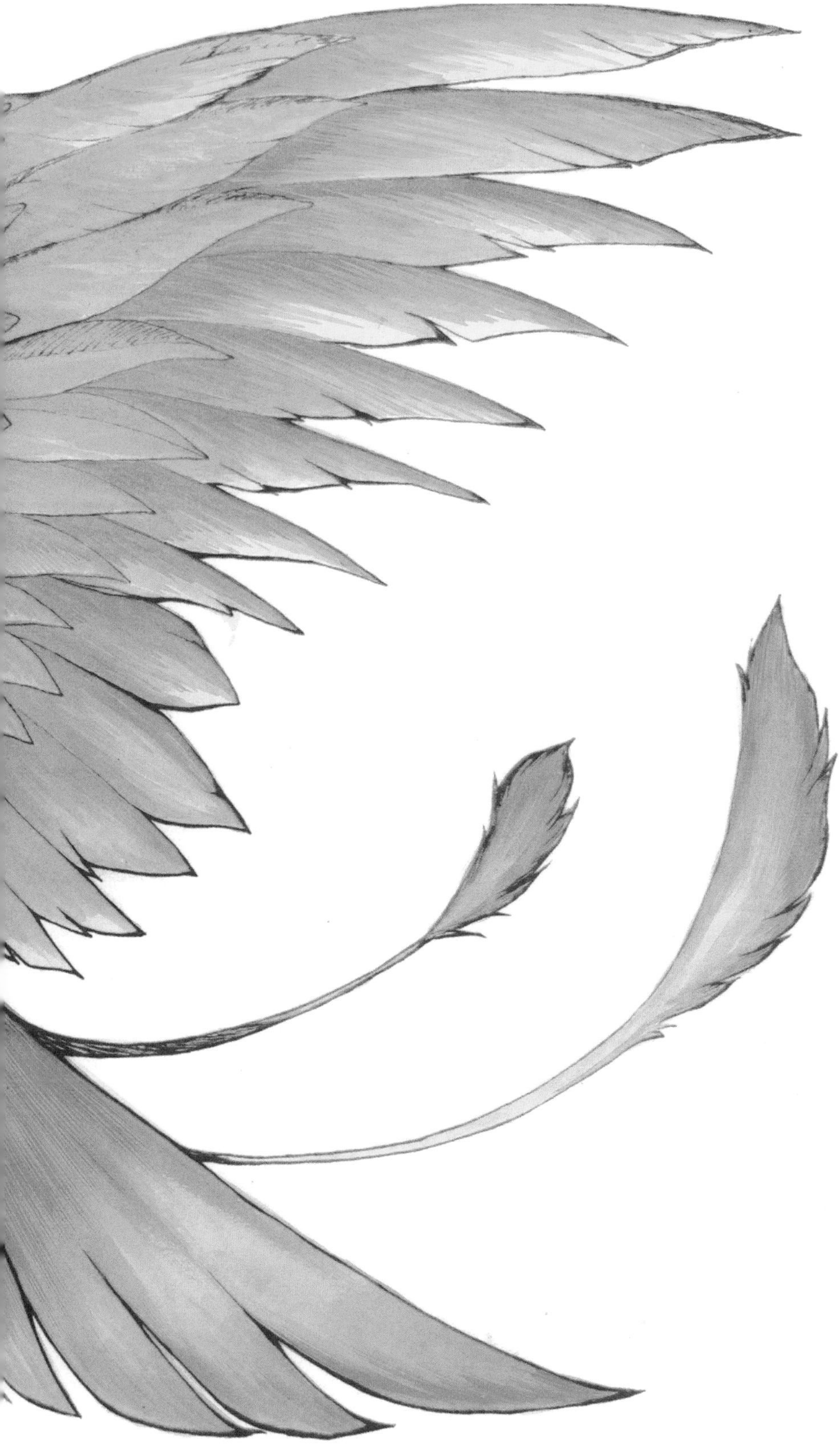

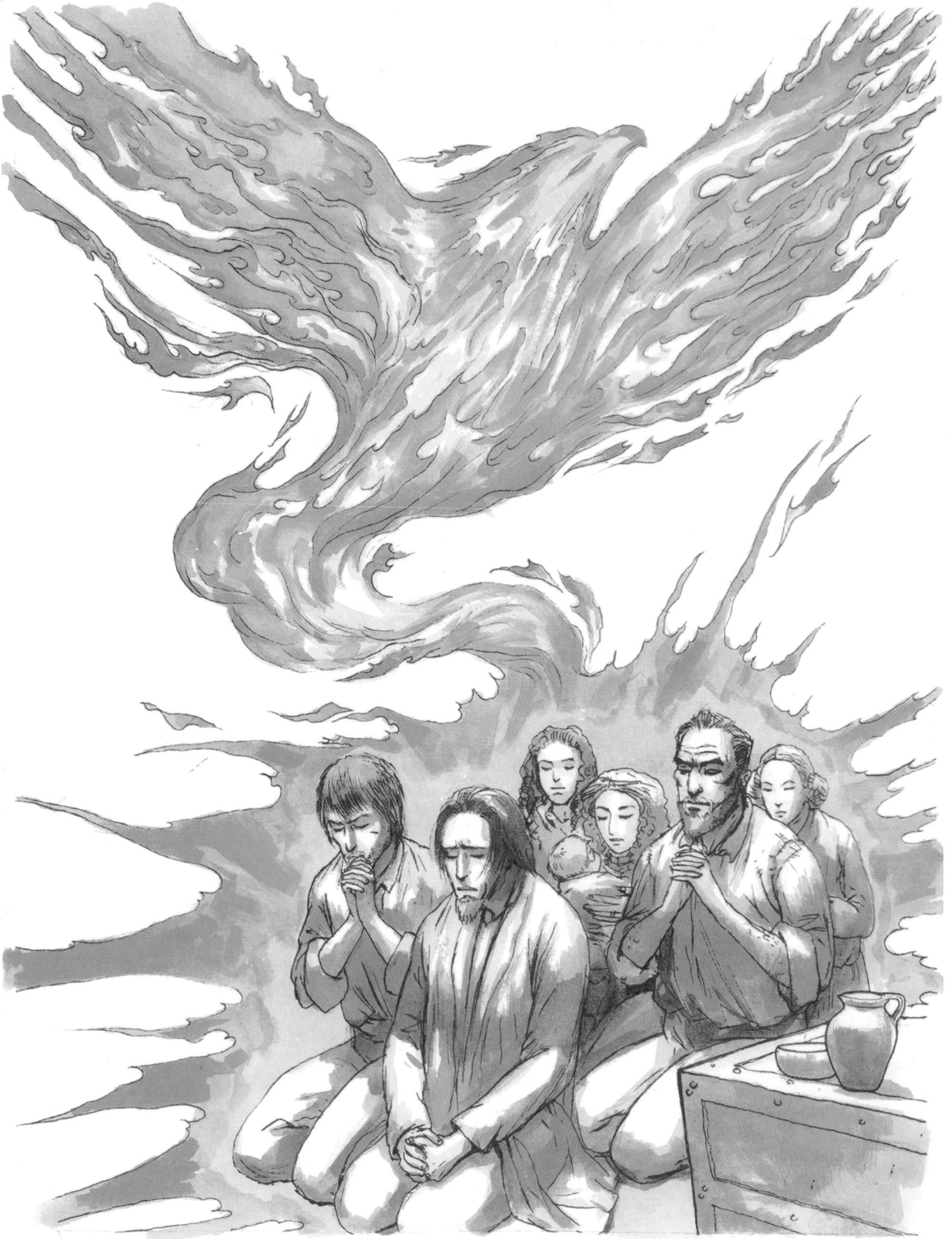

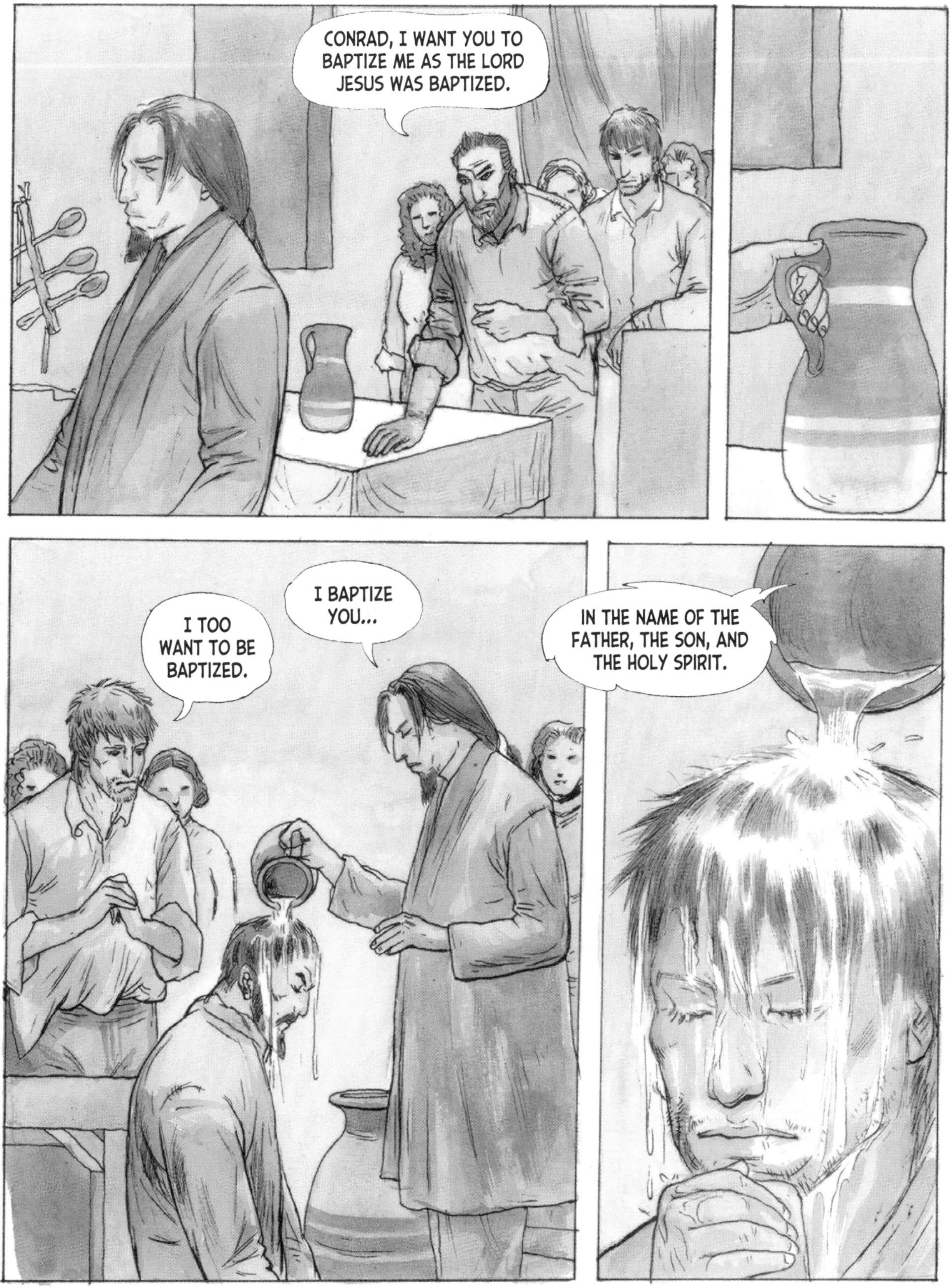
CONRAD, I WANT YOU TO BAPTIZE ME AS THE LORD JESUS WAS BAPTIZED.
I TOO WANT TO BE BAPTIZED.
I BAPTIZE YOU...
IN THE NAME OF THE FATHER, THE SON, AND THE HOLY SPIRIT.

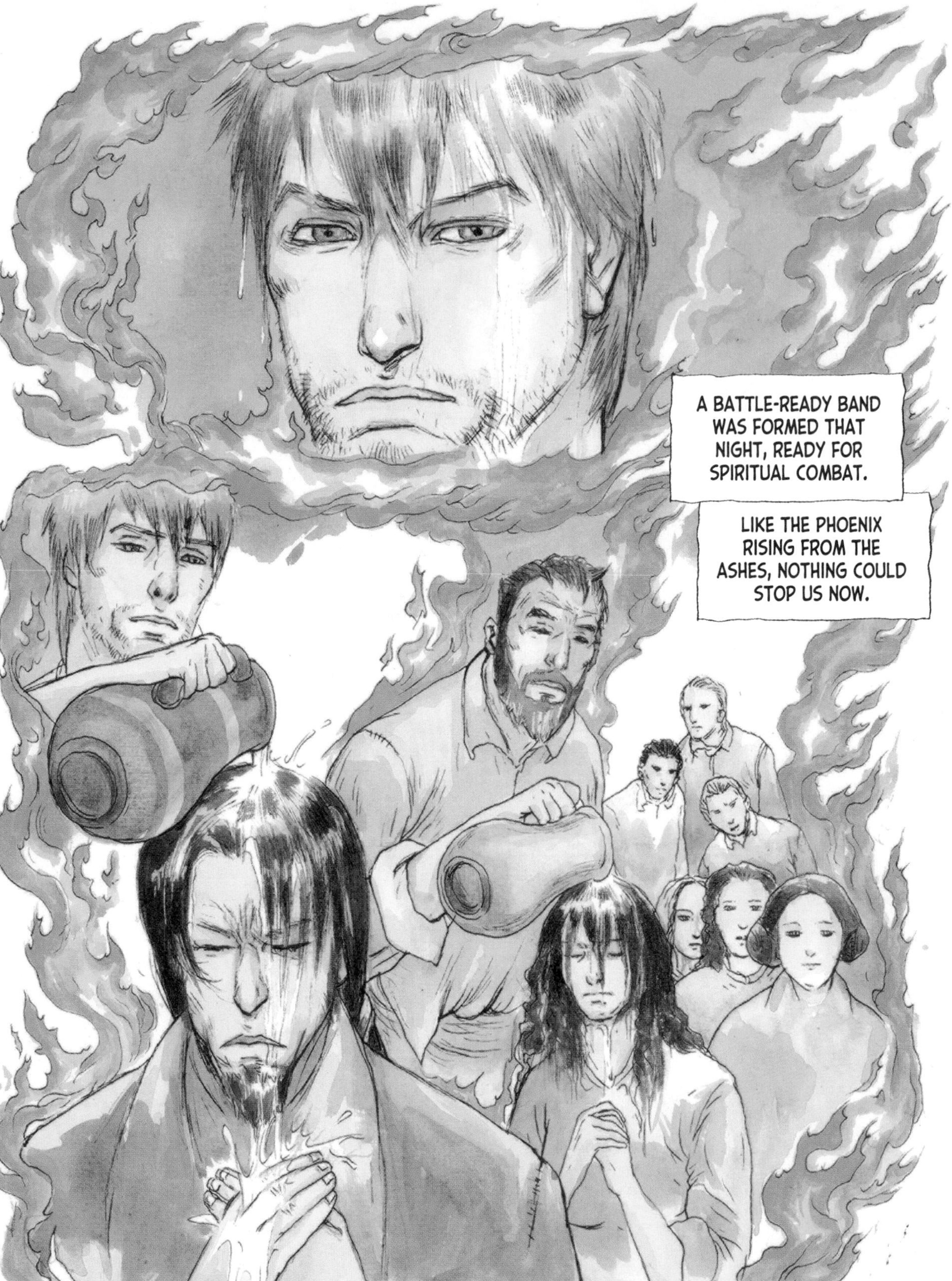
A BATTLE-READY BAND WAS FORMED THAT NIGHT, READY FOR SPIRITUAL COMBAT.
LIKE THE PHOENIX RISING FROM THE ASHES, NOTHING COULD STOP US NOW.

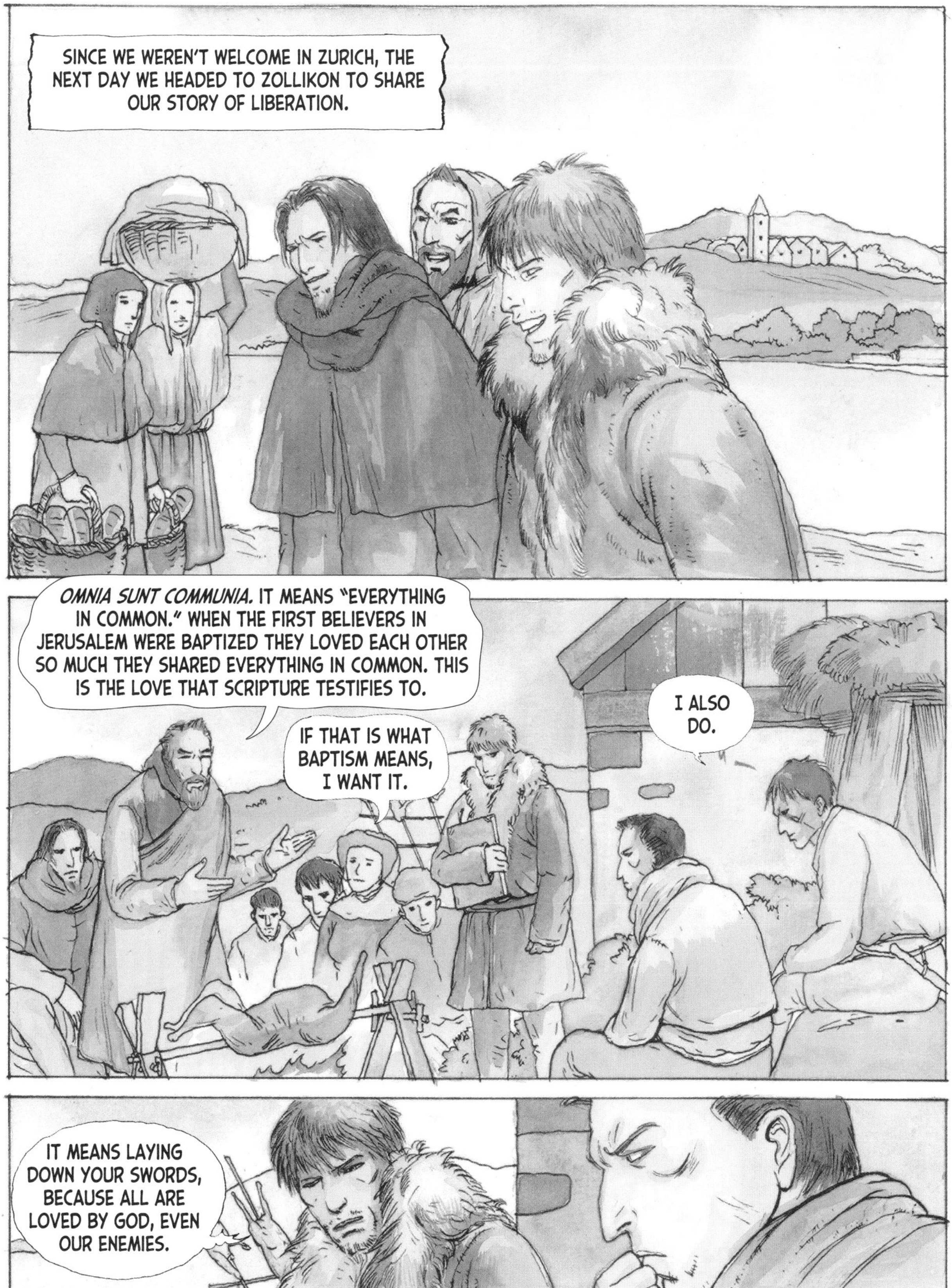
SINCE WE WEREN'T WELCOME IN ZURICH, THE NEXT DAY WE HEADED TO ZOLLIKON TO SHARE OUR STORY OF LIBERATION.
OMNIA SUNT COMMUNIA. IT MEANS "EVERYTHING IN COMMON." WHEN THE FIRST BELIEVERS IN JERUSALEM WERE BAPTIZED THEY LOVED EACH OTHER SO MUCH THEY SHARED EVERYTHING IN COMMON. THIS IS THE LOVE THAT SCRIPTURE TESTIFIES TO.
IF THAT IS WHAT BAPTISM MEANS, I WANT IT.
I ALSO DO.
IT MEANS LAYING DOWN YOUR SWORDS, BECAUSE ALL ARE LOVED BY GOD, EVEN OUR ENEMIES.

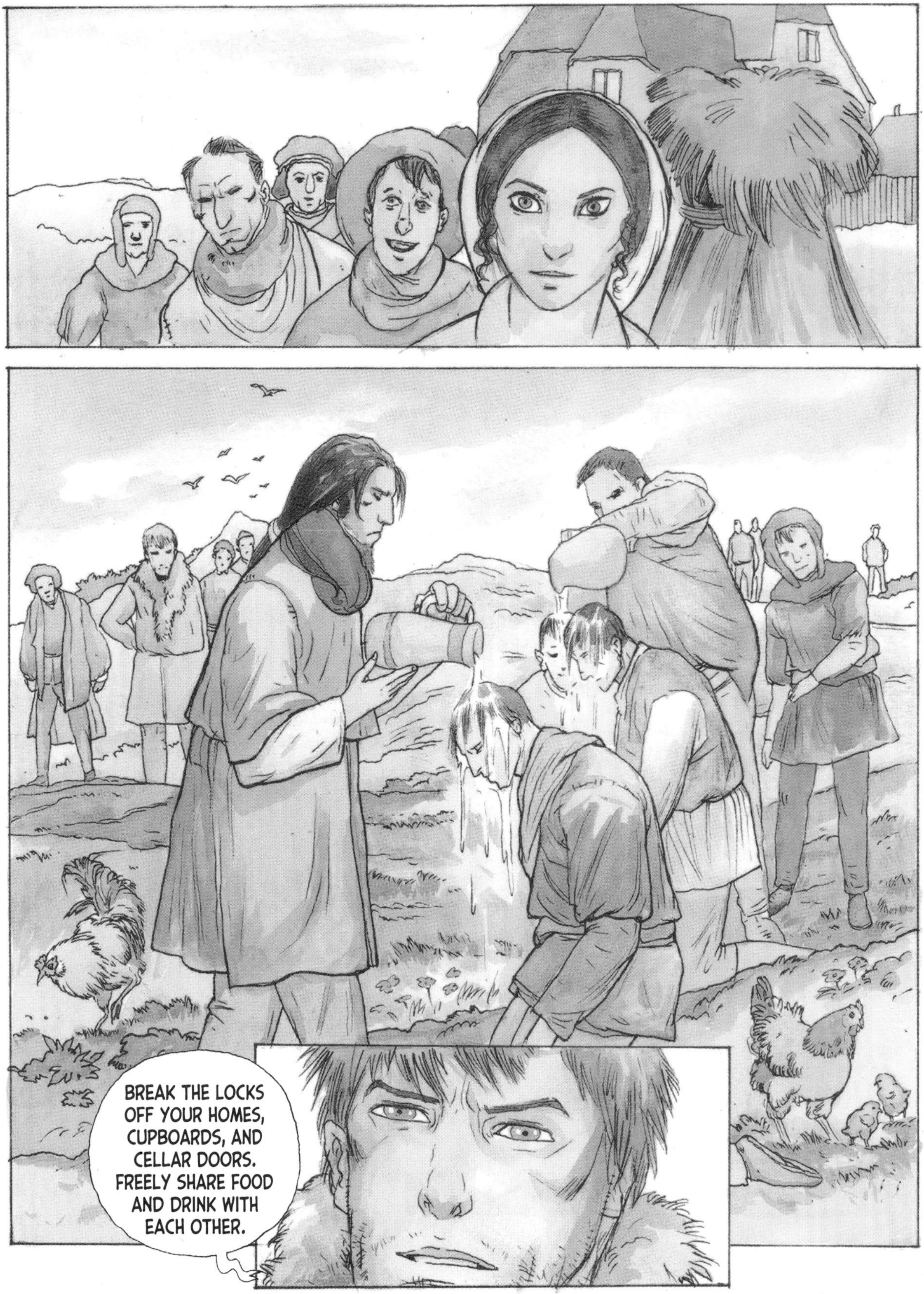
BREAK THE LOCKS OFF YOUR HOMES, CUPBOARDS, AND CELLAR DOORS. FREELY SHARE FOOD AND DRINK WITH EACH OTHER.

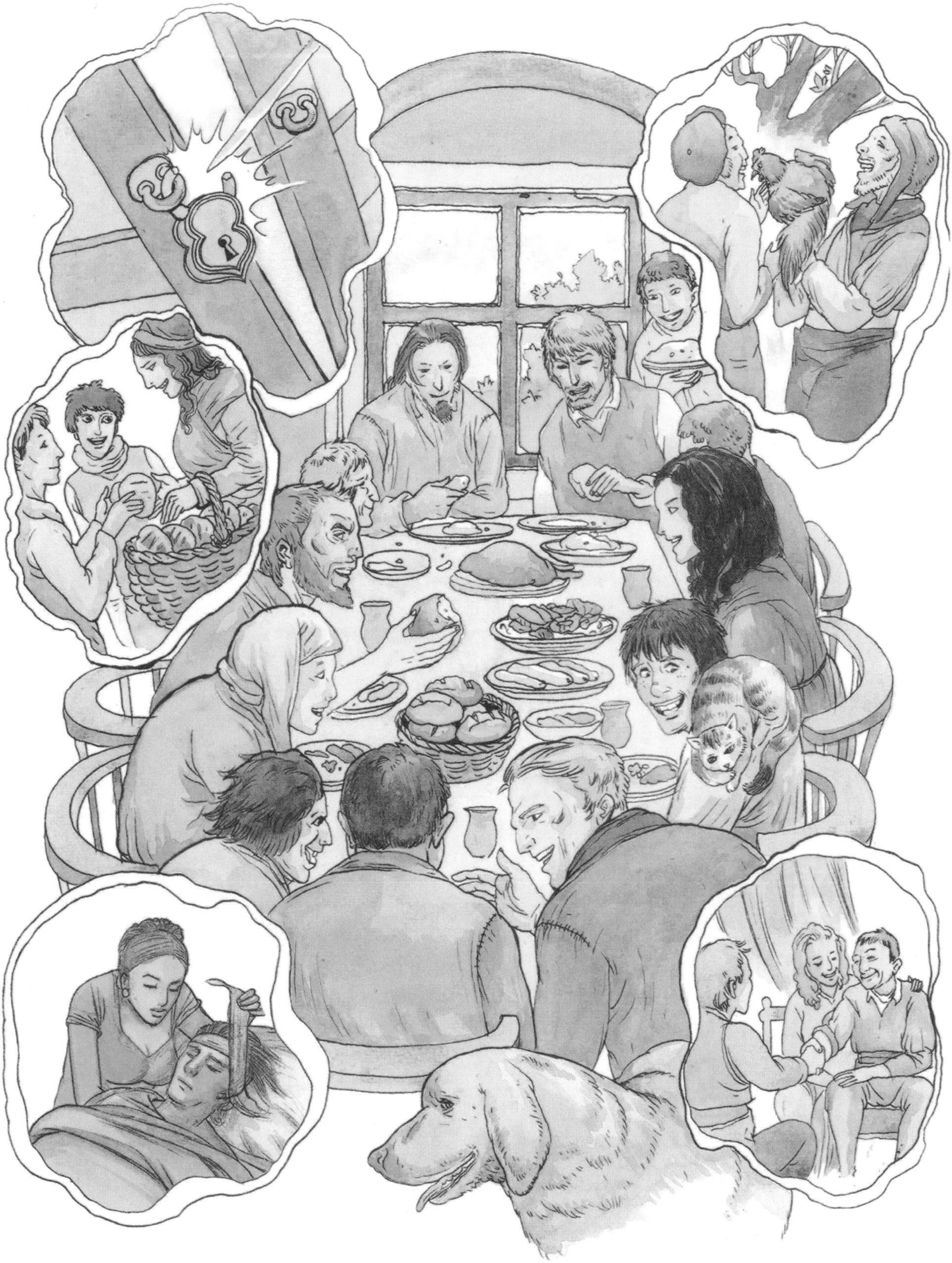

Episode Seven
THE CAPTIVE

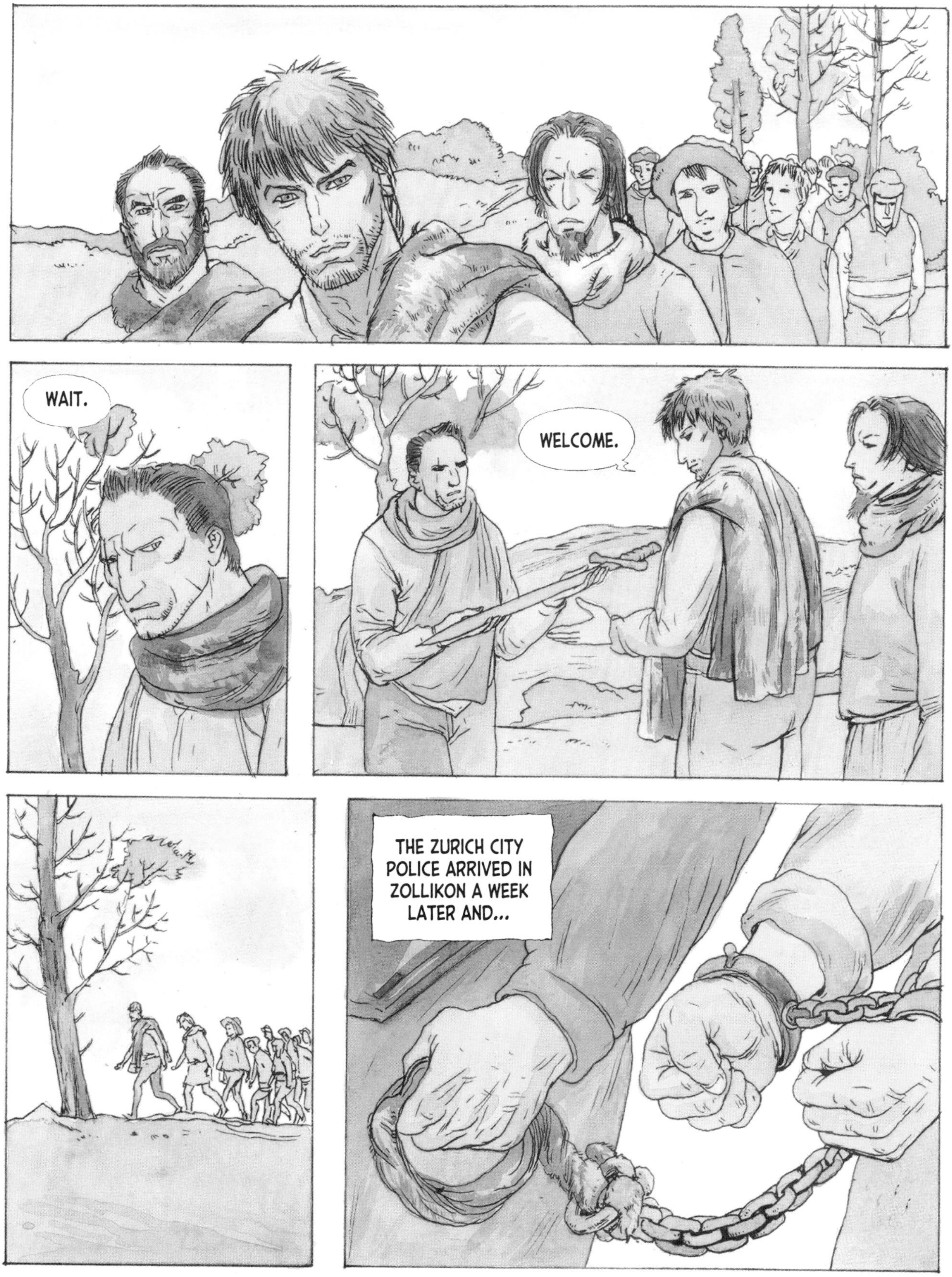
WAIT.
WELCOME.
THE ZURICH CITY POLICE ARRIVED IN ZOLLIKON A WEEK LATER AND...

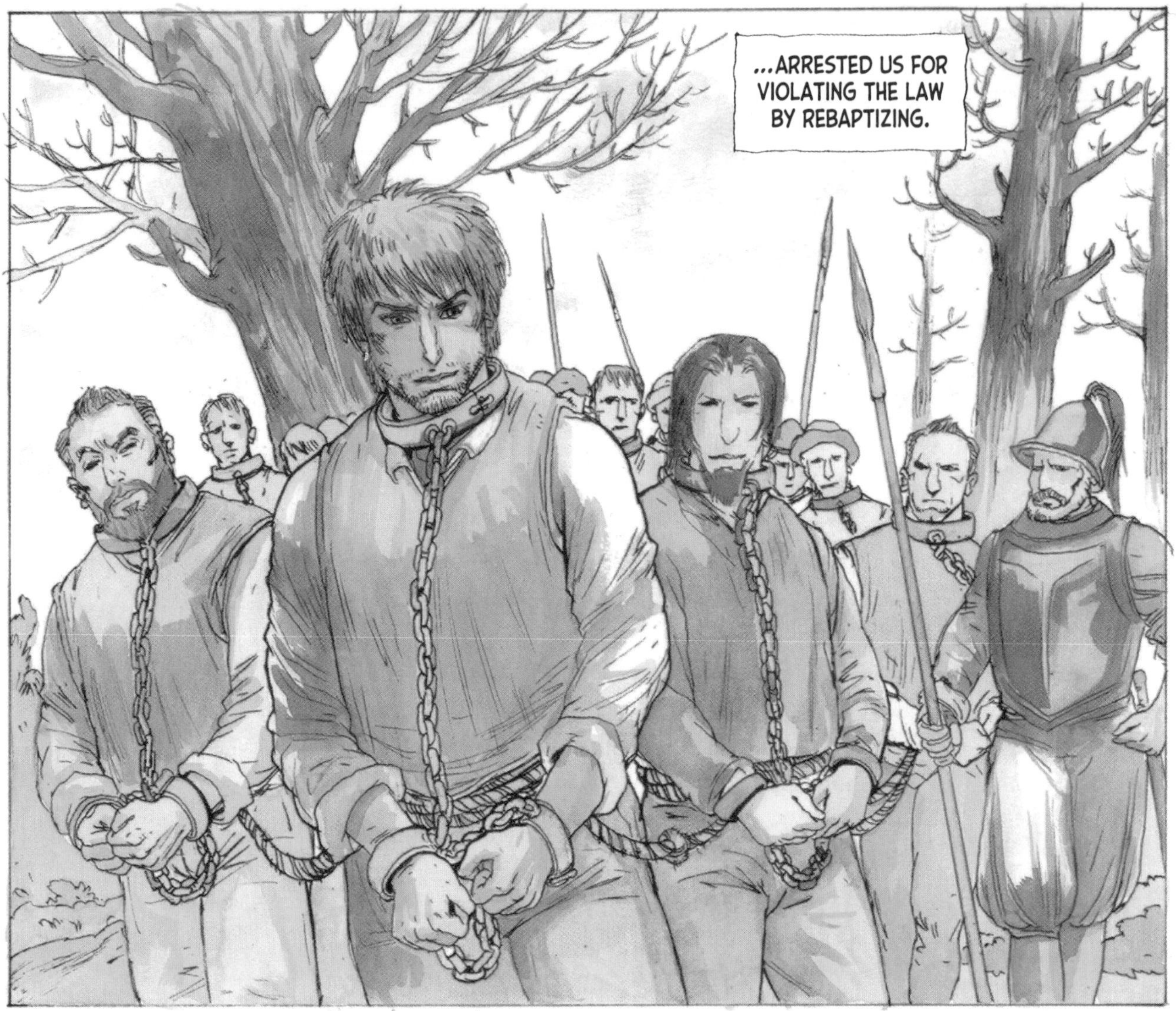
...ARRESTED US FOR VIOLATING THE LAW BY REBAPTIZING.

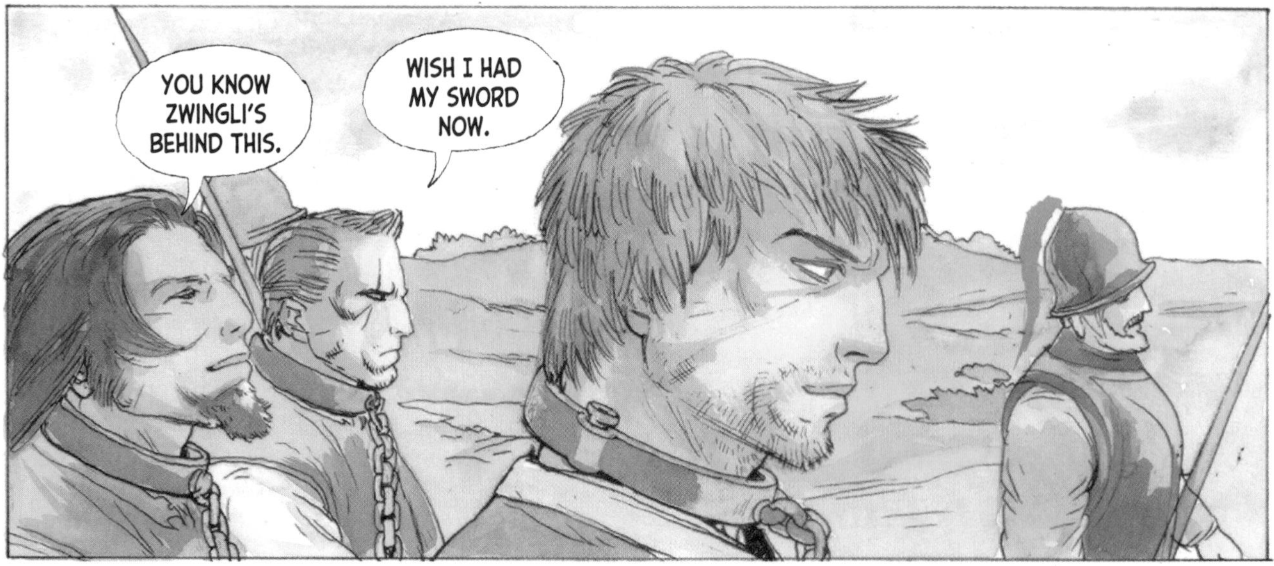
YOU KNOW ZWINGLI'S BEHIND THIS.
WISH I HAD MY SWORD NOW.

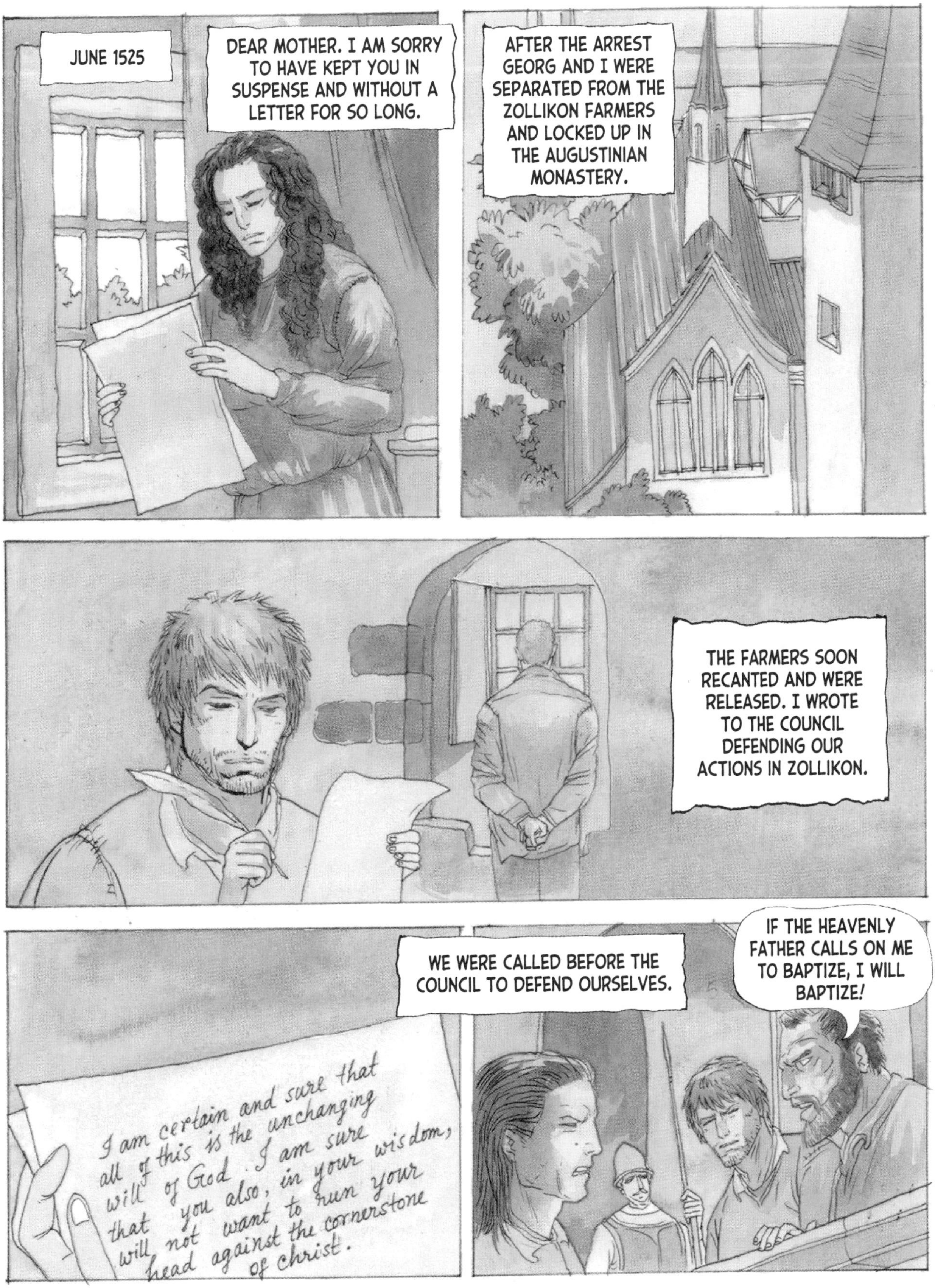
JUNE 1525
DEAR MOTHER. I AM SORRY TO HAVE KEPT YOU IN SUSPENSE AND WITHOUT A LETTER FOR SO LONG.
AFTER THE ARREST GEORG AND I WERE SEPARATED FROM THE ZOLLIKON FARMERS AND LOCKED UP IN THE AUGUSTINIAN MONASTERY.
THE FARMERS SOON RECANTED AND WERE RELEASED. I WROTE TO THE COUNCIL DEFENDING OUR ACTIONS IN ZOLLIKON.
I am certain and sure that all of this is the unchanging will of God. I am sure that you also, in your wisdom, will not want to run your head against the cornerstone of christ.
WE WERE CALLED BEFORE THE COUNCIL TO DEFEND OURSELVES.
IF THE HEAVENLY FATHER CALLS ON ME TO BAPTIZE, I WILL BAPTIZE!

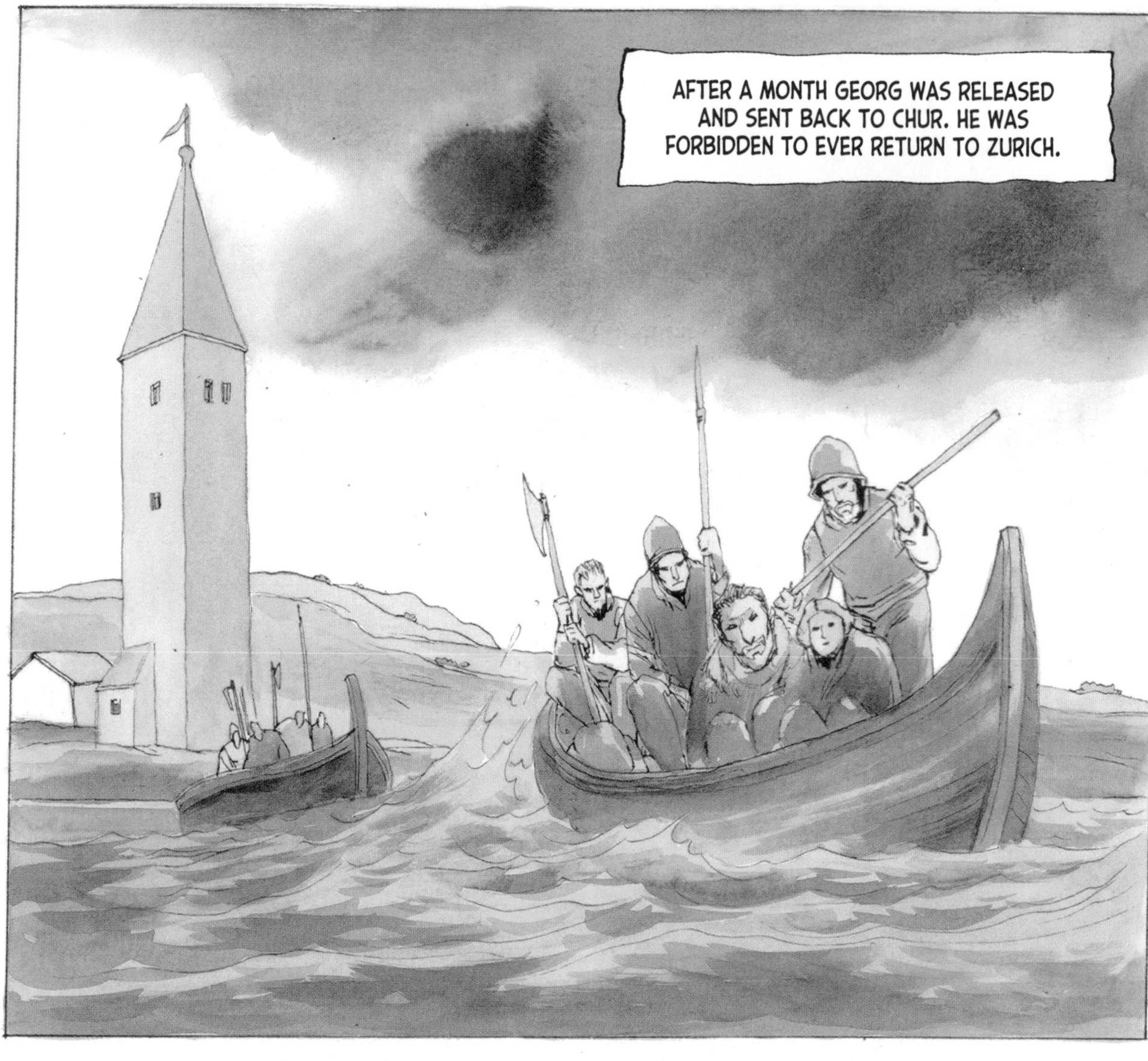
AFTER A MONTH GEORG WAS RELEASED AND SENT BACK TO CHUR. HE WAS FORBIDDEN TO EVER RETURN TO ZURICH.

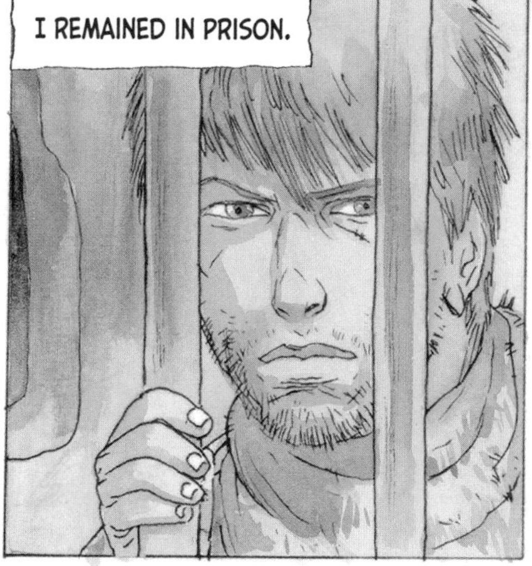
I REMAINED IN PRISON.

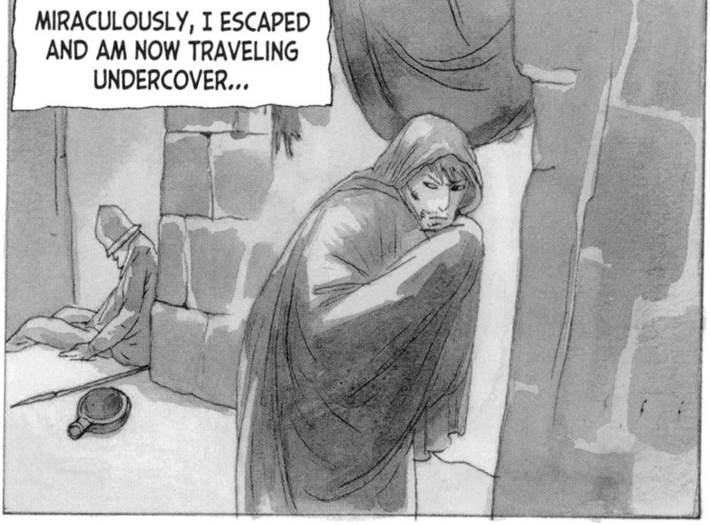
MIRACULOUSLY, I ESCAPED AND AM NOW TRAVELING UNDERCOVER...

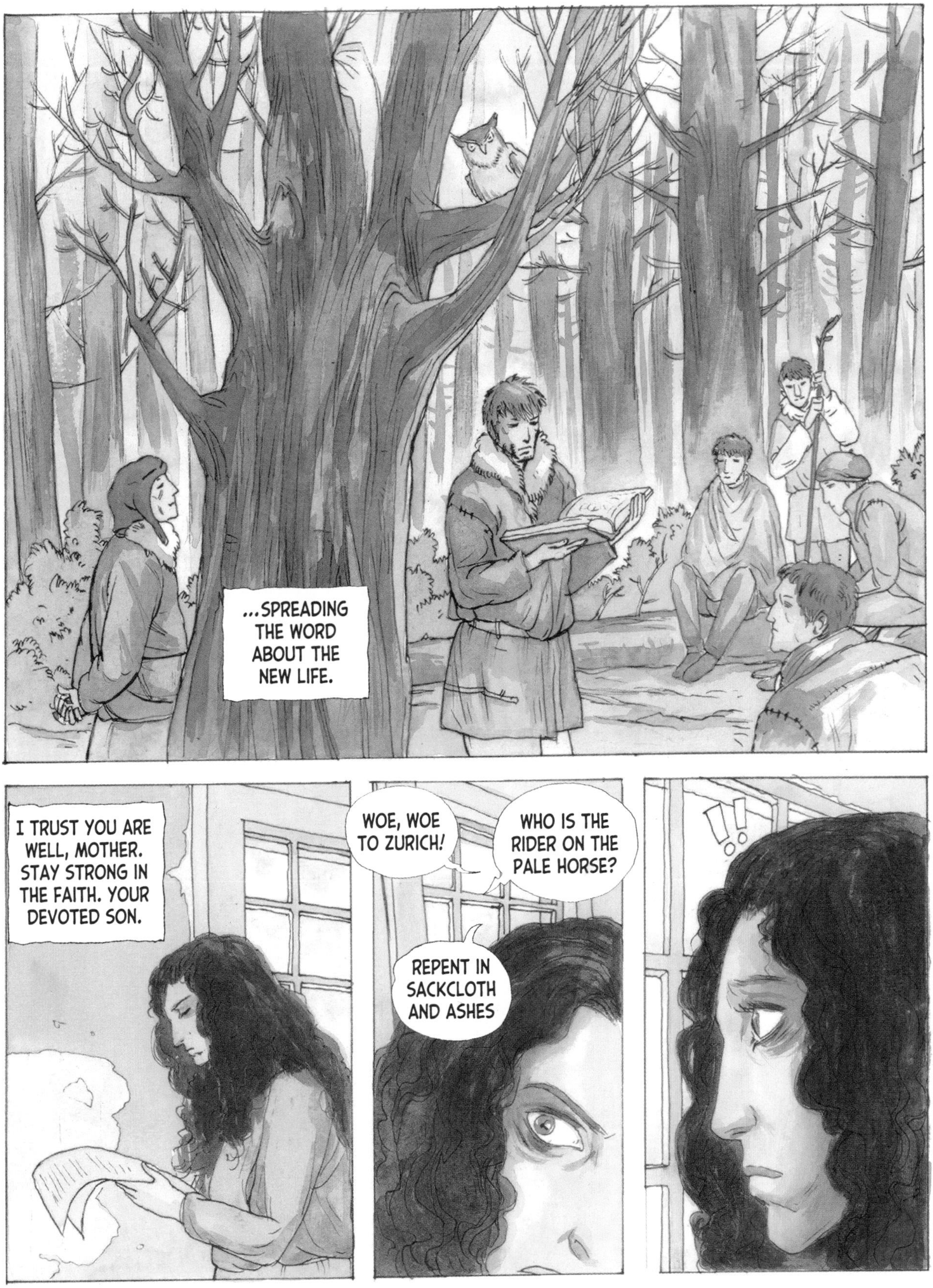
...SPREADING THE WORD ABOUT THE NEW LIFE.
I TRUST YOU ARE WELL, MOTHER. STAY STRONG IN THE FAITH. YOUR DEVOTED SON.
WOE, WOE TO ZURICH!
WHO IS THE RIDER ON THE PALE HORSE?
REPENT IN SACKCLOTH AND ASHES
!!

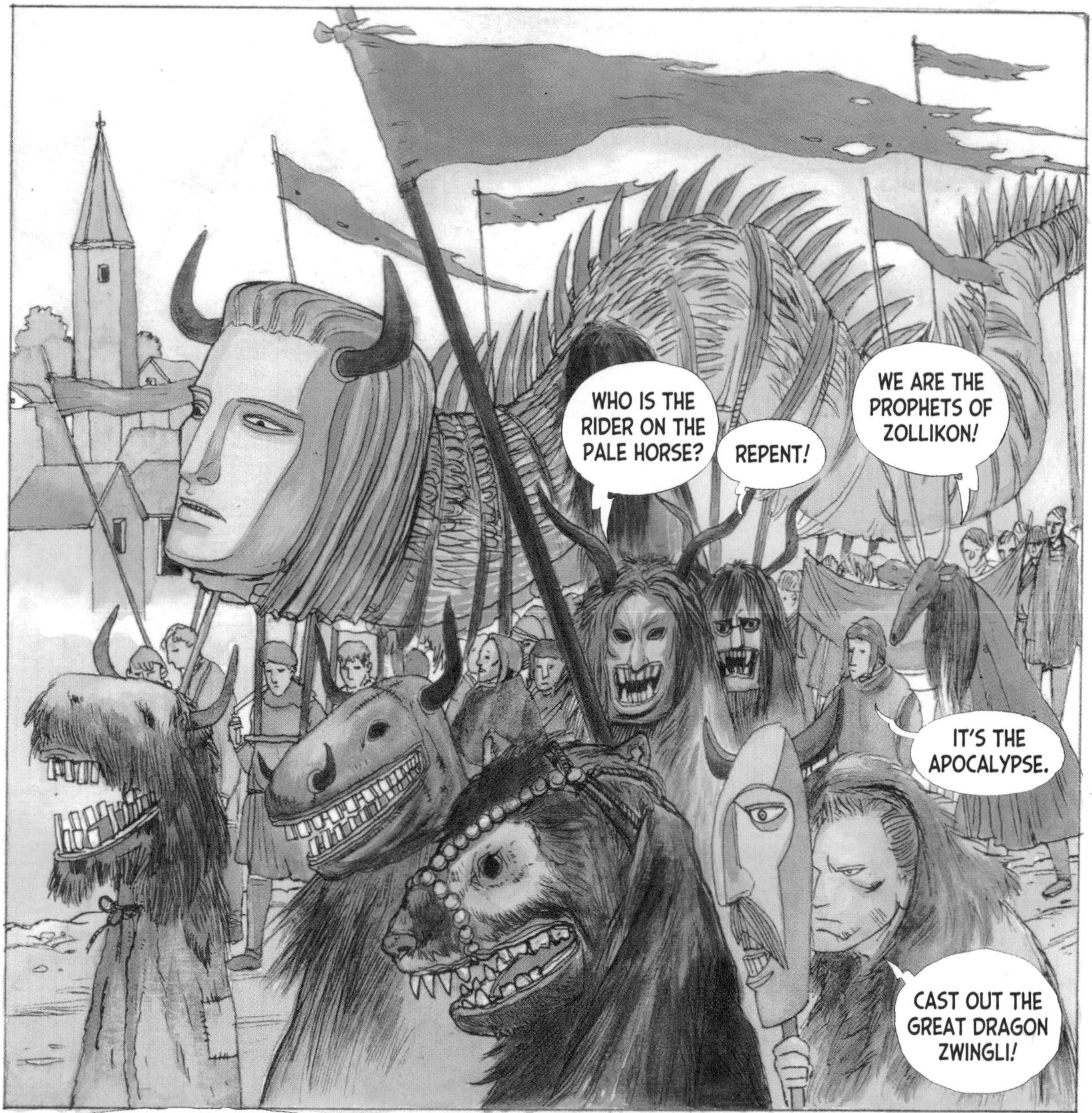
WHO IS THE RIDER ON THE PALE HORSE?
REPENT!
WE ARE THE PROPHETS OF ZOLLIKON!
IT'S THE APOCALYPSE.
CAST OUT THE GREAT DRAGON ZWINGLI!

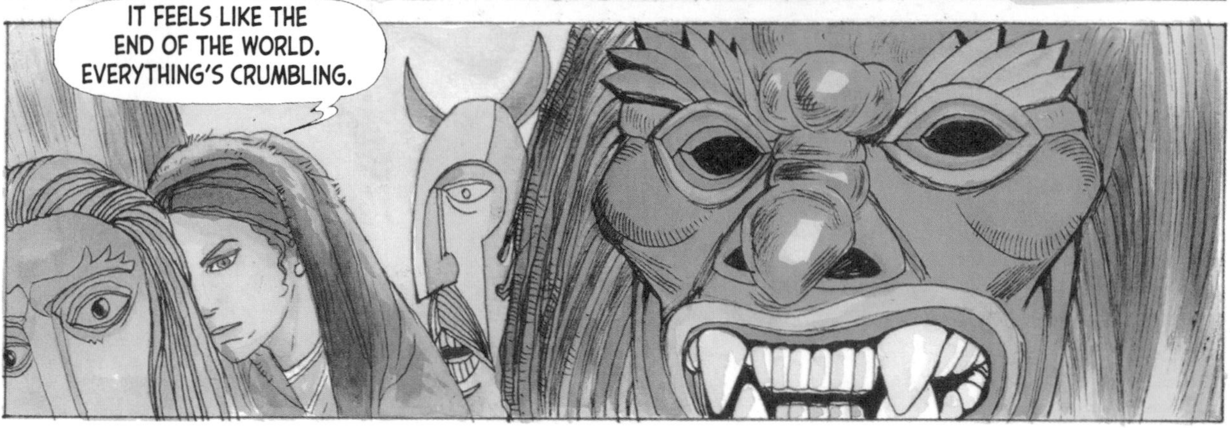
IT FEELS LIKE THE END OF THE WORLD. EVERYTHING'S CRUMBLING.

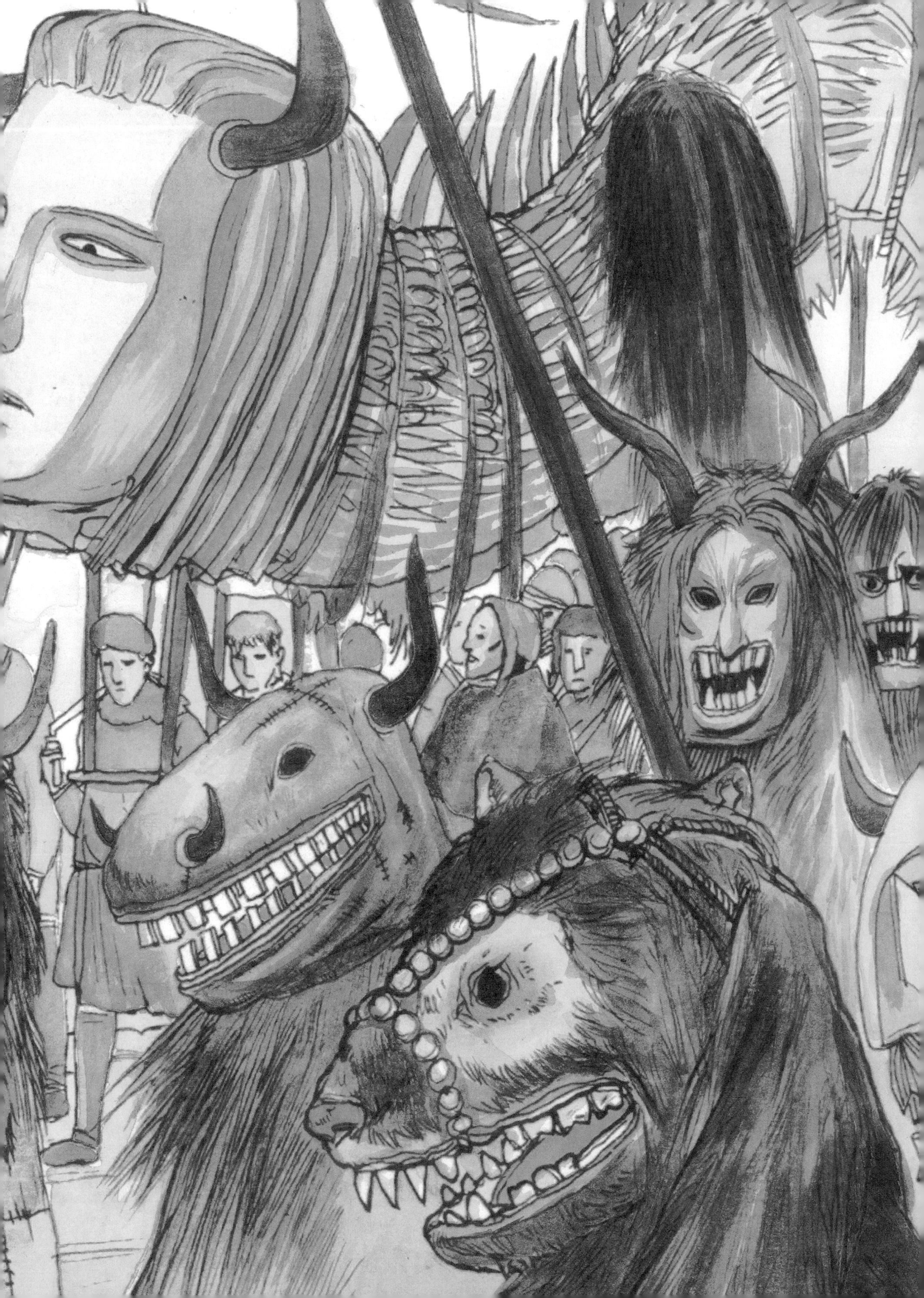

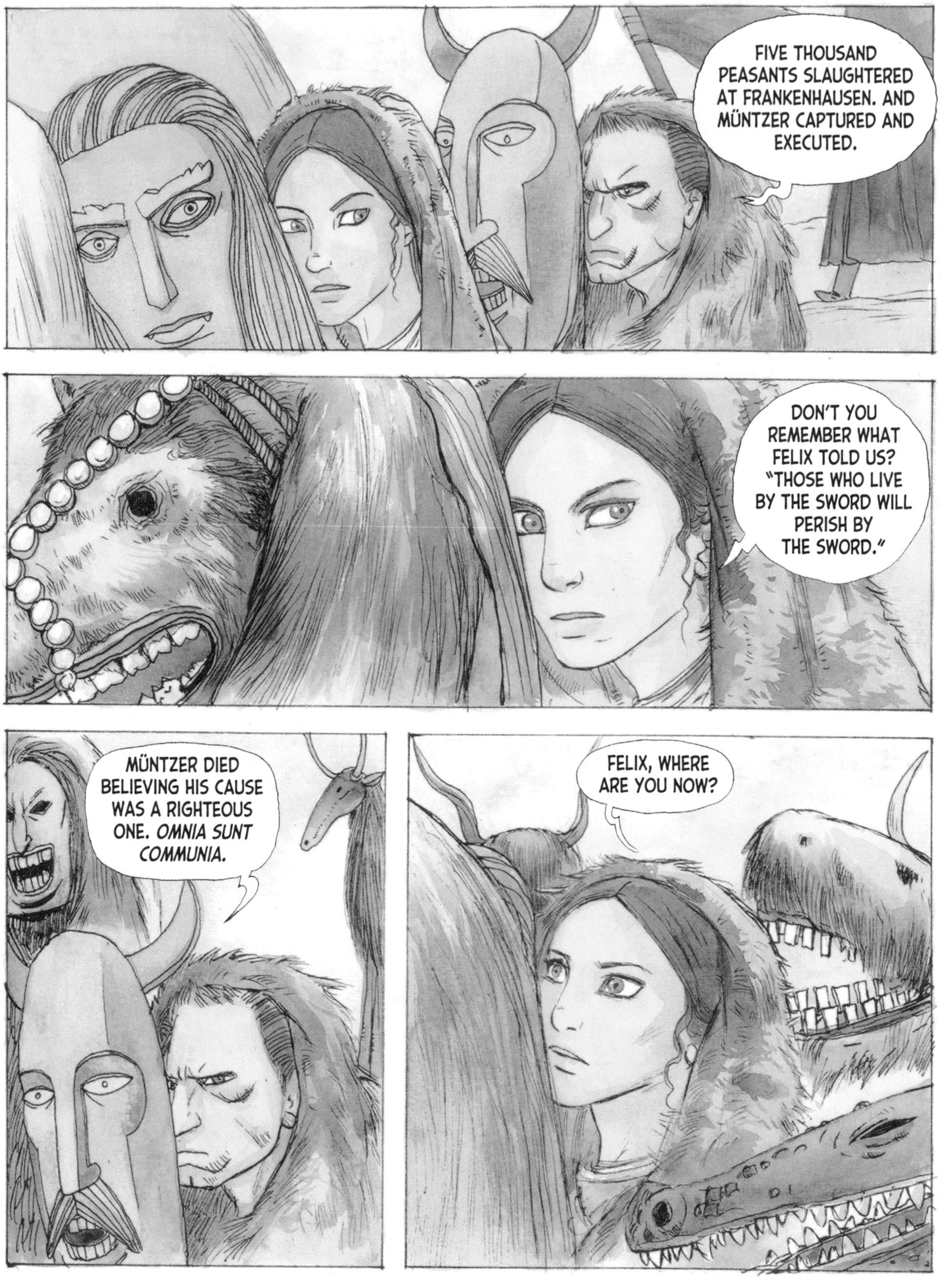
FIVE THOUSAND PEASANTS SLAUGHTERED AT FRANKENHAUSEN. AND MÜNTZER CAPTURED AND EXECUTED.
DON'T YOU REMEMBER WHAT FELIX TOLD US? "THOSE WHO LIVE BY THE SWORD WILL PERISH BY THE SWORD."
MÜNTZER DIED BELIEVING HIS CAUSE WAS A RIGHTEOUS ONE. *OMNIA SUNT COMMUNIA.*
FELIX, WHERE ARE YOU NOW?

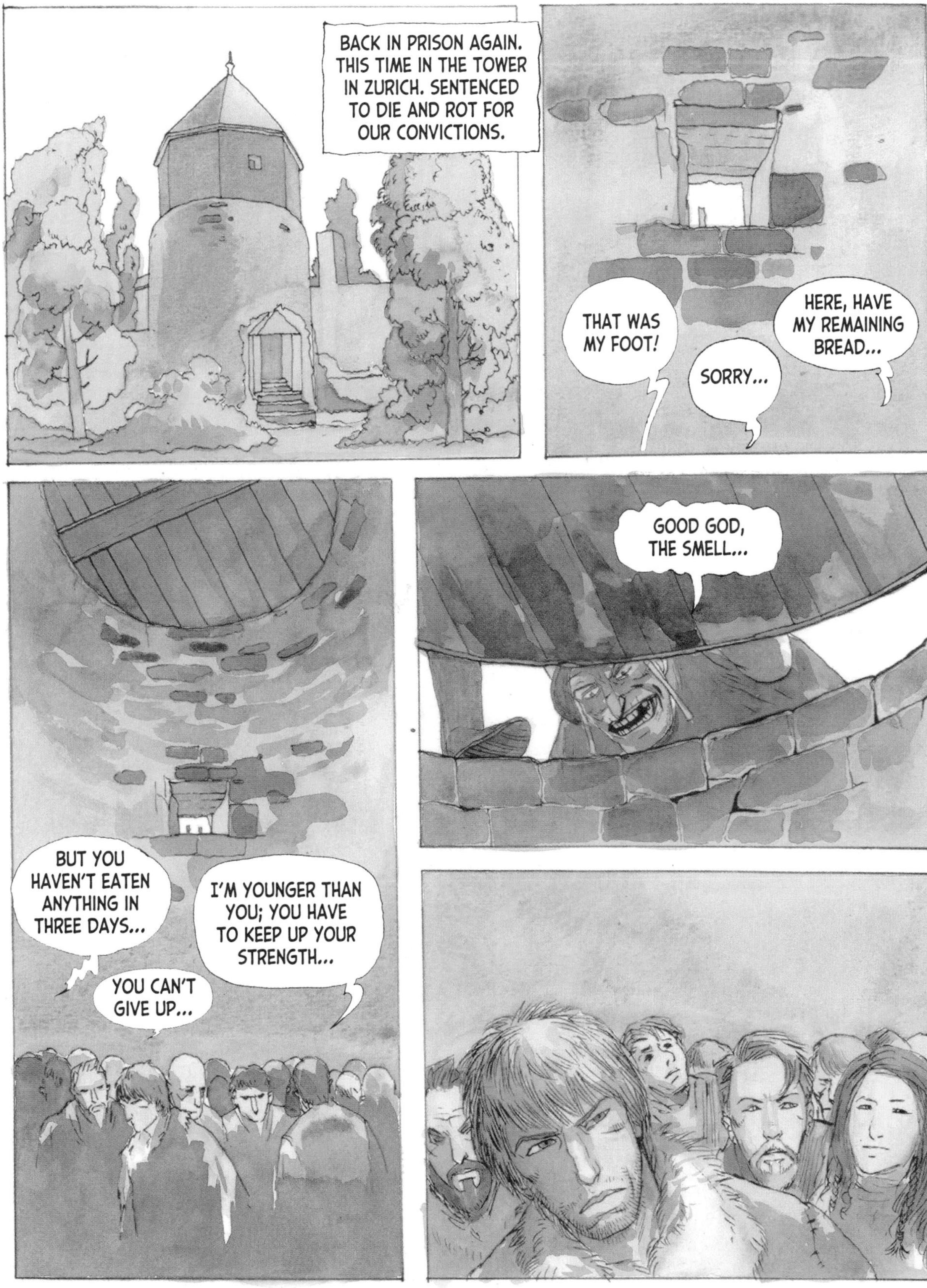
BACK IN PRISON AGAIN. THIS TIME IN THE TOWER IN ZURICH. SENTENCED TO DIE AND ROT FOR OUR CONVICTIONS.
THAT WAS MY FOOT!
SORRY...
HERE, HAVE MY REMAINING BREAD...
BUT YOU HAVEN'T EATEN ANYTHING IN THREE DAYS...
YOU CAN'T GIVE UP...
I'M YOUNGER THAN YOU; YOU HAVE TO KEEP UP YOUR STRENGTH...
GOOD GOD, THE SMELL...

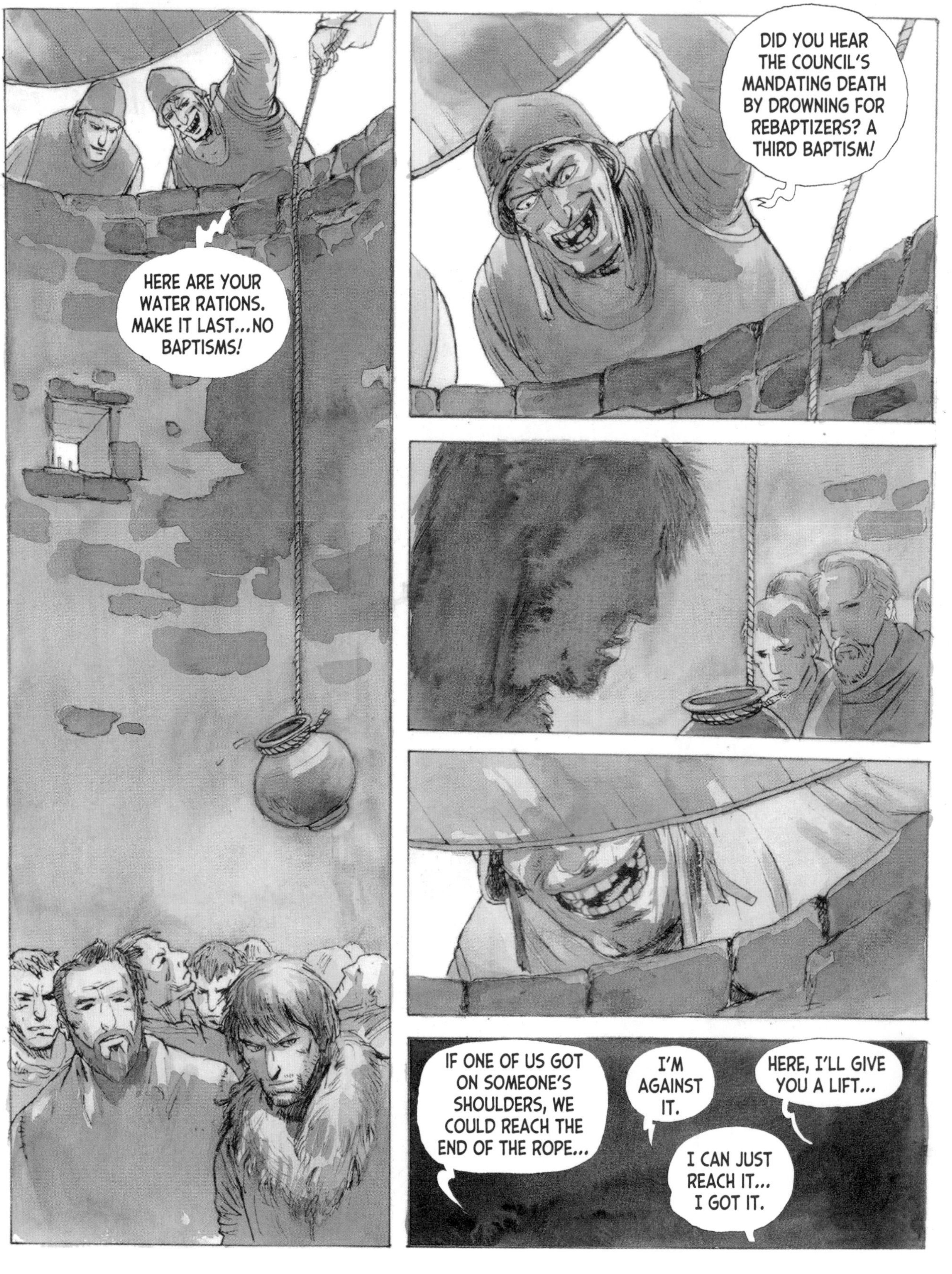
HERE ARE YOUR WATER RATIONS. MAKE IT LAST...NO BAPTISMS!
DID YOU HEAR THE COUNCIL'S MANDATING DEATH BY DROWNING FOR REBAPTIZERS? A THIRD BAPTISM!
IF ONE OF US GOT ON SOMEONE'S SHOULDERS, WE COULD REACH THE END OF THE ROPE...
I'M AGAINST IT.
HERE, I'LL GIVE YOU A LIFT...
I CAN JUST REACH IT... I GOT IT.

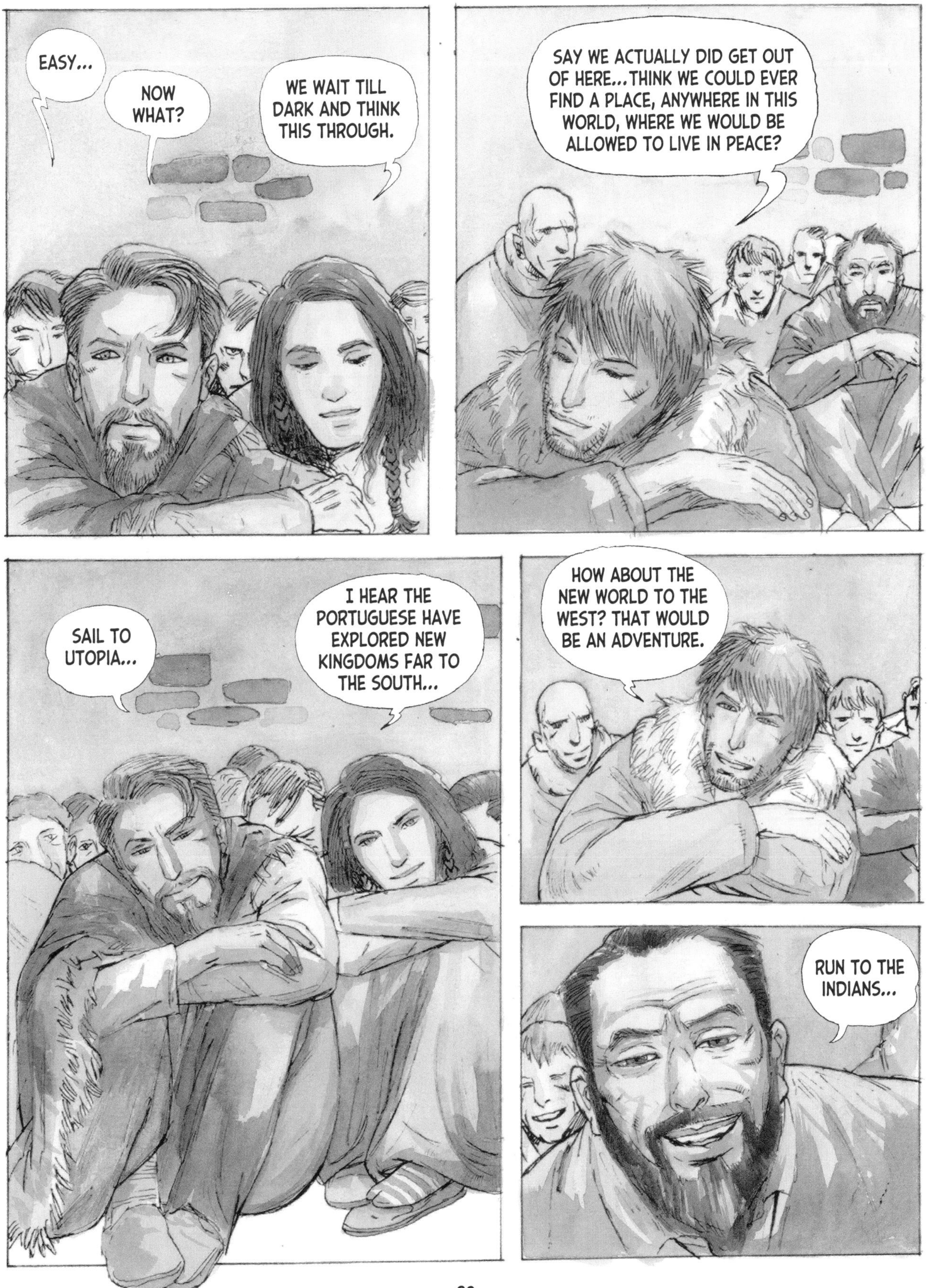
EASY...
NOW WHAT?
WE WAIT TILL DARK AND THINK THIS THROUGH.
SAY WE ACTUALLY DID GET OUT OF HERE...THINK WE COULD EVER FIND A PLACE, ANYWHERE IN THIS WORLD, WHERE WE WOULD BE ALLOWED TO LIVE IN PEACE?
SAIL TO UTOPIA...
I HEAR THE PORTUGUESE HAVE EXPLORED NEW KINGDOMS FAR TO THE SOUTH...
HOW ABOUT THE NEW WORLD TO THE WEST? THAT WOULD BE AN ADVENTURE.
RUN TO THE INDIANS...

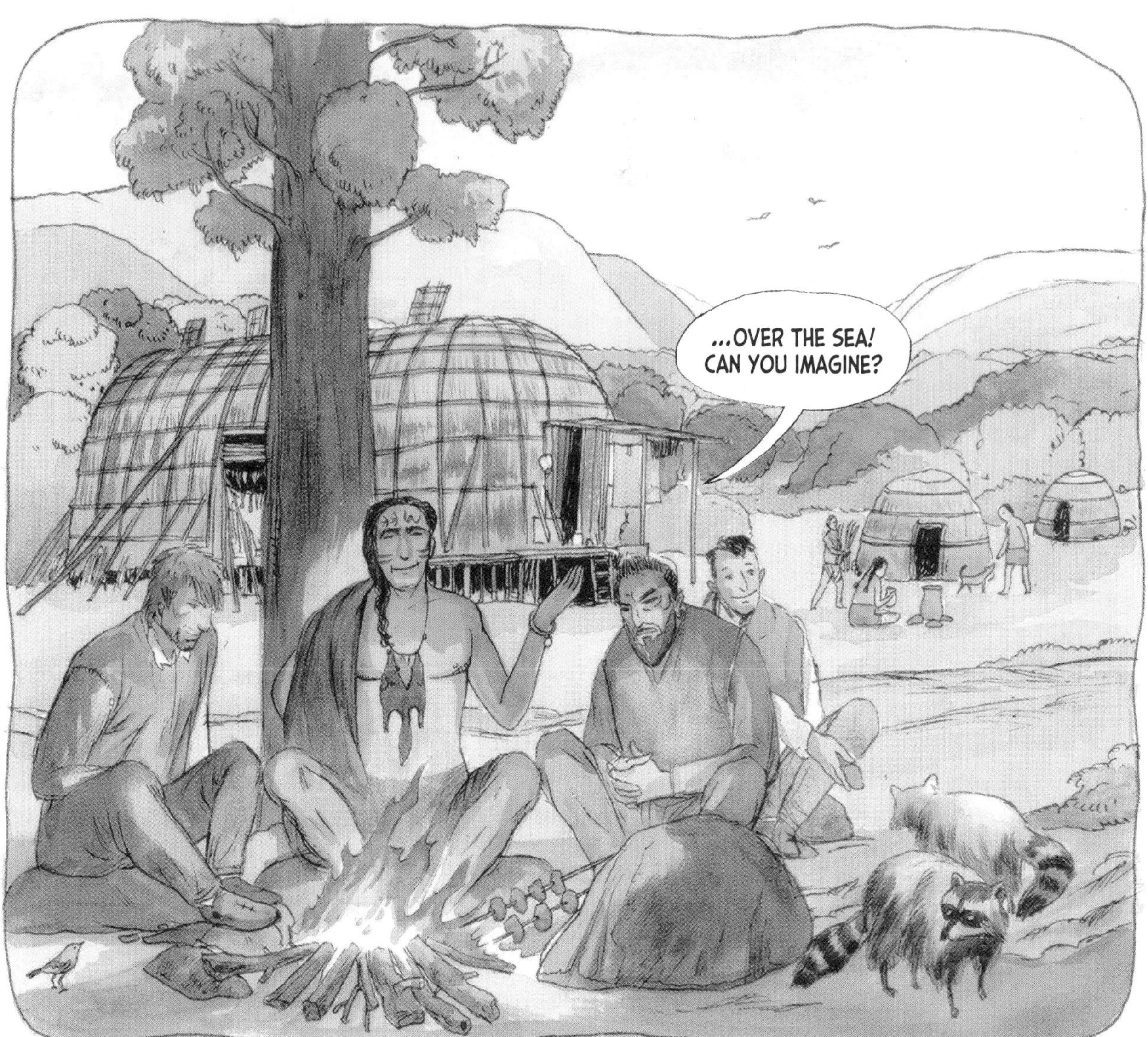
...OVER THE SEA! CAN YOU IMAGINE?

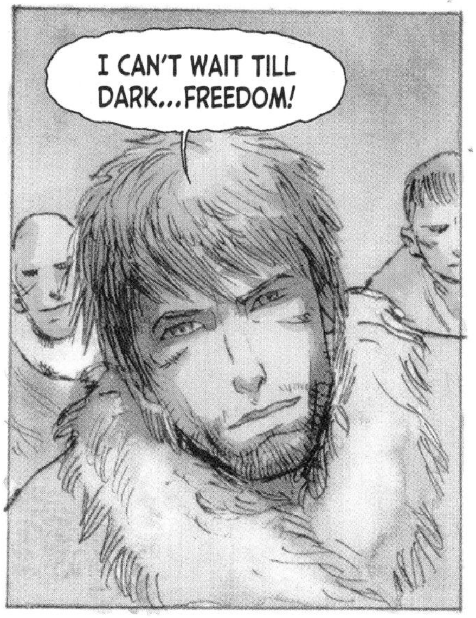
I CAN'T WAIT TILL DARK...FREEDOM!

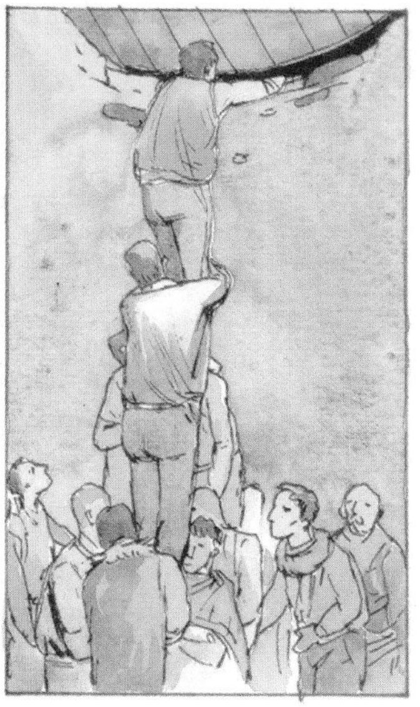

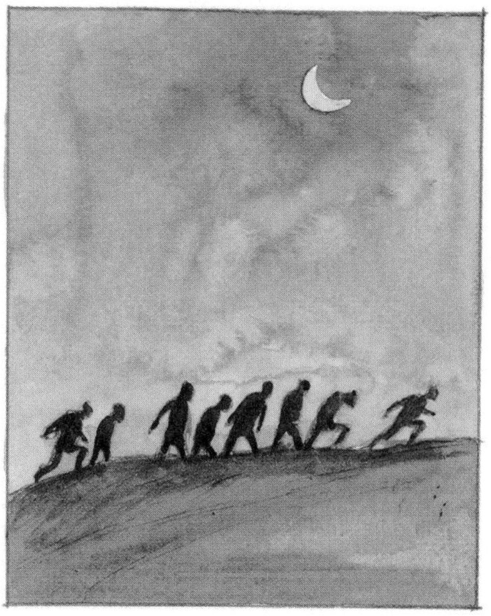

Episode Eight

THE EXILE

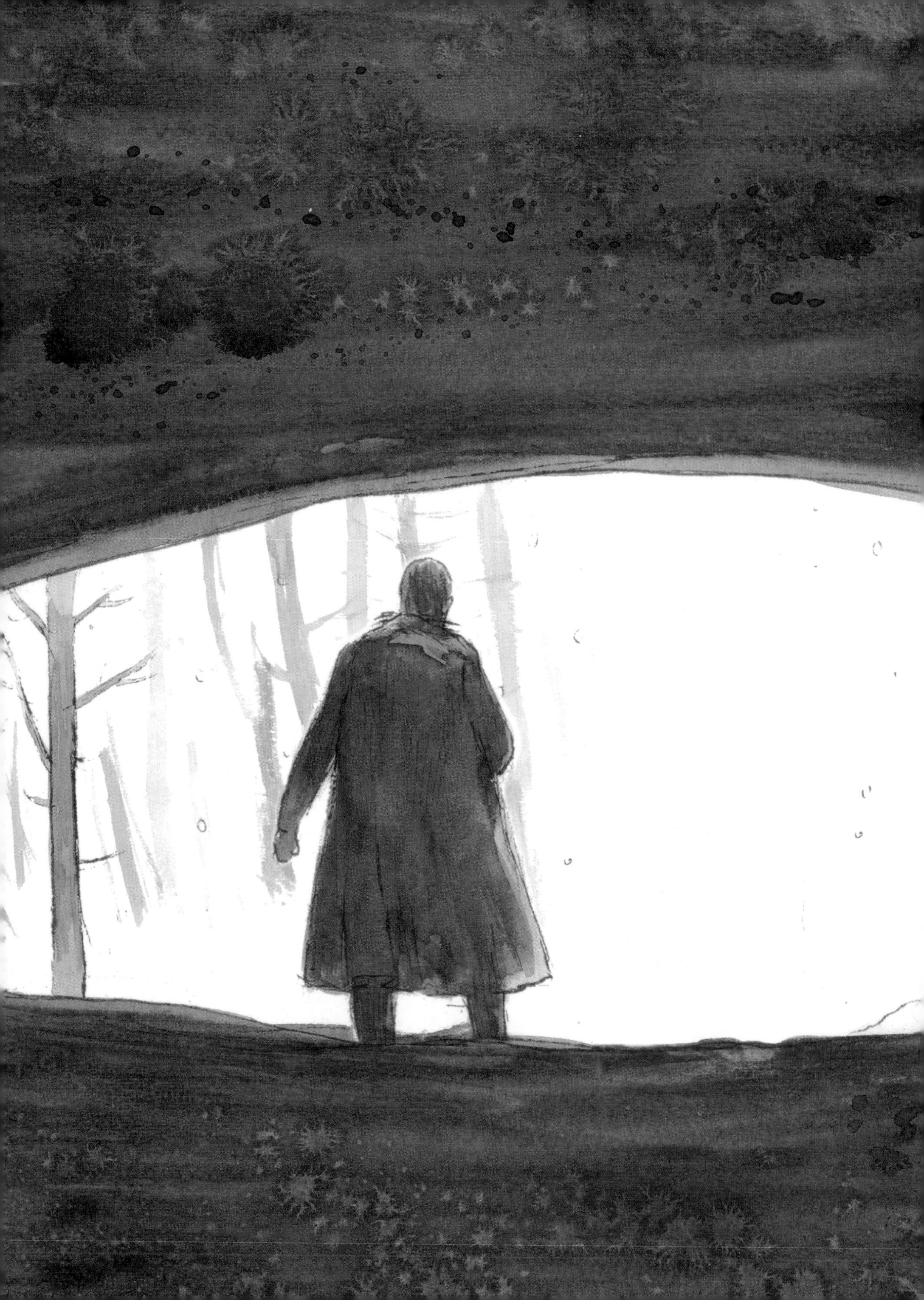

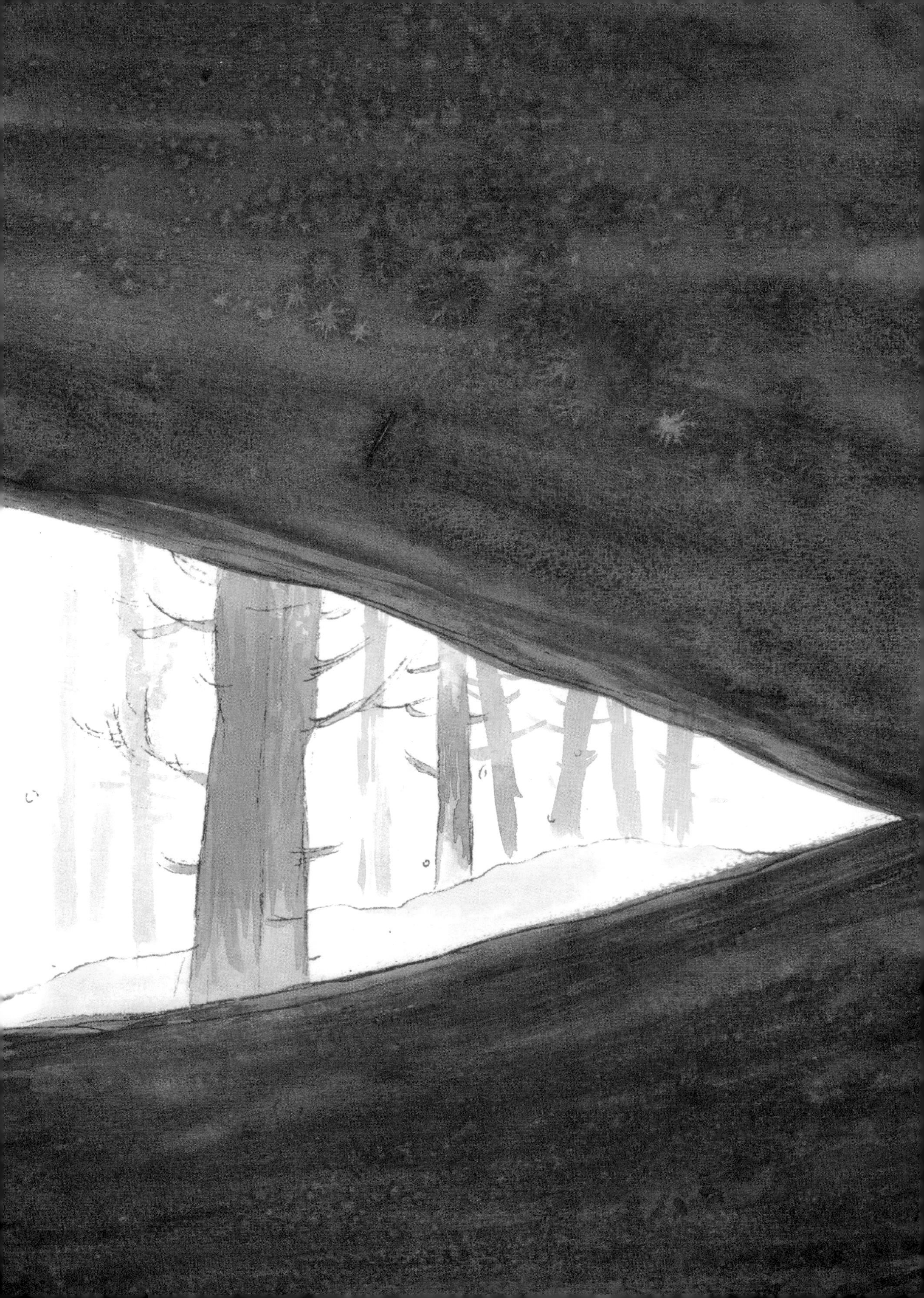

DECEMBER
1526

I'VE BROUGHT
FOOD FOR YOU.
THE FARMERS WERE
GENEROUS.

THANK YOU!
WHAT NEWS HAVE
YOU HEARD?

PEOPLE CAN'T STOP TALKING
ABOUT HIM. ABOUT HIS TEACHING
AND HOW HE INSPIRES THEM.
THEY SAY HE'S AN APOSTLE.

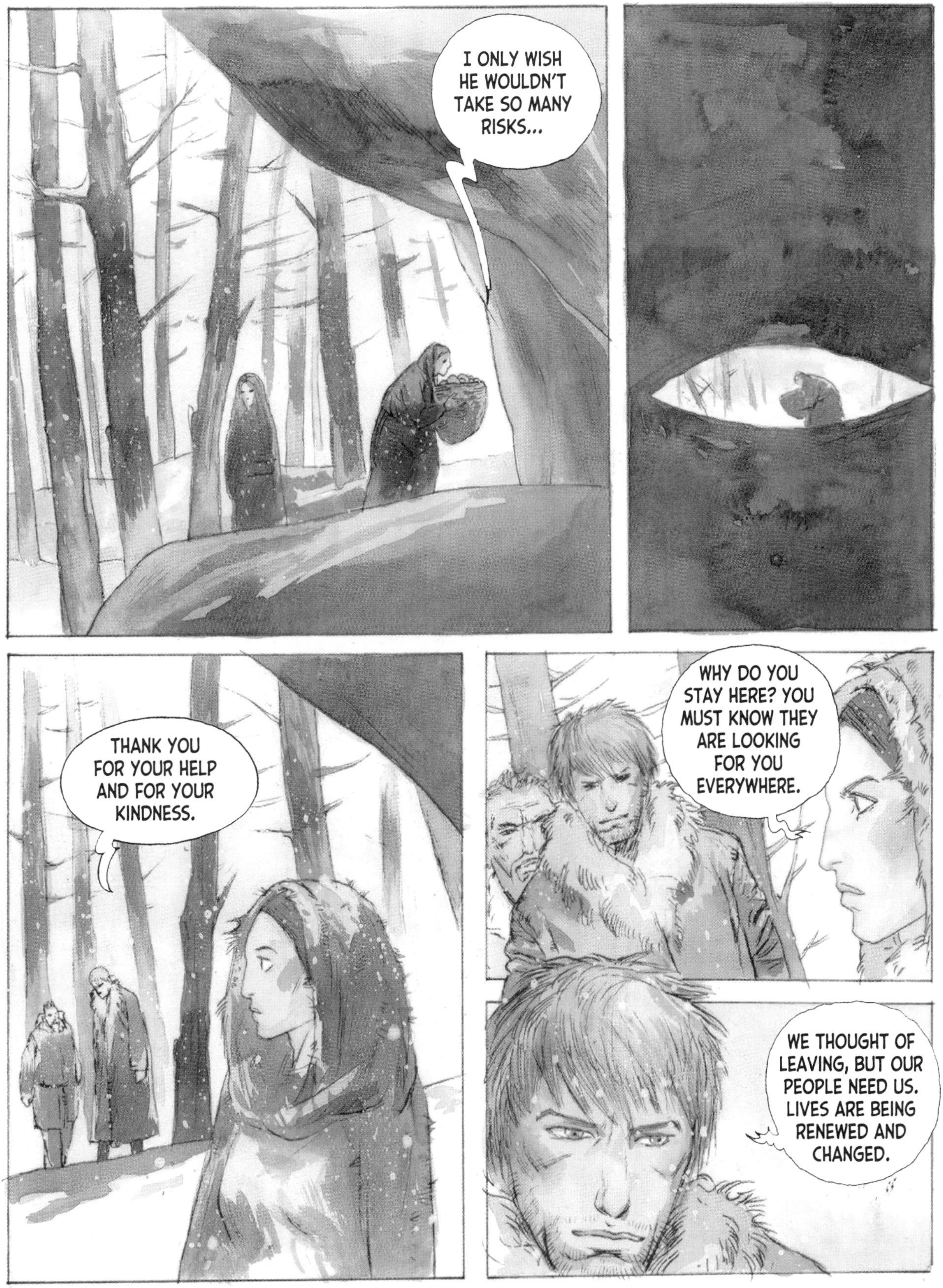
I ONLY WISH HE WOULDN'T TAKE SO MANY RISKS...
THANK YOU FOR YOUR HELP AND FOR YOUR KINDNESS.
WHY DO YOU STAY HERE? YOU MUST KNOW THEY ARE LOOKING FOR YOU EVERYWHERE.
WE THOUGHT OF LEAVING, BUT OUR PEOPLE NEED US. LIVES ARE BEING RENEWED AND CHANGED.

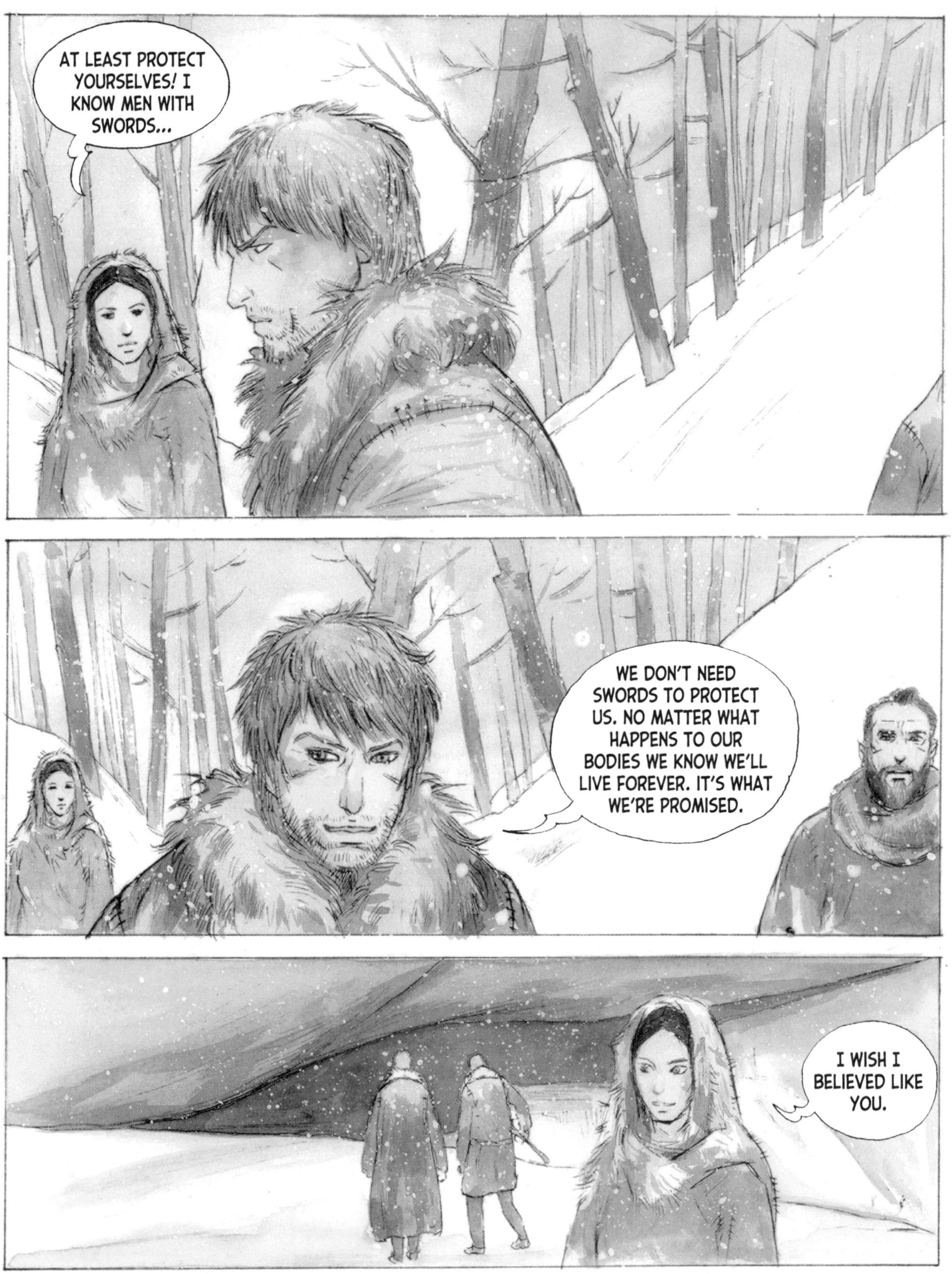
AT LEAST PROTECT YOURSELVES! I KNOW MEN WITH SWORDS...
WE DON'T NEED SWORDS TO PROTECT US. NO MATTER WHAT HAPPENS TO OUR BODIES WE KNOW WE'LL LIVE FOREVER. IT'S WHAT WE'RE PROMISED.
I WISH I BELIEVED LIKE YOU.

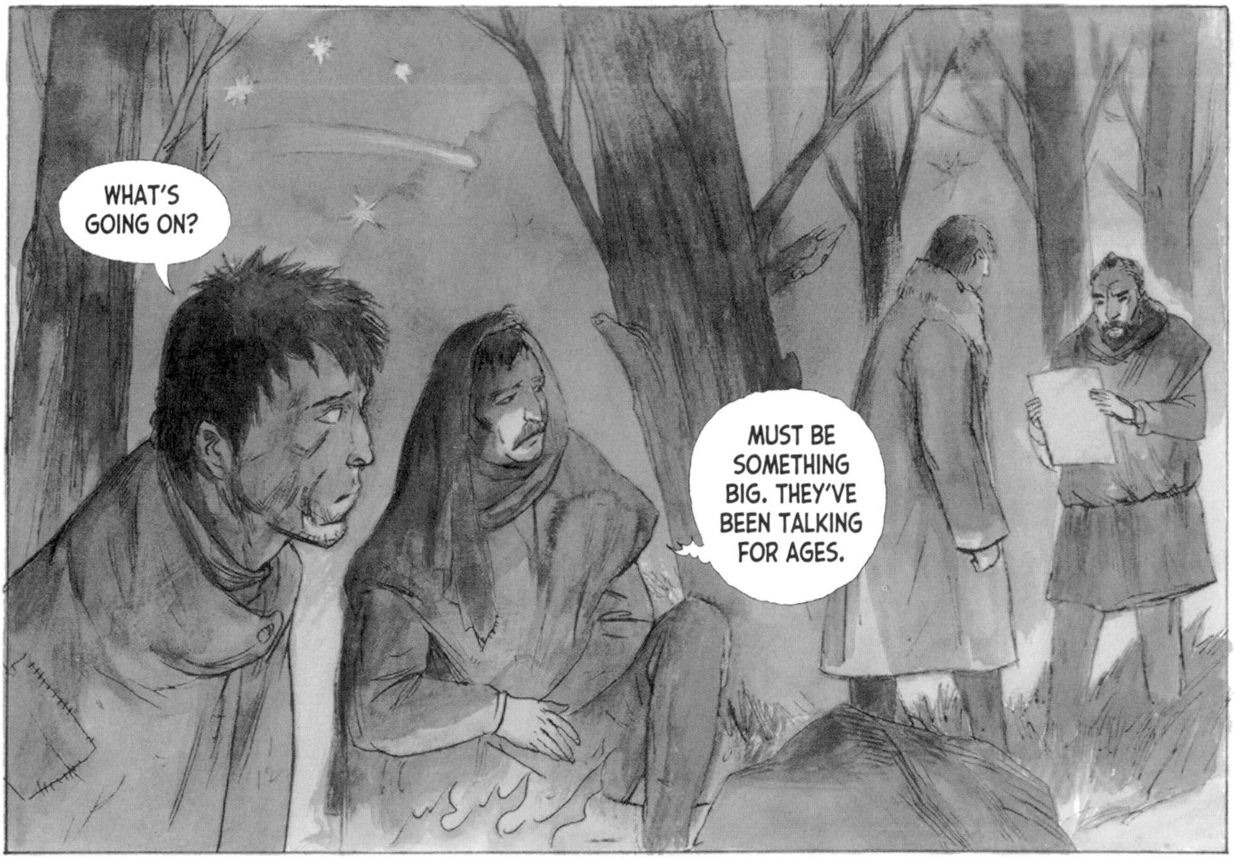
WHAT'S GOING ON?
MUST BE SOMETHING BIG. THEY'VE BEEN TALKING FOR AGES.

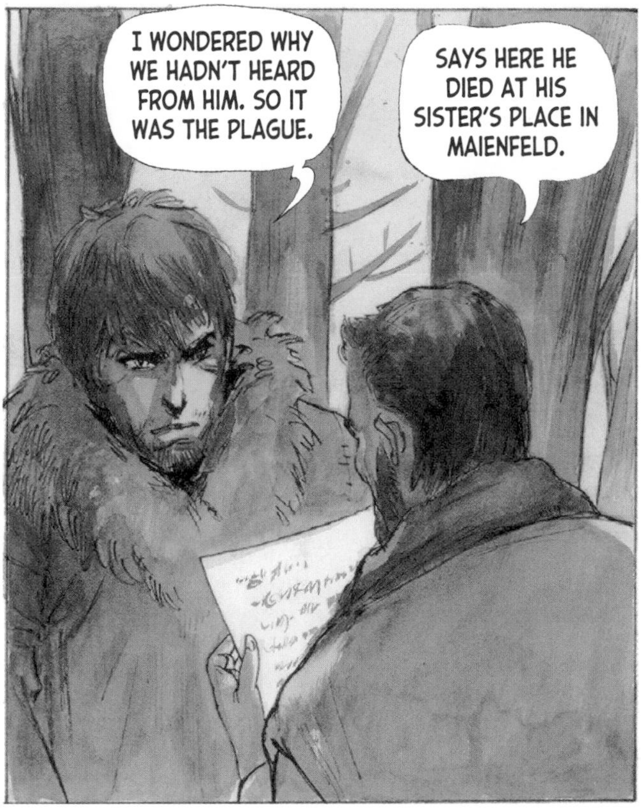
I WONDERED WHY WE HADN'T HEARD FROM HIM. SO IT WAS THE PLAGUE.
SAYS HERE HE DIED AT HIS SISTER'S PLACE IN MAIENFELD.

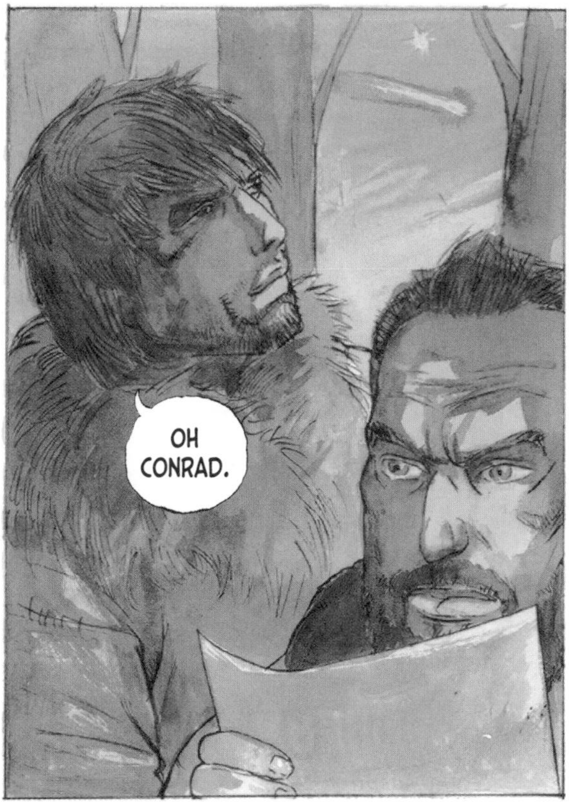
OH CONRAD.

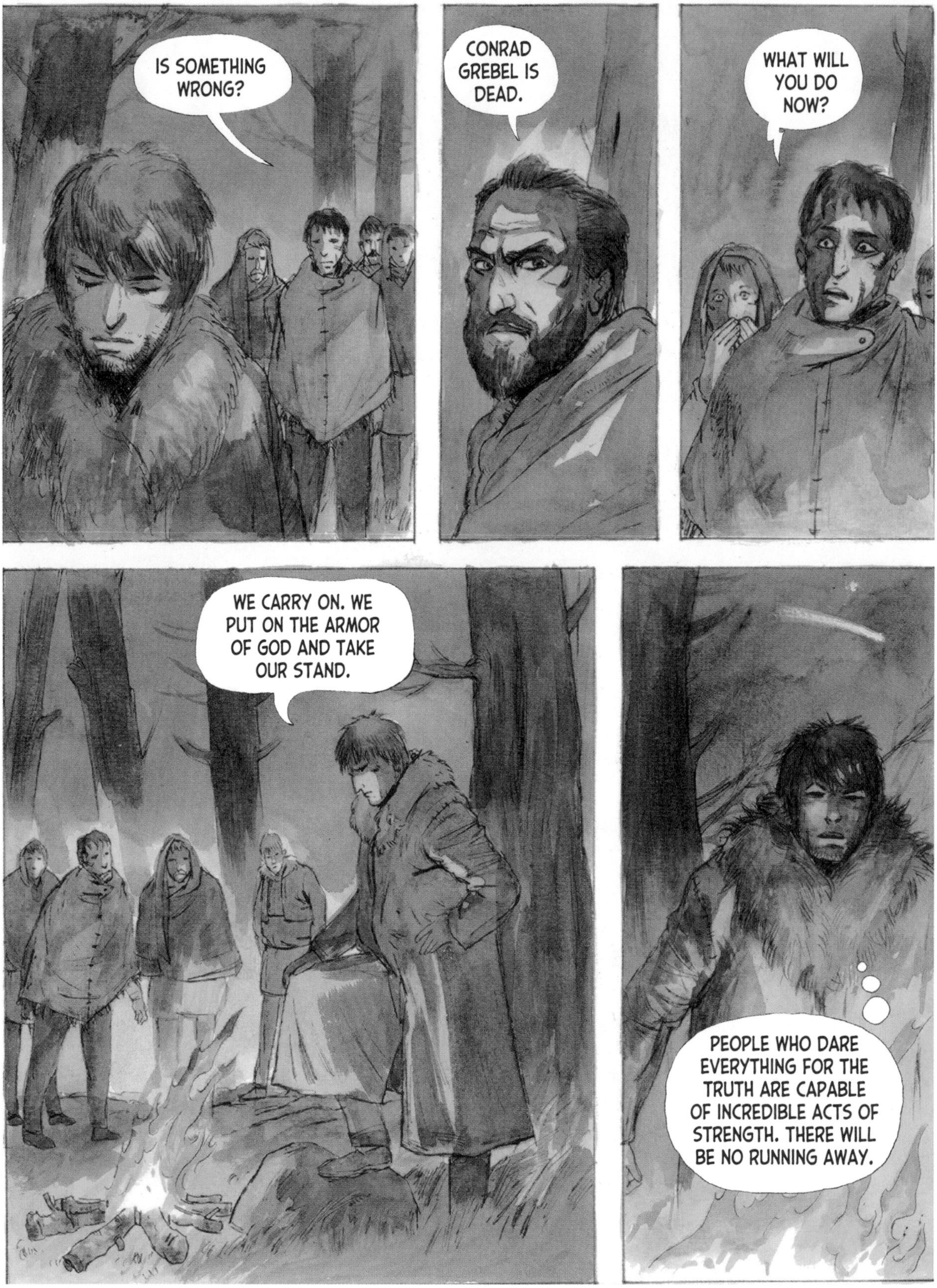
IS SOMETHING WRONG?
CONRAD GREBEL IS DEAD.
WHAT WILL YOU DO NOW?
WE CARRY ON. WE PUT ON THE ARMOR OF GOD AND TAKE OUR STAND.
PEOPLE WHO DARE EVERYTHING FOR THE TRUTH ARE CAPABLE OF INCREDIBLE ACTS OF STRENGTH. THERE WILL BE NO RUNNING AWAY.

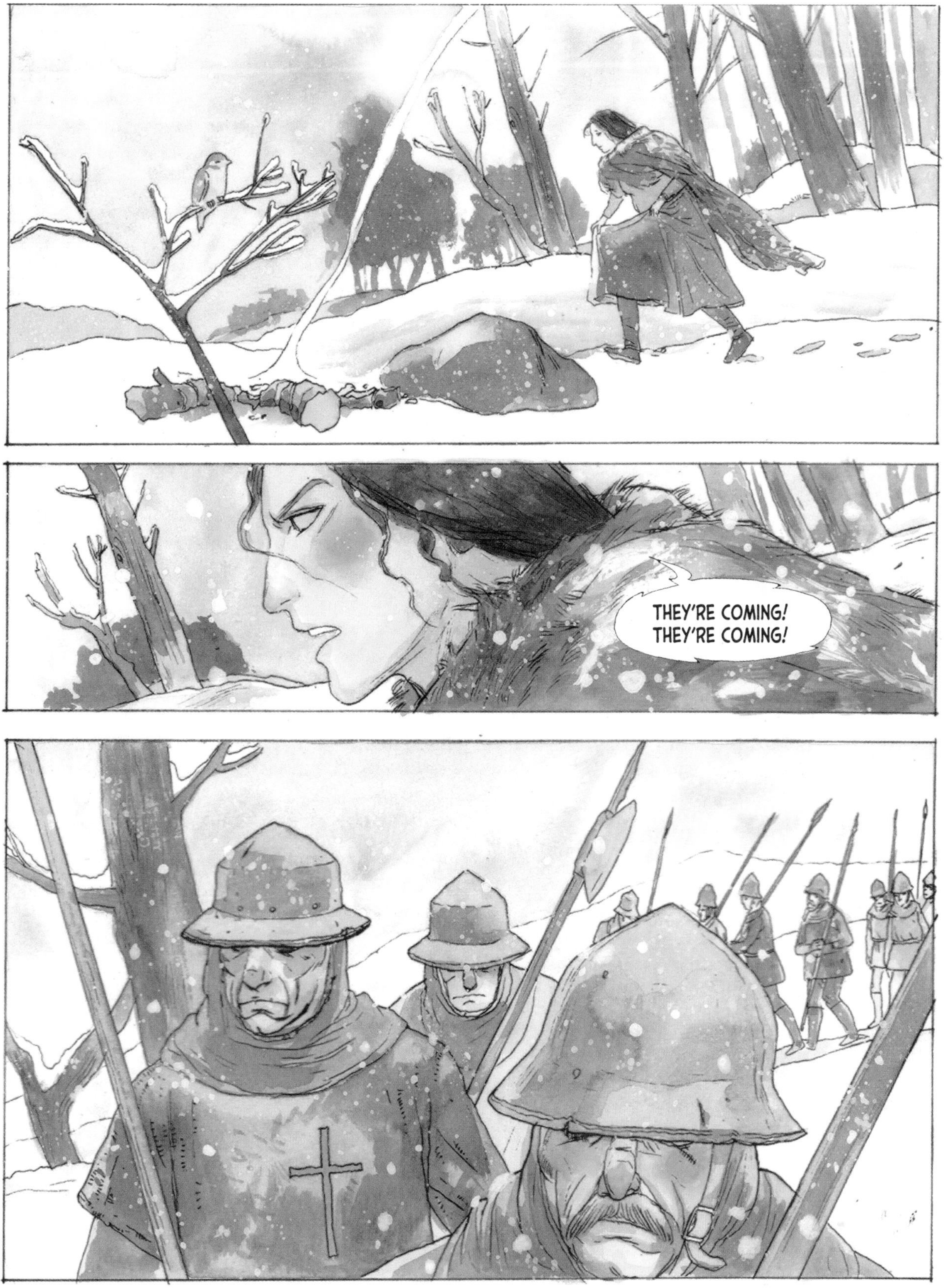
THEY'RE COMING! THEY'RE COMING!

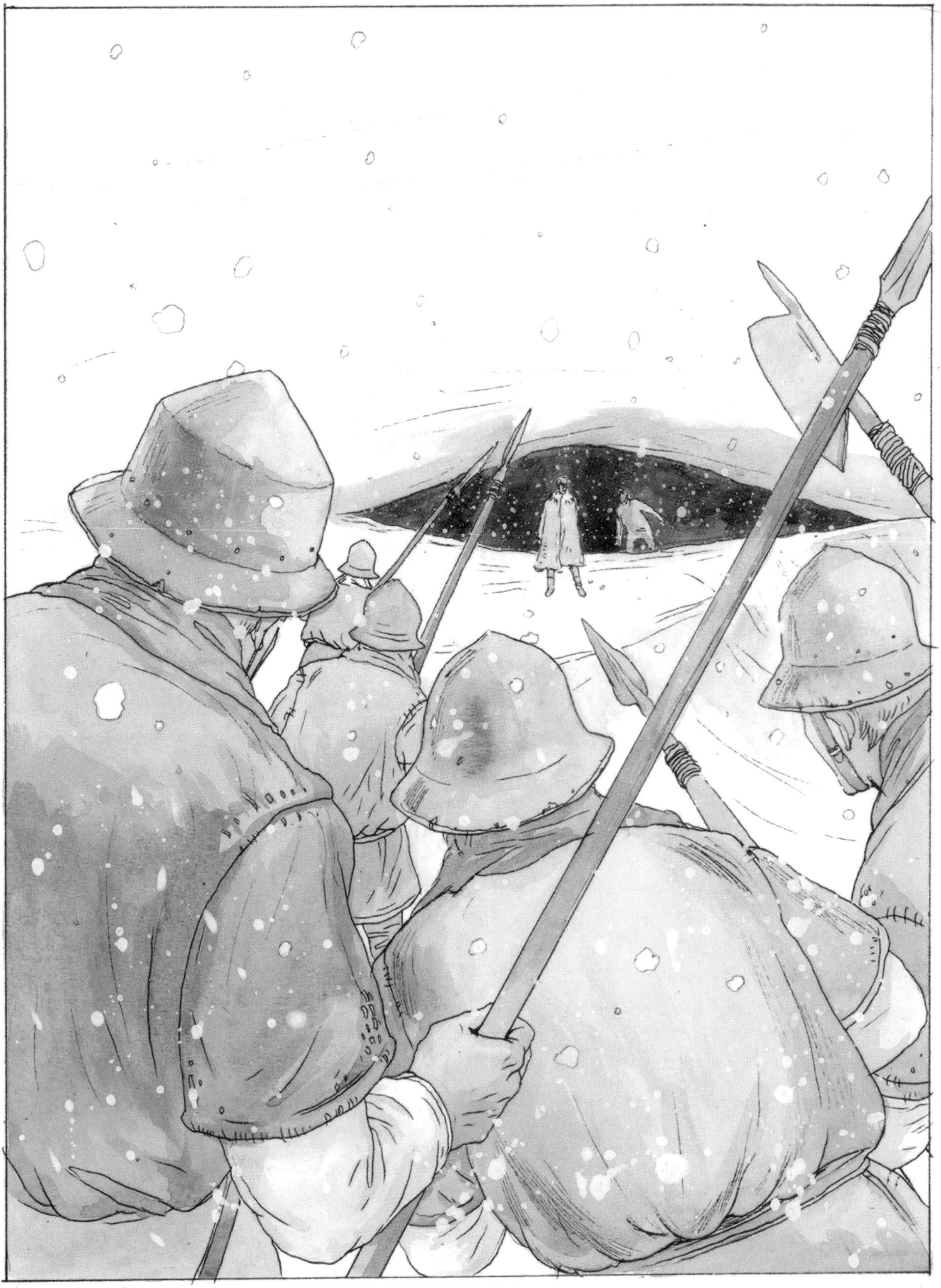

Episode Nine
THE PASSION

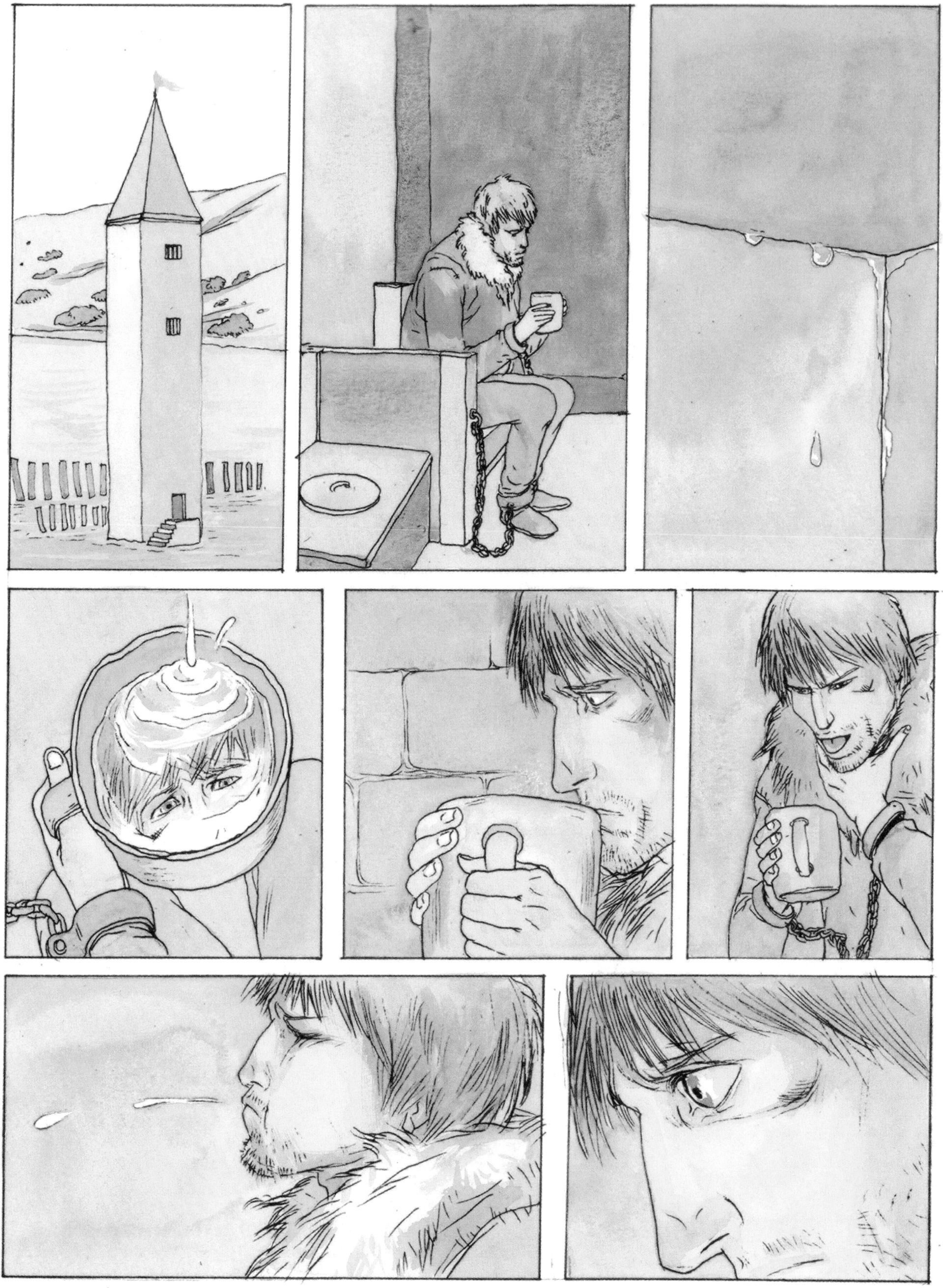

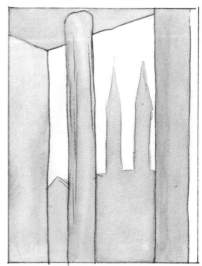

"WHEN THE PERISHABLE HAS BEEN CLOTHED WITH THE IMPERISHABLE, AND THE MORTAL WITH IMMORTALITY, THEN THE SAYING THAT IS WRITTEN WILL COME TRUE..."

"...DEATH IS SWALLOWED UP IN VICTORY."

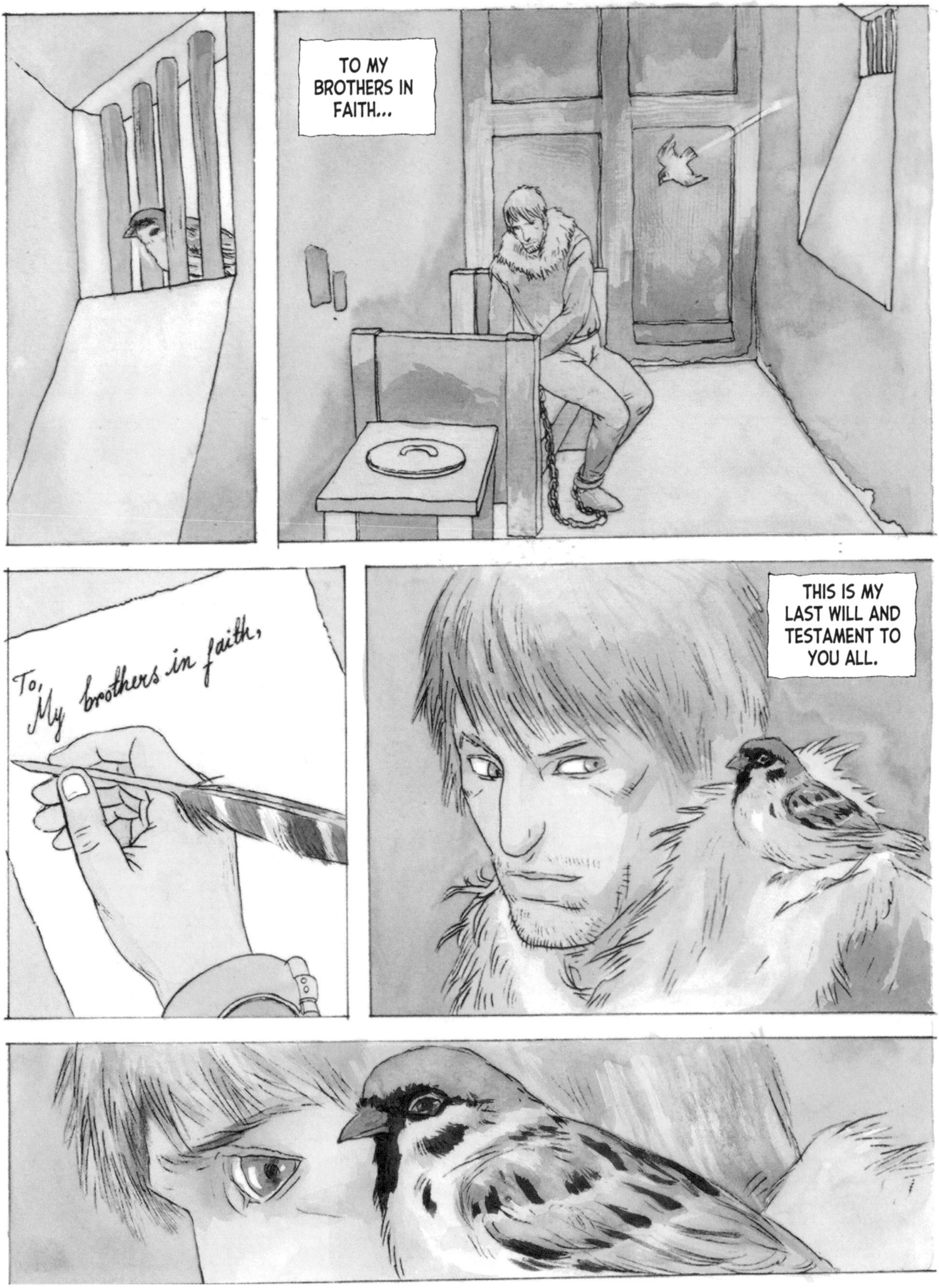
TO MY BROTHERS IN FAITH...
To, My brothers in faith,
THIS IS MY LAST WILL AND TESTAMENT TO YOU ALL.

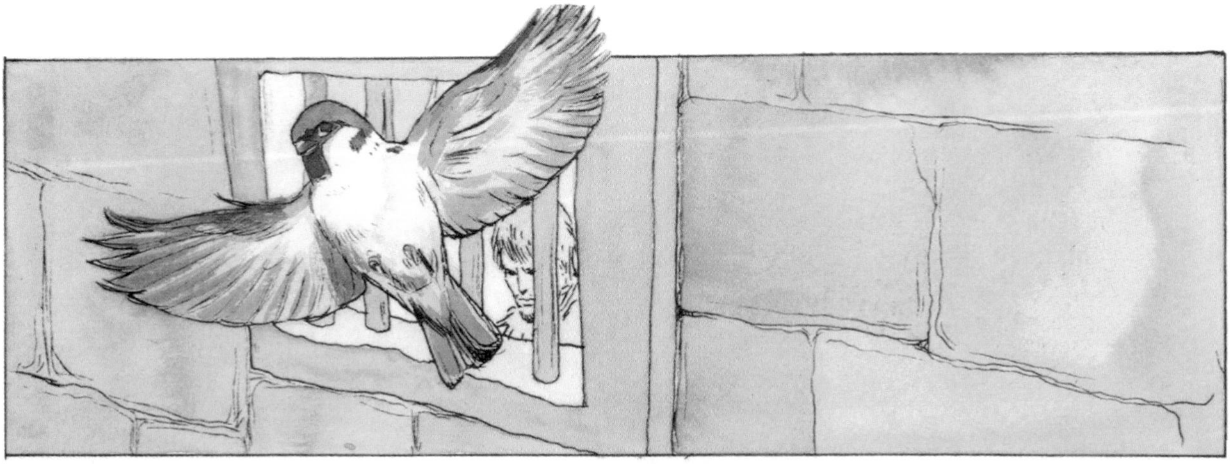

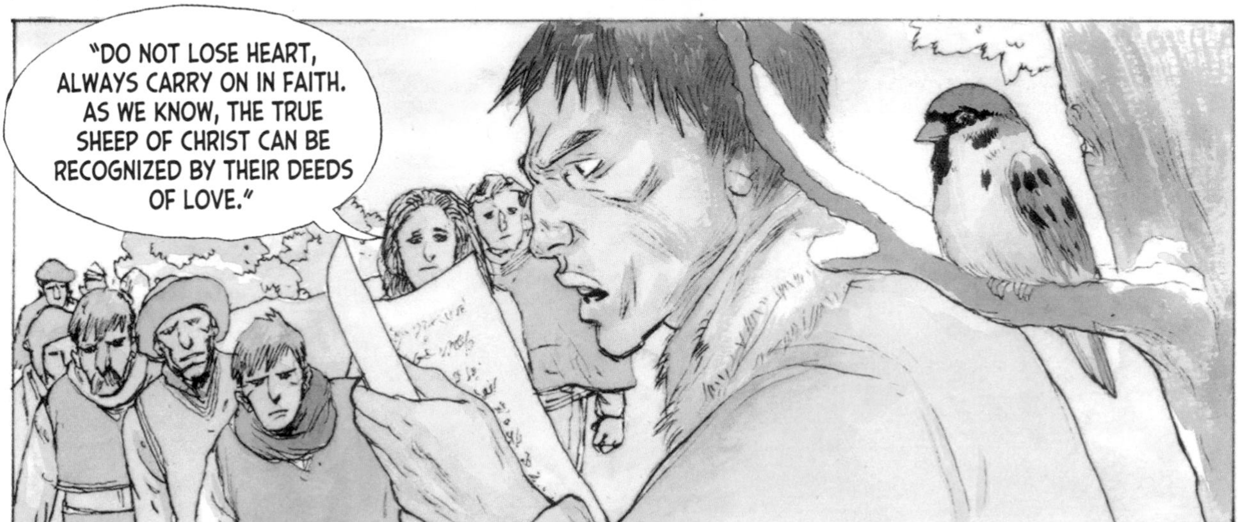
"DO NOT LOSE HEART, ALWAYS CARRY ON IN FAITH. AS WE KNOW, THE TRUE SHEEP OF CHRIST CAN BE RECOGNIZED BY THEIR DEEDS OF LOVE."

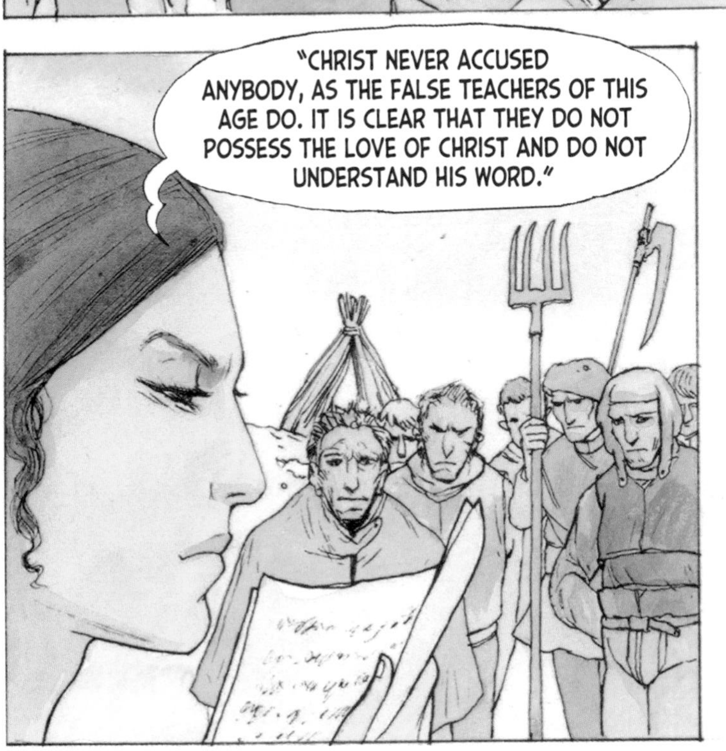
"CHRIST NEVER ACCUSED ANYBODY, AS THE FALSE TEACHERS OF THIS AGE DO. IT IS CLEAR THAT THEY DO NOT POSSESS THE LOVE OF CHRIST AND DO NOT UNDERSTAND HIS WORD."

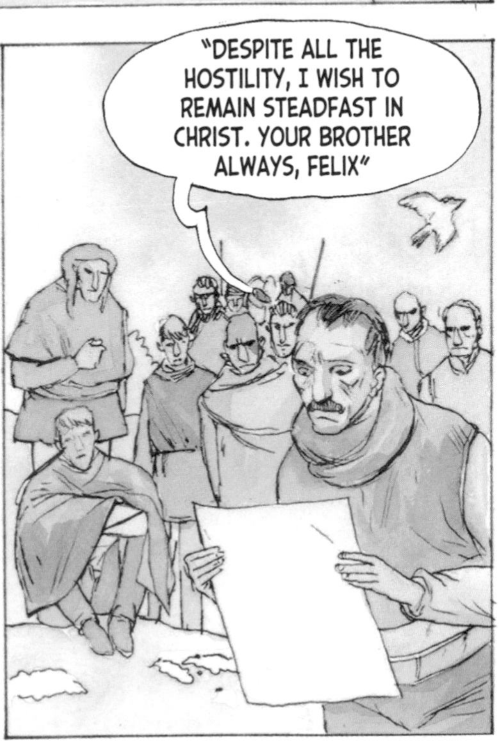
"DESPITE ALL THE HOSTILITY, I WISH TO REMAIN STEADFAST IN CHRIST. YOUR BROTHER ALWAYS, FELIX"

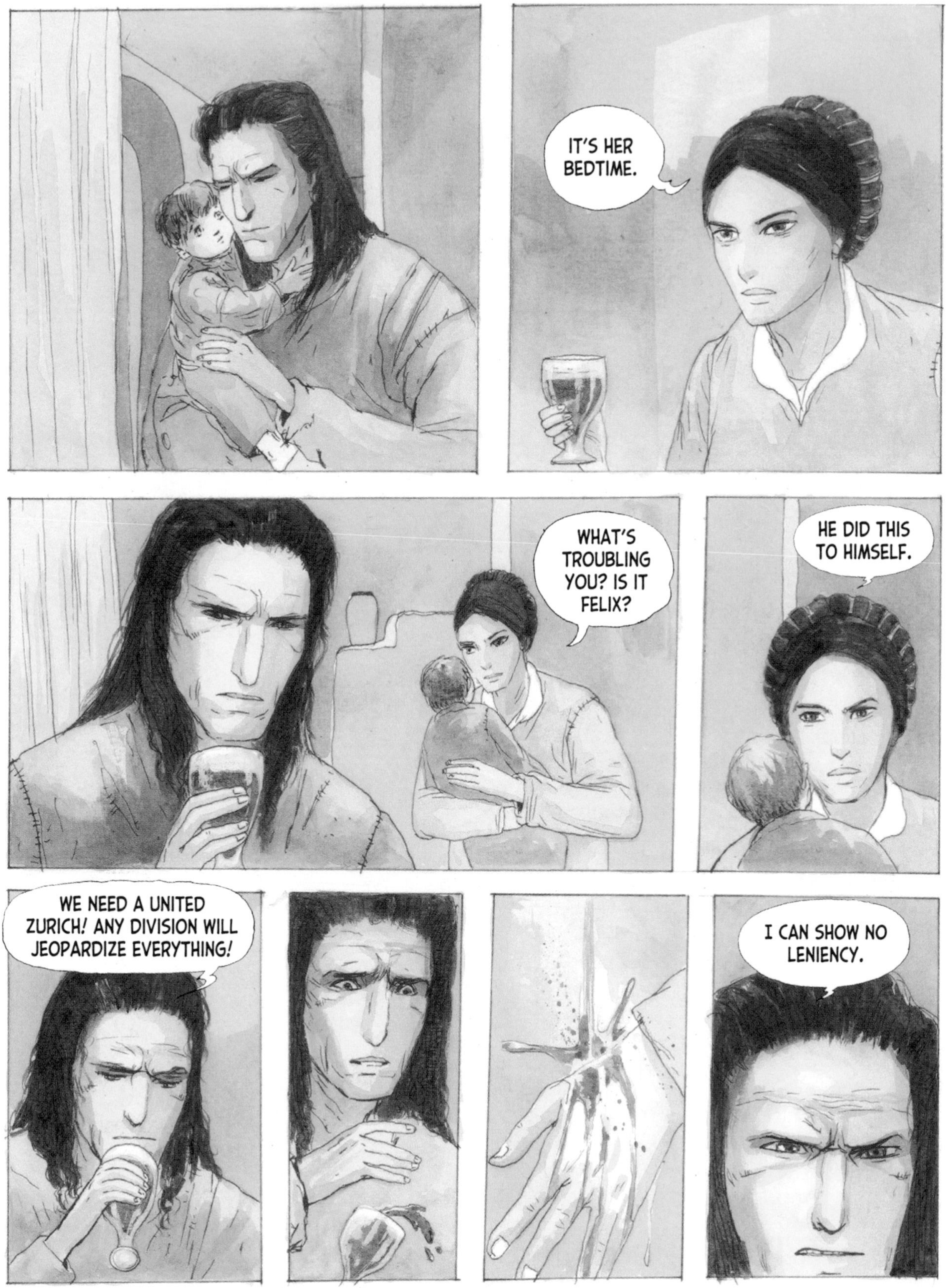
IT'S HER BEDTIME.
WHAT'S TROUBLING YOU? IS IT FELIX?
HE DID THIS TO HIMSELF.
WE NEED A UNITED ZURICH! ANY DIVISION WILL JEOPARDIZE EVERYTHING!
I CAN SHOW NO LENIENCY.

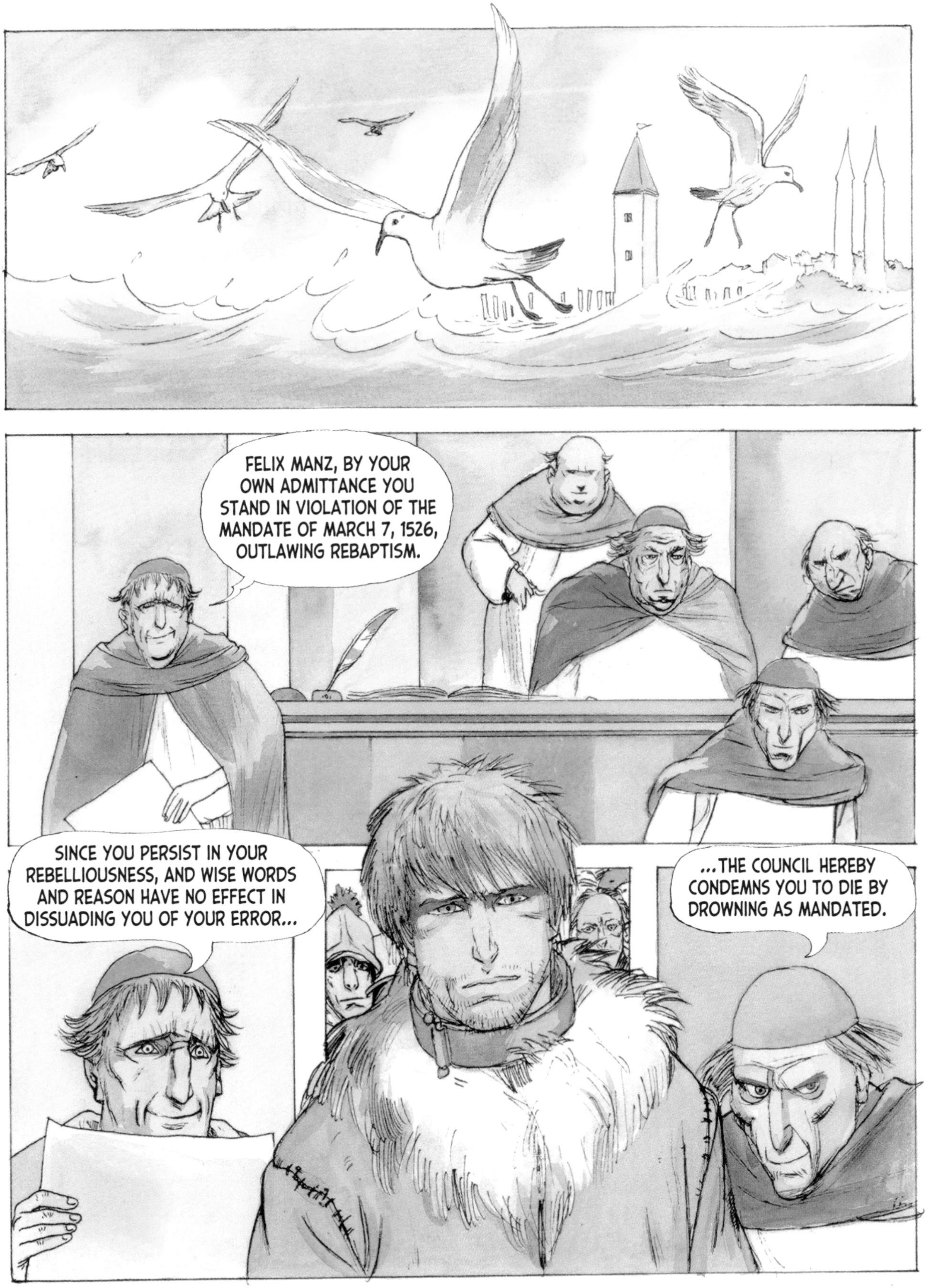
FELIX MANZ, BY YOUR OWN ADMITTANCE YOU STAND IN VIOLATION OF THE MANDATE OF MARCH 7, 1526, OUTLAWING REBAPTISM.
SINCE YOU PERSIST IN YOUR REBELLIOUSNESS, AND WISE WORDS AND REASON HAVE NO EFFECT IN DISSUADING YOU OF YOUR ERROR...
...THE COUNCIL HEREBY CONDEMNS YOU TO DIE BY DROWNING AS MANDATED.

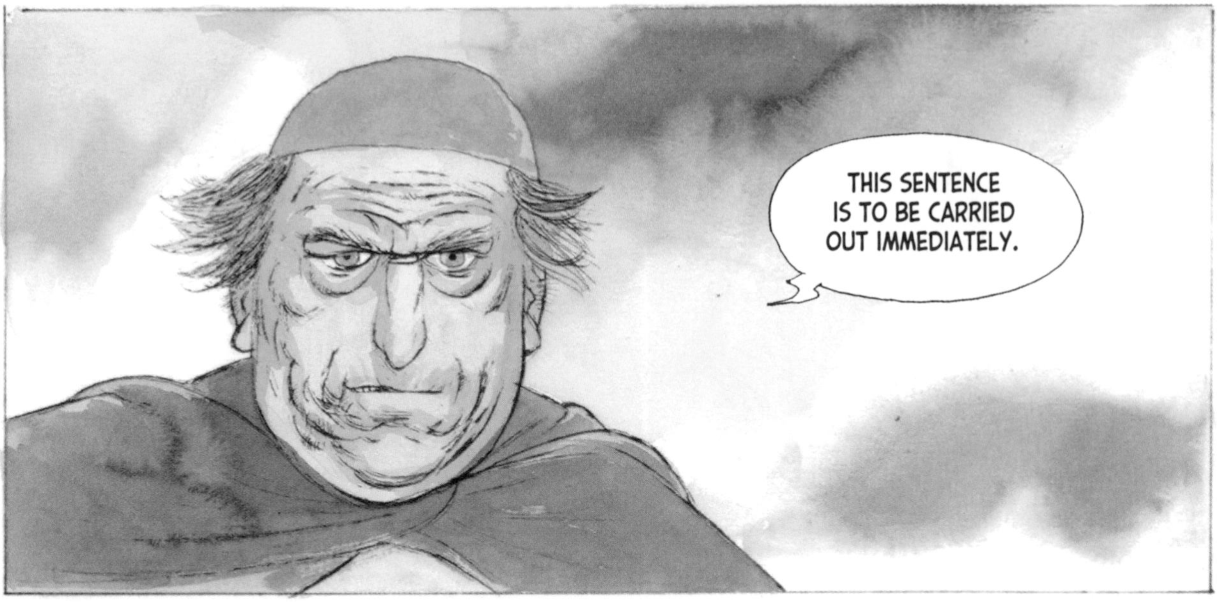
THIS SENTENCE IS TO BE CARRIED OUT IMMEDIATELY.

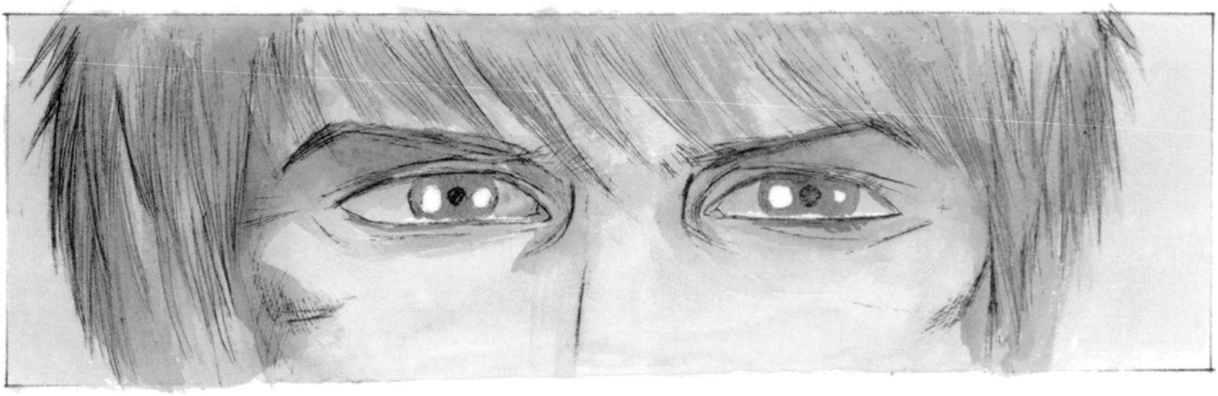

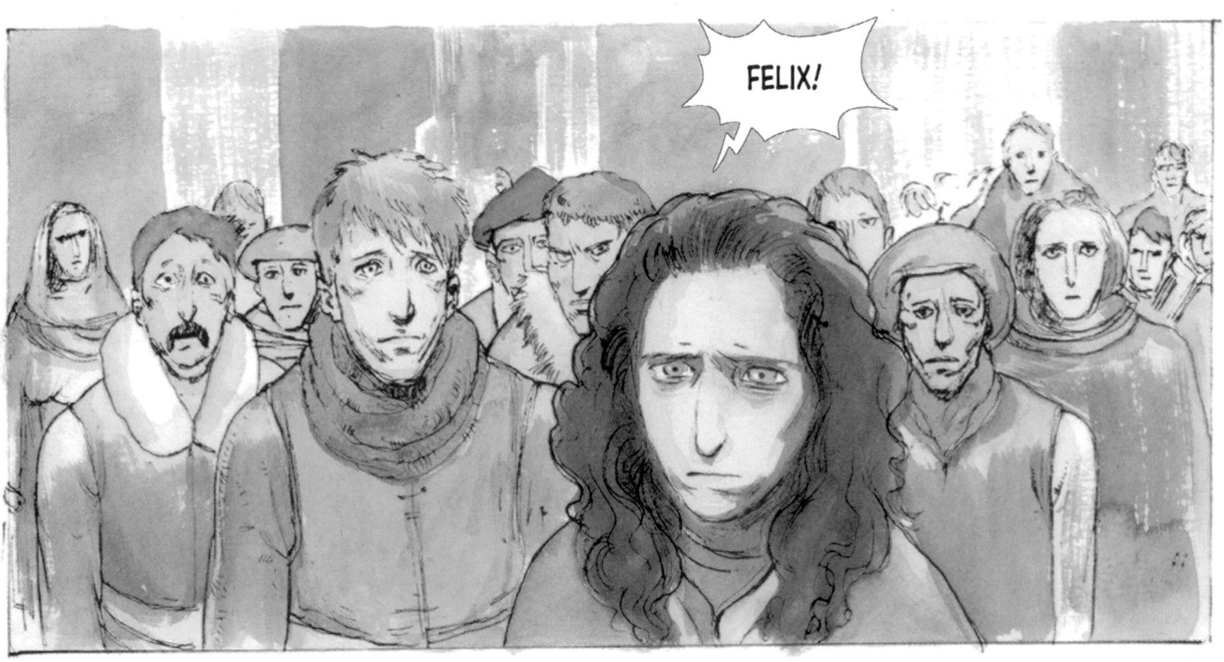
FELIX!

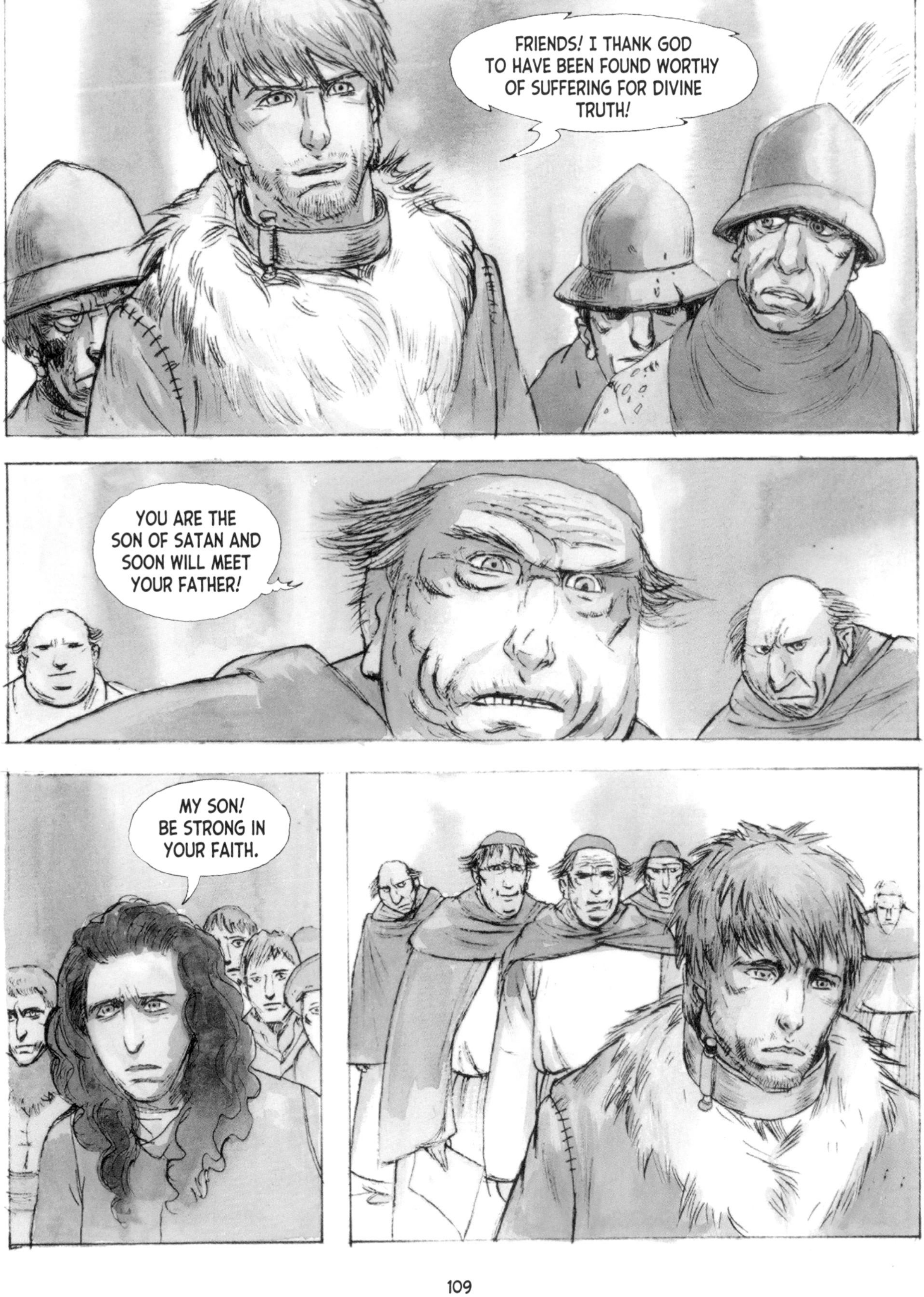
FRIENDS! I THANK GOD TO HAVE BEEN FOUND WORTHY OF SUFFERING FOR DIVINE TRUTH!
YOU ARE THE SON OF SATAN AND SOON WILL MEET YOUR FATHER!
MY SON! BE STRONG IN YOUR FAITH.

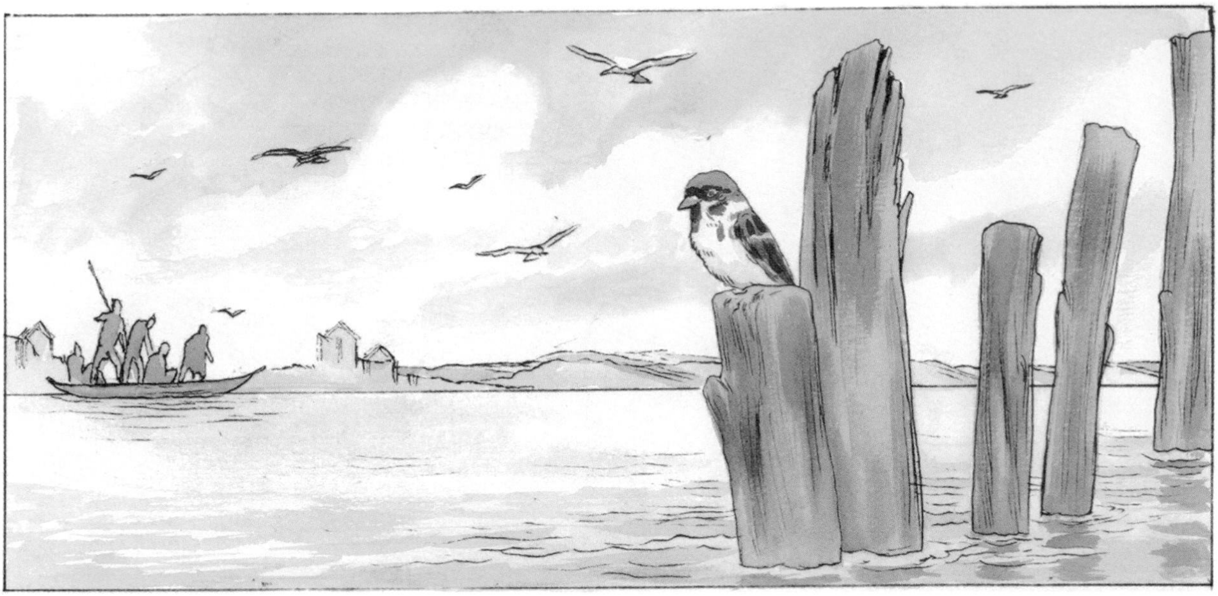

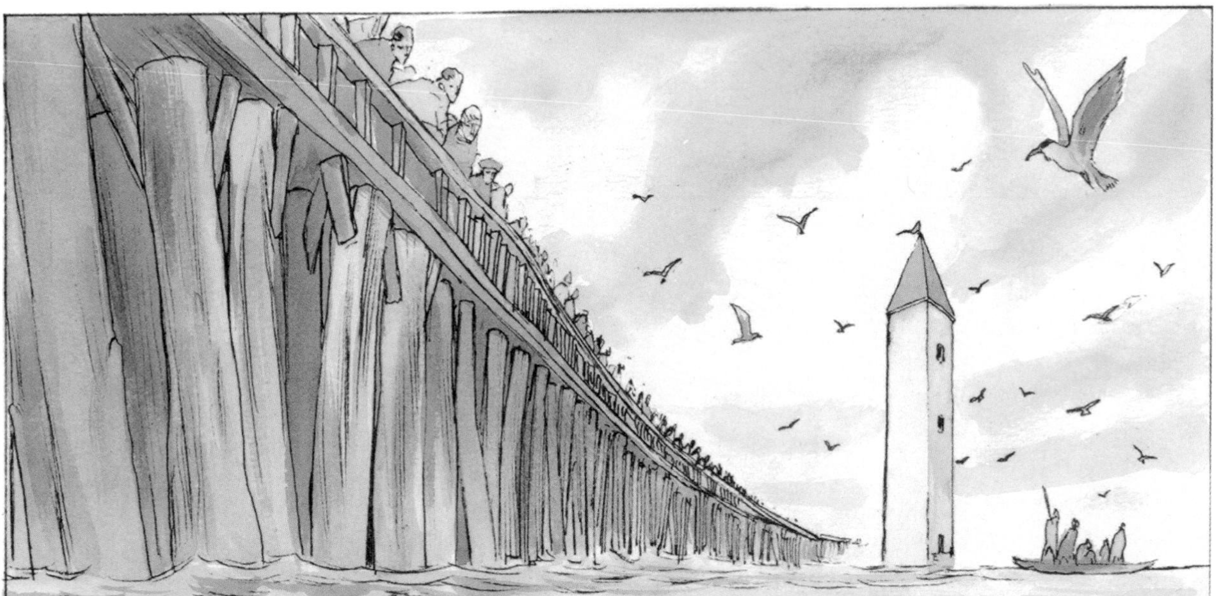

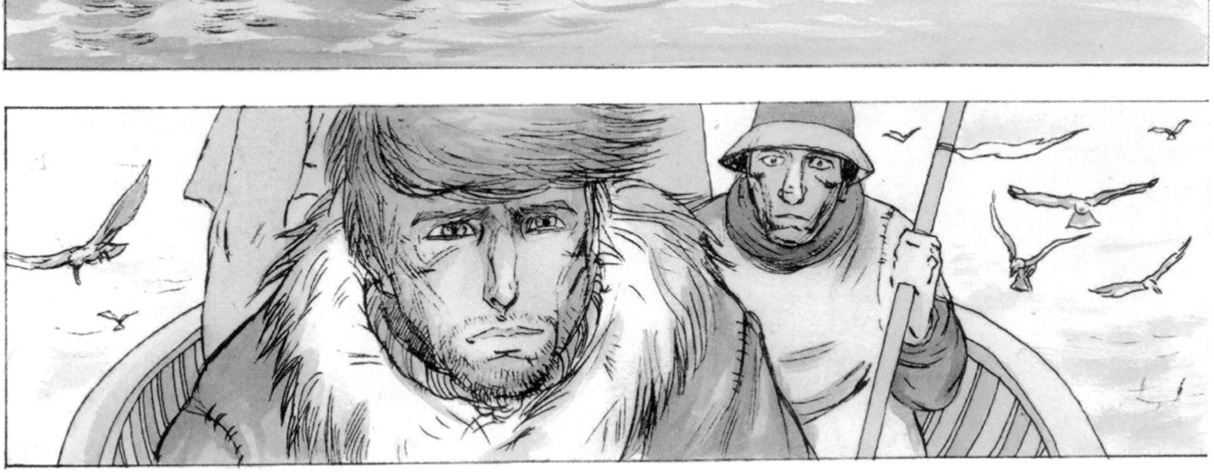

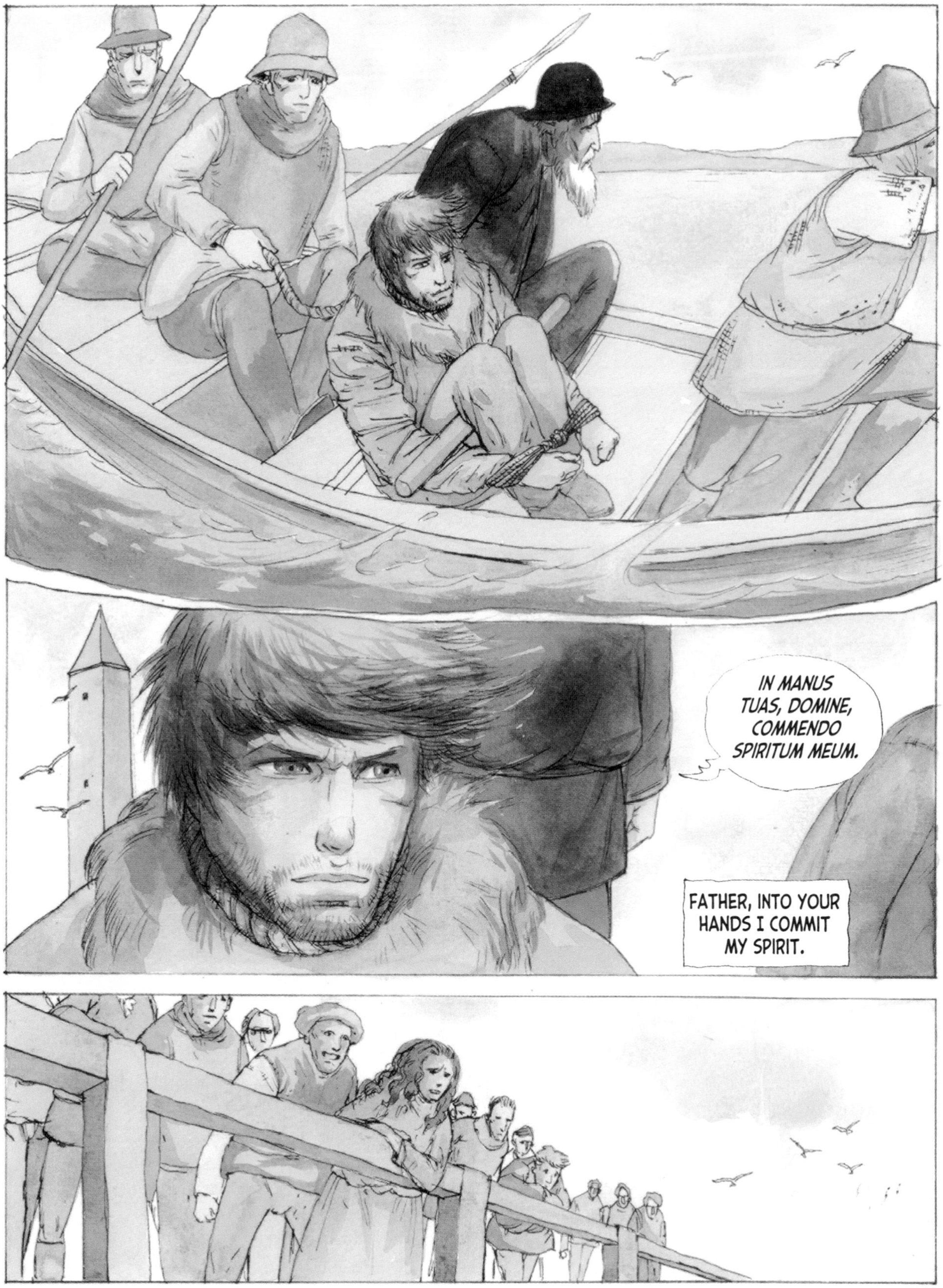
IN MANUS TUAS, DOMINE, COMMENDO SPIRITUM MEUM.
FATHER, INTO YOUR HANDS I COMMIT MY SPIRIT.

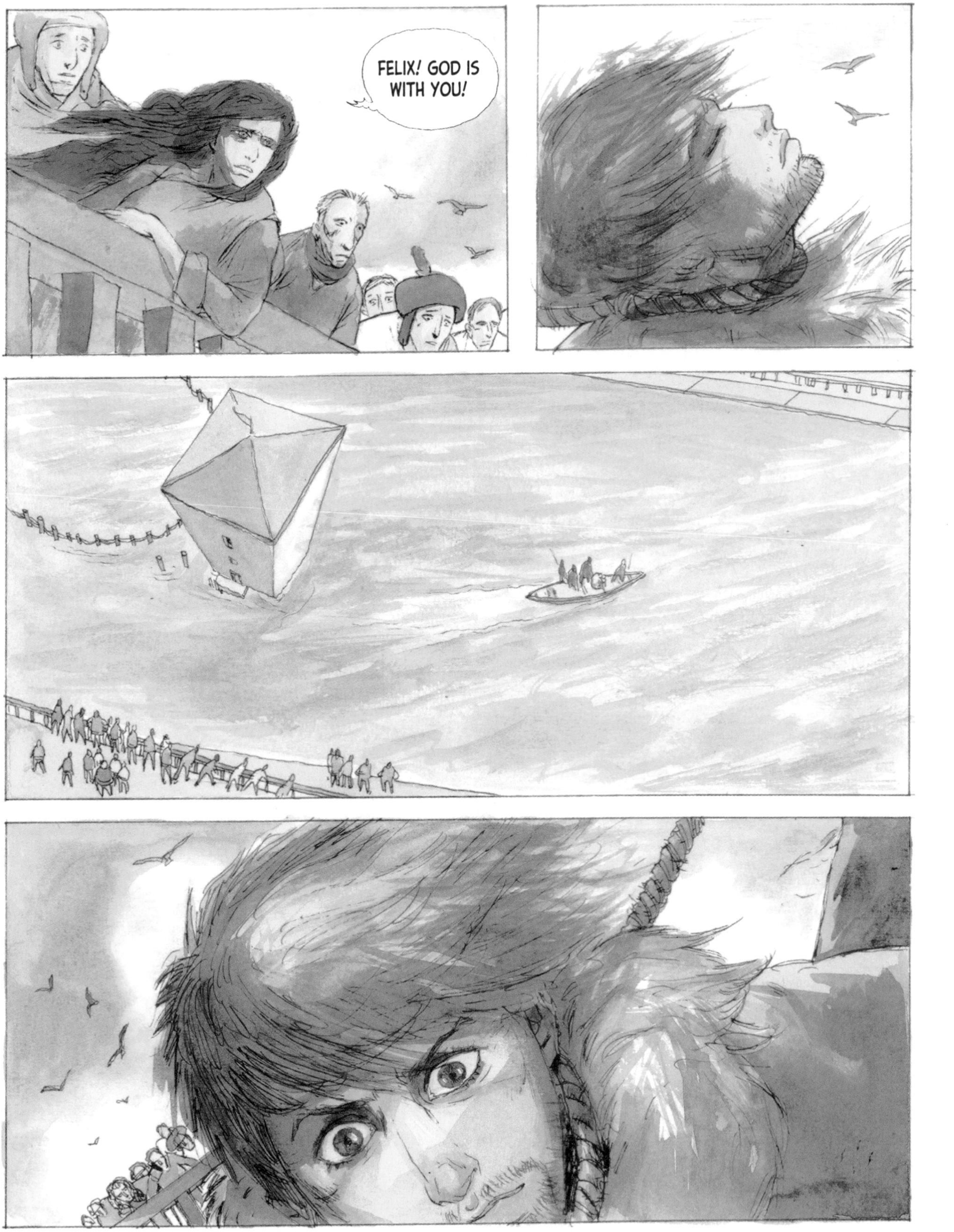
FELIX! GOD IS WITH YOU!

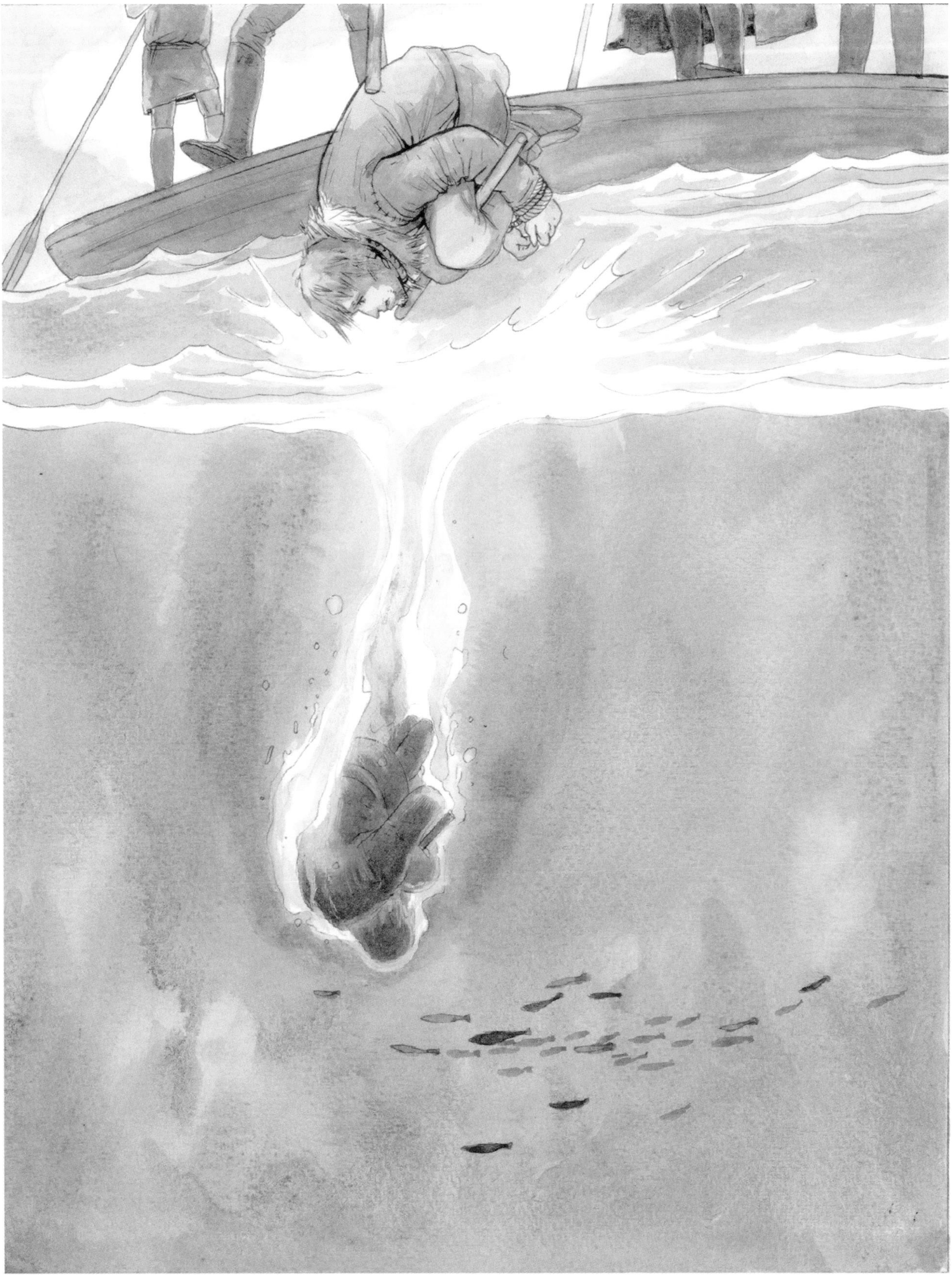

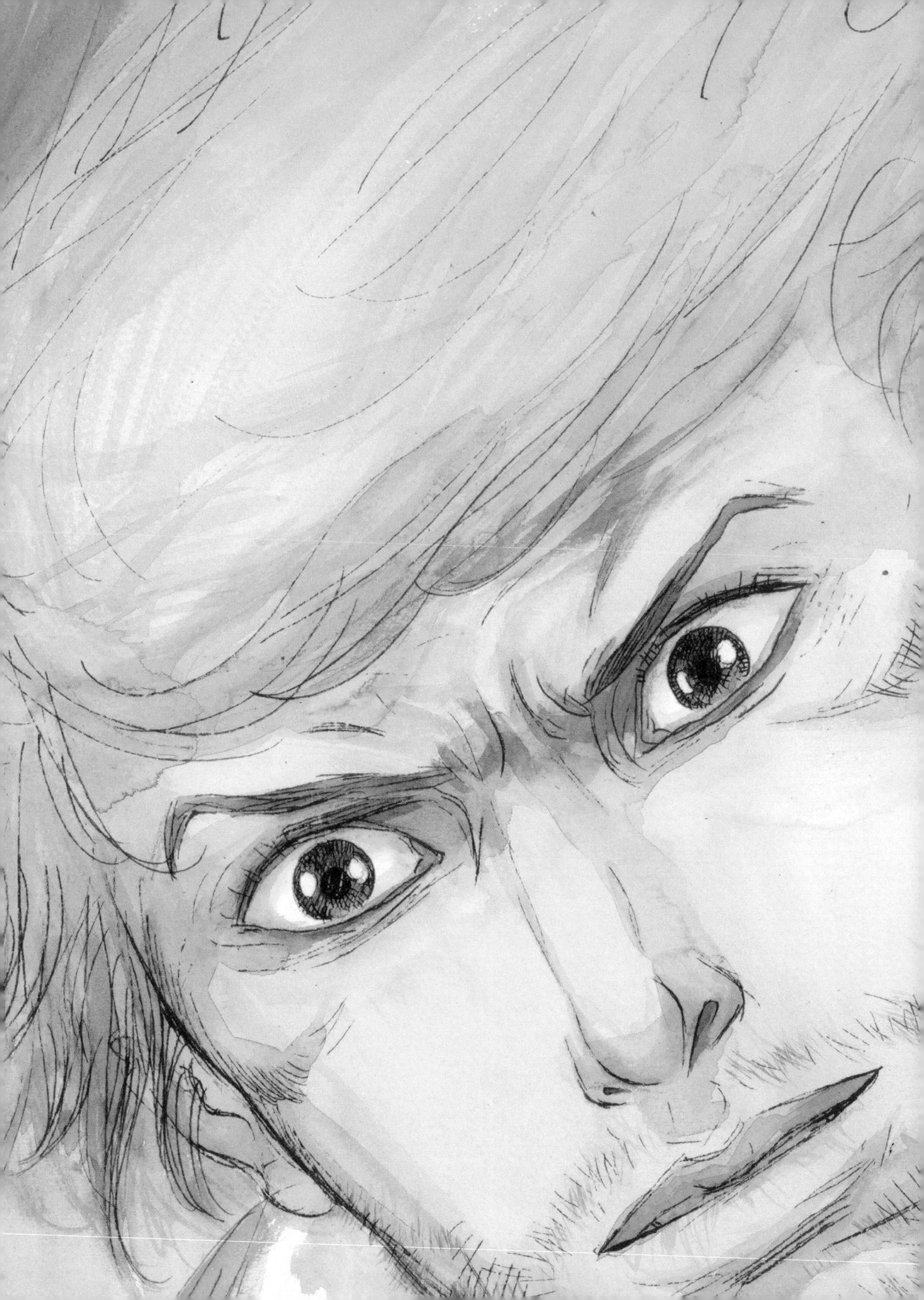

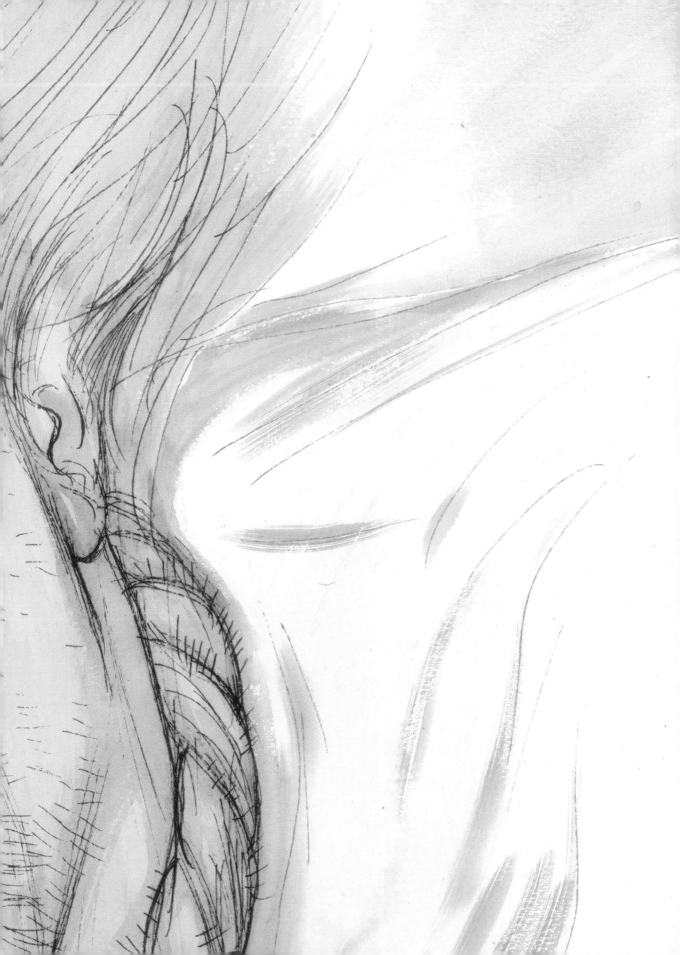

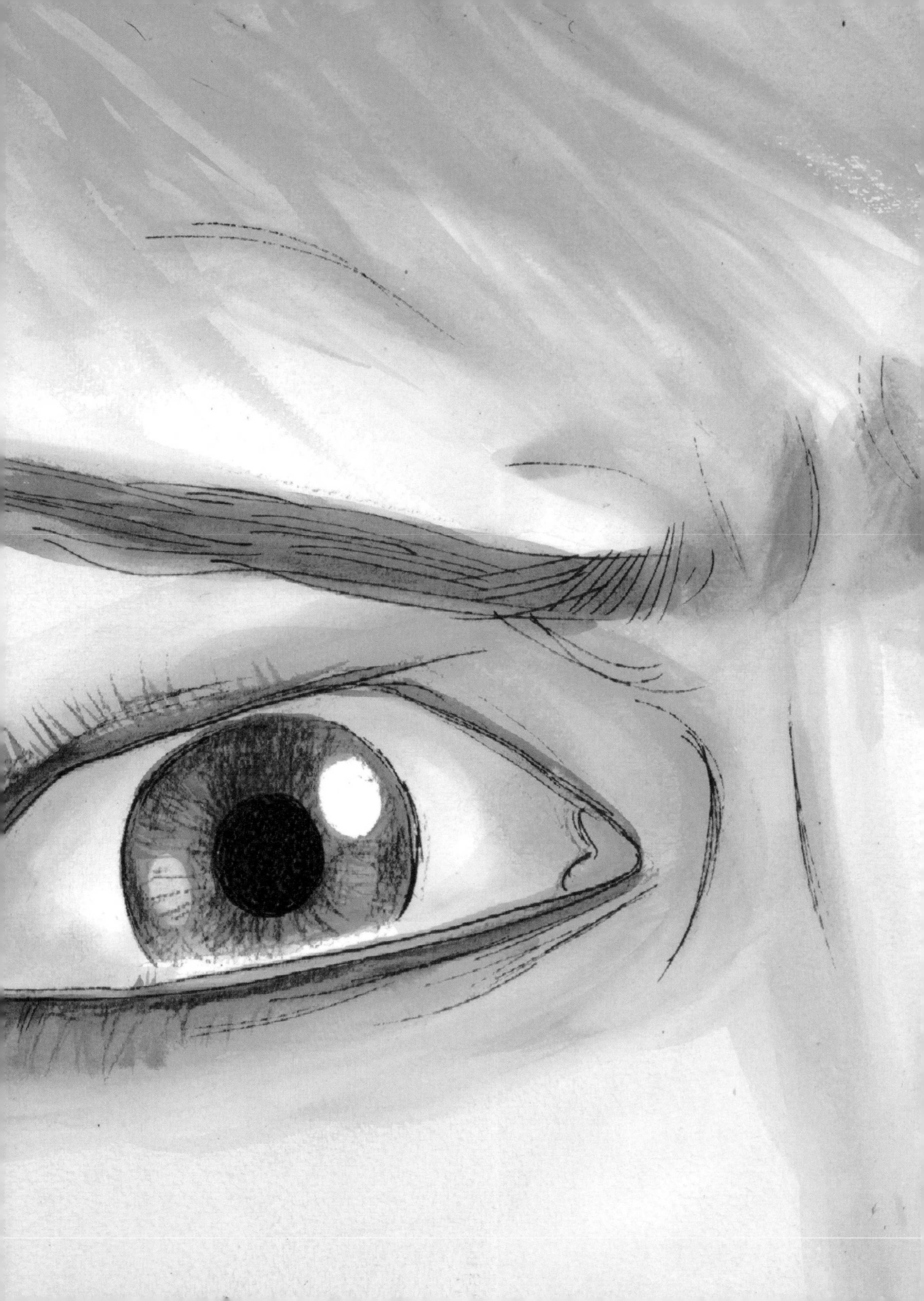

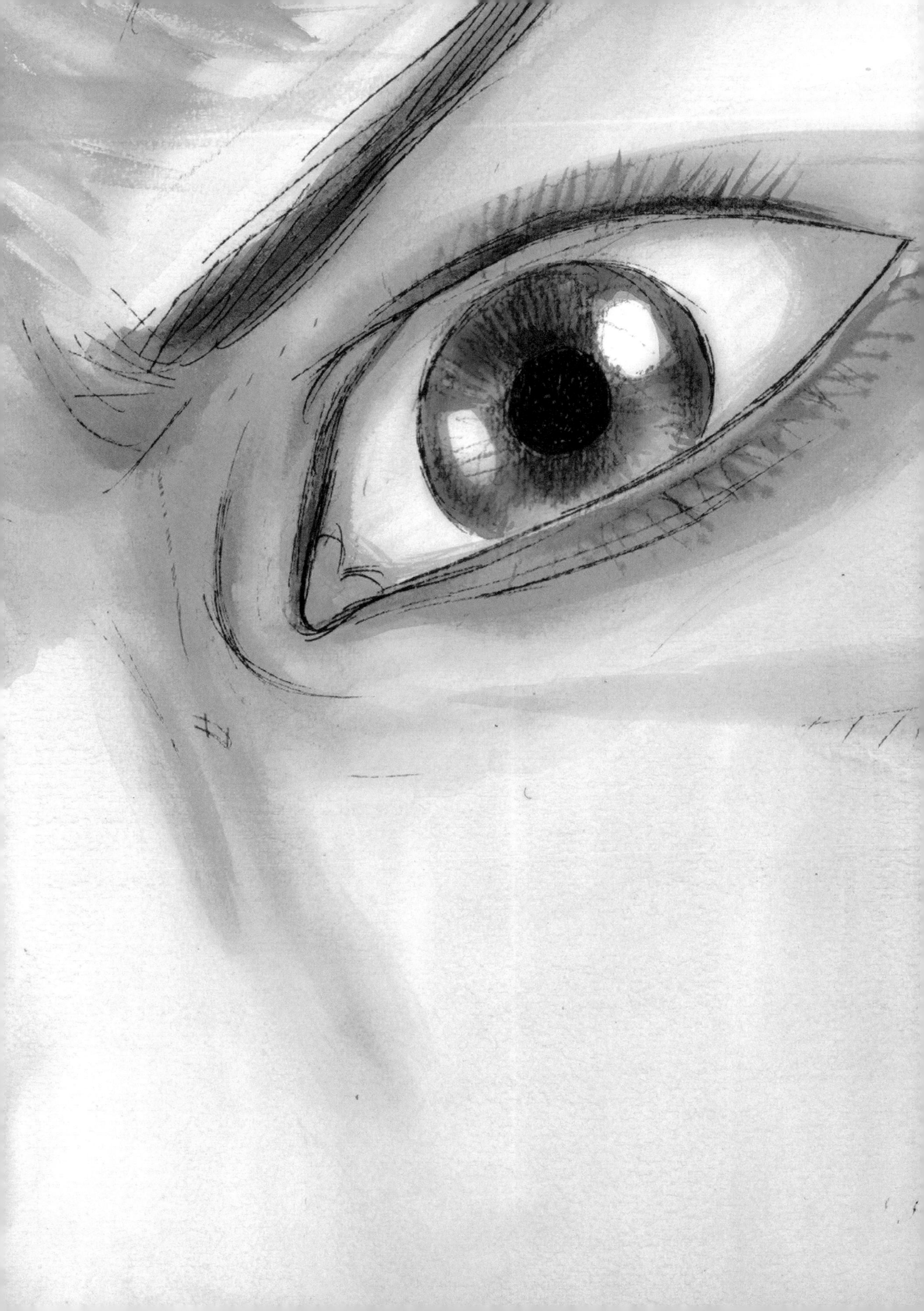

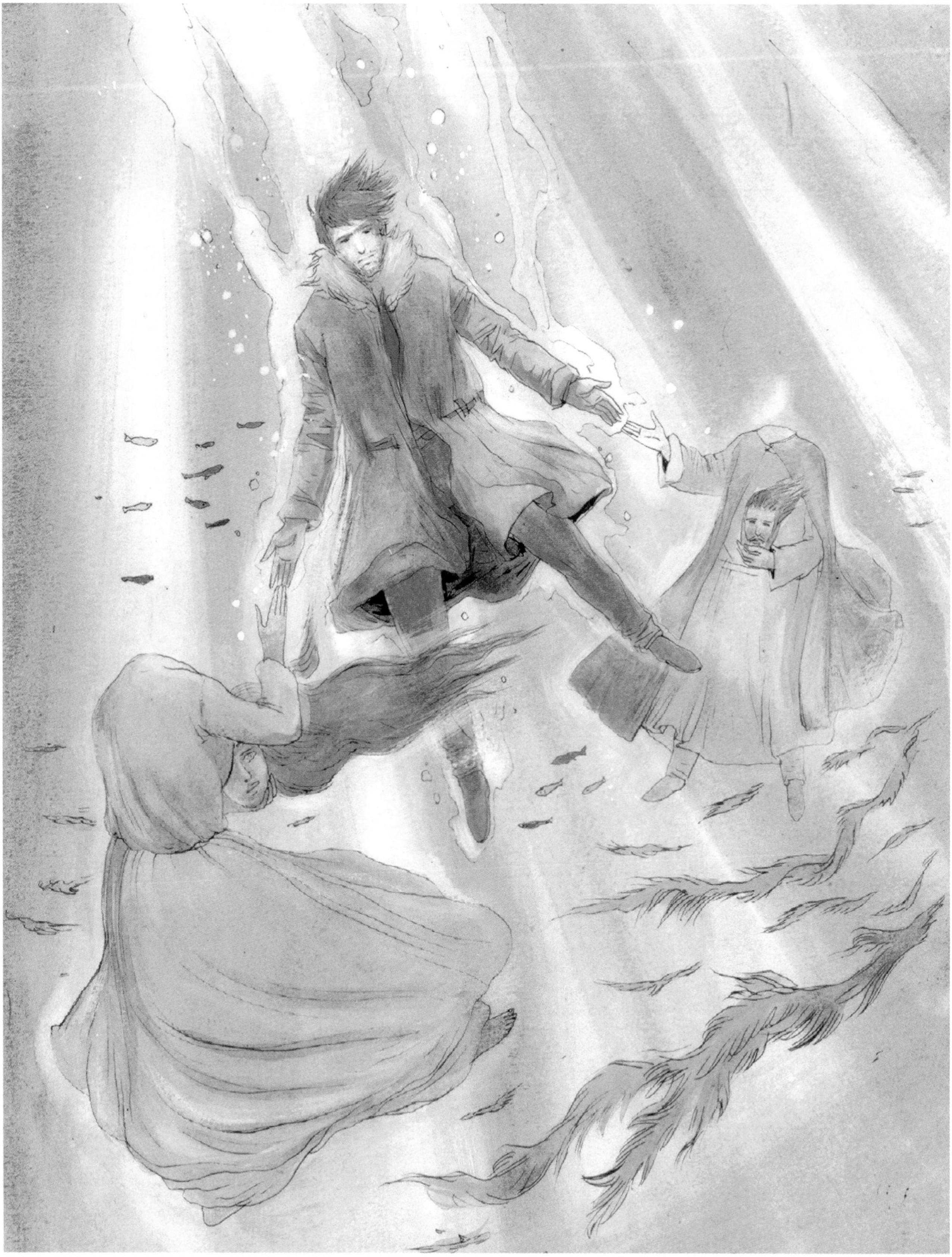

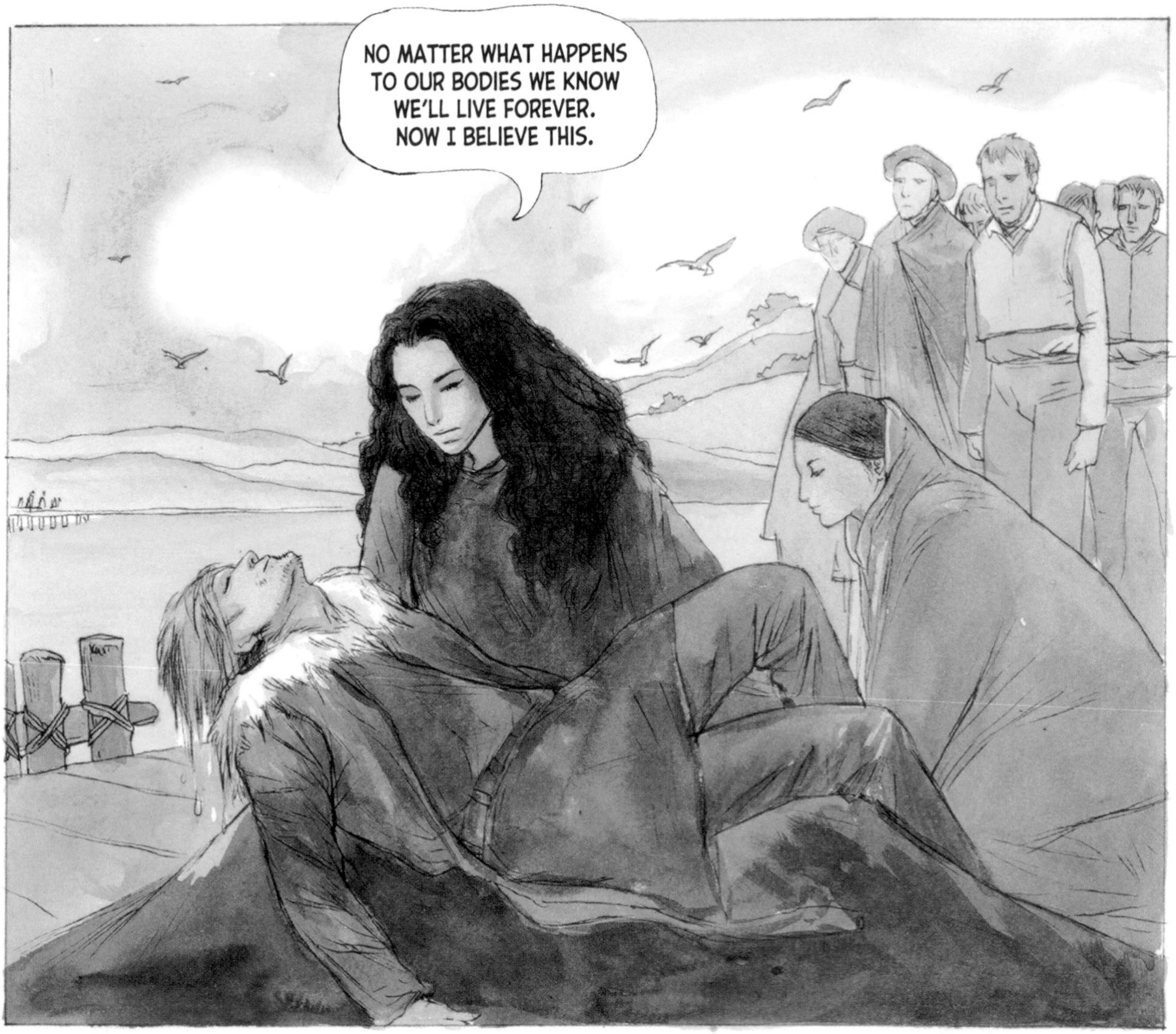
NO MATTER WHAT HAPPENS TO OUR BODIES WE KNOW WE'LL LIVE FOREVER. NOW I BELIEVE THIS.

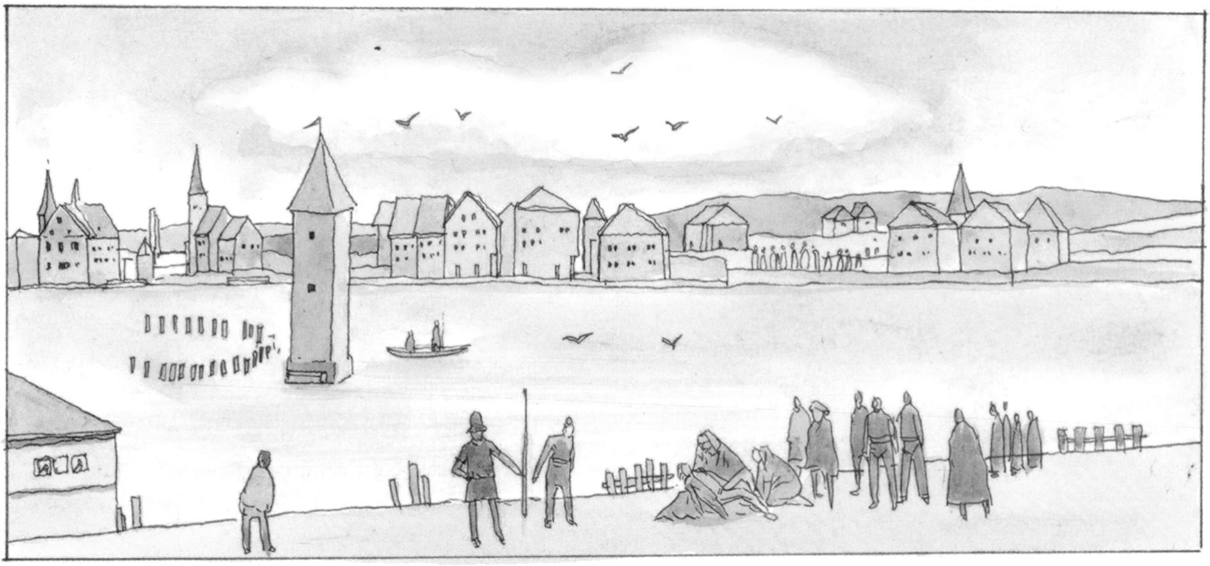

EPILOGUE

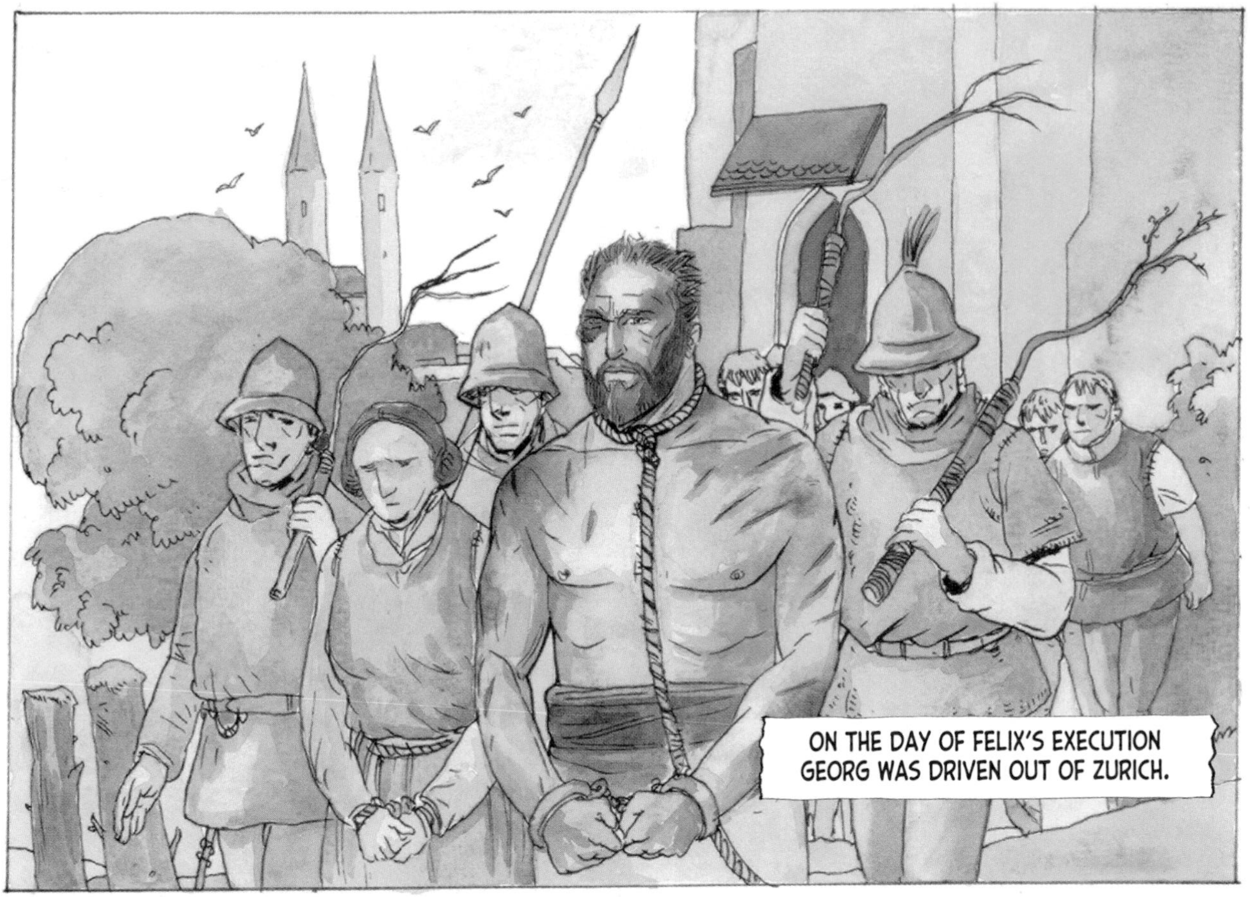
ON THE DAY OF FELIX'S EXECUTION
GEORG WAS DRIVEN OUT OF ZURICH.

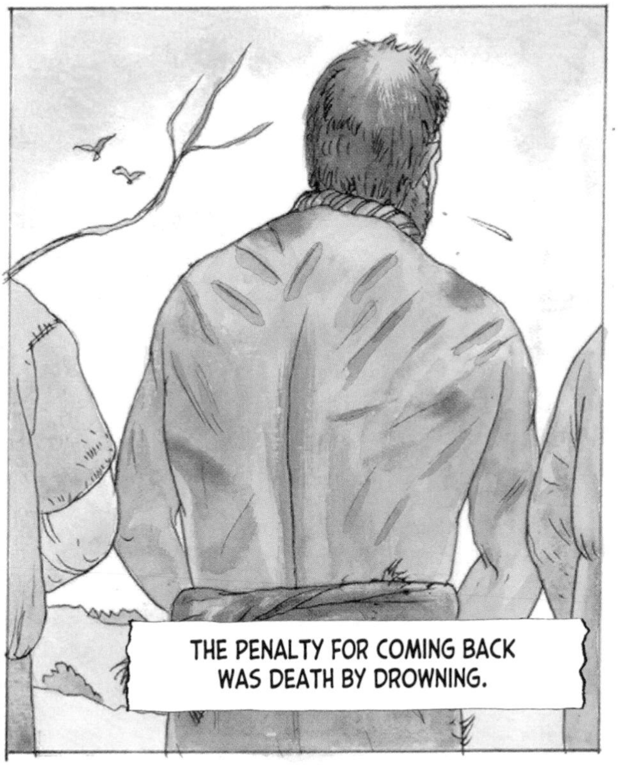
THE PENALTY FOR COMING BACK
WAS DEATH BY DROWNING.

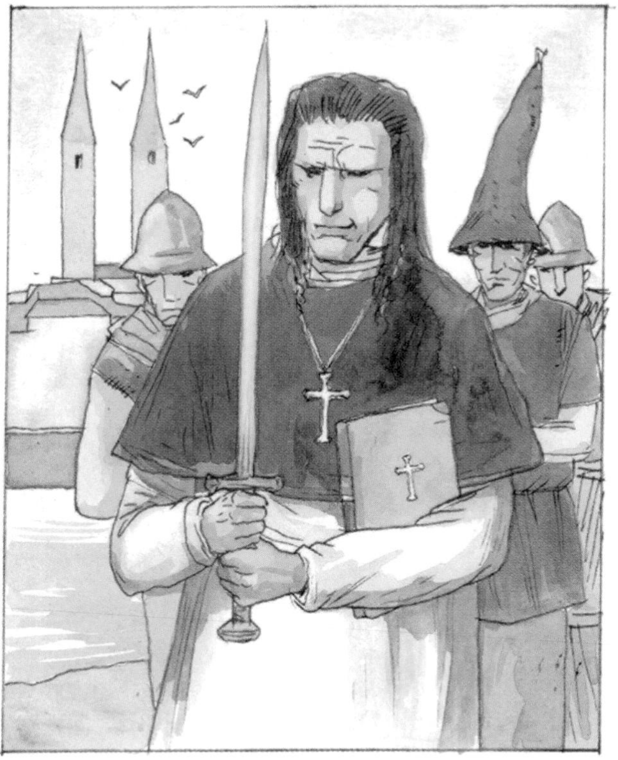

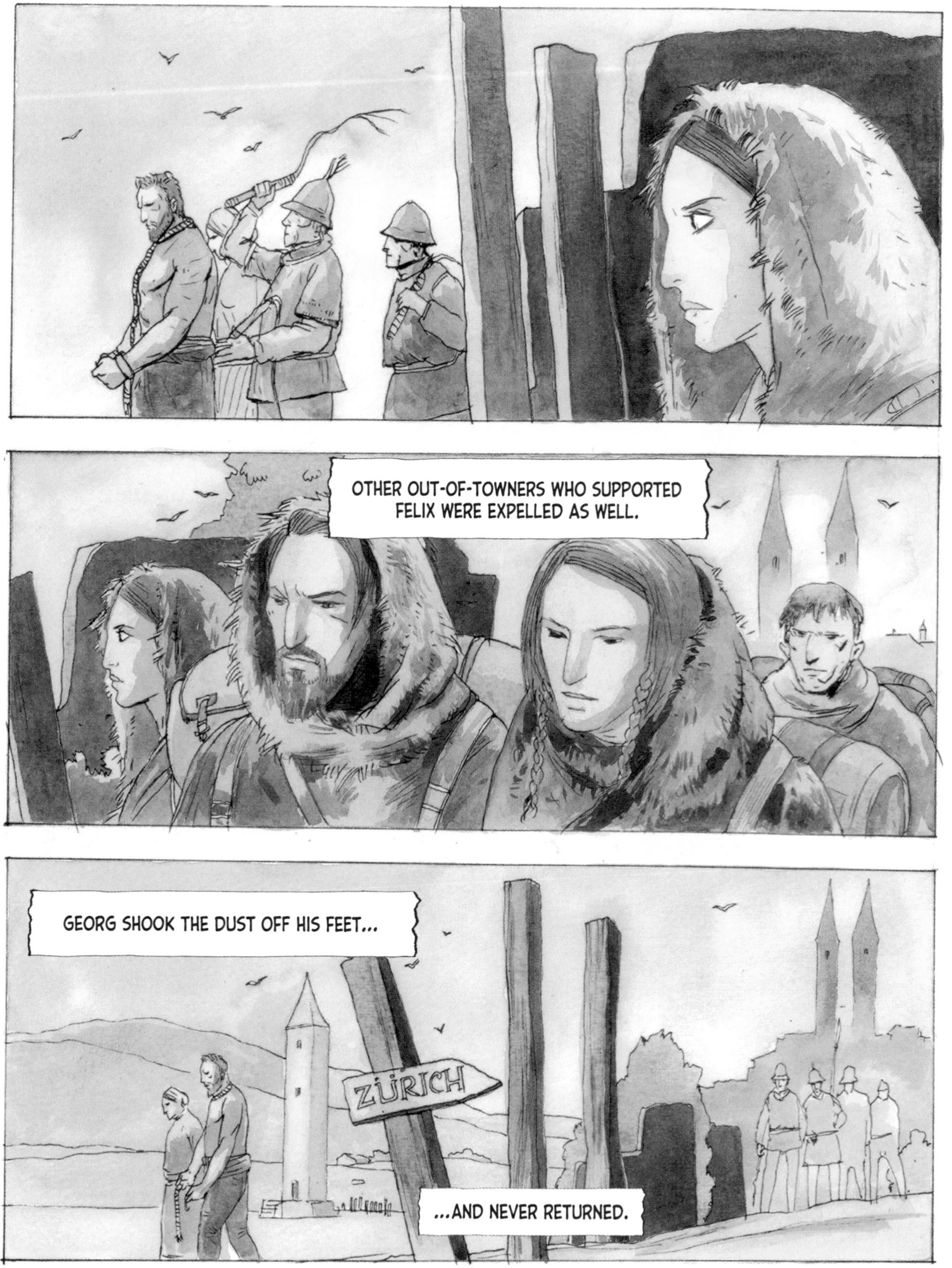
OTHER OUT-OF-TOWNERS WHO SUPPORTED FELIX WERE EXPELLED AS WELL.
GEORG SHOOK THE DUST OFF HIS FEET...
ZÜRICH
...AND NEVER RETURNED.

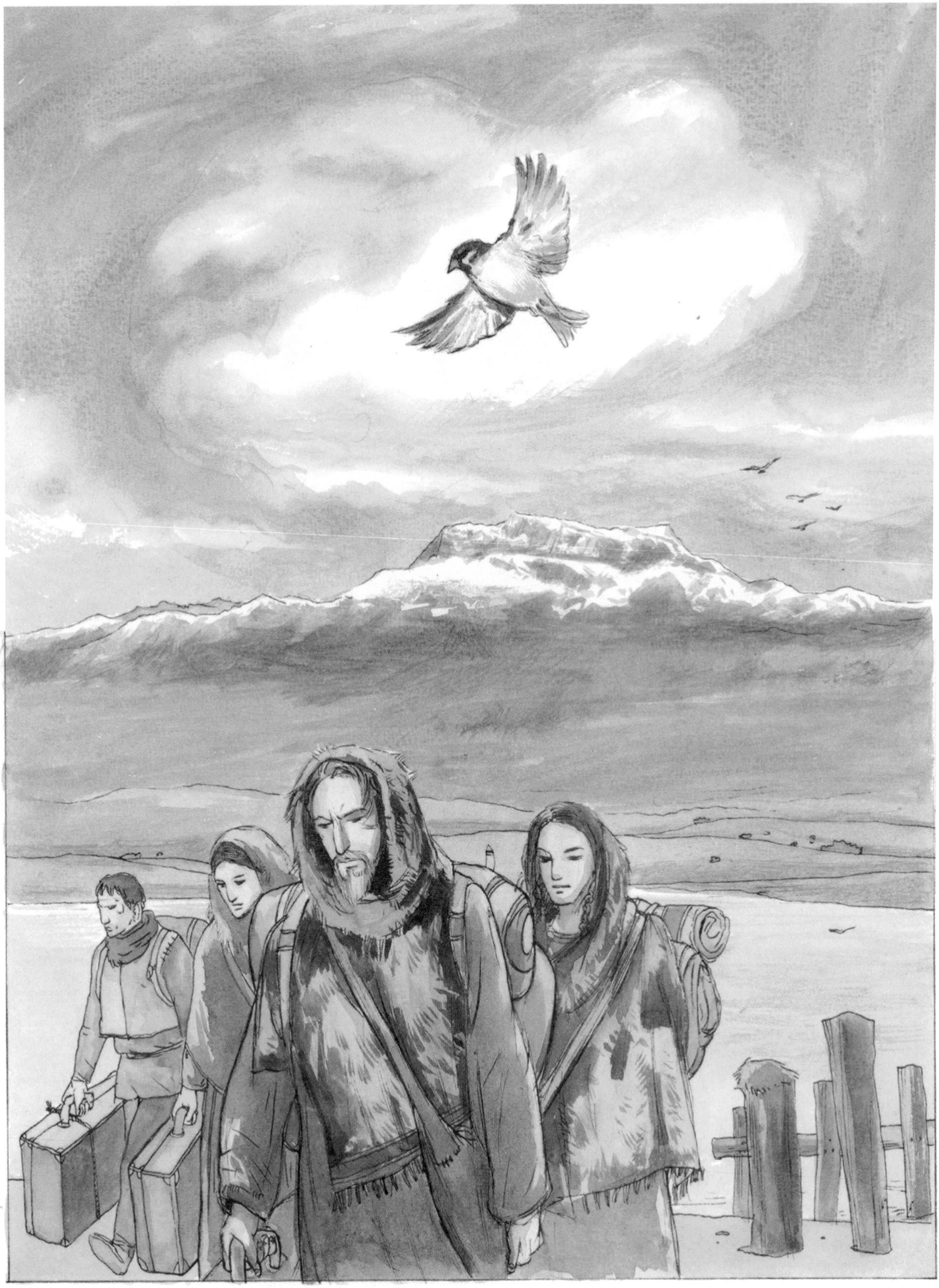

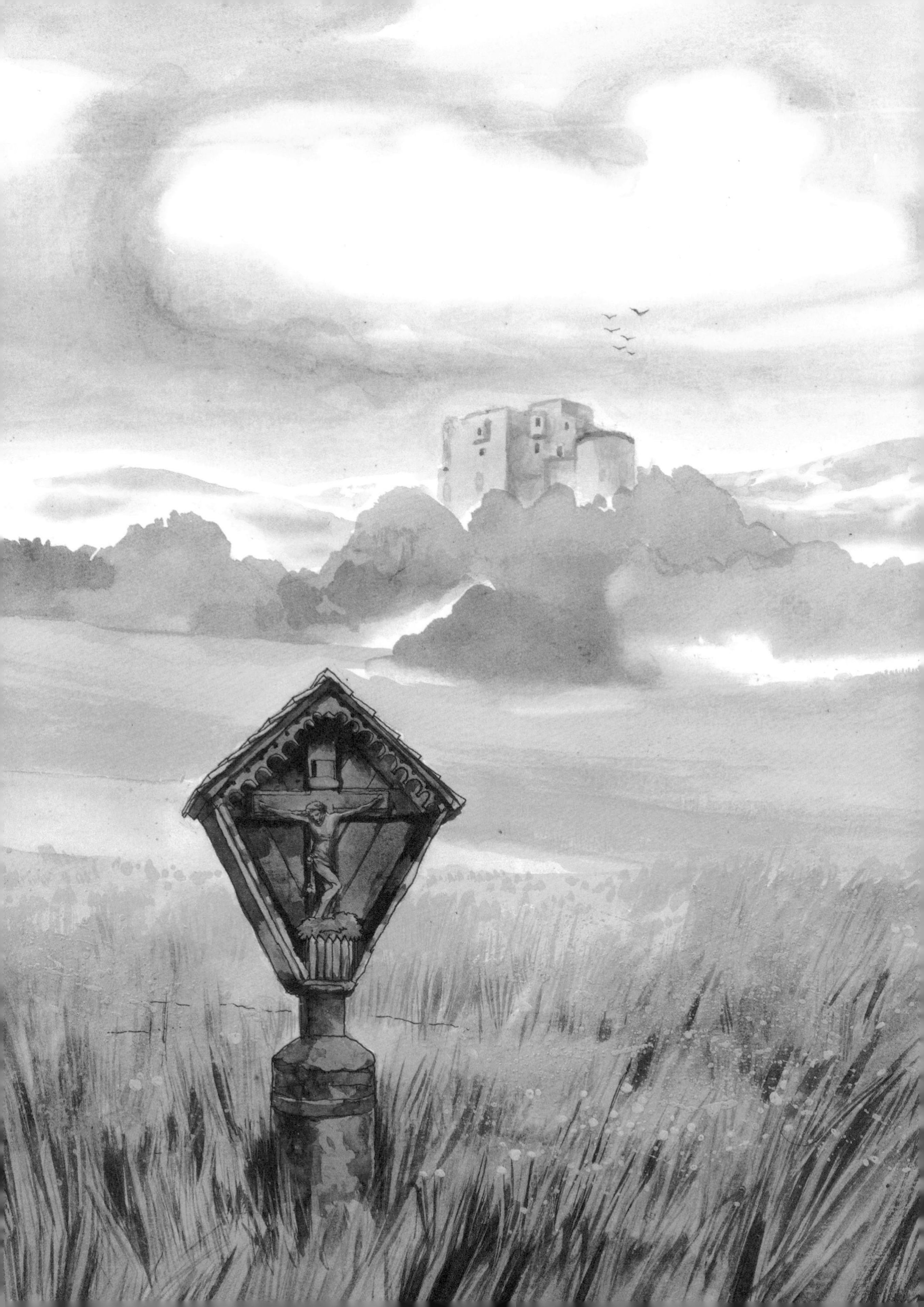

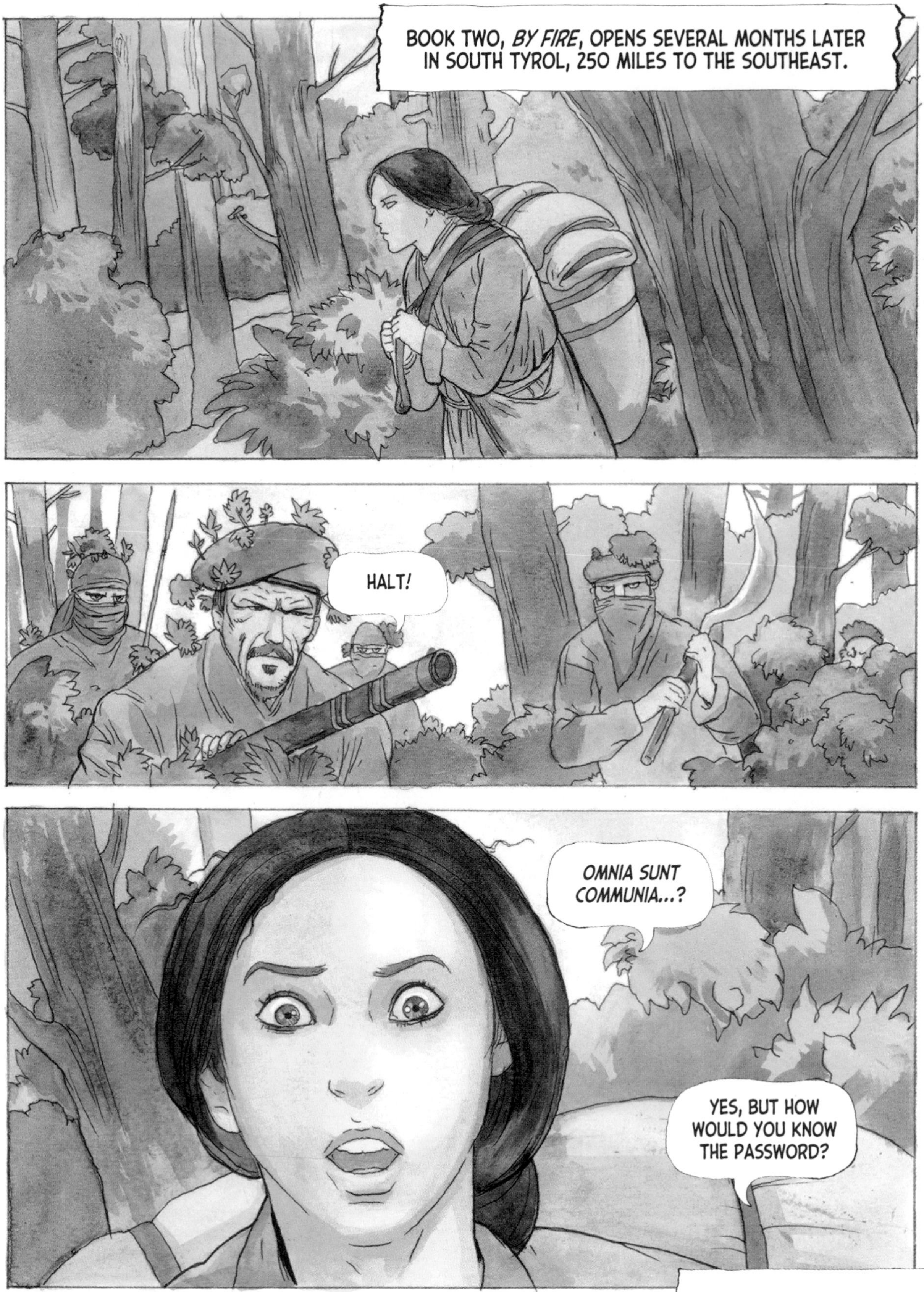
BOOK TWO, *BY FIRE*, OPENS SEVERAL MONTHS LATER IN SOUTH TYROL, 250 MILES TO THE SOUTHEAST.
HALT!
OMNIA SUNT COMMUNIA...?
YES, BUT HOW WOULD YOU KNOW THE PASSWORD?
TO BE CONTINUED...

Two panels of a panoramic altar painting of Zurich by Hans Leu the Elder showing the Grossmünster and the Wellenberg tower, late 1400s.

HISTORICAL FIGURES

Felix and Regula, brother and sister, were executed at Zurich in AD 286 for becoming Christians. According to legend, after they were decapitated, they picked up their heads, walked forty paces, prayed, and lay down in death. On the site where they died and were buried, the Grossmünster of Zurich was built, and they became the city's patron saints.

Ulrich Zwingli (1484–1531) was born to a respectable family in the Swiss canton of St. Gall. He studied in Basel and Vienna and served as a priest. He became a follower of the humanist Erasmus in 1514. In 1519 he became the leading pastor of Zurich. During an illness in the winter of 1520 he began to question many Catholic practices. He eventually resigned from the priesthood and gathered younger men around him to discuss questions of faith. He worked closely with the city council to break from Roman Catholic authority, believing that change would come through the Protestant church's alliance with political power. He died in battle.

Felix Manz (ca. 1498–1527) was born out of wedlock, the son of a canon in the Grossmünster of Zurich. He received a good education and had a thorough knowledge of Hebrew, Greek, and Latin. He became a follower of Ulrich Zwingli, who led church reforms in Zurich. He was among the first group to baptize one another, breaking with Zwingli and the Protestant state church. He was arrested several times, the last time on December 3, 1526. He was sentenced to death and drowned on January 5, 1927, becoming the first Anabaptist martyr.

Anna Reinhard (1487–1538) was a widow with three children, an attentive follower of Zwingli's. When he contracted the plague, she nursed him back to health. They married privately in 1522; Zwingli was still a priest, vowed to celibacy. In 1524 they made their marriage public.

Katharina von Zimmern (1478–1547) was the daughter of a German noble family. She became abbess of the Fraumünster Abbey in Zurich in 1496 at the age of eighteen. In this role, she had significant political power. She chose to accept Zwingli's reforms, which included closing the monasteries. In 1524 she surrendered the abbey to the city and married.

Conrad Grebel (ca. 1498–1526) was born into a respectable Zurich family. He studied in Basel and in Vienna, where he was exposed to humanist ideas. Continuing his studies in Paris, he became involved in student brawls and returned to Zurich in 1519 without a university degree. There he experienced a conversion through Zwingli's preaching. Grebel was an eager follower of Zwingli's until a debate in October 1523, after which Zwingli deferred to the city council and retracted his demands. Grebel rebaptized Georg Blaurock on January 21, 1525. From there, he traveled through Switzerland, preaching and baptizing. Imprisoned in October 1525, he escaped six months later. He died of the plague that same year.

Georg Blaurock (ca. 1492–1529) was born in the Swiss village of Bonaduz. He became a Catholic priest and served as the vicar of Trins in the diocese of Chur from 1516 to 1518. When he arrived in Zurich he had already left the priesthood and married. He became the first to receive adult believer's baptism, and a leader among the Anabaptists, spreading the new teachings boldly despite repeated imprisonment. On September 6, 1529, after refusing to recant under torture, Georg Blaurock was burned at the stake for his religious beliefs in Klausen, South Tyrol (now Italy).

Christoph Froschauer (ca. 1490–1564), a publisher in Zurich, was an early follower of the Reformation. He began publishing Luther's German translation of the Bible, working with Zwingli to give it a Swiss flavor. Starting in 1525, he published parts of the New and Old Testaments, completing the Bible in 1529.

TIMELINE

Felix, Regula, and Exuperantius. Altarpiece in the Spannweid Chapel, Zurich, 1506

Albrecht Dürer, *The Bath House*, 1496

AD 286: Early Christians Felix, Regula, and their servant Exuperantius are beheaded at Zurich.

1450: Johannes Gutenberg develops movable type, starts printing Bibles.

1484: Ulrich Zwingli is born.

1492: Christopher Columbus lands in the "New World."

ca. 1498: Felix Manz is born out of wedlock to Anna Manz in Zurich; his father was a priest.

ca. 1506: Felix Manz is thought to have started attending the Latin school attached to Zurich's Grossmünster church.

1506: Pope Julius II orders work on St. Peter's Basilica in Rome; Leonardo da Vinci paints *Mona Lisa*.

1513: Inspired by humanists such as Erasmus with their emphasis on *ad fontes* ("back to the sources"), Zwingli begins to study ancient Greek.

1515: Zwingli serves as an army chaplain at the Battle of Marignano, where Swiss infantry are defeated by France. This experience turns him against the mercenary system in which Swiss soldiers were hired out to foreign rulers.

1516: Thomas More publishes his book *Utopia,* which describes a fictional country whose inhabitants share all things in common.

1517: Martin Luther publishes his "95 Theses," questioning practices and teachings of the Catholic Church.

January 1, 1519: Zwingli gives his first sermon in Zurich's Grossmünster church. Rejecting the traditional liturgy, he begins reading straight through the Gospel of Matthew, using Erasmus' translation.

Zwingli in his study, where he wrote sermons and pamphlets. Heinrich Thomanns, Bullinger's *History of the Reformation*, 1605.

1519: Felix Manz and Conrad Grebel are both university students in Paris, where Grebel has a reputation for womanizing and fighting.

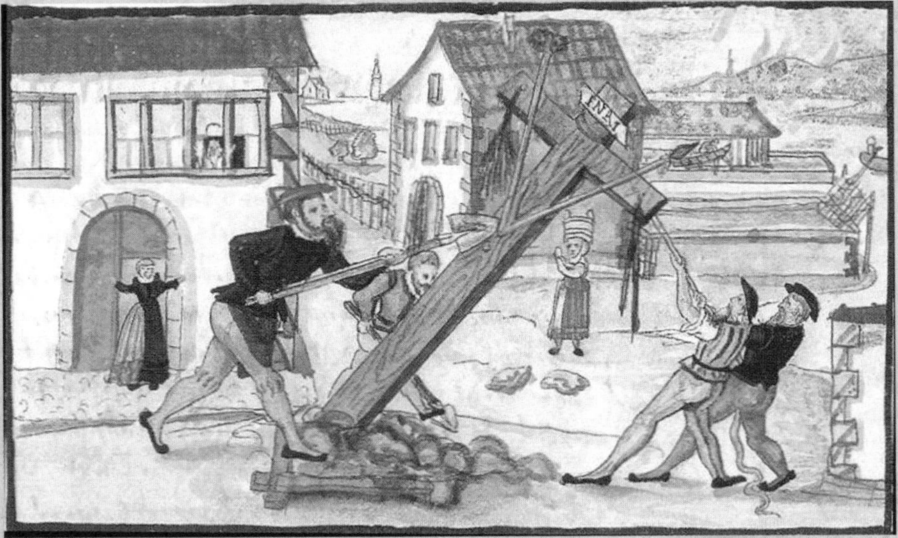
INRI

Reformers pull down a wayside cross in 1523, conisidering it idolatry. Image from Heinrich Thomanns' illustrated manuscript of Heinrich Bullinger's *History of the Reformation,* 1605

1519: Starting in August, the plague sweeps through Zurich. Zwingli contracts the plague, but recovers.

1522: Ferdinand Magellan's sailing expedition completes the first circumnavigation of the earth.

1522: Christoph Froschauer sponsors a sausage party during Lent, defying Catholic tradition. Zwingli is present but does not participate.

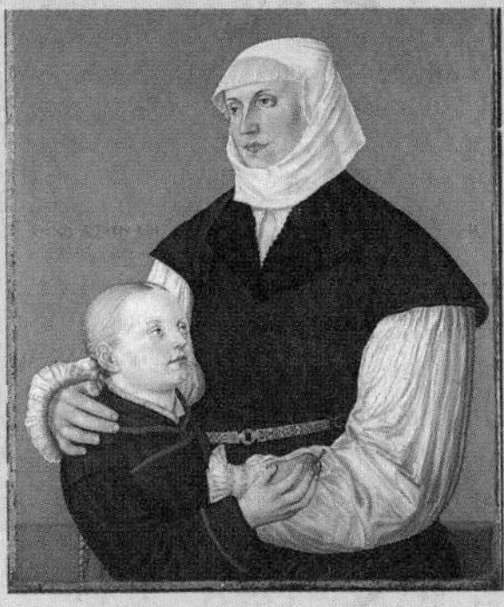

Portrait of Anna Reinhard and one of her daughters.

1523: Iconoclastic riots take place in Zurich and surrounding towns.

April 2, 1524: Abandoning the show of clerical celibacy, Zwingli publicly marries Anna Reinhard. She gives birth to their daughter three months later.

January 17, 1525: Felix Manz and Conrad Grebel debate Ulrich Zwingli publicly on the question of infant baptism.

January 21, 1525: Conrad Grebel, Felix Manz, and Georg Blaurock meet in the home of Manz's mother and baptize one another, breaking with Zwingli and the state church.

January 1525: The first Anabaptist congregation is established in the nearby village of Zollikon.

May 15, 1525: The Battle of Frankenhausen in the German Peasants' War leaves 7000 dead. Radical reformer and insurrectionist Thomas Müntzer is captured, tortured, and executed on May 27.

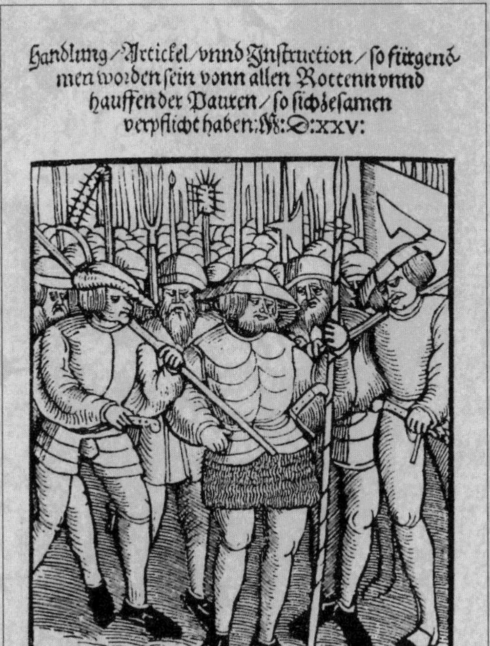
Handlung/Artickel/unnd Instruction/so fürgenōmen worden sein vonn allen Rottenn unnd hauffen der Pauren/so sich zesamen verpflicht haben: M:D:XXV:

Title page from the *Twelve Articles of the German Peasants* pamphlet of 1525

Execution of an Anabaptist by "drowning without mercy".

June 1525: Anabaptist "Prophets of Zollikon" parade through Zurich, declaring Zwingli the dragon described in Revelation.

March 7, 1526: The Zurich council passes an edict making adult rebaptism punishable by drowning.

ca. July 1526: Conrad Grebel dies of the plague.

December 3, 1526: Felix Manz is captured and imprisoned for the last time, along with Georg Blaurock.

1528: Anabaptists later known as Hutterites pool their possessions, reestablishing community of goods described in Acts.

September 6, 1529: Georg Blaurock is burned at the stake in Klausen, South Tyrol (now Italy).

The Täuferhöhle, an Anabaptist hideout. Photo by Jason Landsel.

Erhard Schön, *A Monk as the Devil's Bagpipes*, 1535

January 5, 1527: Felix Manz is drowned. Blaurock, a nonresident, is banished from Zurich.

February 24, 1527: Michael Sattler draws up the Schleitheim Confession, articulating seven distinctive articles of faith among Swiss Anabaptists, including believers' baptism, nonviolence, and refusal to take oaths.

September–October 1529: Ottoman Turks besiege Vienna, but are repulsed.

1534–1535: Some Anabaptists take up arms, establishing a short-lived sectarian government in the city of Münster.

1536: Menno Simons leaves the Catholic Church and becomes a leader among nonviolent Anabaptists in the Low Countries (Netherlands) later called Mennonites.

THE TWELVE ARTICLES OF THE PEASANTS' REVOLT

The Twelve Articles summarize the demands of the peasants during the German Peasants' War of 1524 and 1525. Drafted by Sebastian Lotzer, a traveling furrier and lay preacher, with the preamble added by another preacher, Christoph Schappeler, they were first printed in March 1525 and widely disseminated.

Peace to the Christian reader and the grace of God through Christ: There are many evil writings put forth of late which take occasion, on account of the assembling of the peasants, to cast scorn upon the gospel, saying, "Is this the fruit of the new teaching, that no one should obey but that all should everywhere rise in revolt, and rush together to reform, or perhaps destroy altogether, the authorities, both ecclesiastic and lay?" The articles below shall answer these godless and criminal fault-finders, and serve, in the first place, to remove the reproach from the word of God and, in the second place, to give a Christian excuse for the disobedience or even the revolt of the entire peasantry.

In the first place, the gospel is not the cause of revolt and disorder, since it is the message of Christ, the promised Messiah; the word of life, teaching only love, peace, patience, and concord. Thus all who believe in Christ should learn to be loving, peaceful, long-suffering, and harmonious. This is the foundation of all the articles of the peasants (as will be seen), who accept the gospel and live according to it. [. . .]

In the second place, it is clear that the peasants demand that this gospel be taught them as a guide in life, and they ought not to be called disobedient or disorderly. Whether God grants the peasants (earnestly wishing to live according to his word) their requests or no, who shall find fault with the will of the Most High? Who shall meddle in his judgments or oppose his majesty? Did he not hear the children of Israel when they called upon him and save them out of the hands of Pharaoh? Can he not save his own today? Yea, he will save them and that speedily. Therefore, Christian reader, read the following articles with care and then judge.

1 First, it is our humble petition and desire, as also our will and desire, that in the future we should have power and authority so that **each community should choose and appoint a pastor,** and that we should have the right to depose him should he conduct himself improperly. The pastor thus chosen should teach us the gospel pure and simple, without any addition, doctrine, or ordinance of man.

2 According as the just tithe is established by the Old Testament and fulfilled in the New, we are ready and willing to pay the fair tithe of grain. The word of God plainly provides that in giving rightly to God and distributing to his people the services of a pastor are required. We will that for the future our church provost, whomsoever the community may appoint, shall gather and receive this tithe. From this he shall give to the pastor, elected by the whole community, a decent and sufficient maintenance for him and his, as shall seem right to the whole community. **What remains over shall be given to the poor.** [. . .]

3 It has been the custom hitherto for men to hold us as their own property, which is pitiable enough, considering that Christ has delivered and redeemed us all, without exception, by the shedding of his precious blood, the lowly as well as the great. Accordingly it is consistent with Scripture that we should be free and should wish to be so. [. . .] We therefore take it for granted that **you will release us from serfdom** as true Christians, unless it should be shown from the gospel that we are serfs.

4 In the fourth place, it has been the custom heretofore that no poor man should be allowed to **touch venison or wild fowl, or fish in flowing water**, which seems to us quite unseemly and unbrotherly as well as selfish and not agreeable to the word of God. In some places the authorities preserve the game to our great annoyance and loss, recklessly permitting the unreasoning animals to destroy to no purpose our crops, which God suffers to grow for the use of man; and yet we must submit quietly. This is neither godly nor neighborly; for when God created man he gave him dominion over all the animals, over the birds of the air and the fish in the water. [. . .]

5 In the fifth place, we are aggrieved in the matter of woodcutting, for the noble folk have appropriated all the woods to themselves alone. If a poor man requires wood, he must pay. [. . .] It is our opinion that in regard to a woods which has fallen into the hands of a lord, whether spiritual or temporal, that unless it was duly purchased it should revert again to the community. It should, moreover, be free to every member of the community to **help himself to such firewood as he needs** in his home.

6 Our sixth complaint is in regard to the **excessive services which are demanded of us** and which are increased day to day. We ask that this matter be properly looked into, so that we shall not continue to be oppressed in this way, but that some gracious consideration be given us, since our forefathers were required only to serve according to the word of God.

7 Seventh, **we will not hereafter allow ourselves to be further oppressed** by our lords, but will let them demand only what is just and proper according to the word of the agreement between the lord and the peasant. The lord should no longer try to force more services or other dues from the peasant without payment, but permit the peasant to enjoy his holding in peace and quiet. The peasant should, however, help the lord when it is necessary, and at proper times, when it will not be disadvantageous to the peasant, and for a suitable payment.

8 In the eighth place, we are greatly burdened by the holdings which cannot support the rent exacted from them. The peasants suffer loss in this way and are ruined; and we ask that the lords may appoint persons of honor to inspect these holdings, and **fix a rent in accordance with justice**, so that the peasant shall not work for nothing, since the laborer is worthy of his hire.

9 In the ninth place, we are burdened with a great evil in **the constant making of new laws**. We are not judged according to the offense, but sometimes with great ill-will, and sometimes much too leniently. In our opinion, we should be judged according to the old written law, so that the case shall be decided according to its merits, and not with partiality.

10 In the tenth place, we are aggrieved by the appropriation by individuals of meadows and **fields which at one time belonged to a community**. These we will take again into our own hands. It may, however, happen that the land was rightfully purchased. When, however, the land has unfortunately been purchased in this way, some brotherly arrangement should be made according to circumstances.

11 In the eleventh place, we will entirely abolish the due called heriot [death tax], and will no longer endure it, nor allow **widows and orphans to be thus shamefully robbed** against God's will.

12 In the twelfth place, it is our conclusion and final resolution that if any one or more of the articles here set forth should not be in agreement with the word of God, as we think they are, such article **we will willingly retract** if it is proved really to be against the word of God by a clear explanation of the Scripture. Or if articles should now be conceded to us that are hereafter discovered to be unjust, from that hour they shall be dead and null and without force. [. . .]

English translation from James Harvey Robinson, ed., *Readings in European History*, Vol. 2 (Boston: Ginn & Company, 1904), 94–99.

THE FIRST ADULT BAPTISM

This account of the first adult baptism in 1525, written down during the 1560s by Kasper Braitmichel in The Chronicle of the Hutterian Brethren, *is among the earliest known written accounts of the event, thought by some scholars to be based on a report by Georg Blaurock, one of the participants. It gives a sense of how the story was recounted among early Anabaptists.*

It began in Switzerland, where God brought about an awakening. First of all a meeting took place place between Ulrich Zwingli, Conrad Grebel (a member of the nobility), and Felix Manz. All three were men of learning with a thorough knowledge of German, Latin, Greek, and Hebrew. They started to discuss matters of faith and realized that infant baptism is unnecessary and, moreover, is not baptism at all.

Two of them, Conrad and Felix, believed that people should be truly baptized in the Christian order appointed by the Lord, because Christ himself says, "Whoever believes and is baptized will be saved." Ulrich Zwingli (who shrank from the cross, disgrace, and persecution that Christ suffered) refused to agree – he said it would cause an uproar. But Conrad and Felix said that was no reason to disobey the clear command of God.

At this point a man came from Chur, a priest named Georg from the House of Jakob, later known as Georg Blaurock. Once when they were discussing questions of faith, Georg shared his own views. Someone asked who had just spoken. "It was the man in the blue coat (blauer Rock)." So he was given this name because he had worn a blue coat. This same Georg had come because of his extraordinary zeal. Everyone thought of him as a plain, simple priest; but he was moved by God's grace to holy zeal in matters of faith and worked courageously for the truth.

He, too, had first approached Zwingli and discussed questions of faith with him at length, but he had got nowhere. Then he was told that there were other men more on fire than Zwingli. He inquired eagerly about them and met with them, that is, with Conrad Grebel and Felix Manz, to talk about questions of faith. They came to unity about these questions. In the fear of God they agreed that from God's word one must first learn true faith, expressed in deeds of love, and on confession of this faith receive true Christian baptism as a covenant of a good conscience with God, serving him from then on with a holy Christian life and remaining steadfast to the end, even in times of tribulation.

One day when they were meeting, fear came over them and struck their hearts. They fell on their knees before the almighty God in heaven and called upon him who knows all hearts. They prayed that God grant it to them to do his divine will and that he might have mercy on them. Neither flesh and blood nor human wisdom compelled them. They were well aware of what they would have to suffer for this.

After the prayer, Georg Blaurock stood up and asked Conrad Grebel in the name of God to baptize him with true Christian baptism on his faith and recognition of the truth. With this request he knelt down, and Conrad baptized him, since at that time there was no appointed servant of the word. Then the others turned to Georg in their turn, asking him to baptize them, which he did. And so, in great fear of God, together they surrendered themselves to the Lord. They confirmed one another for the service of the Gospel and began to teach the faith and to keep it. This was the beginning of separation from the world and its evil ways.

English translation from *The Chronicle of the Hutterian Brethren*, Vol. 1 (Rifton, NY: Plough, 1987), 43–45.

THE FIRST ANABAPTIST CONGREGATION

Persecution of Anabaptists in Zurich's Oberland region. Bullinger's *History of the Reformation*, 1605.

This account of the first community to embrace the Anabaptist teaching was penned by Johannes Kessler, chronicler of St. Gallen, writing objectively from a state church perspective.

Now when the founders of Anabaptism noticed that not much room was granted them in Zurich for their activity, they turned to the countryside into the villages again and again. Always their teaching and preaching was about rebaptism against infant baptism. They asked nothing but: Why don't you get baptized? Why do you have your child baptized? This occurred mainly in a place not far from Zurich called Zollikon, where they had their center. There water was prepared and if anyone desired baptism they poured a panful of water on his head in the name of the Father, Son, and Holy Spirit.

Now because Zollikon in general had itself baptized, and they assumed that they were the true Christian church, they also undertook, like the early Christians, to practice community of temporal goods (as can be read in the Acts of the Apostles), broke the locks off their doors, chests, and cellars, and ate food and drink in good fellowship without discrimination.

. . . But when they became aware of the activities at Zollikon, their honorable wisdom, the governors of the city of Zurich, were as unwilling to tolerate such separation in their canton as in their city, but issued their command and prohibition also throughout their domains. But because the Zollikon people persisted, the burgomaster and council decreed that the baptizers and baptized be seized and imprisoned in the Wellenberg (which was done).

English translation from Leland Harder, ed., *The Sources of Swiss Anabaptism* (Walden, NY: Plough, 2019), 344–345.

SENTENCING OF ANABAPTISTS BY ZURICH COUNCIL

Anabaptist debate with Zurich City Council in 1525. Bullinger's *History of the Reformation*, 1605

Mandate of the Zurich Council, November 30, 1525

In spite of imprisonment, two disputations, and the consequent promise to desist from rebaptism, many Anabaptists have backslidden. [...] Because of this, it is our prohibition and serious judgment that henceforth everyone – men and women, boys and girls – abstain from all rebaptism, no longer practice it, but baptize the infants. For whoever acts to the contrary, whenever it occurs, shall be fined a silver mark. And

if anyone shows himself to be disobedient, we will deal further with him, and we will penalize those who are disobedient in this regard in accord with their deserts, and we will not let up. Everyone will know how to conduct himself. All by virtue of this open letter sealed with the city's seal and proclaimed on St. Andrew's Day, 1525.

Resentencing by the Council, March 7, 1526

Wednesday after St. Fridolin's Day in the presence of Lord

Walder, senior burgomaster, and the Large and Small Councils.

The following Anabaptists are definitely known to be in Milords' prisons: Felix Manz, Georg Blaurock of Chur, Conrad Grebel, Uli Hottinger of Zollikon, Ernst of Glätz of Silesia, Anthony Roggenacher of Schwyz, Hans Hottinger, Rudolf Hottinger, Hans Ockenfuss, Karl Brennwald, Fridli Ab-Iberg of Schwyz, Hans Heingarter of St. Gallen, Agli Ockenfuss, Elizabeth Hottinger of Hirslanden, Margaret Hottinger of Zollikon,

Detail from the Murerplan, a map of Zurich, printed in 1576 by Jos Murer.

Winbrat Fanwilerin of St. Gallen, Anna Manz, and Widerkerin at the Green Shield.

Concerning these Anabaptists, it is declared that upon their answers which each one gave and their opinions persisted in, that they shall be put together into the new tower; and they shall be given nothing to eat but bread and water and bedded on straw. And the attendant who guards them shall under oath let no one come to them or go away from them. Thus let them die in the tower unless anyone desists from his acts and error and intends to be obedient. That should then be brought to [the attention of] Milords' councilors and representatives. And then they shall be asked how further to punish them. No one shall have the authority to alter their confinement, behind the backs of said Milords, whether they are sick or well.

Similarly, the girls and women shall be placed together and treated in every respect as stated above.

It is further decided to issue an open mandate everywhere indicating the severe imprisonment of the Anabaptists. And [that] anyone who baptizes hereafter will be drowned without mercy and thus brought from life to death, etc.

Mandate of the Council, March 7, 1526

Inasmuch as Our Lords, burgomaster, [Small] Council, and Large Council, which are called the Two Hundred of the city of Zurich, have for some time earnestly endeavored to turn the deceived, mistaken Anabaptists from their error, etc., but inasmuch as some of them, hardened against their oaths, vows, and pledges, have shown disobedience to the injury of public order and authority and the subversion of the common interest and true Christian conduct, some of them – men, women, and girls – were sentenced by Our Lords to severe punishment and imprisonment. And it is therefore the earnest command, order, and warning of the said Our Lords that no one in their city, country, and domain, whether man, woman, or girl, shall henceforth baptize another. Whoever henceforth baptizes another will be seized by Our Lords and, according to this present explicit decree, drowned without any mercy. Hereafter, everyone knows how to avoid this so that no one gives cause for his own death.

This judgment shall be announced in the three parishes on Sunday and in the districts of the land and announced by public written mandate. Put into force on Wednesday after Oculi Sunday, 1526.

English translations from Leland Harder, ed., *The Sources of Swiss Anabaptism* (Walden, NY: Plough, 2019), 443, 447–448.

THE DEATH SENTENCE
OF FELIX MANZ

The drowning of Felix Manz in 1527. Bullinger's *History of the Reformation*, 1605.

The Zurich Council's Sentencing, January 5, 1527

Felix Manz of Zurich and others of his relatives and followers had gotten mixed up in rebaptizing, contrary to Christian order and custom. They embraced it and taught it to others, and Manz was an instigator and leader. Our Lords, the burgomaster, the Council, and the Large Council (as the 200 of the city of Zurich are called) explained and expounded to the aforementioned Manz and others by their preaching and holy scripture,

the Old and New Testaments, that rebaptizing cannot stand according to the word of God but must be repudiated. It is contrary to Christian order. Infant baptism, which has been practiced throughout Christendom, is right and in accord with God's word. With all possible diligence and seriousness, out of the truth of divine scripture and evangelical teaching [they urged] him and the others to renounce their error and stubborn opinion, to reconcile with general Christian practice and accept brotherly admonition.

However, some of them continued to insist on their obstinate ideas and refused to give in. Despite Christian admonition, neither friendly nor threatening words helped, and anxious that further evil and outrage would follow, Our Lords had a solemn order or mandate proclaimed publicly in their towns, counties, and districts as follows: from now on, anyone who sympathizes with or practices rebaptism or teaches such, shall be drowned without mercy be they women or men, young or old.

Even though Felix Manz (as explained above) is a primary instigator of such rebaptism, causing great unrest and conflict, Our Lords released him from prison, with clear instructions to desist from baptizing or defending rebaptism from now on, but to diligently obey Our Lords. Felix Manz swore an oath to hold to this. However, two weeks after he and his fellow believers broke out of prison, when he came to Embrach he instructed a woman in his ideas and baptized her. He also insisted that if any man or woman comes to him, asking to be instructed and baptized, he would consent and would not drive them away.

Further, he confessed and said that he and others who want to accept Christ, obey his word, and follow him, plan to come together and unite through rebaptism and stay with those of their faith, so that he and his followers would separate themselves from the Christian church and establish a sect and conspiracy under the disguise of a Christian fellowship or church.

This Felix Manz also claimed, without any exception, believing and teaching it as the truth, that no Christian may bear a government office nor execute anyone with the sword or punish anyone. As an indication of his erroneous, seditious ideas, in order to gain followers for his evil, shameful plans, he claimed that once or twice, when he was in prison, some of St. Paul's epistles had been unveiled to him. He had a vision as though he were present at their writing. In this way he presented his wickedness in the form of something good.

Felix Manz's opinion, his practice and teaching of rebaptizing and what it entails is contrary to the word of God and is not founded therein. It conflicts with and destroys the praiseworthy, general custom that has been practiced throughout Christendom. In addition, it is plain as day that so far it has led to nothing but terrible insurrection, outrage, and revolt against the Christian authorities; destruction of the general Christian peace, brotherly love, and civil unity; and all kinds of evil.

Felix Manz has not changed or renounced his own stubborn, erroneous ideas but publicly before crowds of people as well as secretly in corners, homes, and villages he has not only taught and preached but actually baptized people. Despite warnings, fatherly discipline, and serious decrees that have been published, he has separated from the Christian church and [established] his own sect, faction, or conference under the guise of something good. He has seduced other Christians and poor simple people, led them astray from obedience to authority and thus given excuse for robbery, murder, and all kinds of evil. Felix Manz has confessed to this and further proof is not necessary.

Because of Felix Manz's mutinous character, sedition against the authorities, Christian government, and civil unity he

Wellenberg Tower where Anabaptists were imprisioned.

is sentenced as follows: He shall be delivered to the executioner, who shall tie his hands, put him into a boat, take him to the lower hut, there strip his bound hands down over his knees, place a stick between his knees and arms, and thus bound, push him into the water and let him perish and die in the water; thereby he shall have atoned to the law and justice.

If anyone present is upset about his death and retaliates in word or deed, secretly or openly, he shall receive the same punishment.

His property shall be confiscated by Our Lords.

Saturday before Three Kings Day, 1527, in the presence of Mathis Wyssen, bailiff of the kingdom; Diethelm Röist, burgomaster, and councilors and citizens, sealed by Herr Röist.

English translation by Emmy Barth Maendel for this book.

FELIX MANZ'S HYMN

This song is a poetic setting of Felix Manz's last letter to fellow Anabaptists from prison shortly before his execution. It is possible that Manz himself reworked his letter into a song, but more likely that it was adapted later by another Anabaptist. There are eighteen verses in the original; here are four:

I sing with exultation, all my heart delights
In God, who brings salvation, frees from death's dread might.
I praise Thee, Christ of Heaven, who ever shall endure,
Who takes away my sorrow, keeps me safe and secure.

Whom God sent as example, light my feet to guide.
Before my end he bade me in his realm abide.
That I might love and cherish his righteousness divine;
That I with him forever bliss eternal might find.

Sing praise to Christ our Savior, who in grace inclined,
To us reveals his nature, patient, loving, kind.
His love divine outpouring he shows to everyone,
Unfeigned and like his Father's, as no other has done.

Christ bids us, none compelling, to his glorious throne.
He only who is willing Christ as Lord to own,
He is assured of heaven who will right faith pursue,
With heart made pure do penance, sealed with baptism true.

English translation by Marion Wenger from *Songs of Light* (Rifton, NY: Plough, 1977), 70.

BIBLIOGRAPHY

Amman, Jost and Hans Sachs. *The Book of Trades (Ständebuch).* New York: Dover Publications, 1973.

Bender, Harold Stauffer. *Conrad Grebel, c. 1498–1526, the Founder of the Swiss Brethren Sometimes Called Anabaptists.* Goshen, IN: Mennonite Historical Society, 1950.

Blanke, Fritz. *Brothers in Christ: The History of the Oldest Anabaptist Congregation, Zollikon, Near Zurich, Switzerland.* Translated by Joseph Nordenhaug. Eugene, OR: Wipf and Stock, 2005.

Borchert, Till-Holger and Joshua P. Waterman. *The Book of Miracles.* Cologne: Taschen, 2013.

Dangelmaier, Ruth. *Dürer.* Cologne: Könemann Verlag, 2017.

Duby, Georges, ed. *A History of Private Life: Revelations of the Medieval World.* Translated by Arthur Goldhammer. Cambridge, MA: Belknap Press, 1988.

Fingernagel, Andreas, Stephan Füssel, and Christian Gastgeber. *The Book of Bibles: The Most Beautiful Illuminated Bibles of the Middle Ages.* Translated by Karen Williams. Cologne: Taschen, 2016.

Goertz, Hans-Jürgen, ed. *Profiles of Radical Reformers: Biographical Sketches from Thomas Müntzer to Paracelsus.* Scottdale, PA: Herald Press, 1982.

Grebel, Conrad. *Conrad Grebel's Programmatic Letters of 1524.* Translated by John Christian Wenger. Scottdale, PA: Herald Press, 1970.

Harder, Leland, ed. *The Sources of Swiss Anabaptism: The Grebel Letters and Related Documents.* Walden, NY: Plough Publishing House, 2019.

Harrington, Joel F. *The Faithful Executioner: Life and Death, Honor and Shame in the Turbulent Sixteenth Century.* New York: Farrar, Straus and Giroux, 2013.

Hutterian Brethren. *The Chronicle of the Hutterian Brethren,* Vol. 1. Rifton, NY: Plough Publishing House, 1987.

Klaassen, Walter, ed. *Anabaptism in Outline: Selected Primary Sources.* Walden, NY: Plough Publishing House, 2019.

Krajewski, Ekkehard. *Leben und Sterben des Zürcher Täuferführers Felix Mantz: Über die Anfänge der Täuferbewegung und des Freikirchentums in der Reformationszeit.* Kassel: Oncken Verlag, 1958.

MacCulloch, Diarmaid. *The Reformation: A History.* London: Penguin Books, 2005.

Merle d'Aubigné, Jean-Henri. *For God and His People: Ulrich Zwingli and the Swiss Reformation.* Translated by Henry White. Greenville, SC: BJU Press, 2000.

More, Thomas. *Utopia.* Cambridge: Cambridge University Press, 2002.

Packull, Werner O. *Hutterian Beginnings: Communitarian Experiments during the Reformation.* Baltimore: Johns Hopkins University Press, 1999.

Robinson, James Harvey, ed. *Readings in European History,* Vol. 2. Boston: Ginn & Company, 1904.

Sattler, Michael. *The Legacy of Michael Sattler.* Translated and edited by John H. Yoder. Walden, NY: Plough Publishing House, 2019.

Stayer, James M. *The German Peasants' War and Anabaptist Community of Goods.* Montreal: McGill-Queen's University Press, 1991.

Swan, Laura, *The Wisdom of the Beguines: The Forgotten Story of a Medieval Women's Movement.* Katonah, NY: BlueBridge, 2016.

OTHER TITLES FROM PLOUGH

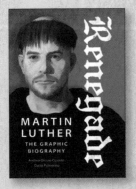

Renegade
MARTIN LUTHER
THE GRAPHIC BIOGRAPHY

Renegade
Martin Luther, the Graphic Biography
Andrea Grosso Ciponte and Dacia Palmerino

Five hundred years ago Martin Luther confronted the most powerful institutions of his day, sparking the Protestant Reformation that marked one of the great turning points in history. His story comes vividly to life in this graphic novel.

Paperback | 160 pages | $19.95

FREIHEIT!
THE WHITE ROSE GRAPHIC NOVEL

Freiheit!
The White Rose Graphic Novel
Andrea Grosso Ciponte

The dramatic true story of a handful of students who resisted the Nazis and paid with their lives, now in a stunning graphic novel.

Hardcover | 112 pages | $24.00

JOHN CARLIN – ORIOL MALET
MANDELA AND THE GENERAL

Mandela and the General
John Carlin and Oriol Malet

The struggle for racial justice will be won when we win over our adversaries. Find out how Nelson Mandela earned the trust of a white nationalist leader in this graphic novel.

Paperback | 112 pages | $19.95

Julian Peters
POEMS TO SEE BY
A Comic Artist Interprets Great Poetry

Poems to See By
A Comic Artist Interprets Great Poetry
Julian Peters

A fresh twist on twenty-four classics, these visual interpretations by comic artist Julian Peters will change the way you see the world.

Hardcover | 160 pages | $24.00